THE
BLACK
DOOR

Tyner Gillies

In Praise of The Watch

"First class…riveting…I made the mistake of opening it and I
didn't get a lick of work done until I'd finished it."
–Jack Whyte, International Best Selling Author.

"…[a] thrilling story…a page-turner right to the end. Tyner
Gillies presents his debut novel with a fresh voice—an
exciting new Canadian talent!"
*– kc dyer, Author and Director of the Surrey International
Writers' Conference*

In Praise of Dark Resolution

"Taut writing, gripping action and sly wit in a perfect blend of
police procedural and demonic horror. Gillies has hit another
one out of the park."
–CC Humphreys, Winner of the Arthur Ellis Award

"…builds the suspense from the first chapter and keeps the
relentless pace throughout the entire book…twists are intricate
and will keep you guessing…I highly recommend!!!"
–R. Kyle Hannah, Award Winning Author

Also By
Tyner Gillies

Resolution Cove Trilogy
The Watch
Dark Resolution
The Black Door

Shadowboxing

THE BLACK DOOR

Tyner Gillies

Dark Dragon Publishing
Toronto, Ontario, Canada

The Black Door

Dark Dragon Publishing
88 Charleswood Drive,
Toronto, Ontario
M3H 1X6
CANADA
www.darkdragonpublishing.com

Printed in the United States of America.

For more information on Tyner Gillies

www.tynergillies.com

For my friend, uncle, mentor;
Jack Whyte.
I miss you.

Also for my wife, Sayeh.
I'd be lost without you.

FORWARD

The Black Door is not a pandemic novel; meaning, I did not write it during the pandemic. Instead, it is a novel that almost died because of the pandemic.

I wrote this story during the spring and summer of 2019, and submitted it to the publisher in early autumn. My long-time editor, Karen Dales, sent me the substantive edits at the ass-end of winter in early 2020. I was excited and optimistic, and looked forward to getting another Quinn Sullivan story out into the world.

Then, the pandemic hit.

Where I live, in British Columbia, Canada, the state of emergency was declared on March 12th, 2020. I am a full-time police officer, and at that time my role was the NCO i/c (Non-commissioned officer in charge) of the Emergency Planning unit. In the space of a couple hours, my role shifted from planning upcoming major events for spring and summer, to trying to figure out how to see a major police agency through the first world-wide pandemic in a hundred years. I worked, without reprieve, for months on end. Don't get me wrong, I am extremely grateful that I was employed and worked in a role that allowed me to leave the house and see people, but holy shit was I ever tired.

Like all of my writing-life friends, I was riding the creative struggle bus. In fact, I was driving the struggle bus down the struggle highway, onto the struggle turn pike, and drove right into the centre of struggle town where they presented me with the key to the city...and elected me mayor.

And so the edits for this story sat for a year. A couple of times I went so far as to sit in my little home office and open the document on my computer. I would stare at the first few lines of editing notes without comprehending them until I decided a better course of action would be to go back to the living room and watch a few re-runs of the Big Bang Theory and play some Candy Crush on my phone.

It wasn't until I attended the virtual version of the Surrey International Writer's Conference where I sat in on one of Liza Palmer's workshops, that I had the slightest creative spark. She said (and I'm paraphrasing due to my imperfect memory): *Now is the time when your writing is even more important, because people need stories.*

It took me a couple more months and several stuttering false starts, but eventually I ground through the edits on the story. And now you, dear reader, are sharing it with me. I am sure you have struggled; probably much worse than I ever did, and dammit, I am glad to see you.

This story is dedicated to you, as much as to the people I mentioned in my dedication. I am excited you're here to read my book. My wish is that it gives you hope and brings with it the belief that the light can conquer the dark.

Tyner Gillies
Langley, BC
June, 2022

CHAPTER 1

The naked man fled across the patchy lawn of the small house, and the Mounties followed.

"God's truth will not be bound by likes of you!" the wiry man screamed, his sweaty skin glistening in the sparse light shed by the street lamps.

Corporal Quinn Sullivan gave chase, his boots squelching across the damp earth as he pursued the man. "Dammit, Earl!" Quinn shouted between huffing breaths. "You need to go to the hospital."

Quinn lunged for the sweaty man, but Earl turned a tight circle and the Mountie missed, lost his balance and tumbled across the damp yard.

"I swear to Christ I'm gonna shoot this guy in the ass," Constable Dave McLeod growled. He dodged around Quinn's sprawling form and hustled after the naked man. "Earl, you idiot, come here!"

Dave, the quicker of the two Mounties, caught up to Earl and grabbed his wrist, but the man shrieked and twisted his sweaty arm from Dave's grip before taking off across the street, his bare feet slapping the blacktop.

"Please, Quinn," Dave said, his voice plaintive. "Please, let me shoot him."

"You're not shooting the crazy guy." Quinn picked himself

up and wiped a handful of torn turf off the front of his body-armour and flung it into the cold, October night. "Come on."

They took off down the street, chasing Earl who pin-wheeled his arms and screamed, "Help me! The agents of Satan seek to lock me away!" Lights began to flick on in the densely packed houses that lined the street. "They persecute me because I won't shut up about the gospel!"

"Resolution, this is Charlie-Five-One," Quinn said into the shoulder mic on his radio. "Our SOC is in the grip of some kind of psychosis and is running east down Sixteenth Street from the dispatch location."

The radio crackled. "Is it Earl again?" the dispatcher asked in a somewhat staticy feminine voice.

"That's a big ten-four," Quinn said, the exasperation heavy in his voice.

"Does he have any pants on?"

"That would be negative."

Earl, quick despite his bare feet and continuous screaming, ran, zigzagging, down the street, shouting about angels, demons, and the gospel. People were coming out of their houses, and Quinn saw the glow of cell phone flashes as people began recording Earl's antics.

Rounding a corner in the street, Earl looked over his shoulder at his pursuers and failed to see the big, dark shape that stepped out from behind a telephone pole. That shape extended an arm as thick as a tree trunk, and Earl slammed into it at chest height, his momentum sending him spinning through the air to land on his stomach, on the grass, in a wheezing heap.

Quinn and Dave, only a few steps behind, saw the massive form of Sergeant Charles Raife bend over the crumpled Earl, and snap handcuffs onto narrow wrists. Raife hauled the wheezing man up by one arm, easily supporting his weight with one hand, and reached for his radio mic.

"Resolution, this is Echo-Five-Five," Raife said in his rum-bling voice. "We have one crazy bastard in custody and need another car for transport."

Quinn shook his head, suppressing a chuckle. Only Raife could get away with calling someone a 'crazy bastard' over the radio and not get his ass chewed.

"We had that well under control, Sergeant," Dave wheezed as he leaned over and put his hands on his knees and sucked in deep breaths. "I had him right where I wanted him."

"Sure you did." Raife ran his thumb and forefinger over his heavy, handlebar moustache. "We don't have time for this foolishness. We have another job needs doing." He hauled up on a sagging Earl. "Heavy work."

Whenever Raife said, 'heavy work,' it meant one thing.

"Is it one of *those* calls?" Quinn asked.

Raife nodded. "Yup. A few people called about their cats going missing and seeing something in an abandoned duplex in the north part of their neighbourhood."

"Ah, fuck," Dave huffed, standing upright. "That's the third one this month."

"It's getting worse," Quinn said.

"You bet your ass it is." Raife nodded his chin towards the headlights of an approaching car.

A white Ford Crown Victoria, the RCMP emblem on the doors and a light bar on the roof, pulled up and came to a stop. Gerritt Hauk, the junior man in Resolution Cove detachment, got out of the driver's seat and grinned at Raife over the hood of the car. "Hiya, Sarge."

Raife nodded. "Run this idiot down to the hospital, will ya?"

The young man, barely in his twenties, closed his door and hustled around the front of the car to grasp Earl's limp arm and steer him towards the back door. "Not much need to search him, is there?" Gerritt's grin grew wider. Quinn chuckled, and Dave let out a loud guffaw.

The front passenger window of the car rolled down. Sandy Harding, Gerritt's field trainer, cocked an elbow out the window.

"He's doing better," Quinn said, looking at Gerritt.

When the young, blonde constable had first arrived in

Resolution, there had been a significant debate as to whether he had actually graduated from training, or if someone suffering from a traumatic brain injury had stolen a police uniform and shown up looking for a job. In the last three months, however, Gerritt had shown some aptitude, a little initiative, a healthy serving of courage and an abundance of loyalty. There had been more than enough events in his brief service to make a seasoned street cop question their own sanity, but he had stuck with his team without complaint.

Gerritt had only been a handful of days into his field training, when a creature, a Demon, the second of its kind, had arrived in Resolution. The Demon had nearly killed both Quinn and Raife, and had taken the life of Quinn's friend, Autumn Donnelly.

That wasn't entirely accurate, Quinn thought, as he looked west, toward the black expanse of the ocean. Autumn wasn't necessarily dead, but she was certainly gone. Quinn had been so busy keeping his town from being ripped apart that he hadn't been able to figure out if there was a way to get her back.

The Demon, the most powerful force of evil Quinn had ever encountered, had come to Resolution seeking a child of exceptional abilities. Abby McRae had the ability to open doors—portals—to anywhere on Earth, as well as to places that no man could, or should, walk. Abby's father, Kord McRae had fled to Resolution seeking the protection only Quinn could provide.

Quinn was shaken from his reverie when Sandy opened her door and climbed out, her dark hair pulled into a tight pony-tail and shining in the light from the street lamp. "Hey, Gerritt?" she said as she slammed her door.

The recruit looked up at her as he shoved Earl into the back passenger seat of the car. The naked man had begun to regain his breath and was winding himself up for another diatribe.

"I know he's crazy," Sandy said. "But read him his Charter and Caution anyway, okay?"

Gerritt nodded and pulled out his notebook.

"Get in the car and do it, please." Sandy gestured towards the driver's seat.

Without question, Gerritt stepped to the driver's door and climbed in. The rest of the watch had never actually sat him down and explained to him that they'd done battle with a few supernatural creatures, but Quinn was certain the youngest member of their team had figured out Resolution was not an average town. Some conversations he didn't need to hear.

When the recruit was sealed in the car with the, once again, squalling Earl, Sandy turned and regarded the other three men. "Is there any particular reason you can't transport this guy yourself?"

"Yeah," Raife said. "The Inspector called. He's got a job for us. The kind only we can do." The big man's words were short and clipped, and he worked his mouth around them as though they tasted bad. He had changed since the day he had fought the demon. He had nearly lost his life, and only Autumn's intervention had saved him. The change worried Quinn, and he made a mental note to try and talk to Raife about it later. If there was a later.

Sandy pressed a slim hand to her forehead. "Another one? How many is that? Six?"

"Eight," Quinn said. "If this is another one of *them*, it will be the eighth one in three months." Only three short months since some of them had nearly been killed and Autumn had been lost into one of Abby's portals, along with the demon who had nearly destroyed their town. Quinn felt like they should have had some time to recover, to regroup, to mourn, but within days of Quinn and Raife being released from the hospital, they'd had to go back to work.

The detachment had received a call of a tall, hairy, naked man in a park, eating someone's poodle. Two members from the detachment had responded and had quickly called for backup to deal with something that was certainly not a man, since it didn't die when they shot it.

After shots had been fired, the watch commander on duty

called Inspector Donald Green, who had immediately called Quinn.

The Inspector, who was still recovering from the loss of his son—murdered in a plot to draw Quinn away from Resolution, so the demon could claim Abby McRae—had been brief. *"The members on duty met another one of those things,"* he said. *"I need you to go and take care of it."*

Limping from his house, leaving his love, Carrie, crying on the doorstep, Quinn had gone to find whatever had attacked the members on duty. *"I'm the only one who can do this,"* he'd told Carrie. *"There isn't anyone else."*

"But why does it have to be you?" Her voice cracked and tears ran down her face. *"When will you have done enough? When you're dead?"*

He wasn't able to answer, and had turned his back on her, unsure if she'd welcome him home if he returned.

Armed with Donnel's dagger—the weapon given to him by Autumn, once carried by her ancestor, Donnel of Inverness—Quinn had called Raife and Dave, who also limped from their homes, leaving behind crying wives. Together, they found the creature, a great, hairy, ape-like beast, shuffling through a park on the edge of town. They had been able to kill it, without losing too much blood, and had hobbled home.

Quinn had hoped it would be over after that, but he was disappointed. Like moths to a flame, more creatures, each one stranger and more vicious than the last, were drawn to Resolution. Autumn had suggested that Resolution was a place of power. She thought strange forces, both good and evil, would be naturally drawn here. But Quinn suspected that it had something to do with Abby and her incredible ability to open doors to anywhere that drew them. Now with Autumn gone, there was no one to ask questions, no one to tell him what to do.

"Are you carrying what we need?" Raife asked.

Reaching to the small of his back, Quinn touched the handle of the ancient dagger where it rested in the special, concealed sheath he'd had made for it. He nodded. "Always." He tilted his chin at Dave. "Are you?"

Dave reached beneath his vest and pulled out a tarnished set of brass knuckles, and bounced them in the palm of his hand.

When Kord McRae had arrived with his daughter, he'd been carrying the weapon. Like Quinn's dagger, it burned with white fire in the presence of a demon. It did not work for Dave, or Raife, or anyone else who held it, the same way it worked for Quinn. Quinn still wasn't so sure what it was that made him so special—what made him the Guardian—but the weapons turned from a muted glow to an inferno in his hands.

"Are we ready?" Raife asked, as Dave slipped the brass knuckles back beneath his vest.

"No," Quinn and Dave said in unison.

"Well saddle the fuck up cause we're going anyway."

Quinn nodded. There was no question they were going. No question they were ready. It seemed like they'd been doing nothing but fighting for months, and though he might deny it, Quinn knew he was growing accustomed to it.

As he glanced at Dave and Raife, he realised they had all been subtly but definitely changed. They were harder now. Quicker. Always the first and last to strike. Whenever they were asked to respond to regular calls for service and deal with normal people who weren't trying to eat each other, they moved with a brutal decisiveness that was unmatched by any other member of the detachment. The other Mounties in Resolution knew that the three men, who always seemed to be together, were doing something different, even if they didn't understand what it was, and did their best to stay out of the way. When they stepped aside, it was with fearful, side-long glances.

They were not the men they'd once been, and Quinn was not sure it was a good thing.

With final glances at each other, they went their separate directions to find their vehicles. Heavy work needed to be done.

CHAPTER 2

In the years he'd lived in this place, he had almost forgotten what his real name was, but he began to remember it as he dug his fingers into the dark earth. He knelt in the rectangle of yellow light spilling from the window of the well-kept house behind him, the knees of his pants soaking through on the soggy lawn that bordered his rose garden. He ignored the chill and worked his hands in the rich dirt and thought about his name. His human tongue could not pronounce it, and even if it could, the sound would deafen this fragile body he had formed.

The important thing was that he remembered.

When he had first come to this world, weak and terrified, he crouched, hidden, for a very long time, waiting until he was strong enough to step into the light. He had appeared and behaved as a human for so long that he almost believed he was one.

Now, he thought as he worked the soil, was the time to remember what he once was.

He had put out the call, summoning others of his kind. Humans, in their rank stupidity, believed that they were the dominant force in the world. They had no idea what lurked in the shadowed places, where no one could see, where none but the strongest could survive. He knew. Just like he knew his call would be answered.

He lowered his head and cast his will down through his hands and into the churned soil. He gathered power to himself, drawing from the deep reservoir of raw energy that infused the very rock. When he had so much energy flowing through him that he felt he would crack, he sent it out.

Come to me, he shouted into the earth. *It is time*, he screamed with the wind.

When all the power he had summoned was expelled, he stood and slapped his hands together, sending a shower of black dirt onto the clean leaves of his rose bushes. He had tended that garden for more than a decade, shaping the bushes, growing roses that won ribbons and human acclaim. He had grown the garden so he could wear it like a cloak, hiding who, *what*, he was behind the mundane act of tending a pointless growing thing. He stared at the bushes, the late fall blooms full and red, and hated them. They were a symbol of all the old strength he had forgotten and he wanted to rip them from the ground.

Many times, during his long, long life, he had come to this town. Many human lifetimes he had spent working one trade or another, waiting several generations between each return to ensure he was not remembered. Each time he came back to this place the humans called *Resolution*, he convinced himself he would harness the power of this place, do something great, but he'd only forgotten his true name and become more human-like. The profession he had chosen this time had been one of service, and it sickened him each time he crawled from his bed, as though he should have any need of something so mundane and weak as sleep, and went out to his *job*.

Now, he knew, things were different. Everything had changed. He had something to fight for, and he would not fail.

He glared down at the hated roses and flexed his hands, ready to claw them from the powerful earth, and stopped. He sighed. Instead of ripping them out by the roots, he picked up the heavy burlap sacks that he had pulled from the small shed in his back yard and covered them to keep the frost off.

The time was close, but had not quite arrived. And, he thought as he carefully arranged the thick cloth around the plants, he was not ready to give up every trapping of his human life either.

"Are you almost done?"

He turned and smiled at his wife as she stepped carefully down the wet steps of the back porch. He did not have to pretend or force affection when he looked at her. Though he sometimes hated himself for feeling something as pitiful as *loneliness*, he had been glad of every moment he had ever spent with her. His love for her had weakened him, but it was an acceptable loss for everything she had allowed him to accomplish. Soon, his weakness would not matter and she would sit as his queen while he ruled this world. She would be his partner for all eternity, though she had no idea. Yet.

"Just finishing." He turned back to his roses and settled one last sack into place.

"Come inside." She slid her arms around his lean waist and settled her head against his chest. Her long, black, silken hair settled over his chest and he lowered his face to kiss her tanned brow. "It's cold tonight, and I need you to warm me up."

"There is nothing I would rather do more."

She glanced around the garden. "Did you get everything done that you wanted to do?"

He lifted one dirt caked hand and rested it on the swollen curve of her huge belly and felt the small life moving there. A smile lifted his face when he thought of his child and of the brethren that would answer his call to help him usher his child into the world.

"Yes," he said. He rubbed his hand in a small circle, knowing she would be furious at the muddy hand prints, but also knowing that she could not see what was hidden in the dark. "I've done what I needed for tonight." He looked around the garden. "But there is more work to be done. Heavy work."

CHAPTER 3

The old duplex smelled of rotten drywall, wet carpet and death. Quinn stood on a narrow landing just inside the front door and swallowed heavily as he looked around. The house, a typical 'BC Box', had the entrance halfway between the floors. A set of stairs, directly in front, led up to a main floor and another led down into a basement. Though he knew they would have to, he did not want to go downstairs. Since he, Raife and Dave had faced the first of Resolution's demons in the basement of Joe Robowski's house more than two years ago, he'd had trouble going into any subterranean space.

He did not have to wonder if the abandoned dwelling contained an unnatural presence. Everywhere he looked laid the littered remains of small animals, mostly torn apart rather than actually eaten. He smelled a strong, heavy, animal stink, like the baboon cage at the zoo. It filled the air and almost overpowered the stench of rotting dead things.

Also, the dagger at the small of his back burned hot.

"Is this the place?" Raife asked. He stood in front of Quinn, a black Remington shotgun in his hands.

"Yeah," Quinn said, his voice coming out in a croak. He drew his pistol with his right hand, his flashlight in his left. "It's here. I can feel it."

"Up or down?" Dave asked from behind Quinn, adjusting his grip on his pistol.

"What do you think?" Quinn asked.

Raife racked the shotgun, pumping a round into the chamber, and switched on the light fixed to the bottom of the fore-stock. "Down it is."

They moved down the stairs in a tight stack, one after the other. Bile rose in Quinn's throat as his boots squelched through several torn, furry little bodies littering the stairs. At the bottom they found a perpendicular hallway, floored in pale, cracked linoleum. Raife peeled to the left. Quinn followed while Dave watched the hallway on the right.

It had been three months since Quinn and Raife had nearly been killed by the demon that had orchestrated the murder of Inspector Green's son, Patrick. Quinn and his team had not been idle during that time. Once they were able to limp from their beds, they had begun to train; both in group tactics and hand to hand combat. They trained with knives and fists, for the times they would be called upon to use Autumn's dagger or Kord McRae's brass knuckles, and drilled constantly in building clearing and firearms. They were, all of them, Sandy and Gerritt included, hard and sharp as any team of cops you'd find. Following Raife into the dark basement of the duplex, Quinn knew exactly what Raife would do and what he needed to do in turn.

The first room they came to was an empty bedroom, containing nothing but a water-logged carpet and fragments of broken drywall. Raife moved inside while Quinn held the hall-way.

"Clear," Raife growled, once he had entered the room and checked the empty closet.

As Raife emerged, Quinn moved down the hallway and checked the next room. He found a bathroom, the toilet broken off and lying on the floor, the bathtub half full of brackish muck. "Clear," he said, once he had checked under the vanity holding up the sink.

One more room stood at the end of the hall. It, too,

appeared empty. They turned and stacked up behind Dave, who still watched the dark hallway, his flashlight off but his gun pointed into the gloom.

Quinn settled himself as he felt Raife move up behind him. He waited for the big man's hand to squeeze his shoulder, and reached up in turn to squeeze Dave, signalling they were all ready. Dave blew out a snorting breath and nodded.

Dave moved forward smoothly, his steps short and efficient. They passed a shallow closet filled with bits of old debris and one rubber boot, and came to the entry of what appeared to be a large room. Without stopping, Dave switched on his light and swung right into the room. Quinn swung left and Raife followed Dave.

The moment Quinn stepped across the threshold, the dagger secreted at the small of his back flared with intense heat, making the previous sensation feel luke-warm. He slammed his pistol into its holster and reached back under his vest to yank Autumn's dagger free.

The weapon blazed with a searing white light, throwing the room into a stunning brilliance that burned Quinn's eyes. Dave, also holstering his pistol, drew the set of brass knuckles from under his vest and slipped them onto his right hand. The small weapon glowed, although with only a fraction of the intensity of the dagger. The knuckles would turn to an inferno in Quinn's grip, but they agreed that two of them armed with weapons that could actually harm the creatures would be better than relying on Quinn alone.

In the light of the dagger, Quinn saw a small, hunched shape in the corner of the room. When the light from the dagger landed on its slouched shoulders, the green figure turned and glared at them with black, bulbous eyes, the torn body of what might have been a cat, held to its chest. The demon was shaped much like a frog, but the size of a Great Dane. It had a wide mouth that spanned the front of its round, basket-ball shaped head, and opened it to show them several rows of needle-like teeth. Bits of flesh and fur were stuck between its teeth, and dark blood mixed with the creature's slobber to drip onto the filthy carpet with a wet plop. The thing tossed away the carcass while its flat black eyes fixed on the dagger in Quinn's grip. It let out a long, drawn out hiss.

Quinn swallowed, tamping down his gorge, and glanced over at Dave, who nodded once. Together, they rushed across the room, their weapons held up and ready to strike.

The demon dropped to all fours and let out a sharp, barking croak that scraped painfully through Quinn's ears. The creature began to shake, vibrating so violently that it became a blur in Quinn's vision. Both he and Dave skidded to a stop, and glanced at each other.

The vibrations continued, speeding up until Quinn could hear a high-pitched whine. He tried not to stab himself as he fumbled the dagger to press his palms over his ears. Dave did the same, and behind them, Raife let the shotgun dangle from its sling and slapped his big hands to the sides of his head. The eye-level window in the room cracked from the sound, and Quinn felt as though his eardrums would burst. As the sound grew to a pitch that Quinn was sure would either deafen him or drive him mad, the demon abruptly stopped vibrating.

Only, now there were two of them.

"That's probably not good," Raife said, his voice barely trickling through the whine in Quinn's ears.

The two creatures opened their wide mouths in unison and leapt towards them.

Raife stepped between Quinn and Dave, and pulled the trigger on the shotgun. One of the demons—the one lunging for Dave—was thrown backwards into the wall. Quinn pivoted out of the way of the other, swinging the dagger in a wide arc. He caught the demon across the belly and felt hot blood splash against his hand. The demon landed, staggered like a punch-drunk boxer, then turned and leapt at Quinn again. Meeting the lunge, Quinn drove the dagger forward and punched it into the mottled green flesh of the creature's chest.

The animal smell that filled the house struck Quinn in the face. He churned with his thick legs, driving the demon backwards. The creature hissed and spit and clawed at Quinn's face and shoulders, but he shrugged the blows away and slammed the demon into the wall. He ripped downwards with the dagger, dragging the blade through the demon's belly, spraying himself with hot, black blood and spilling its slick innards onto the soggy carpet. Fire leapt from the jagged wound and soon consumed the remainder of the demon's body.

Turning away from the burning demon, Quinn saw its twin hauling itself up from the stained floor, its chest a jagged ruin from where the shotgun blast had struck it. The thing turned its bulbous head, seeking an escape route. Shrieking, it leapt at Dave, smashing its clawed feet onto his chest, knocking him back. It used Dave as a launching pad and hurled itself through the already cracked window and into the night.

"Son of a bitch," Raife snarled. He turned to hustle from the room and up the stairs.

Quinn hesitated only long enough to ensure that Dave got up, with a plethora of cursing, and both ran after Raife's huge form.

They burst through the front door of the duplex into the cold night air. Quinn saw the demon scuttling across the soggy, overgrown lawn, towards the street. Raife lifted the shotgun and tucked it into his shoulder, sighting along the barrel at the fleeing creature. Quinn stopped beside him, gritting his teeth in anticipation of the blast of the gun, when he saw a sight that made his heart come to a lurching stop in his chest.

A figure, full-hipped and slim waisted, dressed in a long skirt, with a poof of curling hair, stepped from behind an old Ford pickup, and directly into the path of the frog-like demon. Quinn's heart started beating again in time for him to lunge at Raife, slapping his hand against the side of the shotgun. The gun roared, but the shot went wide, pellets hitting the side of the old Ford with a chorus of *plinking* snaps.

"God dammit, Quinn," Raife hollered. "It's going to get away."

"Raife," Quinn said, pointing at the figure. "Look. It's her."

"Who—" Raife started, but stopped short as he saw the figure stepping quickly across the lawn, its hands raised in front of it.

"It's Autumn," Quinn breathed, his voice barely above a sigh as his heart soared in his chest.

Quinn gave a strangled cry as the demon streaked toward the woman, covering the space between them in a single lunge. But she spread her feet and gave a hard shout, moving her hands forward as though she were pushing against a heavy door. A bright white light, like the flash of a camera, pulsed from the palms of her hands. The demon smacked into the light as though it had hit a wall and sprawled on the ground. It bounced up and leapt again, once more crashing into the barrier of light.

Illuminated by the light from her hands, Quinn felt hope in fizzle away. Though she was almost identical in height and stature, Quinn saw that she was not Autumn. The woman's hair was grey, rather than blonde, and the lines around her face etched deeper, more pronounced. The elated feeling that had lifted Quinn so high, fled, and despair crashed on him in a tide. He staggered back a step, nearly dropping the dagger burning in his fist, and had to clench his teeth against a sob that struggled to free itself from his throat.

"Quickly, Guardian!" The woman shouted, taking a step forward, hammering the demon with the light from her hands. "I cannot hold this thing forever."

The woman's shout broke the shackles of Quinn's despair, and he shook his head, clearing it of the image of Autumn's face. He charged across the swampy lawn and threw himself toward the demon with the dagger raised above his shoulder.

The creature saw him coming and tried to dart sideways, but collided with Raife, who smashed into it with the shotgun held across his chest like a cross-checking hockey player. Dave raced out of the front door of the house and across the front lawn, the brass knuckles glowing mutely in his grip, to cut off the creature's other avenue of escape.

The demon flipped from its back onto all fours and faced Quinn, letting out an ear-splitting shriek.

"Now is the time, Guardian," the woman said between

gasping breaths.

Quinn flicked his glance up to her face, bathed in both the glow from her hands and a sheen of sweat, and then lunged at the creature. The demon howled and leapt to get away, but Quinn caught one of its legs, the texture of its skin rough and greasy beneath his hand. He pulled down, hard, and smashed the frog-like shape into the ground. Its clawed hands scrabbled in the dirt, but Quinn dragged it towards him with a yell, and drove the dagger into its mottled back at the base of its skull. He released his hold on the creature's leg and shoved downwards with both hands, pinning the creature to the earth.

As he pushed, the big muscles of his back and shoulders bunching beneath his uniform, he thought of the night Autumn had died. He had foolishly taken her to what he knew would be a deadly confrontation with the demon who had orchestrated the murder of Patrick Green. The creature had kidnapped Abby McRae and planned on forcing her to open a gate to its own home-plane. Quinn had been fighting a losing battle and, certain he was about to die, tried to push the demon into a portal that Abby had opened. Quinn knew he'd have to go in with the bastard, but before he could, Autumn had leapt onto the thing's back and tumbled into the portal with it. He had tried to get Abby to open the door again so he could go in after her, but the exhausted child hadn't been able to manage it.

Autumn had been alive when she tumbled away into the dark, but Quinn couldn't believe that she would be able to survive in the blackness with what lived in there. He had asked Abby to open other portals, but each time she did, she was unable to tell him where the door might lead, and Quinn saw nothing but endless black. Each time he talked the child into opening another door, he swore he was going to take his dagger in his grip and go after Autumn. Each time he quailed in the face of the infinite dark and turned away, his courage failing him.

The thought of Autumn alone in the black, of his own quaking fear, drove Quinn to a fury. As the anger filled him, he willed it down through his hands and into the grip of the dagger. The demon had already been burning where the blade touched it, but its cries lifted in both pitch and volume. It erupted in a pillar of flame that lifted Quinn up and tossed him away.

He landed on his back a dozen feet away, all the air driven from him. Above him, a rolling cloud of flame billowed into the sky, and in its wake came the acrid stink of burning flesh.

"Jesus Christ, Quinn," Dave said, running to Quinn's side to skid to a stop on his knees. "Are you all right?" He looked over his shoulder at the smouldering remains of the demon and the thick pillar of smoke above the charred body. "What was that?"

"That was the Guardian realising his power," the grey haired woman said, dusting her hands together and stepping carefully across the torn lawn.

"I'm sorry," Raife said, stepping between the woman and Quinn. "Who the fuck did you say you were?"

The woman looked Raife up and down and sniffed loudly, like a disapproving teacher. "I am, Gemma Donnelly." She turned her eyes to Quinn. "I believe you know my daughter, Autumn."

"I knew, Autumn," he said, loosing cramped fingers from around the grip of the dagger as Dave grasped his other hand and pulled him painfully to his feet. He sucked in a deep breath and slid the dagger into the sheath at the small of his back. "It's my fault she is dead."

Though he had said it on the inside of his head a thousand times in the months since Autumn tumbled through the black door, Quinn had never uttered the out loud before. The confession felt like a blow to his gut, and his stomach clenched.

Gemma Donnelly brushed her long hair away from her face with both hands—an exact mimic of Autumn—and sniffed again. "Do not speak of my daughter in the past tense, because she is not dead."

Quinn' face heated, as he rubbed his hand over cheeks that

suddenly felt swollen. "Not dead?"

"No, Guardian," Gemma said. "She is merely lost, and it is up to you to find her."

CHAPTER 4

After assuring several nearby residents that the gunfire and pillar of flame was only a response to a loose bear and not an invasion from a foreign country, the Mounties, accompanied by Gemma Donnelly, left the south end of Resolution and headed towards the detachment.

An ugly conversation coming, Raife suggested it would be better had in private. They all agreed and walked to their respective vehicles.

Without being invited, Gemma walked to the passenger door of Quinn's patrol vehicle—a Chevrolet Tahoe marked with the buffalo head emblem and RCMP colours—and waited for him to unlock it. Still in shock, he remembered his manners and stepped around the front of the truck to open her door.

As Quinn pulled the handle of her door and stepped back, he took the opportunity to take a closer look at her face in the pale light cast by a nearby street lamp. She was, simply, an exact copy of Autumn, older by twenty years. The only difference, Quinn could see, was the grey of her hair and the lines of her face. Where the fine lines around Autumn's eyes gave the permanent impression she were about to break into a smile, Gemma always seemed to be on the verge of a frown.

Quinn noted, as she slipped into the passenger seat of the

Tahoe and he closed the door, that her scent was the same combination of incense and flowers that always wafted around Autumn. The memory made his heart ache.

As Quinn climbed into the driver's seat, he could feel an almost tangible tension inside the cab. He started the truck, dropped it into drive and pulled away from the curb as he tried to control his thudding heart. If Gemma felt any of the tension, she gave no indication. She rode in contemplative silence, looking out the window at the dark houses they passed.

"I..." he started, working his dry mouth into speaking.

She cut him off with a wave of her slender hand. "No apologies, Guardian." Her gaze focused on the houses passing by.

"You can call me Quinn," he said, softly.

She turned her head slightly, her eyes flicking to his face. "Quinn, then. No apologies. There is nothing to be done about what is behind us. We can only move forward, and there is much to do if we are going to bring my child home."

Quinn allowed himself a rueful grin. Autumn was ten years his senior and only her mother could refer to her as a child. They rode in silence for a time; Quinn didn't know what to say, and Gemma, it seemed, was unwilling to speak any further.

As they neared the detachment, a question occurred to Quinn. "How did you know what happened?" he asked. "Did someone call you and tell you? I didn't know Autumn had any family. If I had, I would have called you myself."

"I don't own a phone, so there would be nothing for you to call."

His grin came, quickly this time. The acute similarity to Autumn, to her unwillingness to come in contact with any technology that belonged in the last century, broke through his apprehension and made him want to laugh. Gemma glanced over at him again and sniffed once more.

"I do not need a phone to hear news of my daughter, Guardian," she said, looking back out the window. "I did not need you to tell me to know that she was lost."

Her words slapped away any hint of humour. He felt his

mouth settle into a grim line and kept his attention on the road, saying nothing more until they pulled into the parking lot of the detachment.

He backed into a parking spot near the rear door, turned off the ignition and got out. Beside him, Raife and Dave parked their vehicles as well.

"This is where you work?" Gemma asked as she got out of the patrol car.

Quinn nodded. "Yup."

She sniffed again. "It smells like fear. And anger." She wrinkled her nose. "And unwashed feet."

"You'll never find an angrier bunch of assholes than a group of cops," Dave said, grinning as he walked up with his energetic, bouncing gait. Even after all the years he'd known him, Quinn could never figure out how the man had so much energy.

"Where you wanna have a sit-down, boss?" Quinn asked Raife, as the big man strode towards them.

He rubbed his thumb and forefinger over his moustache and blew a breath out through his nose. "Don't matter, I think. No one here but us."

Quinn knew he was right. At this time of night, there was only his Watch working. Sandy and Gerritt were still at the hospital with Earl. Besides themselves, the building would be deserted.

He pulled his pass card from the pocket of his uniform pants and rubbed it across the grey panel beside the door. Yanking on the handle, he held the door open while Raife and Dave ducked inside. Gemma followed with another sniff. They walked past the detachment's small cell block, the run-down gym and the vague stink of the men's locker room.

They stepped out of the narrow hallway and into the larger space of the general duty pit. As expected, it was deserted. The only sound the faint buzzing of the fluorescent lights overhead. Raife led the way across the pit and into the small board room beside the Inspector's office.

Once they were all inside, Raife closed the door and all

three Mounties turned to face Gemma. The grey-haired woman studied the ubiquitous motivational posters, the assorted Arnold Friberg prints and the various plaques and awards interspersed along the walls. Finished with her examination, she ran her hand across the oblong oak conference table that dominated the centre of the room. When she showed no sign of paying them any attention, Raife cleared his throat, his moustache riffling in the breeze.

"Uh, Gemma," Quinn said. She turned, her arms folded into the sleeves of her billowy white blouse—a gesture so like Autumn that it made Quinn's breath hitch—and raised her pale eyebrows at him. "Can you fill us in on what's going on?" he asked after attempting and failing to meet her eyes.

She pulled one of the high-backed conference chairs from around the long table and sat down, folding her arms and crossing her legs, scrutinizing the three men with a pinched face. While some of her gestures and aspects of her appearance mirrored Autumn, Quinn noted that there was a whole pile of distance separating the two women. While Autumn seemed to be all made up of kind patience, Quinn felt as though Gemma was constantly on the verge of giving someone a good scolding.

"I think it is you who needs to tell me what is going on, Quinn." She glanced from Quinn, to Raife and Dave, and back again. "You and your...companions."

Raife folded his heavy arms across his barrel chest. "Since you're sitting in my detachment, and not," he nodded his chin toward the window, "wherever it is you came from, we can draw the general conclusion that you know something happened, lady. So, why don't you tell us what you already know and we'll do our best to fill in the blanks."

Gemma pursed her lips even tighter. "I know that you battled with something darkly powerful here. That you," she turned her eyes to Quinn, "lost my daughter in the process."

Once again, Quinn tried to meet her gaze and failed.

"I also know that your town has suffered deeply since then. Something is calling the things that dwell in the dark places of the world, and they are answering the call."

"Fuck, she's good," Dave said, hitching his thumbs behind his gun belt and leaning back against the wall beside the door.

Quinn lifted his gaze from the grey carpet in front of his boots and looked at Gemma. "How do you know all this?"

Gemma unfolded her arms and clasped her hands on her crossed knees. "Autumn and I had been in touch, in a mystical form unknown to the people of your generation, called a 'letter'. She told me of the child with the remarkable gift, the ability to open doors to elsewhere. And when Autumn passed from this plane, I felt her loss as keenly as if you'd cut off my arm. I could only assume she'd gone through one of these doors, as I would have known if she had simply died." She stood from the chair and walked to the dark window, looking out over the water of the Rivers Inlet. "I could also feel the power that is calling all these creatures to this place. I didn't hear it the same way they did, but I felt it just the same."

"What call?" Raife asked. "I didn't hear anything."

"You don't hear it with your ears, Mr..."

"Sergeant Raife," the big man said.

"You don't hear it with your ears, Sergeant," she said, moving towards Quinn. She didn't walk so much as glide. "You feel it here." She tapped Quinn on the centre of his chest, her long fingernail making a soft sound against the bulk of his body armour. "And here." She tapped the centre of his forehead, making him jerk his head back.

She looked up into Quinn's eyes, and he forced himself to meet them. "And you, of all people, Quinn, should be able to hear it."

"Oh, this sounds familiar," Dave said.

It was deeply familiar, Quinn knew, to all of them. Autumn had tried, without much success, to lead Quinn away from the conventional beliefs that he entrenched himself in, and make him see the world the way she did. She still believed in magic, and that the powers of good—of the light—must battle against the things that dwelled in the dark. She tried to show Quinn the world that existed at the edge of his vision, where he couldn't quite get a look at it.

Autumn saw things with her heart, where Quinn saw only what was obvious and tangible. He wished, just then, that he'd listened to her a little more carefully. Perhaps he should have listened with his heart.

Gemma let her gaze touch each of them. "If I'm not mistaken, things in your town have been degrading sharply. Your time is running out. Both to save yourselves and to recover my daughter. If we don't act soon, we won't be able to act at all."

"What is it you want us to do, Gemma?" Quinn asked, his voice soft. He felt like he would do almost anything to bring Autumn back. He should have done more.

Still looking at Dave, she stepped back from Quinn. "First, you need to open another door and find Autumn."

"I've tried that," Quinn said, thinking with a chill of the doors he'd had Abby open in the last three months, and of the gut churning terror he'd felt every time he looked into that long, trackless darkness. "When I get Abby to open the doors, I can't see anything except more black. I can't find her."

"Just like every door," Gemma said, "it has to start in a certain place in order to lead to the right spot."

"Okay," Dave said. "Where do we need to open the door?"

Gemma folded her hands into her sleeves again. "That is the part I'm not sure of. This town stands on a natural confluence of power. When we find the nexus of that power, we'll know where to open the door. Then we'll be able," she looked into Quinn's eyes, "you and I, to bring her to our door."

"You're sure of this?" Raife asked in a rumbling growl.

"I am sure of nothing," Gemma said. "I can only believe."

Raife snorted and rubbed a big hand over his bald head. "Yeah, well your belief and a dollar will buy a cup of shitty coffee."

"You said finding the right place for the door was the 'first' thing," Quinn said. "What's the second?"

"You need to find whatever is calling others of its kind to this town," Gemma said, "and kill it."

"That sounds suspiciously like one of those things that's easier said than done," Dave said.

"I did not say it will be an easy task," Gemma said. She looked back at Quinn and raised a pale eyebrow. "But we have a Guardian, and he is well armed."

"Anyway," she continued, turning away from the three men to move back to the window. "I did not find you tonight so that we might find the solution to all our problems at once. Solutions will come later, I think. For now, my goal was to get a look at this town's Guardian and see if he is left wanting."

"And," Quinn said. "Am I?"

She looked over her shoulder at him, her lips pursed, making the lines of her face deeper. "I haven't decided... yet."

Quinn didn't know what to say, so he examined the carpet some more.

Gemma sighed and ran her fingers through her long hair. "I think I've battered you enough for now, Quinn Sullivan. You will have to excuse a mother's anger. I know it is not your fault that Autumn is gone, and you have done what you can to get her back. Now that I am here, with you, it is time for us to do more."

"That is something we can all agree on," Raife rumbled.

Quinn stood mutely and nodded. He had carried such a weight since the moment Autumn tumbled into the black door; a sacrifice she had made in order to save him. Gemma's words, her affirmation that she didn't blame him for her daughter's death, or exile, whatever it really was, made the burden a little lighter. For the first time in months he felt like there might be a way forward.

Gemma tapped her sharp chin. "There is something more to be explored, as well. If I understand things correctly, the battle you fought most recently was a losing one." Her eyes focused on his face. "Am I right?"

Quinn said nothing, shifting his weight uncomfortably.

"I see," she said. "You are a Guardian, Quinn. This is not a mantle that is draped on every man who takes up arms to defend the light. The dark should tremble when you step into it, and there should be nothing that dwells there that can stand against you. You have not yet reached your potential, and that is something we have to mine a little deeper."

The role of Guardian was still something that Quinn did not fully understand. He did not know why it was up to him to take up this battle, or how he was 'chosen'. Autumn had told him, almost constantly, that he was special and that he carried a heavy responsibility. But he didn't really know what was expected of him, or why. If it was something he could give away, he would do it in a heartbeat.

Anxious to change the subject, Quinn cleared his throat and sniffed while he wiped his hand under his nose. "Where are you staying while you're here, Gemma?" he asked.

She shook her head. "Don't worry about me, I will see to myself." She stepped past Quinn, towards the door to the conference room, but on the way, she gave his forearm a brief, hard squeeze.

Without prompting or direction she walked through the general duty pit, and through the waist high door that gave access from the front counter to the main lobby. Quinn followed, Raife and Dave in his wake. As she reached the double glass doors that led out to the parking lot, she stopped and turned back towards him.

"I cannot tell you the exact how and why of everything that is to come, Quinn, but I know there is a great deal of," she paused, "*darkness* coming our way. I can also tell you, with equal certainty, that you will be the one to cast a light against it. There is power in you that you don't know, but together we will find it." She tipped him a wink, a gesture that was all her own and had no trace of Autumn in it, and her lined face lifted in a slight smile.

She turned, punched the latch to open the door with palm of her hand and stepped out into the chill air.

Quinn gazed out through the glass door as it closed and saw Gemma get into the passenger side of a battered, white Ford cargo van that idled in the visitor parking lot. A wide, slope-shouldered man with a fringe of dark hair around his bald head sat behind the steering wheel. The big man saw Quinn through the window and gave a nod. Quinn returned the gesture. Once Gemma had closed the door, the big man pulled the gear shifter down and drove the van out of the small parking lot and onto the street.

Turning away from the window, Quinn faced Raife and Dave.

"What the fuck are we supposed to do with that?" Dave asked.

"That woman was big on frowns," Raife said, frowning himself. "But not especially plentiful with the solutions."

Shaking his head, Quinn crossed his arms. "I don't know. I have no idea where we would even hope to begin." He looked back and forth between his two partners.

Neither had been with him during the final battle with the demon. Raife had been unconscious in a hospital bed and Dave had been forced to remain at the hospital to fend off the things that came to finish Raife. But, despite their absence, he believed they understood the burden of guilt he carried over the death—or, perhaps, loss was more accurate—of Autumn.

There was not a day that went by that he did not replay the entire battle through his head, thinking of everything he might have done differently to produce a result that would still have Autumn living in the small apartment above her little book store. Often annoyed with her 'feelings' and 'visions' and nagging admonitions that Quinn was some kind of chosen one, destined to protect Resolution Cove from all the evils of the world, he would cut off his hand if he thought it would bring her back. He would even happily listen to her prattle about a shape she saw in her oatmeal that she was convinced spelled certain doom for the town and its occupants, which would be near as bad as losing a hand.

No matter what protests Gemma might make about not blaming Quinn for Autumn's loss, he could see the reproach on her face as clearly as if she held a sign.

He met the gazes of his two closest friends. "I don't know what to do. I don't know where to go."

"For right now, son," Raife said, "you have to go back to work. You've got," he glanced at his watch, "five hours of night shift left to go." He turned and hulked his way towards the hallway to the rear parking lot.

"Where are you going?" Dave asked.

Raife turned and looked over his massive shoulder. "Me? I'm taking my old ass home. This is Quinn's team, not mine. I just came to help with the heavy lifting." He turned back for the door. "Don't call me unless something bites your arm off."

CHAPTER 5

He sat on the edge of the bed, his left leg jittering up and down as he wrung his hands. He looked down at his leg and snarled, slapping his hand down on it to keep it still. He had almost been asleep when he felt the surge of power from somewhere across the town. It had been a roar in his head that jerked him upright in his bed. His wife had stirred, reaching out for him, murmuring in her sleep. He had placed his hand on the warm swell of her belly, murmuring back until she stilled.

Now, he sat, infuriated that he had developed things like nervous ticks and the need to sleep, and dug his fingers into the meat of his thigh as his leg continued to bounce.

He knew what the power of the Guardian felt like, had tasted it in the air, and this was not it. This felt like old magic, like that wielded by the Guardian, but the source was different.

Someone new had entered the arena and that someone was very dangerous to him and his.

He looked over his shoulder at his sleeping wife, at the swell of her stomach, and for a moment the jittering of his leg stopped. Then he thought about all that he needed to do to ensure the safety of his child, and his leg began bouncing again.

He could not allow this new person, this new power, to

interrupt his plans. The time for action had come, time to remember his savage past, to reclaim what he had been in order to secure his future.

He stood from the edge of his bed, slowly so that his wife did not hear him, and padded toward the doorway. He thought of the work he needed to do, and of the tools he would need to do it. The call he'd put out had been answered, and while he could send some of his brethren to take on this task, he did not believe in half measures. He reached with his will, calling out silently, gathering others to walk with him. He would summon more of his kind, but he had always believed that if you need something done right, you should do it yourself.

He shook out his arms, casting his will down into them, felt them swell and lengthen. His face began to feel tight and the skin across his shoulders rippled as it expanded.

He was ready for what was to come, and he knew where to go. He remembered who he was.

CHAPTER 6

Gemma Donnelly sat in the front passenger seat of the Ford van and ran her hand through her hair, sighing heavily. She had come so far and was exhausted, but knew there were countless miles to go.

The Guardian, the young Quinn, was powerful. She could almost see it rippling off him like waves of heat off hot concrete, but he was woefully unprepared. She thought Autumn would have taught him better, helped him prepare, but it was evident the young man was head-strong and stubborn, and would have been a challenge for anyone. She believed that Autumn had done her best, but Gemma's eldest daughter had always been a soft touch, and Gemma could see that Quinn Sullivan needed a firmer hand.

She hoped it was not too late.

As clearly as she could feel Quinn's power, she could feel a darkness spreading over this town. Autumn had talked, in her letters, about the shadow that hung over Resolution, and Gemma could feel it as soon as she had cleared the mountains and descended towards the inlet. She could sense the obvious taint of the Guardian's recent battle, like acrid smoke that had not quite dissipated, but something else as well. Something more subtle. A black root, somewhere in Resolution, grew every day, spreading its branches further and further.

She turned in the seat and looked into the back of the van. Her sweet Bobby lay on the seats that folded down into a wide bed, a small lamp turned on above him, as he read a battered paperback novel. He had a rumpled sleeping bag pulled up to the centre of his bare chest, the lamp-light glinting off his bald head. He saw her looking at him and laid the book on his broad chest. His arms, covered in old, blue tattoos, were hard and thick with muscle, despite the gray that nested in the thatch of hair on his chest. He did not look quite as he had when she'd met him thirty years ago, after the death of Autumn's father, but he was a long way from over the hill, and the sight of those arms still put a tickle in her belly.

"What is it Gigi?" he asked, his soft voice. She smiled at the sound of his nickname for her, the same thing he'd called her since the day they met. "Why don't you come lie down and talk to me?"

She shook her head. "I know I should, but I can't get settled. There is so much..." she paused and looked out the window at the empty lots of the campsite that surrounded the van. "It feels like there is so much that needs to be done. I haven't earned the right to rest."

He stuck a sliver of torn paper in the pages of his book to mark his place and turned towards her, propping his head up on one thick hand. "It has been a long day and you spent a lot of energy helping the Guardian."

"You saw that?" She could not conceal a smile, as she looked at him.

He shrugged, the motion small because his shoulders were so big they didn't have far to travel. "I know that you're capable, but I've been looking out for you for so long that I'm not sure that I know how to stop. I stayed out of the way, but close enough to help if the Guardian did not meet your expectations."

"Expectations..." She chewed on a fingernail as she looked out the window. She had not known what to expect, but had hoped for so much. Quinn's problem was that he still thought in terms of only himself, only this small town. He thought the battles he fought were only about the creature he faced. He had no idea that he was a champion of the light, while the demons represented the dark. He needed to think beyond himself, on a bigger scale, and past his own guilt. They all did.

"Come on, Gigi," Bobby patted the bed next to him and held out a broad hand. "Come here with me and have a little rest."

Gemma sighed again and moved to kick off her shoes and crawl into the bed when she felt something she had not known in years.

It was a certain tang in her nose, like a sneeze that wouldn't quite come, and a tingle that ran up her scalp. Her mouth turned dry and her breath came in quick gasps.

"Gigi?" Bobby sat up in bed, the sleeping bag falling away from his thick chest to pool around a belly that had grown a little in recent years. "Gigi what is it?"

"Something is coming," Gemma said, her voice hard and hollow in her own ears.

"How much time do we have?" he asked.

She turned around and looked out the windshield. She saw several figures moving at the edge of the glow cast by their dying campfire. All had eyes that glowed red in the dark. "None at all."

Gemma opened the passenger door and slid off the seat to stand on the hard-packed dirt of the campsite, while Bobby scrambled from the bed, dressed only in a pair of old jogging pants, cut off below his knees. He kicked open the swinging back door and dropped to the ground. He groped around under the bed for a moment and came up with a heavy, bearded axe, the haft as long as his arm and covered in steel studs.

"How many?" he asked, as he rushed to stand beside her.

"Too many," Gemma said, as she stepped towards the fire. She summoned her will, drawing power from the earth she stood on, and reached down into the fire pit. She came back up with her hands wreathed in flame and stepped forward, making a throwing motion. A wall of white flame, three feet high, sprang up in a circle around them and the van.

Bobby stepped in between Gemma and the wall of fire, his axe gripped in both broad hands. One of the creatures outside the wall screamed. Bobby roared back.

"My love?" Gemma said. He turned and looked at her. "You made my life worth living."

"And you mine, Gigi," he said. "But save that for later on. I've not been laid low just yet."

"Yet," Gemma whispered, too quiet for him to hear.

Quinn sat in the Watch Commander's office, a windowless cave crammed in beside the front counter, and stared at his computer. It had reached the last quarter of the shift and the radio was quiet, which meant that he should be getting caught up on his team's paper-work. He tried, he really did, but every time he began correcting one of Dave's terrible reports—they looked like they might as well have been written in crayon—he found himself replaying the conversation with Gemma over in his mind.

He had only been in Resolution Cove a matter of months the first time he'd encountered the touch of something truly evil. A demon, what he later learned was really a lesser of its kind, had broken through the barrier between the human plane and the place where demons existed and had begun affecting people in Resolution. Quinn had shot and killed a high school student who had held his classmates hostage with his father's handgun. Then, Quinn had confronted a local homeless man who had shot up a strip mall with a machine pistol. In both situations, the people Quinn had been forced to kill had come into contact with the same creature, and both had been terribly and irrevocably changed.

It was after the second confrontation that Quinn had met Autumn.

Autumn Donnelly, who possessed power of her own, tried to tell Quinn that he was special and convinced him that something was horribly wrong in his town. She had shown him that it was okay to see things with his heart, instead of only his eyes. But most importantly, she had believed in him.

It was her belief that got her killed.

She had accompanied Quinn in a confrontation with an extremely powerful demon; one that made Resolution's first visitor look like a whipped dog. The new demon had carefully planned Quinn's removal from the town so it could move about—and eat a lot of people—unopposed. Quinn had attempted to kill it, but instead was hardly able to slow it down. Abby McRae had opened the portal that saved Quinn and the town.

Quinn couldn't stop thinking about Gemma's appearance in town. She had not outright blamed Quinn for Autumn's death—or loss, as she put it—but the inference was clear. If she looked to put him on the guilt train to Regretville, he didn't need anyone else to punch his ticket for him. He had spent the last three months punishing himself. With the appearance of Autumn's mother, that guilt struck him all the harder.

He looked at the clock on the wall above his desk. It was almost three in the morning and he was completely and utterly out of steam. He had just made up his mind to give up on work and close his computer down, when the radio mic attached to his body armour crackled.

"Resolution to Resolution cars, prepare for a tone alert," the dispatcher's voice said.

Bee-do bee-do bee-do bee-do, the tone that preceded any true emergency call pierced Quinn's ears.

The radio crackled again with the dispatcher's voice. "Need cars to clear for a report of a fight, and a vehicle that has been set on fire at Resolution campground. 9-1-1 caller reports several people fighting with what he believes are axes. Caller reports seeing several flashes of white light from an apparent explosion and the screaming of a wounded animal." There was a pause. "Cars to respond?"

Quinn keyed his mic, as he stepped briskly from his office, his exhaustion forgotten. "Send it to all of us, Resolution."

Dave stood up from his desk on the other side of the pit.

"Is this what I think it is?" he asked. He fell in behind Quinn, as he reached the narrow hallway to the back door and broke into a trot.

"Can it be anything else?" Quinn asked, as he reached the back door and shoved it open.

Sandy and Gerritt were already in their car, going over a report, when Quinn cleared the door and began running towards his truck.

"Do you want us to come with you?" Sandy asked, leaning from the passenger window of her Crown Victoria.

The answer was 'no', he did not want her and Gerritt to come. With the reports of the bright white light, he knew that they weren't going to be dealing with a handful of rednecks in a drunken brawl. It was going to be something far worse. He had been doing his best, for months, to insulate Sandy and Gerritt from those kinds of files, but given the description of the event from the caller, he didn't think he and Dave could handle it on their own.

"I think this is going to take all of us," he called back, as he slid in the driver's seat of the supervisor's Chevy Tahoe and started the ignition. Yanking the gear shift into drive, he hammered on the accelerator and guided the big vehicle, skidding and thumping, from the parking lot and onto the roadway.

Resolution Campground was the nicer campground in town, where actual tourists came to stay, instead of the more interesting of the town's denizens who, by choice or circumstance, lived in shabby travel trailers all year round. It was on the highway heading north from the town and was only a few minutes away from the office. Quinn knew the way, and the engine of the Tahoe roared as he pushed his foot down as hard as he could.

Silent houses streaked by, lit red and blue by the roof lights of the truck while the sirens called forth his passing. Within a handful of heartbeats, he cleared the densely packed houses of the city centre, passing into the less populated neighbourhood that lined the highway. His headlights flashed in the eyes of various animals that stood on the sides of the road like sentinels. Unless they were in the roadway, he ignored them. He would only get interested if they glowed red instead of white.

During the previous encounters with demon-kind, the recurring theme had been 'red eyes in the dark'; something agreed upon—or perhaps uttered—by anyone who had come in contact with a demon. It was one of the only sure signs of a demon that Quinn knew, but he had also been fooled before.

The demon that had killed Patrick Green—the son of Donald Green, Resolution detachment's commanding officer—had carefully concealed itself as a member of the Cranbrook RCMP detachment. It had killed and assumed the identity of one of the detachment members, and then killed Patrick to lure Quinn into leaving Resolution to investigate the young man's death. Quinn had no indication he rode around in a car or shared the investigation with a demon until it had chosen to reveal itself.

Quinn had vowed he would not be fooled again, but he didn't know if it was a vow he could fulfill.

He crested a rise, and the entrance to the campground came into sight. Behind the sign bearing a flannel clad cartoon frontiersman, the sky lit orange with fire, the color interrupted only by flashes of brilliant white light.

Quinn guided the Tahoe between the sign and the open gate that marked the driveway into the campground, squeezing the brakes as the tires of the big vehicle thumped and bounced through the washboard pot-holes of the gravel surface. Once he had the vehicle roughly straight, he hammered on the accelerator, spitting gravel behind him. He glanced in his rear-view mirror to see Dave's vehicle close behind, with Sandy and Gerritt's car coming only a heartbeat after.

Whatever it was they were about to face, at least they'd be facing it together.

Thick-trunked cottonwood trees lined the way into the campground, their leaves long since fallen and littering the twin wheel-ruts that marked the drive. The trees zipped past on either side of Quinn, obscuring the bright orange glow that came from one of the camp-sites near the end of the park.

As Quinn undid his seatbelt, preparing to move from the vehicle, he felt the dagger hidden at the small of his back grow scorching hot. He cursed softly, as he snatched the radio mic off its hanger on the dash. "Be ready, Dave," he said. "Heavy work."

He dropped the mic onto the floor and stared, open-mouthed, at the apocalyptic sight before him.

The van that had picked up Gemma was surrounded by a ring of fire, and outside that ring were several huge, hunched shapes. The ground was scorched in a broad circle where the fire appeared to have burned the grass away, but the flames dwindled, shrinking to no higher than the height of Quinn's knee. Just outside the ring were half a dozen shapes, pacing back and forth. Some of the shapes stood on two legs, some on four, but they were all hunched-shouldered, their long limbs corded with muscle.

In their midst stood a tall, straight-backed creature, its skin black as ebony. When the lights from Quinn's Tahoe hit it, the creature turned. Arms crossed its broad chest, its face was nearly featureless, and the mouth little more than a line and its nose not much more than two holes. The eyes above the face glowed red, and its thin mouth turned downward in a sharp frown when it saw Quinn.

In front of the van, Gemma stood, her arms raised high above her. Between her and the ring of fire, was a thick-shouldered balding man, almost as wide as Raife, if not near as tall. He had a big, protruding gut above the waist band of a pair of ragged, cut off jogging pants, but his wide chest bulged with undeniable muscle. He gripped a big axe in hands covered with tattoos, roaring at the demons surrounding them.

Quinn twisted the wheel of the Tahoe and slammed on the brakes, bringing the vehicle to a skidding halt, the passenger side towards the van and the demons that surrounded it.

The ebony skinned demon spread its arms wide and let loose a mind-numbing howl, the sound of it rattling the windows of the truck. It charged, lowering its shoulder and striking the front passenger door.

The passenger side of the vehicle collapsed inward, the side windows exploding in a shower of safety glass, as the truck rocked on its wheels. Quinn, devoid of his seatbelt, bounced painfully around the inside of the cab, cursing as he threw up one arm to shield himself from the shards of glass and fumbled for the handle on the driver's door with the other.

The demon took several rapid steps backwards and lowered its shoulder to charge again, when it disappeared suddenly from view. In its place stood Dave's patrol car, the brakes smoking and a large dent in the centre of the hood. Making a note to thank Dave later, Quinn yanked on the door handle of the Tahoe and slid from the driver's seat. He drew his pistol from the holster and crouched low as he made a sharp turn around the back of the truck.

Dave stepped out of his vehicle and looked down at the hood of his car. "That's my third crash this year," he said. "The Inspector's going to murder me."

"We have bigger problems right now, Dave," Quinn said, lifting his pistol and firing rapidly at a black, red-eyed shape that turned and charged towards him.

Quinn's pistol locked open, empty, and the creature barely slowed. Dave drew his own gun, but was knocked sprawling backwards by his own door as the demon smashed into it. Quinn dropped his spent magazine and pulled a fresh one from his gun-belt, when Gerritt appeared beside him, a newly-issued patrol carbine in his hands.

"This is fucking weird," the young constable said, as he shouldered the long weapon and fired at the charging creature, striking it in the head and knocking it backwards.

"Sure is," Quinn said, slamming the magazine into his pistol and yanking on the slide to chamber a new bullet.

The demon Gerritt had shot picked itself up off the ground and shook its head, gore flying from the newly acquired hole above its left eye.

"Well?" Quinn shouted, holstering his pistol and reaching

for the dagger at the small of his back. "Shoot it some more." When he pulled the dagger free, it hummed with white light, heat pouring off it in shivering waves.

Gerritt looked from the knife, to the demon in front of them, back to the knife and swallowed thickly.

"Today, Gerritt," Quinn said with a snarl.

"As you say, Corporal," Gerritt said, a nervous tremor in his voice. He lowered his eye to the optic on the top of the carbine and began pulling the trigger rapidly. The bullets punched into the demon. It threw its clawed hands in front of its face and howled.

When Gerritt's rifle went dry, Quinn charged past him and drove the dagger into the creatures neck so hard the blade punched through the other side. As Quinn pulled the blade free, fire spewed from the wound to quickly consume the demon. It turned and ran towards the other dark shapes, arms pin-wheeling while it screamed. Several of the others broke and ran.

The ebony giant, however, did not run. It picked itself up off the ground and casually dusted wet dirt from its shining skin and smirked at Quinn. It was such a typically human gesture that it gave Quinn pause. About to step out and meet it, Quinn faltered.

Seeing Quinn's reluctance, the demon tilted its head back, laughed, and then lifted a muscular arm to crook a clawed finger.

Sandy came up beside Quinn, a shotgun in her hands, and fired a shot at the ebony demon. The creature threw an arm across his eyes, but did not stagger when the shotgun blast hit it.

Glancing around, Quinn saw Dave on one knee, shaking his head while blood dripped from his nose and mouth.

"The knuckles," Quinn shouted. "Dave, give 'em to me."

Glancing up, Dave stuck a hand beneath his vest and produced the glowing brass knuckles and tossed them towards Quinn. Awkwardly, he caught them with his left hand and juggled them about until he could get his fingers through the holes. As he squeezed, they burst into a white radiance. Quinn turned to step past Sandy and stopped to face the Demon. He spread his feet and planted himself, a scorching hot weapon in each hand.

"Sandy, grab Dave and get those people out of here," he ordered. He glanced over his shoulder and saw Sandy lower the shotgun from her shoulder, but she made no other move. "Now!" he barked.

"Gerritt," Sandy said, turning and opening the back door of her car.

Without being given further instruction, Gerritt turned to hustle where Dave knelt on one knee and hauled him up by the arm.

Quinn turned back to his opponent and took several sliding steps to his right, placing himself between the demon and the people in the dwindling circle of fire. If the creature was strong enough to demolish Quinn's truck and shrug off a shotgun blast, he didn't think he could stop it. But he was going to have to try.

"Come on then," Quinn shouted. "Come for me, if you're coming."

The creature grinned, pointed black teeth showed between flat lips, and lifted its arms. Many of the demon-kind had fled into the dark, some remained. Quinn counted three hunched shapes shuffling up behind the ebony giant.

Now, Quinn knew, he couldn't hope to win. The best he could do was slow them down enough that Sandy could get everyone else away. What they would do when they had escaped was currently unclear to him, but he had to give them the chance. He shifted his left foot forward and ground his back foot into the gravel of the drive, gripping his weapons tighter.

"Hang on, Guardian. We are coming."

Quinn glanced over his shoulder. Gemma knelt in the ring of fire and placed her hands on the ground. The fire died and the huge man charged forward, skidding to a stop at Quinn's side.

"No one fights alone," the man roared, talking to Quinn but facing the gathered demons. "Not today. Not while I live."

"No," Gemma agreed, pushing up the sleeves of her blouse as she hustled forward. "We will stand as one, or we will fall together."

Sandy, seeing Gemma and her companions form a line on Quinn, ran to join them, pumping a fresh round into her shotgun. Gerritt, too, with one arm around Dave and the other holding his carbine out from his hip pointed it at the demons. Dave, his face pale and his mouth set in a grim line, pulled his pistol from his holster and held it in shaking hands.

Quinn wanted to tell them to run, but did not think they would, and was glad of it. He let a growl crawl up his throat and felt the weapons in his hand grow hotter.

The ebony demon lowered his arms, crossed them, and tilted his head. He examined the line of people facing him, his black gaze landing on each face in turn, then lifted one clawed finger and tapped on his flat lips. The thing gave a short bark, which might have been a laugh, and then made a flicking gesture with the hand at its lips. The three hunched shapes behind him gave howls, before charging forward.

Quinn gave a roar in answer and lunged to meet the quickest of the creatures. It would have been far taller than Quinn, had it been standing upright, but its long back was bent almost double and it galloped forward on all four clawed limbs. Short protrusions of jagged bone stuck out along its spine and from its joints. Eyes the colour of hot iron glared out from spiked brow ridges.

About to collide with the creature, Quinn rolled to his left. The creature swung a jagged limb at him, but missed. Quinn came to his feet in a crouch, just out of reach. When the creature skidded and tried to turn, Quinn lunged, punching forward with the dagger and the brass knuckles, his hands streaks of light. The demon howled as the dagger punched through its mottled skin and the brass knuckles smashed through jagged bones. The creature slumped forward, black blood boiling from its wounds. Quinn raised the dagger for a killing stroke, when something slammed into him from behind, sending him crashing and tumbling through the gravel.

He landed face down, particles of sand in his eyes and mouth. He raised himself on his elbows and turned to see the demon that had hit him, squat and hairy, shambling towards him with a strange, rolling gait. Quinn struggled to get to his knees when the shirtless man appeared in front of him. The big man held his bearded axe in front of him, and when the demon came within striking distance, he made an efficient twisting motion and buried the blade where the creature's head joined its squat shoulders.

Quinn scrambled to his feet as gunshots and bursts of white light exploded all around. The thick man yanked his axe free and chopped down a second time, driving the squat creature to its knees. Quinn rushed in behind him and drove Donnel's dagger into one of the things eyes. White flames burst from the wound. Quinn ripped the dagger away and rammed it in again. The demon howled and thrashed as white fire consumed it. Both Quinn and the thick man pulled their weapons free and stepped back.

Looking around, Quinn saw that the hunched demon he'd already stabbed lay twitching on the ground, while another had been pinned up against Gemma's van by gunfire and bursts of white fire.

Both Sandy and Gerritt shot at it, while Gemma stood behind Dave, leaning against his back. She clenched a fist that glowed white. A lance of fire erupted from her hand and slammed into the demon.

Knocked backwards into the van, it caved in the sliding door, the brilliance scorching the white paint. The demon turned and fled, crashing through a picnic table and the structures that held the campgrounds showers and the main office, trailing tendrils of white fire.

Turning, Quinn saw the ebony demon, its head still tilted to one side and its arms crossed. It nodded, slowly, as though it were thinking carefully about something, before turning to disappear into the night, another shadow in the dark.

"Bloody coward," the shirtless man growled, and then turned to Quinn. He leaned his axe on his shoulder and held out a hand approximately the size of a small block V-8 engine. "Robert Morrow," he said. "But my friends call me Bobby."

Quinn thought he'd never met anyone who looked less like a 'Bobby' than the burly, tattooed man in front of him, but he grinned and shook with him. "Glad to meet you, Bobby. I'm glad you were here."

"It is us who are glad of you, Quinn Sullivan," Gemma said as she staggered forward, arm in arm with Dave. Quinn wasn't sure who was leaning more heavily on whom, but he was sure that if one moved away, with other would go head long onto the ground.

Bobby moved forward and looped one of his thick arms around Gemma's waist, pulling her away from Dave, who would have fallen had Gerritt not reached out with one hand and gripped him by the elbow.

"Are you hurt?" Bobby asked, his deep voice soft as he lowered his face to Gemma's and held her close.

She shook her head, grey hair shivering about her. "No, I am not wounded. I have just given a little too much today, I think."

"What do we do now?" Dave asked.

Quinn sheathed the dagger and tucked away the brass knuckles, both of which were now cold, and glanced around the campground. Everywhere he looked, the grass was either scorched black or still on fire. Several picnic tables and a jungle gym lay in splintered ruin, and Gemma's van, riddled with bullet holes, sagged on two flat tires.

"Uh, Quinn?" Sandy said, her voice low.

Quinn turned to her, as she tilted her chin in the direction of the office. Quinn looked where she indicated. The campground's owner, a thin, wizened man named Irwin Jones, stood in plaid pyjamas. A flashlight drooped from his hand and his mouth hung open as he stared at the carnage.

"What we do now," Quinn said, with a sigh, "is figure out how the hell we are going to explain this to the Inspector."

46

CHAPTER 7

He ran through the dark trees, the after image of the Guardian's white fire still burning in his eyes. He had known the Guardian a long time, had time to observe him and, he thought, understand him. Tonight, however, he had met a man he did not know. The witch and her companion had made a difference, yes, but the Guardian proved to be far more formidable than he had suspected.

He would have to change his plan, alter his approach. Yes, he must remember his old strength, but he also needed to utilize reason and planning, and move these humans like pieces on a game board to achieve the result he wanted—the result he needed.

As he grew closer to his home, a strange anxiety seized him, along with anger that he would feel such a thing as anxiety. If he had misjudged tonight's events so badly, was it possible that he had misjudged other things? He had left his wife and unborn child, believing them safe in the fact that no one knew the magic of the thing growing in his wife's belly. If he had failed to predict the outcome of this night's confrontation, had he failed to protect his family?

He slipped unseen, quick as a sharp breath, down side-streets and between houses. He sped up footpaths, knowing every turn, where every street-lamp cast its circle of light, and soon leapt over his precious roses and in through his own back door. He vaulted up the stairs and down the hallway to his bedroom, willing his claws to grow that he might rend apart whatever threatened his family, and his future.

His bedroom was still, undisturbed, and his wife lay on her side, knees pulled up beneath the bulge of her belly. Her breathing was deep and even, a small snore whistling through her finely shaped nose. He strained, reaching out with all his senses, seeking out the threat. Nothing.

His wife murmured and reached out to his side of the bed. Her hand slid back and forth along the sheet for a moment before she raised her head.

"Babe?" she asked the dark, her voice thick with sleep. "Are you all right?"

He ducked silently out into the hallway, willing himself back into the form she was familiar with. It took several, agonizing seconds. Though he had worn the form for many human generations, it was an ill fit after an hour in his true form.

"Babe, are you there?"

He coughed, as he completed the change. "Yes," his voice hoarse. "I'm here." He padded toward the bed and slipped onto the mattress, pulling the comforter over his waist. His wife turned away and pushed her hips back against his.

"You're cold," she said, giving a small shiver. She reached for his hand and pulled it across her body, placing his palm on a swollen breast. "Let me warm you up."

He pulled her against him, nuzzling his face into her dark hair. She made a satisfied sound in her throat and wiggled her shoulders against his chest.

"Is everything all right?" she asked.

He opened his eyes and laid his head onto his pillow, looking into the dark. He had been surprised in the confrontation with the Guardian, but if there is one thing he had learned in his long life, it was that mistakes were opportunities to learn. His mistake had been significant, but so would be his improvement.

He opened his mouth to reply, when the cell phone beside his bed rang. He sighed and flicked on the bedside lamp before reaching for the phone, lifting it up to look at the screen. It was his office. It could only mean that someone from the public had called in about the battle in the campground.

His wife turned to him, her eyes bleary, and he kissed her forehead before swiping his thumb across the screen. "No, I don't think everything is all right. But it will be."

CHAPTER 8

Jesus leaping Christ, Quinn," Raife said, his hand rubbing across the pillow marks in his face. "I leave you alone for five minutes and you try to burn down the entire town?"

"It was more like five hours," Dave pointed out from his seat on the bumper of an ambulance, as Al Blaker, a paramedic that Quinn's team knew well, shone a small light into Dave's eyes.

"Shut up, Dave," Quinn and Raife said in unison, which made Raife look even more annoyed.

"And it wasn't the town," Gerritt said, apparently trying to be helpful. "We aren't even in town." He swept the campground with a wave of his arm. His smile abruptly faded as Raife turned the full weight of his glare on him.

The gradually lightening sky made the scene around him look even worse than Quinn feared. An ambulance and a fire truck crowded onto the grassy common area of the campground with the marked police cars, two of them destroyed. All around them lay scorched earth, spent shell casings and chunks of charred, broken wood. The dishevelled caretaker spoke animatedly to Staff Sergeant Steve Faulk, who solemnly nodded and wrote quickly in his notebook. The forensic identification member, who had joined the detachment last year, marked out the bullet holes in all of the outbuildings, while continually looking over her shoulder at Quinn to shake her head.

"How do you expect to explain this, Quinn?" Raife asked as he attempted to smooth his moustache, which was even more bristly than usual.

"I'm trying to figure that out, Sarge," Quinn said, wincing as Al Blaker's partner, a slender South-Asian man named Gary, rubbed an alcohol wipe on a bloody cut on Quinn's forehead.

"You don't need any stitches, Quinn." Gary's his thick eyebrows drew together as he tilted his head back to look down his nose at Quinn's forehead. "But I wanna put a couple butterfly bandages on it."

"Okay," Quinn said. He sat on the ambulance bumper beside Dave, and Gary deftly placed the small white bandages on his cut. Once the medic was done, Quinn stood up and walked away from the ambulance. Raife followed, his big shoulders bunched up as he studied the ruins of the campground, wincing. Dave patted Al Blaker on the arm and then hobbled after, rubbing at his forehead.

When they were out of ear shot of the medics, Quinn stopped and turned to Raife. "Just so we're clear, Sarge, it's not as though I was sitting in my office after you left, thinking up ways I could possibly get myself killed while destroying tens of thousands of dollars of detachment property."

"I will freely admit, Sergeant, that I was totally doing that," Dave grinned.

Raife rubbed a big hand over his bald head and let loose with a whooshing sigh. "I know that, Quinn, but this is fucked."

"You don't know the half of it," Quinn muttered.

As he gingerly touched the cut on his forehead, he hissed. Quinn saw a black Chevy Tahoe pull down the washboard driveway of the campground. "Ah, fuck."

"What?" Raife asked.

"Speak of the Inspector and he shall appear," Dave said.

Inspector Donald Green pulled the Tahoe in behind a fire truck and climbed out. A portly man of later years, his bald head was surrounded only by the slightest fringe of greying hair. Though Quinn had not cared for him at all when he first arrived in Resolution, he had grown to love the slump-shouldered man. He had covered for Raife, Dave and Quinn when they killed the first demon they encountered more than two years ago, and then again when Quinn had done battle with the demon that had orchestrated the death of the Inspector's son. He had kept their heads above water, able to do their jobs and away from any boards of inquiry that would ruin their careers and their ability to fight the darkness that threatened to overwhelm their town.

As the Inspector approached, Quinn glanced behind him, subtly sidling to his left to try and block the Inspector's view of the collapsed side of the watch commander's Tahoe. Raife saw what he was doing and gave a snort, the air riffling his moustache.

Halting in front of Quinn and Raife, Inspector Green put one hand on the butt of his pistol, while the other patted at his fringe of hair. He slowly turned, his hand continually patting, and then faced Quinn.

"How bad is it, Quinn?" the Inspector asked.

"You mean in a general sense, or just here?"

Inspector Green lowered the hand that patted his head and glanced at it. "You know, corporal, I'd slap you, but it would be unbecoming of a commissioned officer. Give me the whole story."

Beginning at the confrontation with the frog-like demon in the collapsing duplex and culminating with the battle in the campground, Quinn told the Inspector everything that had occurred in the last few hours. As Quinn spoke, checking over his shoulder often to ensure they didn't have an audience, the Inspector looked at the ground, his lips pursed in apparent thought.

"And these people, the mother of the Donnelly woman and her companion, where are they now?" the Inspector asked.

Wrapped in scratchy grey blankets provided by the fire department, Gemma and Bobby sat on one of the few picnic tables that appeared still intact. Bobby had managed to get a shirt out of the mangled van and had stowed his axe in the trunk of Sandy's patrol car before anyone else arrived. Quinn pointed them out, and led Raife and the Inspector to them.

"Miss Donnelly?" the Inspector asked and extended his hand.

"That's me," Gemma said. She extended a pale, trembling hand from the wrappings of the scratchy blanket, and gripped his hand briefly.

"I'm Inspector Donald Green, the detachment commander here in Resolution. Is there any way you could shed some light on exactly what happened here tonight?"

"A battle happened, Inspector."

The Inspector shifted his weight and gave an irritated grunt. "I'd prefer if you would answer me succinctly and not play silly games." His tone, one Quinn had only ever heard him use when he was well and truly pissed off, was sharp. "I've no time for your bloody sarcasm."

As the Inspector spoke, Bobby's face grew dark. He pushed the blanket off his shoulders, stood up and moved towards the Inspector. As Bobby moved, Raife stepped in front of him, so close their chests almost touched.

"You need to back up," Raife growled.

"I'll not have that midget talk to my girl that way," Bobby said, the same dangerous note in his voice.

"I said, back up." Raife's massive hand balled into a fist.

Raife was almost a foot taller than Bobby and had to stoop slightly to glare into the other man's face, but they were the same girth. With their bald heads and prominent noses almost touching, they looked like two rhinoceroses about to fight.

"That's enough, Charles," the Inspector said.

The use of Raife's given name, which Quinn was quite certain was only ever used by his mother, made him break eye contact with Bobby and glance at the Inspector.

"I apologize for my tone." The Inspector patted Bobby's heavy shoulder. "I mean no offense. I'm just anxious to ensure that none of my residents are eaten, or the town they live in burned merrily to the ground."

"I apologize as well, Inspector," Gemma said, standing to loop her arm around Bobby's. "I must confess, I am not a great fan of authority figures, and must remind myself that I am here to help."

"Right, so what is your sense of what occurred here?"

Gemma looked around the campground, before turning her gaze to Quinn. "How much does he already know?"

"You can assume he knows everything I do," Quinn said.

After the first confrontation with the demon, the Inspector had asked for as few details as possible so he could retain some kind of plausible deniability. But, when his son had been murdered, he'd pressed Quinn for every fine detail he possessed. There had been many hard conversations, but the Inspector had come out the other side with his sanity intact.

"Then, what I can tell you, Inspector, is that we were attacked by a very powerful demon. One that has the ability to summon others of its kind."

"Others?" Inspector Green's greying eyebrows climbed towards his bald pate. "As in, plural?"

Quinn nodded. "There were at least six, maybe more. We killed three of them, but the rest fled."

"You killed them, boss," Dave said. "Some of us were lying on the ground."

"I think we have to expect that more will come," Gemma said.

"Well, that's troubling." Inspector Green's mouth turned down in a deep frown, pulling his eyebrows down with it. "And what is it they want?"

Quinn let out a sighing breath. "I'm not sure, sir, but I have a suspicion that it has something to do with Abigail."

At the mention of the child's name, the Inspector's face hardened, his jaw flexing as he clenched it. When her father had been killed, Inspector Green and his wife, Geraldine, had taken Abby McRae into their home. From what Quinn could see, they had gone a long way towards healing each other. The girl was the light of Donald Green's life.

"Abby is not in any danger is she?" Inspector Green asked, his hand drifting towards the butt of his pistol. "My wife will be dropping her off at school this morning."

"I think not," Gemma said. "In fact, she is probably safer there than anywhere else. If the demon is looking for her, it will be reluctant to reveal itself and the child will be most secure in a crowd of people."

"What does this thing want with my Abigail?" The Inspector's voice dropped and took on that pissed-off note, again.

It made Quinn smile to hear the Inspector refer to the child as his own, but it set off a tinge of worry. "I," he glanced at Gemma. "Well, we, think it wants to open a door somewhere."

The Inspector let out a small growl. "Those bloody doors. To what end?"

"That is the hard question," Gemma said. "I believe that if we can determine where this door needs to be opened, and to what purpose, we will know how and when to stop this demon."

"Are you not able to put it down like you did the last one?" Inspector Green asked, turning to Quinn.

The question made Quinn shift his shoulders uncomfortably. "I didn't exactly put the last one down, sir." He glanced at Gemma again. She studied the trees behind the members. "If Autumn hadn't saved me, I'd be dead."

The Inspector pointed at a particularly dark, greasy burned smear on the ground not far from where they were standing. "You stopped these ones here, today, didn't you?"

"We did, sir. But the one leading them is a different matter."

Gemma tightened her grip on Bobby's arm. "And it was something much different."

Inspector Green rubbed a finger under his nose and snorted noisily. "What do you suggest, then? What should we be doing? How do we avoid—" he stopped rubbing his nose and waved his hand at the general carnage of the camp site "—any more of this?"

"I need time to think," Gemma said. "And I need access to my daughter's home. She might have some things there that will help me."

"Can you arrange that, Quinn?" the Inspector asked.

Quinn nodded. "I can."

The Inspector grunted in assent as Staff Sergeant Steve Faulk approached. Quinn glanced at Gemma. She met his gaze, raising one eyebrow. Quinn interpreted the look as a question, as to whether or not Steve Faulk knew of the things that they had faced here tonight, and he surreptitiously shook his head.

"How's the caretaker, Staff?" Raife asked as the tall, wiry, staff sergeant stopped in front of them, looking over the chicken scratch characters in his notebook.

"Scared shitless." Faulk snapped his notebook shut. "That man is convinced that a small war broke out on his front lawn, and that our members had a firefight with a group of marauders in Halloween costumes." He glanced from Quinn to Gemma and Bobby, and back again. "Is that accurate?"

"Pretty close, Staff," Quinn said.

"And why was...well, everything, set on fire?"

"Molotov cocktails," Raife said, rubbing his moustache.

"Molotov cocktails?" Steve Faulk asked.

"Big ones," Dave confirmed.

"Is there any way you can hazard a guess as to why a band of marauding trick or treaters, toting firearms and Molotov cocktails, came into this campground and starting lighting things on fire?"

"They were trying to rob us," Bobby said.

"Rob you?" The staff sergeant looked over at the battered Ford van. "Of all your riches?"

"They looked desperate, Staff Sergeant," Gemma said. "They were probably on drugs."

"Can someone also explain to me how you all collectively seem to have fired several hundred rounds but hit nothing except that shitty van and the caretaker's house?" Faulk folded his arms.

"Well, you see, Staff," Dave said, rubbing at his forehead. "Gerritt is new and, frankly, a really terrible shot."

"And what do you intend to do about this, Corporal?" Faulk asked Quinn.

"I'll immediately schedule remedial firearms training for my entire team, Staff," Quinn said, doing his best to stand at attention without looking like he was standing at attention.

"No, Sullivan, I mean about this group of firearm toting robbery suspects." The Staff Sergeant's face grew darker with every word.

Quinn opened his mouth to reply, hoping that something intelligent would spill out, when Inspector Green put a restraining hand on Steve Faulk's shoulder. "'C' watch has had a hell of a night, Steve. I'm sending them back to the office to submit their reports and then go get some sleep. I've also called our G.I. team to come and manage the scene." The General Investigation team, a corporal and two constables in plain clothes who tackled some of the more complex investigations, was another new addition that the Inspector had paid for by hectoring the mayor for more resources.

"Donald, you cannot seriously be satisfied with this explanation." The Staff Sergeant grew a livid red and his voice climbed.

"I am, Steve," the Inspector said, his voice still even.

Faulk turned to Quinn. "Why is it that every time something ridiculous happens in this town, you're at the centre of it, Sullivan?"

"Just lucky, I suppose."

Faulk looked like he wanted to hit him, but took in a deep breath instead. "Sir, you do what you want with this. I'll be submitting my own report on the file."

"You do what you think you have to, Steve," the Inspector said patiently.

Faulk nodded and stared up at the sky. "All right then. If you'll excuse me, I need to stop at home before I head to the office. It looks like it is going to be a nice day, and I want to take the frost covers off my roses."

Quinn looked at the front of the house and gritted his teeth. He was not looking forward to what awaited inside.

"Are you sure you want to go in there alone?" Dave asked from the passenger seat of the old, poop-coloured Dodge Caravan that served as the detachment utility vehicle. Quinn had asked for a different car, but Steve Faulk was still in a rage and refused to allow him to drive any of the detachment's nicer vehicles.

Drumming his fingers on the ragged steering wheel of the old van, Quinn thought about all the things he would rather do like undergo dental surgery or smash his thumb with a ball-peen hammer. Finally, he blew out a big breath through his nose and gathered his resolve.

"I'm just going to go and get it over with." He reached for the door handle.

Bobby leaned forward and tapped Quinn on the shoulder. "You mind telling us who lives here?"

Quinn let out another big breath. "I do."

Bobby leaned back and exchanged a glance with Gemma. "Then why are you so scared to go inside?"

"Because my girl is not going to be happy."

Gemma snorted. "You cannot be serious."

"Oh, he's serious, all right." Dave crossed his arms and hunched lower in his seat. "And you wouldn't catch me going in there for anything."

"You just asked me if I wanted to go in alone," Quinn said.

"Yeah, but I never said I was going with you. I was just trying to talk you out of committing suicide." Dave checked the front of the house again, as though afraid he might be heard.

"This is silly," Gemma said, reaching for the door handle of the van. "It has been a very long night and I cannot sit here while you wring your hands like an old woman."

Before Quinn could stop her, Gemma stepped out of the van and walked briskly towards the front door of the neat house.

"Ah, fuck." Quinn hurried to follow.

He passed Gemma and was halfway up the wide concrete steps leading to the front door when it opened. Carrie, the love of Quinn's life, stepped into the doorway. She was dressed in a pair of Quinn's old boxer shorts and form-fitting tank top that hugged the curves of her breasts, her black hair tousled from her recently vacated pillow. She had only had a few hours sleep, Quinn knew, between closing her uncle's pub and then getting Shawn, her son, ready for school. Despite her fatigue, the sight of her made Quinn's breath catch, just like it did every time he saw her.

She lifted one muscular, tattooed arm and wiped at her eyes while she yawned. "Quinn? Why are you still in uniform? You were off two hours ago."

"Um, hi, babe," he said, rubbing at the short hair on the back of his head. "We had an incident, and I kinda had to bring some people over."

"What?" Carrie asked, rubbing at her face again and stifling a yawn. It was then that Gemma stepped around Quinn and up the stairs, her hand extended.

"Hello," she said. "I'm Gemma Donnelly. I believe you know my daughter, Autumn."

Carrie's eyes widened, as she tried to smooth her hair before reaching out to shake the offered hand. "Um...hi."

"Hiya, Carrie."

Quinn looked over his shoulder to see Dave waving, Bobby striding along beside him on the front walkway.

Carrie looked down at herself and stepped smoothly to the side of the doorway so only her head and shoulders were visible.

"Just give me a minute," Quinn said to Gemma before bounding up the last few steps and into the doorway.

"Jesus, Quinn," Carrie said. "You couldn't give me some warning so I could put myself together before you brought strangers to our house to get a good look at my nipples?"

He looked down and saw the cold air had certainly had an effect on Carrie.

"I'm sorry," he said. "But we had a bit of an incident this morning and I needed someplace to bring these people while we figure it out."

She folded her arms and narrowed her eyes. "What kind of incident?"

"Well...it involved a lot of shooting, and a couple wrecked police cars."

"Jesus, Quinn." She turned away and let her head drop back, looking at the ceiling.

"And we might have burned down a building."

Carrie put a hand on her forehead and let out a long breath, turning back to face him. "I really am surprised you haven't been fired yet."

"If you ask Steve Faulk, my dismissal is not outside the realm of possibility."

She lowered her hand and glared at him, then shook her head. "Okay, what is going on with these people? Did that woman say she's Autumn Donnelly's mother?"

"Yeah. She thinks Autumn is still alive, and she's here to help me find her."

"Still alive?" Her eyes were wide, and then narrowed suddenly. "Wait...this incident you had this morning. Is something going to be looking for these people."

Quinn opened his mouth to reply, and then shut it. The last time he had brought people to their house to hide, Carrie and Shawn had nearly been killed when the demon that killed Patrick Green came looking for them.

"Uh...yeah," He said, finally.

"For fuck sakes, Quinn, I just finished patching the bullet holes in the drywall from the last time." She flapped her arms in frustration. "I cannot do this again."

"You won't have to," he said, reaching out to grip her shoulders. "I'm going to figure this out and get them safely away. I just need somewhere for them to be for today until the Inspector can find somewhere to house them."

She ran her fingers through her long black hair. "You've never lied to me, Quinn, so don't start now. How bad is this going to be?"

He turned and glanced back over his shoulder, to where Dave talked quietly with Gemma and Bobby in the pale morning light. It had been bad in Resolution for months before they arrived, and things had taken a very strange, very dangerous turn in the last few hours.

"I really don't know, Carrie." Quinn turned back to face her. "I can't explain it, but I feel like if I can get Autumn back from whatever dark place she went into, I might be able to stop what's happening in this town."

In the days and weeks that followed Autumn's plunge into Abby's portal, Quinn had not discussed the weight of the guilt he felt with anyone but Carrie. She alone knew the abysmal grief he felt and held him in the dark when the nightmares wouldn't let him sleep.

"I feel," he said, speaking carefully as though his words might take flight and scatter if he tried to grab them too fast. "I feel like now is the last, best chance I have to make this right. If there will ever be a time for me to figure this out, it's now."

Carrie reached up and cupped his cheek, the ball of her thumb rasping against the stubble on his chin. "I love you, Quinn, and you know I am behind you. I'll do whatever you need me to for you to end this, but don't get lost in the dark." She tilted his chin up, her blue eyes looking into his. "I couldn't take it."

"I won't," he said, pulling her close. He wrapped his arms about her and squeezed as hard as he could, pressing his face into the silky mass of her hair, as he breathed in her smell. He would not get lost in the dark, he silently promised. This time, he would step into it and cast a light.

CHAPTER 9

After settling Gemma and Bobby in the small guest room at the back of the house, Quinn sent Dave home with the dilapidated mini-van.

"Get a few hours of sleep," he told Dave at the door of the house. "I'll get Carrie to drop me off at the office and we'll try and figure out a game plan. Hopefully, the Inspector will have made some arrangements for our guests and Steve Faulk will have stopped screaming for my blood."

Quinn locked his pistol in the gun safe he'd installed in the bedroom and slipped Donnel's dagger into a pocket on the back of the headboard of the bed he shared with Carrie. Once everything was in its place, he went into the bathroom, stripped off his uniform and got into a steaming shower to wash off the blood, dirt and soot that had accumulated over the course of the exhausting shift. The hot water washed away all of the grime, if not his worry. As he scrubbed himself and let the hot water pound on his head, he pictured the face of the ebony demon and the smirk on its lipless face.

After the confrontation that nearly killed Quinn and sent Autumn tumbling into the abyss, he believed that he'd met the most powerful of the creatures. Now, after seeing the careless strength of the ebony demon, Quinn knew he was wrong.

Once he'd been in the shower long enough to fear that

he'd used all the hot water, Quinn climbed out, towelled off and shuffled back into the bedroom. He got into bed naked and looked at the pale light dappling the ceiling through the gaps at the edges of the curtain. Knowing what was out in the world, hunting them, Quinn felt guilty about even thinking about sleep. Once again, there was something in Resolution Cove that only he could face, and he lay in bed.

He thought that guilt would keep him awake for a long time, but in what felt like minutes Carrie was running her fingers through his short hair and planting a kiss on his forehead. He opened his eyes to see her kneeling beside the bed, her face close to his.

"Dave just called. He's at the detachment, waiting for you."

He tried to sit up, but every muscle in his body thrummed with a deep ache that a few hours of sleep had no power to banish. Everything hurt, and a little groan leaked through his teeth as he levered himself into a sitting position and swung his legs out of the bed. "What time is it?"

"A little after two o'clock," she said, running a hand across the back of his neck, her strong fingers kneading. "Do you have to go, or can this wait until tomorrow?"

He sighed and leaned forward enough for his head to rest on her flat stomach. The hardened resolve he'd felt in the early morning seemed to have evaporated while he slept. He wanted nothing more than to pull Carrie into bed and spend the rest of the day snuggled up against her. The feel of her hands on his skin almost had him convinced, when a flash of memory sparked behind his eyes; Autumn, tumbling into the black door, her face resigned and flat.

That was enough to push him to his feet, though another groan escaped him. "I better go. The sooner we get this started, the sooner we'll have it finished." He looped his arms around her and pressed his face to the top of her head.

He felt her nod. "I had a feeling you were going to say that, so I got your clothes ready and there's food in the kitchen."

"What would I do without you," he said, pulling back to run his fingers through her dark hair.

She smiled up at him. "You would be filthy and starving." She grabbed his arm and steered him towards the neat stack of clothing on the dresser, smacking his bare ass as he turned. "Now get a move on. I want you clothed when Shawn gets home from school."

Quinn quickly dressed, then stopped in the bathroom to wash his face, apply some deodorant and rub some gel in his hair. When he got to the kitchen, he found Bobby sitting at the table, dressed in faded blue denim overalls with a white t-shirt stretched across the bulk of his chest and shoulders. He had his legs crossed and perused the local newspaper with a pair of tiny reading glasses, that looked like he'd stolen from a much smaller man, perched on the end of his wide nose. He lowered the paper when Quinn stepped out of the hallway and regarded him over the top of his glasses.

"Feeling better?" the heavy man asked.

Rubbing at his face, Quinn snorted. "I feel like I've been dragged through a knot-hole backwards."

"Humph." Bobby lifted the newspaper. "Men were harder when I was your age. We'd fight all night, then put in a full work day before going out and doing it all again." He gave the paper a shake. "And we wouldn't complain about it."

"And you'd walk bare assed through three feet of snow to go to summer school," Gemma said from the living room. "Pay him no mind, Quinn. The last time he had to go to the doctor and get a shot, he fainted."

"I did not faint," Bobby said, snapping the pages of his paper. "I passed out."

"What's the difference?" Quinn asked, feeling a grin tug at the corners of his mouth.

"Passing out is more manly," Bobby said, looking over the paper again and tipping Quinn a wink.

"What is your plan, Quinn?" Gemma asked, moving to stand behind Bobby's chair and rest her small hands on his wide shoulders. He didn't take his eyes off his paper, but tilted his face down to rub his stubbled cheek against the back of her hand like a huge bald cat.

"I'm going to meet Dave at the detachment and try to figure some of this out," Quinn said. "Look for likely spots for this 'nexus' we talked about last night."

Bobby folded his paper and laid it on the table. "You want us to come with you?"

Carrie came out of the narrow kitchen with a round plate of grilled cheese sandwiches in one hand and a steaming pot of soup in the other. She set them down on the old arborite table, kissed Quinn on the cheek, and then shoved him towards a chair.

"Sit and eat," she said as she took a stack of bowls and plates off the kitchen counter and set them on the table. She added a handful of spoons and several glasses, clinking as she set them down.

Quinn took a plate from the stack and topped it with two grilled cheese sandwiches, while Bobby, sitting across from him, did the same.

"I thought about you guys coming," Quinn said, ladling fragrant chicken soup into a bowl and handing it to Bobby, who in turn set it in front of Gemma.

"And?" Bobby asked around a mouth full of grilled cheese.

"I don't think it's a good idea. Dave and I are going to do some research and we might have to be out and about to do that. Having you with us will raise too many questions."

Bobby opened his mouth to speak, but Gemma put a hand on his thick arm. "I think that will be fine," she said. "While you're doing that, I would like to see where Autumn lived. There may be things we can use."

"Things?" Quinn asked as he dunked a corner of a sandwich into his bowl of soup.

"Things," Gemma stated.

After waiting for several heartbeats for an elaboration, Quinn gave up and concentrated on finishing his food.

As Quinn ran the last crust of his sandwich around the inside of his empty bowl, the front door crashed open and Carrie's eight year old son, Shawn, exploded into the room.

"Quinn!" the boy hollered. He dropped his backpack—

which was coming apart at the seams from many such droppings—on the floor of the hallway and sprinted across the space of the living room to launch himself at Quinn.

Dropping his crust, Quinn stood up and caught the boy mid-air. Quinn spun Shawn, squealing, in a circle, then body-slammed him on the couch, which was also coming apart at the seams from many such slamming. They grappled on the couch, both of them laughing until Carrie came down the hallway, dressed in dark jeans and snug-fitting grey hoodie.

"How many times have I told the both of you not to do... whatever that is in the house?"

"I stopped counting at a million," Shawn said between bursts of laughter as he scrambled across Quinn's back and wrapped his thin arm around Quinn's neck. "Sleeper!" he shouted. Quinn pretended to pass out, but fell on his back on the couch, pinning Shawn to the cushions and eliciting another peal of laughter.

"Don't forget, we have guests," Carrie said.

"We don't mind at all," Bobby said, watching the antics with a smile curving one side of his mouth.

Pulling himself from the tangle of Shawn's arms and legs, Quinn stood and straightened his clothing. "I gotta take off for a little while, pal."

"What?" Shawn asked, sitting up on the couch and looking from Quinn to Bobby and Gemma and back again. "I just got home, and you're off today." He gestured to the two guests at the table. "And you haven't introduced me yet."

Quinn smiled and snatched the boy off the couch in a tight hug. "I'm sorry, pal. I have to go back in to work for a while."

"Uncle Sam is going to come and hang out with you for the afternoon," Carrie said, planting a kiss on first Shawn's cheek, then Quinn's.

"I'll be back as soon as I can," Quinn said, setting Shawn back on the couch. He rubbed the boy's head, then turned and headed back down the hallway to the master bedroom.

He retrieved his pistol, strapping it on with a plain clothes holster from the safe, along with Donnel's dagger, and slipped the brass knuckles into his back pocket. Before he walked out, he stopped at a hardwood jewellery box that sat on the antique dresser across from the bed. Sitting beside random sets of earrings was a single brass key. He looked at the key and took a long, slow breath before picking it up and tucking it onto the watch pocket of his jeans. He patted the pocket once and then stepped purposefully down the hallway.

In the kitchen, Shawn stood in front of Bobby, formally introducing himself and shaking hands like Quinn had taught him. Quinn had a swelling moment of pride that almost made him want to cry.

Carrie slipped an arm around his waist. "You ready to go?"

Quinn kissed the top of her head, breathing in her scent. "As ready as I am likely to get."

Carried bent and kissed Shawn, causing the boy to screw up his face and wipe his cheek. "Uncle Sam will be in herr five minutes. Will you be okay for that long?"

Shawn rolled his eyes. "Mom..." he drawled, drawing out the word in a sing-song voice. "I'm not a baby."

Carrie laughed. "You're my baby."

"Do you want a coat of some kind?" Carrie asked Bobby as the big man patted Shawn on the shoulder and thumped towards the front door.

"I used to walk naked through the snow, remember? A little coastal weather is nothing."

Once Gemma had collected her own coat and a small leather bag and joined them on the front steps, Bobby turned to Quinn. "He is quite the boy, Quinn."

Quinn glanced through the still-open door to where Shawn, the child who was not his blood but was his own son just the same, and nodded in agreement.

"Yes, he certainly is."

Gemma Donnelly stared out the window of the dark four door Jeep, as the Guardian's wife drove through the narrow roads of Resolution Cove. She glanced over the young woman's shoulder and saw the ring finger of her left hand was bare. The Guardian, his left hand on her leg from his place in the front passenger seat, also wore no ring. Perhaps they were not wed by law, but in their hearts, certainly. She didn't need a ring to tell her the two of them were bonded together as surely as she and her Bobby. She could not say why, but it made her feel better about this man, knowing he could love a woman as deeply as he obviously loved Carrie. Without thinking about it, she reached out and tucked her hand into the crook of Bobby's arm. He stopped his own study out the window and turned to her, favouring her with a grin as he covered her hand with his own.

Smiling, Gemma turned her gaze back to the window and studied the town as it zipped past. It looked much like any of the hundreds of small towns she'd passed through in her life, but Resolution had a peculiar feeling about it, a *weight* that she had never felt before. There was power here, running through the very rock, and she felt it reaching out to her like a giant's fingers.

Autumn had told her as much in the letters she'd sent once she had settled here. There was always an unspoken question in those letters; *will you come?* they had asked. And for all the time Autumn had lived here, Gemma's answer had always been '*no*'.

Autumn was a woman grown, and the expectation in their family had always been that their women be able to make their own way, to fight their own battles. Autumn had chosen to make this place her home, and it was her job to protect it against whatever might come. She was next in line to assume the burden of leadership of their family, and she knew better than to ask her mother to come and help her. But now that Gemma has seen this place she knew Autumn had been wrong, just as Gemma had been wrong to ignore the unanswered question and leave her eldest daughter to find her own path.

Because the path she had walked had lead her into an abyss.

Gemma knew the Guardian carried a heavy burden of guilt over losing Autumn. Gemma could see it on the young man's face every time someone mentioned her daughter's name. No matter how heavy Quinn's burden, Gemma's was two-fold. If she had come, Autumn, her eldest daughter, her greatest student and heir, might still be with them, and the town wouldn't be overrun with creatures of the dark. As much as Gemma wrestled with the "what-ifs", she had lived long enough to know that they didn't help. The time for "should-haves" and "maybes" was long gone. There was nothing left but the battle ahead.

Carrie steered the Jeep into what Gemma might have referred to as the "down-town" area. Each side of the street was lined with wide sidewalks and small, glass- fronted shops. At this hour, the business day was in full swing and several people tread the sidewalks with purchases secured in customized plastic bags or string-handled paper. Carrie passed several side streets, until they reached the end of this main street, furthest away from the water.

"Here it is," Quinn said, as Carrie pulled into slanted parking spot in front of a row of store fronts.

Quinn looked over at Carrie, and she lifted her chin towards the building. "You guys go ahead. I'll wait."

He nodded, opening the passenger side of the Jeep got out. Gemma and Bobby both followed suit and soon stood on the wide red-bricked sidewalk, looking up at Autumn's business and home.

"'Nature's Song: Books and Gifts'", Bobby read from the sign above the frosted glass window.

"Sounds like a whimsical name my child would choose for her place of business," Gemma said, a scowl pulling down the corners of her mouth. She turned to Quinn, who stood behind her. "Who has been keeping the store in Autumn's absence?"

Quinn shoved his hands in his pockets and looked at the ground in front of Gemma's feet for several long moments before finally looking up and meeting her eyes. "Um...no one, I guess."

"No one at all?" Gemma asked, surprised. "Is she not close to eviction?"

Again, it took several moments for the Guardian to say anything. Finally, he sighed. "I've been paying the rent."

Gemma opened her mouth to protest the cost, but the young man seemed to anticipate her words and waved her off.

"I called her landlord and told him that Autumn had to leave town suddenly on a personal matter, and the guy was very reasonable. He just asked that I cover a portion of the rent until Autumn comes back."

Bobby snorted. "Autumn, much like her mother, does not believe in banks. If you'd had a look around I'm sure you would have found all her money, or at least enough to cover her expenses."

"I thought of that," Quinn admitted. "But I've not set foot in there except to collect a key and make sure the place was locked up."

Gemma thought to ask more, but shut her mouth with a click when the young man turned his head away, tears glistening in the corner of his eyes. She looked at Bobby, and shook her head back and forth, once. Bobby crossed his thick arms and said nothing.

"Thank you for doing what you have done," Gemma said, patting Quinn's shoulder.

He sniffed loudly and nodded. "It was the least I could do."Digging into the watch pocket on his jeans, he produced a brass key and held it out to Gemma. "You'll need this."

She plucked the key from the palm of his calloused hand. "Thank you."

"Autumn doesn't have a phone in her shop, but there is a payphone on the corner." Quinn pointed down the street, towards the water. "When you are done, give Carrie a call and she'll come pick you up." He recited Carrie's cell phone number, and Bobby plucked his reading glasses, a pen and a scrap of paper from the front pocket of his overalls and jotted it down.

The Guardian stood there, for several more moments,

looking at nothing in particular. Gemma thought he might have something more to say, perhaps trying to think of yet another apology. "We'll be fine, Quinn. Thank you."

The burly young man nodded, turned and got into the passenger side of the dark Jeep.

"If that boy doesn't release all that grief, he's going to eat himself from the inside out," Bobby said, as they watched the car depart on the rain-slicked asphalt.

"He has already taken several big bites of himself," Gemma said, folding her arms into the sleeves of her billowing blouse. "What we have to do is show him how to turn that grief onto someone else, instead of himself."

Bobby slung one of his heavy arms around her shoulders. "I don't think we're likely to run short of enemies in this place."

She laid her head against him. "No, love. No we are not."

"Are you okay?" Carrie asked as Quinn climbed back into the car. She pulled away from the curb once he was settled.

He clenched his fist and rubbed his knuckles against the cool glass of the passenger side window. "Yeah," he lied. "I'm fine."

She reached over and gripped the back of his neck with her warm hand. "I know you are."

Quinn had spoken very little about weight he carried since Autumn tumbled through the black door. Dave and Raife had asked him about it, separately and together, but he had always waved them off. Carrie alone knew the depth of his guilt. Only she had been with him when he went to Autumn's shop to find a key and make sure the place was locked. Only Carrie had held him when he took two steps through the front door of the shop and collapsed on the floor. There he screamed, "I'm sorry", at the shelves until his voice was no more than a whisper.

Only Carrie knew how egregious his lie was when he said he was fine, and the fact she accepted, even if she did not believe it, made him love her even more.

They passed the rest of the drive in silence, Carrie rubbing a the Velcro-short hair on the back of Quinn's head, while he looked out the window and peered mistrustfully into the shadow cast by every building they passed.

When they pulled into the parking lot of the detachment, the fatigue that had settled on him since he'd pulled up in front of Autumn's store started to slough off. Gemma seemed convinced that there was a way to bring Autumn back. If Quinn was going to figure out how, this place was where he would start. He had been a cop long before he knew he was supposed to be a Guardian, and this was the place he knew best.

Before he opened the door to get out, he turned to Carrie, grabbed the front of her sweater and kissed her, hard. She made a sound in her throat and pressed her lips onto his.

"Thank you," he said, when he pulled back. "Thanks for understanding this."

"I don't understand, Quinn," she said, smoothing the front of his hoodie. "But I'm here. And I'll be here when you're finished."

"I won't be long." He opened the door to get out. As he closed it behind him and walked towards the back door of the detachment, he looked over his shoulder and saw Carrie watching him. He could see from her face that she knew he was lying just as much as he did.

Quinn passed through the hallway that lead into the centre of the detachment and found Dave sitting at a desk in the middle of the general duty pit, the computer in front of him showing a Google results page. An open dictionary lay on one side of the computer and a stack of file folders, most of them cracked with age, on the other. Dave, dressed in jeans and a bomber-style black jacket, had his elbows planted on the desk, on either side of one of the old file folders, his head in hands as he read.

A moment of deja-vu hit Quinn so hard he stopped dead.

He remembered sitting in much the same position, maybe even at the desk Dave occupied now, researching a run-down house in the south end of Resolution Cove. It had been the location of the last call Sandy went to before she was driven mad and nearly killed herself. As Quinn and Dave had discovered, it was where Resolution's first demon—the first that Quinn had faced, anyway—made its lair, and it was where Quinn and his friends had destroyed it.

Dave looked up at Quinn's approach. Quinn imagined the look on his face then had been much the same as the look Dave wore now.

"How are you making out?" Quinn asked, pulling a chair away from the next desk over and sitting down.

"Not worth two leaping shits," Dave said, crossing his arms. "Or even one for that matter. I've been trying to figure out where this bloody nexus is. So, once I got out a dictionary," he gave the open tome an irritated poke, "and figured out what nexus meant, I started looking."

"You find anything?" Quinn fought to suppress a smile.

"Just this side of fuck all." Dave pushed back his chair a few feet and indicated the stacks of files on the desk with a sweep of his arm. "See these?" Quinn nodded. "Well they're the earliest files I could find in the records room, and the oldest one is from the nineteen sixties. I've read through almost all of them and they're next to useless. Most of them are hand-written on yellow legal pads, and the penmanship is so bad it looks like hieroglyphics."

"So, kinda like yours?" Quinn asked, failing to hide a grin.

"Not now, Corporal, I'm in no fucking mood." Dave picked up an old blue folder. "Did you know that there were no street names or house numbers in Resolution in nineteen sixty-two? The location for this file is 'Joe's House'. Anyway, what I've found here amounts to two things: Jack and shit, and Jack skipped town."

"So where do we look next?" Quinn asked. "The library?"

Dave screwed up his face as though he had eaten something sour. "I stopped there before I came here, with the intention of getting all the local history books I could and bullying the recruit into reading them. You know what they had?"

The thought of Gerritt, surrounded by a stack of books and moving his lips while he read each one of them, made Quinn want to laugh. "Jack Shit?"

"Ha!" Dave barked a laugh and slapped the surface of his desk. "They never even heard of Jack. The thin-lipped old crone at the front desk was wound so tight she hasn't dropped a shit in at least a decade. Apparently, there aren't many professional writers who have taken an interest in Resolution Cove's history. All I found was the typical touristy stuff about the people who settled the town, old black and white pictures of the main street, the town council through the years...blah, blah, blah, blah."

"So, where do we go next?"

"I'm drawing a blank here, man," Dave said.

Quinn sagged in his chair and let out a heavy breath, while Dave gave the still-open dictionary a petulant shove. After several moments they glanced at each other. Dave raised one eyebrow and Quinn shook his head. When he stepped into the detachment he had believed that a solution, and end to his guilt, was just at the tips of his fingers. Now, that elusive solution might as well be on the moon.

"You two look like someone stole your birthdays."

Quinn turned in his chair and saw Inspector Green, dressed in slacks and a cardigan, hand-in-hand with a girl of an age with Shawn, her hair in pig tails. The girl grinned, and then let go of the Inspector's hand to step forward and loop her arms around Quinn's neck.

"Hi, Abby," Quinn smiled.

"Hello, Quinn." The girl spoke in the same measured, precocious tone she always used, but her grip on him was tight. He squeezed her back.

When she released him, she gave him a little wider grin, and turned to hug Dave. The dark circles that had haunted Abigail McRae's eyes when she first came to Resolution, and after the death of her father, were gone. Since she had been living with Donald Green and his wife, she had put on weight and remembered how to smile.

"What are you up to?" the Inspector asked, tucking his hands into the pockets of his slacks and leaning against one of the cubicles. "And why has McLeod stolen all those files."

"I signed them out, sir," Dave said, his voice formal, as he released Abby from his own crushing hug. "As per policy."

Donald Green scowled. "I have serious doubts about that, David. Really, why are you boys here?"

"We were working on that problem presented by our new visitor," Quinn said.

Beside him, Dave pinched Abby's cheek and gave one of her braids a tug, breaking through Abby's demure smile and eliciting a high-pitched giggle. Hearing the child's laugh made Quinn chuckle.

The Inspector cleared his voice. "And?"

"We have found just two things," Dave said. "Jack and—" He glanced sideways at Abby, who, in the fashion of children, now had her undivided attention hanging on his every word.

"Nothing," Dave finished, swallowing with a bob of his Adams apple. "We have found nothing."

The Inspector snorted. "Abby-dear?"

The girl turned towards him.

"How about you go see if the ladies at the front counter have any good colouring books today."

The girl turned back to Quinn and Dave, gave them a wave that would do the Queen proud, then hustled to the front counter, her braids trailing behind her.

"She looks good, sir," Quinn said, hearing the cries of delight from the elderly volunteers that manned the front counter.

"She *is* good," the Inspector said, a smile creasing his face.

It had taken some careful explaining, by everyone involved, to articulate that Kord McRae had fallen to his death from the catwalk in an abandoned warehouse and had not, in fact, been murdered by a demon. The Inspector spoke with the Ministry of Children and Family Development and offered to take Abby into his home, as she had no living relatives.

When Abby and Donald Green had come together, they had both been broken, suffering a deep loss. But in the months since then, they had rebuilt each other. It made Quinn glad.

"All right, fellas." Donald Green clapped his hands together and rubbed them briskly. "What are we looking for?"

Dave glared at the dictionary again. "We're trying to figure out this Goddamned nexus thing."

"Ah," the Inspector said, rubbing a hand over his bald pate. "Any luck at all?"

"None," Quinn said. "We've checked the resources we have here at the detachment, and the library was a bust."

"Well, who do we know who knows the history of this town?" the Inspector asked. "And I mean the real history, not the touristy bullshit."

Dave snorted. "I think you may have forgotten what we do for a living, sir. Our profession doesn't exactly bring us in contact with the educated portion of the population."

"Fair point, McLeod," Donald Green inclined his head. He put his hands back in his pockets and paced between the rows of desks. "Let's think about this critically for a moment. We're all trained investigators here, aren't we? When you start an investigation, what is the first thing you look for?"

"A way to conclude the file so I can go home on time?" Dave asked.

The Inspector stopped and turned, fixing Dave with a glare. "Sullivan, how do you not beat him regularly?"

"I'm quite convinced he is a barbarian and any beatings will only encourage him," Quinn said, his tone dry. "And to answer your question, we look for evidence."

"Right," the Inspector said, continuing to pace. "And if we don't have any readily apparent evidence, what's next?"

"Witnesses?" Dave asked.

The Inspector turned, pointed at Dave and clicked his tongue. "Right. If we can't find the source, we find someone who can point us to the source."

Quinn sat up straight and looked at Dave, as several tumblers fell into place in his head. "Who do we know in this town who has lived here all their lives, and knows absolutely everyone?"

Dave brightened, a decidedly evil grin stealing onto his face. "Well, only our favourite person ever!"

The two men stood together, and in unison said, "Cecil."

Gemma Donnelly closed another book and laid it carefully on the top of a teetering stack that sat on the round, wooden coffee table which dominated the small living room space. She looked around the apartment that Autumn had kept above her shop and blew out a big breath, making her long hair fly up.

Across from her, Bobby sat in one of the four leather chairs that circled the round table, his reading glasses perched on the end of his nose. He stuck a thick finger in the book and closed it. "Still nothing?"

She shook her head and stood up, smoothing down her skirt with a flap of her arms. "Nothing useful, anyway." She indicated the book she'd just put down, which bore the title, *Magic and Phases of the Moon*. "None of these books say anything about doorways or portals, except in the most abstract of fashions."

Bobby opened his book and traced his finger down the centre of the page he'd marked. "'Only when you release the darkness within you can you open the door to your inner self,'" he read.

"Exactly." Gemma ran her hands through her hair. "The people who wrote most of these books have probably never encountered a creature of the dark. Not a real one anyway. They believe magic is Fae whisperings and crystals on strings. They have no idea that magic, real magic, is blood and fire."

"Perhaps that is a good thing." He lay the book on the arm of his chair. "If everyone knew demons were real, we'd probably be overrun with the bastards and hiding in caves."

"Ugh, I know," she said. "But I feel like we're wasting time.

We're sitting here, reading foolishness, while the thing that came for us last night is walking free in this town." She moved to stand in front of the row of bookshelves along the far wall of the apartment. It was crammed to bursting with books of all description. "There has to be something here, I just don't know where it is."

With a grunting heave, Bobby stood from the chair and shuffled around the low table to stand beside her. "I thought you said Autumn had some old books that you needed."

"I thought so," Gemma said, propping her hands on her hips. "But I haven't been able to find them."

"If they're precious, maybe she wouldn't keep them sitting on the shelf with the others."

"That might be true," she said. "But if they're not here, where are they?"

With a shrug, Bobby plucked his glasses off his nose, hung them on the collar of the t-shirt he wore beneath his overalls, and clumped across the floor towards the kitchen. He started pulling open drawers and cupboards, peering into them. Following his example, Gemma moved into the end of the apartment where Autumn kept her narrow bed. Gemma searched the drawers of the dresser, through the nightstand, under the bed and even between the mattress and box-spring. The only unusual thing she saw was an appliance in her daughter's nightstand, that she instantly wished she could unsee.

"Any luck?" Bobby asked, coming to stand beside her.

Gemma cast an uneasy glance at the nightstand then shook her head. "More nothing." She looked around, and opened her mouth to voice her frustration, but a glance of something over Bobby's thick shoulder stopped her.

In a small frame, hanging on the wall beside the bed, was a quote picked out in cross-stitch. "'To know where you're going, you have to know where you came from,'" Gemma read out loud.

"What?" Bobby asked.

"That quote," Gemma said, lifting her chin towards the

frame.

"What about it?"

"It shouldn't be here."

Bobby crossed his arms. "What do you mean?"

"Have you ever known Autumn to do anything crafty? Knit a sweater or anything like that?"

Bobby laughed. "She used to write some terrible poetry when she was in high school."

"I'm serious, love. Autumn never did anything like this."

He shrugged. "Okay, so what does that mean?"

"It means I think it's here for a reason. I think she wanted to lead me to something."

Gemma began walking the perimeter of the room, examining everything, looking for anything else that was out of place. On the wall next to the door that opened onto the stairs that lead down to the shop was an old, blown up picture. It showed a very young Autumn, her thick blonde hair in a dizzying halo around her head, walking beside a much younger Gemma Donnelly. They were in front of the small house that Autumn had grown up in. Gemma remembered the day and how Autumn had been fascinated with the camera her father had used to take that picture. Gemma had seen the picture when she and Bobby first arrived, but gave it no more thought than you would to a passing, pleasant memory. Now she stood in front of it, studying it.

"That was where she came from," Gemma said, to no one in particular.

She grasped the picture by the edges and lifted it off the wall. Behind it was a small cupboard set into the wall. She set the picture on the floor, against the wall, and pulled the small brass knob affixed to the cupboard door. Inside sat four thick, leather-bound books, as well as the box that had held Donnel's dagger on the day she had given it to Autumn.

"Is that what you were looking for, Gigi?" Bobby asked as he came behind her and wrapped his arms around her shoulders to plant a kiss on her cheek.

"It is," she replied, reaching up to grip his forearms. "And it has given me an idea."

CHAPTER 10

en minutes later Quinn and Dave sat, once again in the decrepit Dodge minivan, in front of a dingy hotel on the edge of Resolution's downtown. Quinn had heard that certain places grew on you, the more you saw them. But in the case of the Welcome Beaver, Quinn's loathing of the place increased a little more with each visit.

"Have I mentioned this place is a shithole?" Quinn asked, as he looked out the passenger window of the minivan. The flickering neon bore the establishment's name on a shape that loosely resembled a beaver.

"Only every time we come here," Dave said. He pulled open the glove box, banging the door into Quinn's knees, and began rummaging inside.

"What are you looking for?" Quinn asked.

Dave gave a hoot of triumph as he pulled a small bottle from the glove box. "Hand sanitizer," he said, holding up the container of clear, viscous liquid. "I like to dab some on before I go in there."

Quinn snorted. "Do I have to explain to you how hand-sanitizer works?"

Dave upended the bottle and squirted half the contents into his open hand, then rubbed it vigorously onto his hands and forearms. "You never know what kind of shit you're going to come in contact with in this place."

Quinn was about to make fun of him some more, looked at the sign above the hotel's front door. "You might be on to something," he said, and reached out a hand for the bottle.

Once they were both pre-sanitized, they opened their doors and stepped briskly across the wide sidewalk. They hadn't changed into full-uniform, but had both donned their body armour over their jackets, and Quinn settled the vest, and checked that all his equipment was in place. Dave grasped one of the tarnished brass handles on wooden doors made up of diagonal slats and pulled the door open with hard yank.

On all of Quinn's previous visits, the entry—that could only be loosely referred to as a lobby—was dark, dirty, and smelled of a combination of piss and vomit. The bright light of a standing construction lamp cut the gloom and the smell of fresh sawdust filled the air. The old couch that had once dominated the room was gone, replaced with a stack of lumber. Behind the scarred reception desk, several sheets of drywall leaned against the faded wall-paper. The wall directly across from the entrance, that had once secreted a small room where Cecil held illegal card games, was gone. Beyond was an open space and, what Quinn could only describe as a spectacle.

In the middle of the now-open space was a hastily erected stage with a brass pole sprouting from its centre. A woman, who appeared to be in her late forties and not in particularly good shape, leaned clumsily against the pole, kicking her feet in an offset rhythm from the crackling music pounding from a row of old speakers. Folding chairs surrounded the stage, some of them occupied by scruffy looking men Quinn recognised from dealing with them in Resolution's darker corners. The men held red plastic cups and hooted enthusiastically at the travesty unfolding on the stage.

"What in the suffering name of Christ is this?" Dave asked, his face displaying the same bewilderment Quinn felt sure was painted on his own.

Quinn waved a hand in front of his face, trying to clear some of the dust. "I feel like this is what hell would look like if someone set up a stage in it."

Raising a hand to ward off the glare from the haphazard lights above the stage, and to block the sight of the stage itself, Quinn searched the room. At the back, under the glow of the construction lamp, a diminutive figure was crouched on top of the rough frame of a table, screwing down a piece of plywood. The frame was obviously not square, and Quinn winced as the figure shifted its weight and the frame gave an alarming lurch.

One of the patrons in the folding chairs said something to the figure on the table, and it looked up, let out a screech and jumped off to hustle towards them.

"Here we go," Dave said, hitching up his belt and fighting the grin that dominated his face.

Cecil Brown, a tool belt sagging from his hips beneath the protrusion of his pot belly and white hard hat perched on top of his head, stormed up to them, his face purple beneath a coating of saw dust.

"McLeod? Sullivan? What the fuck are you two assholes doing in here? You got a warrant?"

"I keep telling you Cecil," Dave said. "I don't need a warrant to set foot in your, uh, establishment."

"Fucking rights you do," Cecil said, tilting his hard hat back to show the spider tattoo on his forehead. "And my name is *Spider!*"

"Anyone ever tell you the hard hat makes you look like an angry little penis?" Dave asked, folding his arms and struggling to maintain a serious expression. Quinn wasn't sure why Dave took such pleasure in heating up Cecil, but he had turned it into an art form.

The little man, whose wobbly hard hat barely reached Quinn's chin, grew a deeper shade of crimson and lifted a finger to jab into Dave's chest, when Quinn gestured to the room behind him.

"Cecil, what are you doing in here?"

The short man paused in his finger jabbing and glanced at Quinn. "I'm renovating."

"But, why are you renovating into a strip bar?" Quinn

asked.

"And where did you dredge up that, uh, dancer?" Dave nodded towards the stage.

Cecil glared at Dave. "Never you fucking mind." Then he turned back to Quinn. "Every tourist, work crew and university asshole who darkens my doorway always comes because they see the name and think I run a peeler bar. Then they fuck off when they see," he gestured to the lobby, "this."

"So you slapped on a hard hat and decided to do it all yourself?" Quinn asked.

"Do I look like I'm made of money? Contractors are expensive."

"Might be less expensive than paying for all the people you're gonna kill when that stage collapses and your entertainer rolls over the crowd," Dave said.

"What is it you assholes want?" Cecil said, apparently ignoring Dave for the first time Quinn could remember.

"We need to ask you a couple of questions," Quinn said.

"Oh, good," Cecil said. "I have a couple of answers. 'I didn't do it', and 'call my fucking lawyer.'"

Dave's face turned uncharacteristically earnest. "Not those kinds of questions, Cecil-"

"Spider!" The little man's face regained the crimson glow it had so recently relinquished.

"Right," Quinn said. "We're not here to question you in relation to a crime. We're actually looking for some directions towards someone who might be able to help us."

"And what if I tell you to go pound sand into the eye of your cock?"

Quinn felt his patience take a dangerous slip, and he stepped a little closer to Cecil, causing the little man to pale and take a step backwards. "If you're unable to provide me with any information to further my current investigation, then I will have a surplus of free time on my hands." Quinn held up his hands and wriggled his fingers for emphasis. "I suspect that I would probably use that free time to investigate whether or not you have a permit to carry out these renovations, which considering the state of this little project I am quite certain you do not. I would have a building inspector down here in about fifteen minutes, and shut down any further changes to your merry little shit-hole.

"Once I have that completed, I would check to see if there is a liquor licence in this place for the pissy beer I assume is in those red cups. From the look on your face I assume that is another thing you overlooked, and the resulting fine will put you out of business." Quinn leaned towards Cecil, and lowered his voice to a hissing whisper. "Forever."

Yanking his hard hat off his balding head, Cecil turned away with a growl of frustration and kicked at a couple of loose pieces of lumber, cursing profusely.

Dave leaned in to Quinn. "Have you been taking lessons from Raife?" he asked.

Quinn glanced over at him. "Maybe one or two."

"Good," Dave said. "I dig it."

Cecil slapped his hard hat back on his head and turned again to face them. "Okay. Fuck. Okay, what do you assholes want?" He pointed a finger at Quinn. "And just for the record, the beer I serve is good. It isn't pissy."

"I have some pretty profound doubts about that, Cecil," Quinn said.

"Spider!" the little man shouted, drawing some looks from the audience gathered around the stage.

"Indeed," Quinn said. "My doubts aside, we're hoping you can point us in the direction of someone."

Cecil crossed his arms, his eyes narrowing. "Who?"

Quinn opened his mouth, then shut it and looked at Dave. His partner shrugged, apparently also uncertain of how to explain their problem. The best way forward was discretion, especially when dealing with someone as treacherous as Cecil Brown, but he still had to get his message across.

"We have a, uh, little project going for the city," Quinn said, trying to build the lie as he spoke. "We're looking for anyone local who knows the history of Resolution."

"The history of Resolution?" Cecil's face screwed up like

he'd tasted something sour. "You seriously came down here and harassed me just so you could ask me about the history of Resolution? You ever hear of a little thing called the internet? Google that shit and get out of my face."

Dave pulled out his cell phone. "I think I have the building inspector's number in here."

"No," Cecil said, the arrogant tones dropping from his voice to be replaced by a panicky squeak. "Jesus, you guys are touchy. Why don't you try the library?"

"We did," Quinn said. "All they have is the touristy bullshit. I'm looking for the real history. The weird stuff that only locals would know."

"Why does the city wanna know that?" Cecil asked. "So they can burn it all before someone finds out?"

"Just answer the question, Cecil," Dave said.

The little man tilted his hardhat back to display his spider tattoo and glared at Dave. "Okay, I might know someone."

"Who?" Quinn asked.

"You can't tell him I sent you." Cecil cast a glance around to make sure no one listened. The dancer on the stage had removed her push-up bra, drawing a cheer from her admirers and searing a painful image into Quinn's retinas.

"Go see the furniture maker," Cecil said in a conspiratorial whisper.

Quinn felt his brow furrow. It wasn't a name he'd associate with the awe Cecil seemed to be heaping on it. "I'm sorry, I thought I heard you say 'furniture maker'."

"I did," Cecil said. "He's got a shop down in the south end."

"And what does he do in this shop?" Dave asked.

"He makes furniture, you idiot," Cecil said. "That's why he's called the furniture maker."

"What does this have to do with the history of Resolution?" Quinn asked.

"The guy is about a hundred fucking years old," Cecil said. "His grandfather was one of the first guys to settle in Resolution Cove, and he knows everything about the place.

He's even got books and journals and shit."

"Okay," Dave said. "Why can't we tell him who sent us?"

Cecil looked around again, licking his lips. "Apparently, he's writing a history book and he doesn't want to share his stuff with anyone. He's convinced it'll be worth a million dollars or some shit, although I have no idea who would want to read a book about this fucking place. Anyway, if he knows I told people about him, he'll come down here and beat me to death with a table leg."

"I thought you said the guy was a hundred years old," Dave said. "You afraid of an old man, Cecil?"

"My name is Spider, you ginormous asshole. And when you meet him, you'll be scared of him too."

"If you say so," Dave said, with a huffing smirk.

Quinn nodded. "Okay. We'll get out of your hair."

"If you had any," Dave said.

Cecil opened his mouth and got his pointing finger ready, but Quinn grabbed Dave by the arm and pushed him towards the door before the little man could build up any steam. Outside, Quinn and Dave climbed into the mini-van.

"You think this is worth following up on?" Dave asked.

"It's the best thing we've got for right now," Quinn said and pointed forward with a grand gesture. "To the furniture maker's."

He sat at his wide wooden desk, in the office he hated, and drummed his fingers on the surface. He didn't know exactly what the Guardian was doing, but he was sure it was something he would not like, and was sure to interfere with his plans.

It seemed like his wife was getting bigger and riper every time he looked at her. Soon he would usher his child into the world. If he could not find a way to remove the Guardian and clear the way for his plans, he might lose both his wife and his child, something that he would not, could not, allow.

He continued to drum his fingers, thinking best how to move forward, when his elderly secretary darkened the door of his office.

"Sir?" she asked in a wavering voice.

He stilled his fingers and looked up at her. He cleared his voice and fixed a smile onto his face. "Yes, my dear. What can I do for you?"

"There is a very angry man on line one, demanding to speak with you. I tried to tell him I would get you to call him back, but he has called three times in the last ten minutes and shouts louder every time I talk to him."

"Oh," he said, looking down at the phone on his desk, where a little red light was flashing. "I'm sorry. Don't give it another thought. I'll deal with it right now."

She smiled, the white surface of her false teeth gleaming in the light from his desk lamp. "Thank you, sir."

When she turned away from his door, he picked up the receiver of his phone and punched the flashing red button. He introduced himself and the shrill voice of Cecil Brown filled his ear. Normally, any interaction with Cecil was a scarcely bearable occurrence, but as the little man ranted, a smile spread across his face. He drummed his fingers on his desk as he listened, and had to work not to laugh.

"I'm very glad you called, Mr. Brown. Very glad indeed."

Finding the Furniture Maker proved to be more difficult a task than Quinn had anticipated. After half an hour of driving around the south end and a failed Google search, Quinn had finally called Carrie's Uncle Sam.

"A furniture place in the south end?" Sam said over the phone. "There was a guy who used to make stuff out of the shop at his house, but he was old when I was your age and I'll be surprised if he's still alive."

"Do you remember where his place was?" Quinn asked.

"Down on Second or Third Avenue, I think," Sam said. "Near that store that had the stabbing a few years back. You remember?"

"Yeah," Quinn said. Of course he remembered. A skinny

junkie named Brandon Williams, who had been horrifically changed into a murderous animal by Resolution's first demon, had stabbed a girl in the Jiffy Gas. Quinn had only been moments away and was the first one to arrive. He had lost the suspect in a foot pursuit, but had never forgotten the sight of the teenage victim lying on the floor and kicking her heels in a pool of her own blood.

"Quinn, you still there?" Sam's voice came through the phone.

Shaking himself from his reverie, Quinn swallowed. "Yeah, Sam, I'm here."

"Sorry, I couldn't be more help, but that's the best I can do."

"No worries, Sam. I think we can find it."

He hit the 'end' button on his phone and told Dave what Sam had said. The slender man nodded and turned the mini-van south.

"Does coming down here freak you out as much as it does me?" Dave asked, peering out the window at the run-down houses.

Quinn nodded. "Sure does."

They had not gone down the street where the charred foundation of Joe Robowski's small house lay. They had not discussed it, and did not have to. It was the place where Quinn, Raife and Dave had first faced something made up of pure evil, and it was not a place they ever cared to visit.

After several more minutes of slowly driving up and down the last two narrow streets where Resolution gave way to dense coastal forest, Dave brought the mini-van to an abrupt halt. He pushed the gear lever up into reverse and backed up a car length.

"That sign," he said, pointing past Quinn's nose, at a white, single level house on the north side of the street. "What does it say?"

Quinn saw the sign. Made out of wood, about the size of a shoebox, covered in dark lichen, it was tacked to the end post of an old rail fence. Squinting, Quinn could just barely make out the ornately carved letters.

"It says, 'furniture'," he said, finally.

Dave parked the mini-van in the narrow driveway and they both got out. The house, a neat rancher with freshly painted cedar siding, was dark, but there was a broad outbuilding behind it with lights on in the windows.

"Do you think this is it?" Dave asked, eyeing the workshop.

Quinn blew out a breath through puffed cheeks and shrugged. "Only one way to find out."

They walked past an old Chevrolet pickup parked in the car port and found a single door on the left side of the shop. A wooden sign on the door, this one clear and in better shape than the one on the fence, indicated 'Custom Furniture'. Below that a plastic card hung from a nail in the door, saying 'closed'. Quinn grabbed the knob and it turned easily, allowing them to open it and step inside.

Quinn was greeted with the warm fragrance of freshly sawed wood, not the tang of the cheap lumber Cecil had been using, but the rich smell of oak and mahogany. From the rear of the shop, came the rumbling whir of a piece of machinery. Near the entrance, he saw several pieces of new-looking furniture, each shining with the gloss of new varnish. Facing him stood a china cabinet that was, even to his untrained eye, of an obviously high quality.

As Quinn reached out to run his finger over the ornate scrollwork, the machinery in the back of the shop died and a rough voice called out.

"The sign on the door said closed, didn't it? And keep your goddamned hands to yourself."

Quinn snatched his hand back like a small child that had been caught sneaking a cookie to glance towards the rear of the shop. The man approaching him hadn't quite reached the age of one hundred, but he could probably see that particular milestone from where he stood. The old man might have been tall once, but his lean body was stooped and bent, and his head was bare except for a few determined strands of snow white hair that clung to the fringe of his scalp. There didn't appear to be anything wrong with his hands, however, as he gripped a heavy wooden mallet in one and a wide chisel in the other.

Quinn backed up a step and held his hands out in what he hoped was a placating manner. "Good afternoon, sir, we're from the Resolution Cove RCMP detachment."

The man, dressed in a leather carpenters apron and a chambray work shirt with the sleeves rolled up, stopped a few feet away and pointed at him with the mallet. "I don't give a shit who you are. That cabinet belongs to someone, doesn't it? So keep your bloody fingerprints off it."

Quinn looked down at his hands and self-consciously wiped them on his jeans.

The furniture maker looked back and forth between Dave and Quinn. "Now, why are the RCMP in my shop?"

"We were hoping you would be able to help us," Dave said.

"With what?" the old man asked, his eyes narrowing to slits. He lowered the mallet but still gripped it while the corded muscles in his forearm stood out under his thin, pale skin.

"We were told you knew Resolution's history," Quinn said.

"Who told you that?" There was a harsh note in the old man's voice that made Quinn step back. He saw Dave's hand drift towards the pistol on his hip.

"We just heard it from someone we ran into, and we were hoping you could help us." Quinn didn't feel any particular loyalty towards Cecil, but he had told the ridiculous little man that he wouldn't say who sent them. Quinn wanted his word to mean something, even to someone like Cecil.

The old man stood stock still, except for his eyes that flicked back and forth between Quinn and Dave. At a complete impasse, Quinn could see that Cecil hadn't been exaggerating when he said the furniture maker was angry. He had to do something to dispel the tension between them or this was bound to get ugly in a hurry. Quinn didn't want to be on the news for getting in a fist fight with an eighty year old man.

Quinn shifted forward and extended my hand. "I'm sorry, sir. I should have introduced myself first. My name is Quinn

Sullivan, and I'm a corporal with Resolution detachment." He inclined his head to Dave. "This is my partner, Dave McLeod. If we had known your name or your phone number we would have called before we came to your shop."

The old man looked down at the offered hand, then up at Quinn's face. He didn't move for several heartbeats and Quinn was sure he was going to refuse to shake with him, but the old man slipped the mallet through a loop on the side of the leather apron he wore and gripped with Quinn.

"My name is Ted, isn't it? Ted Hill."

"I'm glad to meet you, Mr. Hill," Quinn said, releasing the man's hand. "I really am sorry to intrude."

"What is it you want?" Hill asked. The note of anger hadn't quite burned off his voice, but it was down to a flicker.

"We've been looking into..." Quinn trailed off. He couldn't very well tell this man, who still held a chisel in his left hand that they searched for a magical nexus in Resolution so they could pull someone through a doorway from another dimension. It sounded insane to Quinn, and he knew it was true. "We're...ah..."

"Working on a project for the city," Dave said, intervening seamlessly.

"What kind of project?" Hill asked. He crossed his thin arms and leaned towards Dave, his grey eyebrows drawing down. Quinn looked at Dave with equal interest, hoping that whatever his partner said next would be good.

"The city is looking for a site of particular significance with a mind towards erecting a bit of a monument," Dave said.

"What for? The centennial?" Hill asked.

"Exactly," Dave said.

Quinn didn't know when the town's centennial celebration was, but he hoped it would be close enough to make Dave's lie sound plausible. The old man seemed to relax a little, and Quinn took it as a good sign.

"I wonder if they heard about my book," Hill muttered, scratching his chin with the index finger of the hand still holding the chisel. "Who did you say sent you, again?"

"We asked several local residents who knew the most about Resolution's history, and you came up." Quinn said. "Well, more specifically your shop, if not your name." Since he didn't know the man's name when they walked in here, Quinn didn't think it would be wise to try and push the lie too far.

"I don't generally care to discuss my work, do I?" Hill said. "I've written a book about Resolution, and I hope to have it published and ready to market during the centennial next year."

Quinn nodded agreeably. "I think that's a sound strategy." He had no idea who would want to read a book about a town that no one had ever heard of, but he felt now would be a really poor time to point that out.

The old man continued to scratch his chin. "Do you think the city would be willing to market my book for me if I help you boys out?"

"I think that would certainly be in the realm of possibility," Dave said without a moment's hesitation. Quinn began to think his friend was not nearly as crass as formerly suspected.

"All right," Hill said, turning towards the back of the shop and waving them on with the chisel. "I'll have a look."

The old man lead the way through a collection of partially completed pieces of furniture, past several stacks of lumber and rows of wood working tools. At the back of the shop was a steel door with a heavy pad lock on it. The old man removed a ring of keys from the pocket of his work pants and opened first the padlock, two deadbolts, and finally the lock set into the door knob.

While Hill worked at the locks, Dave leaned towards Quinn. "This guy takes his history awful serious," Dave said in a low voice.

"What was that?" Hill asked.

"I was just telling Corporal Sullivan that you can't take security too seriously,"

"That's the very thing I always say, isn't it?" Hill said. "I've had several people attempt to steal my work before, and it is not something I ever plan on allowing."

Once the locks were open, Hill pushed open the door and led them into a neat office. A wide, cherry wood desk stood against one wall, with a surprisingly new-looking computer on it, as well as a digital camera with a wide lens, and a laser printer. Above the desk was a shelf that ran the length of the room, crammed with thick, black books.

Quinn examined the books. The first of them, on the shelf furthest from the door, looked like they were bound in leather, while the closest of them were covered in something shiny, like vinyl. Hill saw Quinn looking and smiled.

"That there is three generations worth of history," the old man said, an obvious hint of pride in his voice. "My grandfather started it. He was one of the first men to settle this inlet, and was present for the town's incorporation. My father took up the practice and then passed it to me." His face turned sad for a moment. "My boys never saw the point, I'm afraid, and my grandkids are far too busy with their noses in Tweeter to care about history."

"That's 'Twitter'," Dave said.

"What?" Hill asked, turning towards Dave, the look of pinched anger starting to coalesce on his wrinkled face.

Quinn surreptitiously reached up a hand and gripped Dave's elbow hard enough the other man winced. "Nothing," Quinn said to Hill while Dave glared at him.

"Anyway," Hill said, turning and sitting down in the high-backed leather office chair in front of the desk. "I have taken the best parts of all our journals and compiled them into one, concise volume." He selected a key from his ring and slid it into a lock on one of the drawers of the desk. Inside was another locked box that required yet another key.

"Holy Jesus," Dave said.

Quinn elbowed him hard in the ribs. Dave grunted, and did a poor impression of a cough to hide his discomfort.

The old man had not seemed to have heard him, thankfully, and pulled a textbook sized volume from the lock box inside the drawer. It was bound in white cardboard and bore a simple title in black block letters; Resolution Cove. He set the book on the surface of the desk and ran a hand over the cover.

"I've not quite decided what photo I'll put on the cover, have I?" he said. "But once a publisher picks it up, I'll decide." He kept his gnarled hand on the surface of the book, as though afraid one of the Mounties might try and snatch it away from him. "Now, what exactly is it you boys are looking for? What does the city want?"

It was Quinn's turn to scratch his chin. How did he explain this without sounding crazy? After a moment he said, "We're looking for a special place in Resolution. A place where the..."

"Spirit," Dave said.

"Right," Quinn agreed. "Where the spirit of the town can really be captured. A place that really defines what Resolution is."

"That defines what Resolution is, huh?" The old man's hand stayed resolutely on the cover of the book. "What kind of monument is the city looking to build?"

Quinn opened his mouth, then shut it and looked at Dave.

"It depends on the site," Dave said.

"Right," Quinn agreed.

Hill looked between the two of them, his eyes narrowed. "So you say."

He turned to the book and opened the cover. From where Quinn stood he could see old black and white pictures on glossy pages with densely packed script. He had halfway been expecting a collection of scribbles and some pictures taped to construction paper. Quinn was impressed by the old man's work.

"Where do we even start?" Hill asked, himself as much as the two Mounties. "There are so many important places, aren't there? The cornerstone of the court house; the first mooring post at the pier; the entrance to the silver mine." He looked up at them. "There are a dozen places that I would suggest for a monument."

Quinn had a feeling he would know the thing they were looking for when he saw it, and was equally sure the book on the desk in front of Hill would hold the answer. "Is there any way I could have at look at it, sir? If you gave me a couple hours to review it, I'm sure I could find what the, uh, city is looking for."

The old man slammed the cover of the book shut. "'Fraid not."

Quinn looked down at the book and had to fight down a surge of fury, as he thought of Autumn's face looking up at him as she plummeted into the black door. He felt the book was the key that could bring her back, and it was within arm's reach. "If I could just browse your book for a couple of moments."

The old man stood up. "This book is important, Corporal. It is going to be a hallmark of Canadian history and represents my life's work. If you want to touch it, you'll have to kill me and pry it from my hands. Now, you tell the city that I am more than willing to help them find their place in trade for them marketing my book. But you will have to give me time to find the appropriate location. Come back tomorrow and I'll have something for you." He pointed towards the door. "But for now you will leave."

The anger in Quinn's chest burbled up behind his teeth, and he felt a growl trying to escape. He opened his mouth, but stopped when he felt Dave's hand on his shoulder.

"That will be fine, sir," Dave said, being the diplomatic one for the first time in the years Quinn had known him. "We appreciate your help. We'll see you tomorrow."

Quinn had more to say, but he let Dave push him towards the door to the office, through the building and then out into the yard. He glanced over his shoulder once, and saw Hill, silhouetted in the door of his shop with his wiry arms crossed on his narrow chest.

When they reached the road, Quinn turned towards Dave. The sun had set while they had talked to the old man, and the temperature had dropped to the point where Quinn could see his breath misting out of his nose. "We need that book," Quinn said, a hint of the anger he felt inside putting an edge in his voice.

"I appreciate that, but we also need you to not lose your mind and scrog out an old man. We're already in shit over burning the campground down. Can you imagine what Faulk would do if you punch that guy?" He jerked his thumb over his shoulder towards the workshop. "Not even the Inspector would be able to save you then."

"But," Quinn said, licking his dry lips. "But, we're close, Dave. I know we are. And that book might have the answers."

"That might be," Dave said. "So when the old man gives us the likely places tomorrow we'll take Autumn's mum to them and see if she gets any, you know," he waggled his fingers in the air to either side of his head, "feelings."

Quinn did not like it, not one bit, but nodded anyway. "All right," he said, after clenching his teeth for several seconds. "Tomorrow it is."

They got into the minivan and Dave pulled smoothly away from the curb.

As the front of Hill's house disappeared from the rear view mirror, Quinn couldn't help thinking they were making a mistake.

Gemma Donnelly's eyes felt like someone had sprinkled sand in them as she turned another of the thick, vellum pages in the second of Autumn's books. She looked up, towards the windows in the front of the apartment, facing out into the street, and saw that it was dark. When she'd sat down at the small table with the books in hand, it had still been full daylight.

"Any luck, Gigi?" Bobby asked from his seat opposite her. He had another of Autumn's books open in his lap.

She ran her fingers through her hair and looked down at the note pad she had taken from downstairs where there were several densely packed lines of her own writing. "I found a few things," she said, blowing out a big breath. "But nothing that really speaks to what we're dealing with. The problem with these books is that they are all handwritten, and there isn't exactly an index in the back. I can find no mention of these doorways the girl child can open. In that, she seems to be completely unique." She looked up at him. He had his lips pursed and peered down through his reading glasses at a spot in the middle of a page, marked with one of his thick fingers. "Did you find something?"

He flattened his lips and glanced up at her. "You know research isn't my strong suit, but I think you better have a look at this."

She stood from her chair, glad of the excuse to get up and stretch, and moved behind Bobby. She leaned over, one arm draping across his chest, and rested her face on the side of his head. He tapped the page and moved his finger so she could read where he indicated. After a few lines, she took the book from him and walked around the room, as she read.

"Does that mean what I think it means?" Bobby asked.

"This is an account of a powerful, ebony skinned demon that required a determined group of very powerful people, lead by a Guardian, to drive it off. The demon hid in a small town, in the south of Spain, in human form, posing as a priest, of all things." The description went on for several pages, giving details on the deception of the creature and how the group discovered it, but the narrative ended there. "And the account claims to be from several hundred years ago."

"Yes," Bobby said.

"The author of this book believes the demon was old, even then," Gemma's eyes flickered across the page. "And it must have been old, and extremely powerful, to be able to hide among the townspeople without them knowing of it. In her letters, Autumn told me the thing she faced walked in human form but carried the odour of an animal with it everywhere it went." She continued to read. "If the demon is as old as this person thinks it is, it might have walked the earth in the time before Donnel of Inverness."

Bobby nodded in agreement. "Yup."

She stopped pacing and looked up at him. "So what do you think this means?"

He crossed his heavy, tattooed arms. "I think, my love, it means we are in very, very serious trouble."

99

CHAPTER 11

After leaving the furniture maker's house, Quinn and Dave, feeling defeated, drove back to the office. When they walked into the general duty pit, they saw the Inspector, Staff Sergeant Steve Faulk, Raife and Mayor Jay Drummond standing in front of the door to the Inspector's office. Raife and Faulk were both dressed in working uniform, but the Inspector and the mayor were both dressed in jeans and fall jackets, suggesting they'd probably been called at home. Quinn wasn't clairvoyant, but he was smart enough to know that having the majority of the town's most influential people in one room at the same time was never good.

Quinn and Dave stopped at the mouth of the hallway. Dave leaned close. "What the fuck is the Mayor doing here?" he asked, his voice low.

"I'm not sure," Quinn said. "But I'm wondering if it's too late for us to make ourselves scarce."

Steve Faulk lifted his head from where he had it bent in conversation with the other men and saw them. "Corporal Sullivan," he said. "You and Constable McLeod present yourselves."

"It is now," Dave whispered.

"You know he's pissed when he calls us by rank," Quinn said.

"I am *not* asking," the staff sergeant said. "I'm telling." His tone was flat and hard, the voice he used when he was either dealing with a member of the public who was really pissing him off or when a member of the detachment had well and truly fucked something up. Where Raife would yell and bluster and throw people bodily out of the building, Steve Faulk was cold all over when he was angry. Judging from the ice in his stare, Quinn thought he was past the point of furious.

Quinn and Dave approached the group of men. The Inspector looked at them with something approaching disappointment, while Raife rubbed his moustache as he stared at the floor in front of his boots. The Mayor gave a wan grin, as though he were vaguely embarrassed to be involved.

"I received a very disturbing complaint today, Corporal," Faulk said.

He still wasn't using his first name, Quinn thought. Bad was moving on towards worse.

"Two of them in fact," Faulk continued. "A man named Cecil Brown has lodged a complaint, saying you harassed him at his place of business."

"If you call the Welcome Beaver a business," Dave said.

"Jesus, Dave, not now," Quinn said.

"Listen to your supervisor, McLeod," Faulk said. "Apparently you intimidated Mr. Brown into giving you information on local residents, telling him you were working on a special project for the city."

"Yes, we spoke to Cecil," Quinn said. "He is carrying out illegal construction and running a bar without—"

"I conferred with the Mayor," Faulk said, getting louder as he talked over Quinn. "We concluded that you had not, in fact, been tasked with carrying out a special project for the city."

Quinn glanced at the Mayor, who gave him an apologetic shrug and continued to look embarrassed.

"Did you tell him that, Sullivan?" Faulk asked. "Did you tell that man you were working a special project for the city and bully him into giving you information?"

Quinn's mind spun as he struggled to come up with a plausible explanation. "Well, yes, we did tell him that but—"

"BUT YOU FUCKING LIED!" Faulk shouted, spittle flying from his mouth. "You walked into that building wearing your badge on your chest and you lied."

"Steve," the Inspector said, putting a hand on the staff sergeant's arm.

"No, Don," Faulk said, jerking his arm away. "Every time something fucked up happens in this town he," he jabbed his finger at Quinn, "is at the centre of it." He glared at Quinn and Dave, his eyes moving back and forth between the two of them. "Then I got a call from a terrified woman on Second Street, saying that two men with guns went into a workshop at the back of a private residence. The only reason you didn't have the whole detachment land on you was because she gave us the plate of the vehicle you were driving, a detachment vehicle, and I knew it was you. What were you doing there, Corporal?"

Any explanation that had been floating around in Quinn's head evaporated like an ice cube on a July sidewalk. He couldn't very well tell Faulk, who had never been part of their confidence, that he was looking for information on where to best open a door to another plane of existence so he could rescue a friend.

"Nothing from you either?" Faulk asked Dave. For the first time in all the time Quinn had known him, Dave didn't have anything to say.

"Fine." Faulk's nostrils flared as he bunched his fists at his side. "Go ahead and say nothing. I'm initiating a Code against both of you and you're both on administrative duties, effective immediately."

"I'm sorry," the mayor said in a soft voice. "A 'Code'?"

"Means a Code of Conduct review," Raife said in his rumbling baritone. "Kinda like a court martial." He still would not look at Quinn.

"Oh," Drummond said. "If I'm not mistaken, Staff Sergeant, Corporal Sullivan is one of the most decorated officers our detachment has ever had. Surely that is a little excessive."

"Yes, Steve," Inspector Green said. "We should talk about this first."

"No, Donald, we're not talking about this. I don't know what your motivation is, but you can't protect him this time. You can't make this go away like you do everything else he does. In the last eighteen hours, he has burned down an entire campground, destroyed two police cars, fired off over a hundred rounds with no explanation, and now he's lying to people in our town while he carries on unauthorized investigations into private citizens."

"To be fair, Staff, that campground thing was all of us," Dave said.

"Shut up, Dave," Quinn and Raife said in unison.

"We are going to investigate this, and we are going to investigate it right," Faulk said. "I've already called Bill Davis over from the island. He'll be here tomorrow morning and his Major Crime team will manage the investigation."

Quinn felt stiff all over, his ears and cheeks burning in the face of the staff sergeant's fury. He wanted to look to either Raife or the Inspector for help. They knew what he was doing, why he and Dave were out on the road, asking their questions. They knew how much this meant.

He groped for something to say, for some way to explain, but still came up empty. After several long moments, he cleared his throat. "Will that be all, Staff?"

"Indeed it will, Corporal," Faulk said, his tone still fringed with ice. "Go home and await instructions on what your job function is to be while you're on admin duties."

Turning to leave, Quinn looked at Dave. His partner's face was flushed, but with anger of his own, rather than embarrassment. Quinn could read the warnings on Dave's face well enough and snagged him under the arm with one hand, propelling him towards the hallway that led to the rear parking lot. Dave resisted for a few steps, but relented. Behind them, the conversations started up again, heated this time, with

Raife's rumbling voice rising above the others.

Once outside, Dave aimed a kick at the bumper of the nearest patrol car. "This is fucking bullshit," he yelled. Two members from the night shift in the parking lot stared at him. "What the fuck are you looking at?" Dave screamed when he saw them.

The two men exchanged nervous glances and beetled into the detachment.

"Calm down." Quinn laid a hand on his friend's arm.

"No," Dave said. "This is a load of balls and you know it. A Code? Over a complaint from Cecil Brown? That fucking guy complains if he sees a police car on the news for Christ's sake. They've never taken him seriously before. Why are they putting so much weight on the shit he says now?"

Quinn walked away from his friend and rubbed at his chin. With the sun down, near freezing temperatures misted his breath as he huffed. Dave was right. The detachment had paid little heed to the mewling complaints of Cecil in the past. Why was he being taken so seriously now? What was Steve Faulk's motivation in lending him credibility?

"This feels wrong," Quinn said.

"Fucking right, it does." Dave aimed another kick at the previously abused bumper.

"No, Dave," Quinn said. "I don't just mean that it sucks. I mean it feels like Faulk is intentionally trying to take us out of the game."

Dave stilled, instantly. "What are you saying?"

Images flashed through the black space behind Quinn's closed eyes. He opened them and looked at Dave. "You remember when I went to Cranbrook to look into Patrick Green's death?"

"Oh, you mean when we were all nearly eaten by that fucking thing that killed Autumn? I'm not likely to forget."

"The member that was assigned to escort me around the town, Clara Morgan, she was killed by a demon who assumed her identity. The thing hid itself well enough that I had no idea, and Donnel's dagger didn't get hot until it quit hiding and tried to kill me."

Dave crossed his arms. "What are you getting at?"

"What if something happened to Steve Faulk?" Quinn asked. "What if whatever we fought this morning has done something to him, or maybe even replaced him?"

Dave shook his head. "No. I'm not buying it. I've known that man for more than five years. I've seen him every day. I would know if something were up with him."

"You said it yourself, Dave," Quinn said. "This isn't right. This is out of character for him, isn't it?"

Dave crossed his arms and leaned against the patrol car he'd been kicking. After a long moment, he shook his head again. "No, Quinn. I can't see it. We would know. *You* would know."

Quinn took several long breaths, his hands jammed in the pockets of his jeans to warm them against the cold. Would a demon be bold enough to move right into their office, to look him in the face while it assumed the identity of one of his superiors? Perhaps he was just being paranoid, but considering all that he'd been through in the last two years, he had a right to be.

"Okay," he said finally. "Maybe I'm just...I don't know. This if fucked."

"You're goddamned rights it is," Dave said, with none of his former heat. "I think what we need to do is head home and lie low for a bit. Give Faulk a chance to calm down and the Inspector a chance to talk him out of his tree. This will look better in the morning."

Quinn nodded. He hoped Dave was right. He also hoped that morning wouldn't be too late.

He could not help but laugh as he drove through the falling twilight. The complaint about the two men visiting someone on Second Street was a boon that was too good to be true. He began to think that the Fates wanted him to succeed. Perhaps it really was time for his child to be born. Having the Guardian side-lined, his movements restricted and carefully watched by everyone, including that withered old fool, Green, was a streak of genius and dark luck.

The streets of a town like Resolution were nearly dead with the work day done, and he saw very few cars as he drove through the town centre towards the south end. This was almost too easy. If he hadn't been so careful through all of his long life he would have thought this a trap.

He could not be overconfident, he reminded himself as he neared the house the Guardian had visited earlier that day. He could not be careless and call attention to himself. He parked his car a block away and slipped through the hedgerows beside a small house and moved through the back yard, as quiet and unnoticed as a shadow. He passed undetected, unseen, and silent as thought, until he arrived at the old man's door.

The lights shone and he could hear the whir of machinery. He opened the door and slipped inside, shutting it behind him. He smelled fresh-sawn wood, varnish and the stink of the old man. The old man's anger and discontentment hung in the air of the small building like a fog of sweet pipe smoke. He breathed it in, holding it in his lungs, letting it intoxicate him.

The old ways were coming back to him, quicker now that he let them, and he fed the hidden side of himself a diet that it had long been missing.

"Son of a bitch," the old man said, as a machine whirred to a stop. "That goddamned sign says closed, now doesn't it?"

The tang of the old man's anger grew stronger. He took another breath. The old man appeared from the rear of the shop, holding a heavy wooden mallet, which would be about as much use against him as a flyswatter.

"I don't even care who you are or what you want," the old man said, brandishing the mallet. "I just want you to get the hell out of here and leave me in peace."

"Do you not recognise me?" he asked. "Surely you know me."

The old man screwed up his face and stared at him. Whatever the old man saw, he did not find appealing, because the pinched set of his face disappeared, replaced by wide eyes. "I don't know you," the old man stammered.

"Think carefully." He took one slow step forward. He shook out his hands, willing the claws to grow. Several pops and clunks and soon he was ready for the bloody work to come. The old man stared at the hands-turned-claws and began making a high, thin sound in his throat.

The old man turned to flee, dropping the mallet.

Laughing, he lunged forward to cut the old man off. "You can't leave yet. You haven't told me who I am."

The old man took a hasty step backwards, his hands pawing at the air in front of his face as though he were trying to swim away. "I don't know. Who are you?"

His arm shot out and caught the old man by the neck. "I am your death."

As Quinn walked up the front steps of his house, he felt as though he were dragging about a thousand pounds of iron chain behind him. But the moment he opened the door and heard Shawn's piping voice, and Carrie's laughter, part of the weight seemed to slough away.

Shawn was on the floor, his limbs in a strange tangle as he wrestled with Bobby. The stout man was on his knees, one arm locked behind Shawn's neck, the boy's arms flailing uselessly behind his head.

"And then, once you get him like this, you can do this," Bobby said, as he began poking Shawn's ribs with a thick finger. The boy shrieked with laughter and kicked his legs. At the kitchen table, Carrie laughed uproariously while Gemma Donnelly smiled at the spectacle.

"Quinn," Shawn said, trying to crane his head towards the doorway. "Help me!"

"Did he get himself into this?" Quinn asked Carrie.

She stopped laughing long enough to wipe her streaming eyes. "He sure did."

"Then you can get yourself out of it, pal." Quinn closed the front door. He walked past the combatants and bent down to kiss Carrie's forehead.

She looked up at him, and her smile slipped. "Are you all right, baby?"

"Ugh," he said, easing himself into the chair beside her. "It was an... interesting day."

"There is a story here, I think." Gemma took a mug from the centre of the table and filled it with tea from a steaming pot. She pushed it towards Quinn and he accepted it gratefully. Bobby set Shawn loose and planted him in front of the television while he joined everyone at the table.

Quinn told them everything he'd seen and done that day, starting with the dead-end search in the detachment and finishing with the confrontation in the general duty pit.

"You're on admin duties?" Carrie asked, incredulous. She had been around cops enough to know the seriousness of the situation. "Faulk can't be serious."

"Oh, he's serious all right," Quinn said. "Serious as cancer." He glanced over at Gemma, who watched him intently. Her gaze made him want to squirm. "What?"

"There is something you're not saying, here, Quinn. What else is there?"

He pushed at the handle of his tea mug, turning it in a circle with his index finger, while he stared at the contents that had now gone cool. He was unsure how much of his suspicion he should voice out loud. If Dave was right and he was just paranoid, he would be frightening everyone for no reason. If Dave was wrong and there was something to Quinn's apprehension, then it wasn't something he should keep to himself.

"I'm worried," he said finally. "I'm worried about Steve Faulk." He told Gemma about his experience in Cranbrook and the ease with which the demon there assumed the identity of Clara Morgan. "Donnel's dagger didn't even get warm until it physically changed, in front of my eyes."

"And you believe that the same thing may have happened to your staff sergeant." Gemma made it a statement and not a question.

"That's the only thing I can think of," Quinn said. "Steve Faulk has always treated me and everyone else very well. I've never seen him lose his temper before, and certainly not on a complaint from someone like Cecil Brown. It seemed like he was waiting for an excuse to sideline me. He jumped on this like a fat kid on cake. This isn't like him." He paused, turning his mug another quarter turn. "This isn't him."

He caught Gemma and Bobby exchanging a pointed look, at the end of which Bobby nodded and got up from the table. There was an old, leather messenger bag hanging from the chair Carrie kept beside the front door. Bobby opened the flap and produced a thick, leather-bound book, as well as a note-pad. He brought them back to the table and handed them to Gemma.

"I found the books I was looking for in Autumn's apartment," Gemma said, opening it to a page that was marked with a ribbon. "I found something that might have some bearing on what you experienced today."

Quinn inched his chair closer to the table and placed his elbows on the surface, leaning towards Gemma. Carrie put her hand on his arm. He moved one of his own hands to cover it, giving it a squeeze.

"Bear in mind that some of the information, the stories in these books, are something you should take with a grain of salt. Sometimes they've been passed down orally for generations until someone writes them down in a book, which is then passed on. Sometimes, the meaning gets diluted."

"Like kids playing 'telephone'," Carrie said.

Gemma smiled at her. "Exactly. That being said, this talked about a town in the southern part of Spain. The residents there suffered several murders and eventually discovered that it was their parish priest who was committing them. The priest terrorized the townsfolk until a Guardian, assisted by several very powerful companions, confronted the priest and revealed that he was, in fact, a demon."

"When did this happen?" Quinn asked.

"About three hundred years ago," Gemma said.

"Okay," Quinn said, rubbing the heels of his hands against his eyes and letting out a big breath. "What does that have to do with us, in Canada, now?"

Gemma turned the book towards Quinn. There was a drawing in the bottom corner. It showed the ebony demon they had battled in the campground.

Quinn shook his head. "No way. You think the thing we fought this morning was terrorizing villagers in Spain?"

Gemma turned the book back towards herself. "I certainly think it's possible. And the author of this passage believed the demon was old, ancient, even then. A Guardian, armed and trained far better than any of our generation, fought the thing with assistance from several people who had magic of their own. Despite all the power they brought to bear against it, they couldn't kill it, only drive it off."

Leaning back in his chair, Quinn scrubbed a hand over his face and through his short hair. "So, now you're telling me that our new demon is three hundred years old and can't be killed."

"No," Bobby said. "She's saying our new demon might be a thousand years old, and wasn't killed then."

Quinn thumped his elbows back on the table. He studied the surface for a moment, then raised his head to meet Gemma's gaze. "Autumn used to tell me that most of the magic had bled out of the world. Do you believe that as well?"

Gemma folded her hands in front of her and nodded. "Magic still exists, and you have seen it yourself. But it is not what it once was. It is a thing that is sustained by belief. When the world, except for a few of us, stops believing, magic shrinks."

"Okay," Quinn said. "So the Guardian from three hundred years ago is going to be better at this stuff than me, right?"

She glanced at Bobby, and then shrugged. "Potentially."

"If that's the case, and the guy in Spain couldn't kill it, what chance do I have now?" He looked between Gemma and Bobby. "What the hell are we going to do?"

"There is something here that you are forgetting, Quinn,"

Gemma said.

"And what's that?"

"You have not plumbed the depths of your potential. I don't think you've even scratched the surface." She closed the book and pulled the notepad in front of her. "I have found accounts of Guardians being able to turn any weapon into one capable of killing a demon. That is probably how Donnel's dagger was imbued with its own magic; by having a Guardian repeatedly use it."

"But I can't do that," Quinn said.

"You don't know that," Gemma said, an edge in her voice. "When you killed the creature outside the duplex, when I first met you, did you feel anything different then?"

Quinn leaned back again, shrugging. "I don't know. I was mad, I guess."

"And what did you do with that anger?"

He remembered the way he'd felt when he'd seen Gemma's face and mistook her for Autumn. He had been so disappointed, so frustrated when he realised it wasn't her that he'd felt a burning in his chest. "I guess I used it to push on the dagger."

"You burned that creature with your own fire," Gemma said, thumping her fist on table. "That burst didn't come from the weapon, it came from you."

He opened his mouth to voice a rebuttal, when there was a knock at the front door. Shawn turned and leapt over the back of the couch to answer the door. Quinn stood so fast that he knocked his chair over. His hand went first to the pistol still on his hip, and then to the dagger at the small of his back. He was about to tell Shawn to get away from the door when the boy yanked it open and revealed Raife, still in uniform, standing on the doorstep.

The big sergeant stepped inside and closed the door behind him, stopping to give Shawn a bristly kiss on the cheek.

"Geez, Uncle Raife," Shawn said, wiping his hand across his face. "I'm too old for that."

Raife smiled and rubbed the boy's head. "Never. I'm going

to do that when you bring your first girlfriend to meet me and embarrass the hell out of you." Shawn laughed, hugged him briefly around the waist and then flounced back onto the couch.

After bending down to set his chair right, Quinn looked at Raife. "This isn't a social call, is it?"

"No, son, I'm afraid it isn't."

"What's the matter?"

Raife let out a big breath, rippling his moustache. "You might want to sit down."

"I'll stand, thanks," Quinn said.

"Raife," Carrie said. "Jesus Christ, what is it?"

The big man looked down at Carrie for a moment, then back at Quinn. "That old man you and Dave visited today?"

Quinn swallowed. "Yeah?"

"His wife just came home and found him dead."

"Dead?" Gemma asked, standing.

Carrie put her hand on her forehead. "Please tell me he had a fucking heart attack."

Raife shook his head. "The members who responded said his workshop was covered in blood. It looks like he had his throat torn out."

Now, Quinn sat down. "Oh, sweet Jesus."

"There's another problem." Raife said, a pained expression on his face.

Looking up at him, Quinn sighed. "Yeah, and the problem is that Dave and I were the last ones to see him alive."

Raife rubbed his moustache and nodded. "You and Dave are currently suspects in that man's murder."

CHAPTER 12

Raife stuffed himself into an unmarked Ford Crown Victoria, grunting as he leaned over so he could slam the door, and wondered for the tenth time in as many minutes how Quinn could always manage to get himself into so much trouble. If that boy wasn't nearly torn apart by a God damned boogeyman, he was getting himself involved in a bloody murder.

"What the fuck," Raife said aloud to the steering wheel, as he pulled away from Quinn and Carrie's house and headed south.

Raife knew that the Major Crime team from Nanaimo would be here in the morning. Initially, it was only going to be for Quinn's Code, but now Bill Davis, who always seemed to catch the various bags of shit that Resolution threw at the Major Crime team, would be coming out to assume conduct of the murder investigation. Raife had known Bill for a long time. Bill would be fair but brook no bullshit. If Raife wanted to save Quinn's career, he might need to do a little bit of bullshitting.

Within a few minutes he had pulled up in front of the crime scene and saw two marked patrol cars out front. Raife turned off the ignition of the old Crown Vic and levered himself out of the driver's door.

"One day we'll get cars for grown-ups," Raife muttered, as

he slammed the door and hitched up his gun belt.

As he walked towards the front of the house, he saw that both the patrol cars were empty. Passing the fence, to start up the driveway, a uniformed constable slipped out of the shadows of a large tree to Raife's left. Momentarily startled, Raife made a mental note to give a positive word to the kid's supervisor for concealing himself where he couldn't be seen, instead of sitting in his car like a bobble-headed target.

"Hiya, Sarge," the young member, a kid named Grady, greeted him.

"Just Raife," he reminded the younger man for at least the millionth time.

"Whatever you say, Sarge."

Raife sighed and rubbed his moustache. "How does the crime scene look?"

"Well...it's..." the young constable swallowed. "It's pretty bad, Sarge. The old dude was tore up something awful."

"I'll bet. You better show me."

The young man hesitated. "Uh, my corporal said the scene is closed and no one is to go in until the Major Crime team from Nanaimo gets here in the morning."

"Uh-huh. What rank am I, son?"

"Uh, you're a sergeant...Sarge," Grady said, swallowing again.

"And what rank is your corporal?"

"Well...he's a...uh...corporal."

Raife nodded. "And which of those two ranks is higher?"

Grady swallowed and cleared his throat. "Um, well, I guess sergeant is, Sarge."

"Correct. Now bear in mind that I am the operations NCO, responsible for everything that happens in any operational or investigational capacity at our detachment. It is my obligation to survey the crime scene, and your obligation is to assist me in doing so. Do you agree?"

Grady nodded. "Yes, Sarge."

"Good man. Now, lead the way."

The line of shit Raife had just fed the poor kid wouldn't

have worked on a more seasoned street cop. Had he tried to pull that on Sandy, she would have laughed at him and perhaps tasered him in the ass. But Grady still had dew behind his ears. Raife was relatively certain that if he told that kid to build a staircase of green cheese and climb to the moon, Grady would head to the supermarket.

The constable led the way past a newer Chevrolet sedan and an old pickup parked beneath the carport roof to a workshop behind the neat house. A carved wooden plaque hung above the door that said 'custom furniture' and a ubiquitous plastic sign on the door itself that said, 'closed'. The door stood ajar, exhibiting a smear of blood on the threshold.

The constable stopped several feet shy of the door and pointed to it. "The scene is in there, Sarge." Grady looked away from the door and gave no indication that he had any intention of entering the building.

That reluctance gave Raife a sense of just how bad this crime scene was. He reached into the pocket of his coat and pulled out a set of purple latex gloves.

"Who found the body?" he asked the young man whose face shone very pale in the exterior light beside the door.

"The victim's wife returned home from her job down at the Super Value and came out here to check on him. She found him and called it in."

Raife looked around. "Where is she now?"

Grady turned and waved a hand vaguely at the house. "She's inside with Gary. We're going to take her to the detachment for a statement, but we're waiting for victim services to bring a car and transport her so she doesn't have to ride in a PC."

"Good plan." Raife pulled the gloves onto his hairy hands. "Is there anything in here I should know about?" He reached out and put his fingers against the door.

The constable took a step backwards and to one side, where he wouldn't be able to see inside the door. "It's pretty much right there when you walk in, Sarge."

"Okay, son," Raife said. He paused in the act of pushing

the door open to consider the 'closed' sign. He guessed that would hold true for a very long time.

Inside the door exhibited a wreckage of blood and broken furniture. What might have once been a china cabinet now bore a close resemblance to a pile of kindling. The only whole chunk of wood Riafe could see was a piece of ornate scrollwork that lay in a pool of congealed blood so thick it was getting a skin on the top of it.

On the other end of the pool, Raife saw the remains of a man. He had seen some fucked up things in his time as a cop, even more so in the last two years since the demons started appearing in Resolution, but nothing he had ever seen prepared him for the sight of the old man.

He wasn't precisely torn limb from limb, because all the appendages were still attached, but each one of them was broken, the bones protruding from the skin through the ragged strips of cloth that had been his clothes. Raife swallowed, his throat almost gelatinous, and ground his teeth together to keep the contents of his stomach in place. He was going to be in enough shit for this particular act of fuckery without projectile vomiting all over the crime scene.

He stepped gingerly around the congealing blood, carefully placing his size fifteen boots to avoid leaving any footprints—a challenging task since there was blood splatter and drag marks all across the concrete floor. When he reached the other side of the body, he saw that the head was turned about twenty degrees too far. The old man's face was unrecognizable as human, and it took Raife several blinking moments to realise the jaw had been ripped off, exposing the pulpy hole of the throat and the white lumps of the upper molars.

Raife turned away, his hand moving up to cover his mouth as he squeezed his eyes shut. He had experienced many traumatic things in his career, both natural and unnatural. He had seen demons change people, turning them into raving monsters. He had seen the remains of men who had been eaten, their flesh wholly consumed. But he had never anticipated that anything, even something as black and evil as the creatures he had faced over the last two years, could do this to someone. He knew one thing for certain—no human did this. This was the work of something evil. Something that lived in the dark.

Raife hadn't seen the thing that Quinn and his team fought in the campground, but he had heard enough about it to have a pretty fair sense that it was involved.

He cleared his throat, shook himself and moved further into the shop. It got easier to traverse the blood as he got away from the rows of completed furniture and towards the tools. The sawdust on the floor soaked up the blood and turned it into rough, doughy mounds. He couldn't help but leave footprints, though, but there were so many that he didn't think a few more would make any difference.

"What were you looking for?" he asked the empty space of the shop. Before he'd left Quinn's house, Raife had asked why he and Dave had been at the old man's house. Raife knew the old man had extensive knowledge on the history of Resolution that Quinn thought would be able to help him get Autumn Donnelly out of whatever place she had gone into. But Raife had no idea what would lead a creature to come to this old man's house and tear him up like that.

At the back of the shop, Raife found the remains of a doorway. The door that had once occupied it, the steel coated kind that cost a small fortune, lay wrenched and broken beside the ragged opening in the wall. Beyond was a small room, containing mounds of torn paper, broken furniture and jagged pieces of shattered electronics. Raife stood and looked at the detritus for several moments, then shook his head. There might be something valuable in there, but he had no idea what, and no time to go digging through the debris to find it.

He pulled off his gloves and stuffed them in his pocket, while he made his careful way back towards the main door, retracing his steps with care. Whatever he thought he would find by coming here was gone, or maybe never existed.

He stepped outside and closed the door behind him. Near the carport, Grady stood, rocking back and forth on his heels, his gaze moving continually from the street to the workshop. When he saw Raife he let out a big breath.

"So?" he asked.

"He is definitely dead." Raife rubbed his moustache with his thumb and forefinger. "You boys have done a fine job of securing the scene. It doesn't look like any steps have been missed. I'll be sure to let your corporal know."

"Okay, Sarge," Grady said. "You going inside to talk to Gary and the wife?"

Raife thought about beating a retreat before he got himself into any more trouble for fucking about in an investigation that he really wasn't part of, then thought some more and nodded. "Yeah, I'll go inside and see how they're doing."

He went around to the front of the house while Grady resumed his place in the shadows of the carport. Raife knocked softly on the door and then stepped inside without waiting for a response.

The front door opened into a narrow entrance, a closed closet to the right and a boot rack with two sizes of shoes on the left. He wiped his boots carefully on the mat covering the linoleum floor and then took the handful of steps to clear the hallway. The inside of the small house was a neat throwback to the eighties, with brass highlights on the furniture and doilies draped on almost every available surface. The plush white carpet was clean, if a little worn, and the walls were covered in Robert Bateman prints of birds.

A wide couch faced Raife, with a wide-hipped woman in her late sixties or early seventies seated dead in the middle, her back ram-rod straight. As Raife cleared the hallway, she reached down and plucked another tissue from a box on the glass coffee table in front of her and blew her nose with a honk. Beside the couch, his back to the window, stood Gary Sidhu, one of the shift's constables. Gary stared studiously at his notebook, turning one page back and forth, as though he searched for something important. He didn't look at the woman, who was obviously suffering. She did nothing but wipe her nose, stare at her hands, and cry.

Raife cleared his throat and the woman's chin lifted slightly so she could glance at him, then she looked back at her hands. Gary looked over at him and nodded.

"Sergeant Raife," Gary said. He took a pen from a loop on the front of his body armour, clicked the top and held it over his notebook, scanning it some more. He stood like that for several seconds, but didn't write anything.

Raife sidestepped around a plush recliner, to stand beside Gary and looked down at his notebook. The page was blank. Raife felt his eyebrows draw together in annoyance.

"Uh, what are you doing, constable?"

Gary snapped his notebook closed and put his pen away with a flourish. "Yes, Sergeant, this is Joanne Hill, the wife of the..." he glanced down at the woman who still stared at her hands. "That is to say, she found the, uh..."

"No, constable," Raife said doing his best to keep his temper in check. "I asked you what you were doing."

"Well, I'm, uh, I'm...you know."

"I really don't," Raife said. "How about you go check the tire pressure on my car."

"Uh, well, Sarge, I'm supposed to..."

"I wasn't asking."

The young constable made a move towards the pen in his vest, then looked up for the first time and met Raife's gaze. He swallowed thickly and tucked his notebook into a pocket on his vest. "Right away, Sarge."

As Gary hurried past him and towards the front door, Raife called after him. "You come get me right away when victim services arrives."

When he heard the front door close, Raife turned back to the woman on the couch. As Raife watched her, he could see that her shoulders shook slightly.

"Hello, Mrs. Hill," he said. "My name is Charles Raife. I'm a sergeant in the Resolution Cove RCMP detachment. Would it be all right if I sat down?"

The woman didn't look up, but gave a short nod.

Raife eased himself down, perching his bulk on the edge of

the couch next to her so he could stay upright. She didn't look at him; just sat and shook.

In his nearly twenty years a cop, Raife had learned a lot of things about human grief, and it affected everyone differently. Some people raged and shouted. Some bawled and wailed. Others said nothing and curled in on themselves. The thing Raife had always found was reading people enough to figure out what they needed to help them through their time of grief. Gary was one of innumerable cops who didn't understand how to do that. It was his job to stand here with this woman, but he hadn't figured out what to do with her, and his presence made things worse instead of better.

What Raife believed the woman needed, and what most people needed at the end of the day, was a little humanity.

Raife reached out with one huge hand and wrapped it around both of hers. "I am very sorry for what you found today, Mrs. Hill. I am very sorry for your loss."

As he spoke, the stiffness melted from her spine and she sagged against him. He let go of her hands and put his arm around her narrow shoulders. She took in a huge, hitching breath and then let out a wail, screaming into his shoulder. He held her there, for several minutes, while she cried. He said nothing, because he instinctively knew she didn't need words.

When she finished, she sat up and reached out for the box of Kleenex, plucking two from the top and wiping her eyes before honking her nose into them. Raife sat patiently, offering no judgment or opinion.

"I'm very sorry, Sergeant," Mrs. Hill said, swiping at her nose.

"Not at all, Mrs. Hill," he said. "And please, just call me Raife."

She looked up at him and met his eyes for the first time. "Very well, Raife. Please, call me Jo." He nodded while she sniffed and wiped her nose again. "Can you tell me what's going to happen from here?"

"Well, to start with, we're going to have our Victim Services people come down here and talk to you."

She nodded and wiped her nose again. "Yes, the dark-haired statue that you shooed out of here mentioned something about that. But, I mean what are you going to do about my Teddy? How are you going to catch whoever did..." She paused and put fluttering fingers to her lips, then took in a big breath. "How are you going to catch them?"

Raife rubbed his thumb and forefinger over his moustache. "Well, we have our own people taking on the initial steps, but the bulk of the investigation will be handled by the homicide team that should be here in the morning."

"I understand that," Jo said. "But what are they going to do?"

"I'm not sure it's proper for me to give opinions on an investigation I won't be leading, but I can assure you the team—"

"No," Jo said with a quiet intensity that made Raife shut his mouth with a click. "I just lost the love of my life," she paused, pressing the palm of her hand to her forehead, "and every person I've met in the last two hours has whispered meaningless crap. I need someone to speak plainly to me, Raife. And I need it to be you."

He opened his mouth again, and then shut it. He looked at her stricken face and nodded.

"Tell me," she said softly. "Tell me, what they are going to do?"

He thought a long moment before replying. He knew what had done this and knew that the homicide team would find nothing when they showed up except for an ass load of questions they couldn't possibly answer. How did you explain to a woman that a boogeyman killed her husband and tore him limb from limb. He suddenly had an idea how Quinn felt after investigating Patrick Green's death and explaining what had killed him to the boy's father.

"They're going to survey the scene," he began, carefully. "They'll have the forensic team come in, photograph the scene and then process it for any possible evidence."

"Will they find anything, do you think?" The intensity was gone from her voice, replaced with a dull acceptance, as though she knew the investigation was not much more than a broad formality and it was best to keep her expectations low.

"I can't say," Raife said. "I'm not an expert, and I didn't study the scene long enough to get any real idea of what was there."

"Yes," she said, nodding. "It was hard to look at, wasn't it?" She lifted her eyes from her own hands and looked at Raife. He, in turn, glanced away. "Never mind," she said, when he didn't reply. "What else?"

"They will process the scene as best they can and remove your husband so a medical examiner can complete an assessment. They'll have people canvass your neighbours, and they'll want to interview you."

She sniffed again, loudly, and wiped her nose. "Everything you've told me, I could read off my stupid phone." She waved dismissively at the smartphone sitting on the coffee table among a piled of used Kleenex. "If you were the man in charge, what would you want to know?"

"I would want to know why," Raife said after another long pause. "I would be asking what motivation anyone could have to attack your husband."

"Do you have any ideas about that?" She kept her voice intentionally flat, but Raife could hear the querulous need in it.

"I do," Raife said, pausing to smooth out his moustache. "They were looking for something in the office at the back of his workshop. It's torn apart with hardly a thing left whole. If I were in charge of this investigation, I would start there."

"Oh, that bloody office!" Jo pressed the heels of her hands to her eyes.

"Do you have any idea what someone would be looking for in that office?"

She tossed her crumpled tissue on the table and pulled a fresh one from the box. "I can only guess that they must have thought he had money or something in there. Ted was always going on about his goddamned history book and how people were going to plagiarize it. He was convinced if he didn't lock it up, that someone would break in and steal it and publish it without giving him the money for it. I've read the bloody thing and it's terrible, so I can't imagine anyone else actually wanting to read it, let alone want it enough to..." She broke off, putting her hand to her mouth to stifle a sob. Raife reached out and grasped her free hand with one of his and gave it another squeeze. When she looked like she had a hold of herself again, he let go.

"I can't imagine anyone wanting his book enough to do anything about it," she finished. "He said it was ready to be published, but was waiting for the right offer before he let anyone have it."

"Did he get any offers?"

She snorted and smiled sadly. "Not a one. He used to say that his book would be the thing that changed the perception of Canadian History. That it was *important*. And when he tried to sell it to the big publishers in New York or Toronto, all he got back was a photocopied letter that thanked him for the opportunity to consider his work, but that they were going to pass on the project." She looked at him. "Which all just boils down to the fact that no one gave a shit."

Raife nodded, pressing his lips together to keep his mouth shut. Someone had wanted that book, the one the old man refused to show to Quinn and Dave, all right, and wanted it bad enough that the old man's life was cheap by comparison.

"I don't imagine we'll ever know now," Raife said. "There is nothing left in that little office besides shredded paper."

"Oh." She got up from the couch. "You can see the book if you think it would help."

Raife stood up as well. "You have copies?"

She turned and walked into the dining room. "Teddy took it to a little printer's shop in Nanaimo and had them print out a dozen copies. He thought his old pictures were far too precious to be handled by anyone else, so he actually took a course at the community college, bought some fancy camera equipment and formatted the book himself. It bordered on an obsession."

At the far side of the dining room, there was a tall china cabinet, obviously handmade. Jo took a small key ring from the pocket of her slacks and selected a small, chrome key. She inserted the key into a lock recessed in the door of the cabinet and opened the sturdy oak door. Inside was the dull metal of a safe.

She looked over her shoulder at Raife. "You see what I mean about obsessed?"

He let out a whistling breath through his nose and nodded.

She selected another key from the ring and opened the safe. Several identical books bound with glossy covers filled the compartment. She plucked one out and handed it to him. "This is the sum total of my husband's obsessive life's work."

Raife opened the book and flipped through the first few pages. He found a chapter index and scanned the headings: "The First Men", "Blazing the Trail", "A Legacy Begins". It looked exactly the same as any dozen books about small towns. He very much doubted that this book was Quinn's secret key. He was about to close the book and hand it back, when his eye caught the last item in the index.

The Dark Days.

If he'd had any hair, it would be standing on end. "You have more of these?"

Jo wiped at her nose with the tissue still clutched in her hand and gestured at the open safe with the other. "Yes, more than I would ever have use for."

"Do you mind if I take this?"

She shrugged and sniffed. "If you think it will help, then you are welcome to it."

"If you don't mind, I'm going to send the constable back in here, and then leave. The major crime team and the victim services worker shouldn't be long."

Her shoulders sagged, and he felt suddenly guilty about leaving her alone. If he were ever killed, he hoped that the detachment would do a far sight better for his wife than they were doing for Jo Hill.

He reached out and squeezed a hand that hung limply at

her side. "I will check in on you soon. And if they don't keep you updated on the investigation, I'll shake the information out of them for you."

Her eyes met his and she nodded. "Thank you." She pulled in a big breath. "Thank you for...everything."

He gave her hand another squeeze and then turned for the door. As he was leaving, he ran into Gary, notebook still in his hand. Behind him were two people—a tall, pimply faced youth and a handsome woman in her early fifties —wearing blue jackets with 'Victim Services' printed in white letters on the front.

"Victim Services is here," Gary said, looking down at his notebook.

"Your notebook tell you that?" Raife growled. He stepped back and held open the door for the victim services workers. "Mrs. Hill is just in there." He pointed towards the couch where the grieving woman had resumed her seat on the sofa.

"Are you going to hang around until the general investigation guys get back?" Gary asked.

Raife looked down at the book in his hand and rubbed his finger across his moustache. "No, I've got some dark days to look into."

CHAPTER 13

No one spoke for a long time after Raife left. The words 'suspect' and 'murder' seemed to hang like a cloud of smoke in the air above Quinn's head. Even Shawn, who was almost always a source of laughter, sat quietly on the couch.

They all still sat at the kitchen table, mugs of tea forgotten and cooling in front of them. Quinn felt he should say something, but as he thought about the death of the old man, he found that words escaped him.

"Well," Gemma said after several minutes.

"Well, what?" Quinn snapped, looking up at her. His nerves felt as though they'd been rubbed with a cheese grater.

"We know you didn't do it, baby." Carrie reached over to squeeze Quinn's hand.

"No," Quinn said. "I didn't. But I led the thing that did do it right to that old man's door. So it might as well have been me."

"Don't talk such foolishness," Gemma said with a derisive sniff. "You must seek out answers. It is your job—both as a lawman and the Guardian of this place. If you could see the outcome of every action, you would not be human."

Quinn grunted and turned his gaze back to the table's surface .

Sniffing again, Gemma stood up. "Come on, then."

Suppressing the urge to tell the woman to get out of his house, Quinn looked up at her. "Come on, where?" He kept his voice even, trying to keep his anger and frustration at bay. Once again, Carrie reached over and squeezed his hand.

"There are things we should be doing besides sitting here moping," Gemma said.

"Moping?" Quinn rubbed his hands against his face. "Gemma, I'm probably going to get fucking fired for this. I'll be lucky if I don't go to jail."

"Nonsense." She smoothed down her skirt and walked to the coat rack where she pulled her heavy sweater off a hook. "No one who knows you will think you capable of murder. And the only way to clear your name is to find and stop the thing that killed that poor soul."

"And how do you propose we do that?" Quinn asked. "I'm already on admin duties, and I wouldn't be surprised if Steve Faulk is at the detachment right now drafting up the mandate letter for my suspension."

"That may be true," Gemma said. "But that doesn't change the fact there is a very powerful demon in this town, and my child is still lost somewhere in the black. The only one who can solve those problems is you. Now, will you sit here and feel sorry for yourself, or will you get up and start moving?"

Feeling sorry for himself sounded like the most viable option, but his guilt, or perhaps a sense of duty, made him nod. "Okay," he said after letting out a big breath through puffed cheeks. "What do you want to do?"

"The child," Gemma said, pulling on her sweater. "The girl who can open portals."

"Abigail," Quinn said. "Abby."

"Yes," Gemma nodded. "I'd like to meet her."

"Why do you want to see her?"

"I have a feeling that she is central to everything that is happening here?"

Quinn frowned. "Why do you think that?"

Gemma pulled Quinn's coat off the rack and tossed it to

him. "She is certainly the key to opening another door to retrieve Autumn, and she is also what your last enemy sought when it came to this town."

Reluctantly, Quinn stood. "And you think this new demon, the one with the ebony skin, is after Abby as well?"

Gemma shrugged. "I cannot presume to know the mind of a demon, and so can't be certain, but I believe that is it."

Pulling on his coat, Quinn looked at Carrie and Bobby. "Okay," he said. "But we're all going together. No one stays alone."

On the way to Inspector Green's house, Quinn called Dave. He, too, had received a visit from Raife. Dave's reluctance to leave his home paled, however, to the objections his wife put up when she found out that Dave was leaving. Quinn reached for the knob of the stereo to turn down the blue-tooth in the car, as the voice of Dave's wife, Monica, burst angrily though the truck's speakers.

Ten minutes later, Quinn stopped in front of the Inspector's house to see Dave getting out of his Jeep.

"If I get divorced," Dave said, hunching his shoulders against the cold air, "I'm coming to live with you. And I'm not going to apologize when I fart on your couch."

"Hi, Uncle Dave!" Shawn leapt from the back seat of the Tahoe to throw himself on Dave.

"Hiya, Squirt." Dave picked the boy up and spun him in a circle. He halted when he saw Gemma and Bobby climbing out of the truck as well. "You bring everyone?"

"I thought it was a bad idea for anyone to stay at the house alone," Quinn said.

"Fair point." Dave tossed Shawn over his shoulder like a sack of potatoes, eliciting a high peal of laughter. "Come on, Squirt. Let's see if Geraldine has any of those oatmeal chocolate chip cookies."

The Inspector's house, a wide red-brick rancher, had a sprawling green lawn leading up to the doorway. Warm yellow light glowed above the red-tiled porch, and more warm light spilled through the cut-glass windows of the front door. As everyone crowded onto the porch, Quinn rang the doorbell.

Half a minute later, dressed in black slacks, a billowy white blouse and fluffy pink slippers, Geraldine Green opened the front door. Her carefully styled blonde hair matched her makeup applied with similar care. The Inspector had joked more than once that his wife never left the house in anything less than her best. Apparently answering the door was no exception.

When she saw Quinn she gave him a wide, white smile. "Quinn." She pulled him into a tight hug. "What a pleasant surprise." She stepped back and saw everyone else behind him. Her smile faltered a little. "Oh...you brought friends."

"Do you have any cookies?" Shawn pushed his way to the front of the crowd.

Geraldine looked down at him and her smile brightened again. Geraldine Green was a sucker for children. "Of course I do." She hugged Shawn to her prominent bosom and looked up at Quinn. "You and your, um, friends, come on in out of the cold, Quinn. Donald is in the living room with Abby."

Quinn stepped through the door and ushered everyone into the spacious, white-tiled foyer, closing it behind them. Geraldine smiled and greeted each person in turn, hugging Dave and Carrie and shaking hands with Gemma and Bobby. Gemma, in her long flowing skirt, baggy homemade sweater, and scarf around her head, looked as dissimilar to Geraldine as a pinecone to a rose petal. Gemma also appeared so uncomfortable that it made Quinn itch just to look at her.

He bent close to her. "It's okay," he said into her ear. "These are good people."

She glanced up at him. "I do not doubt the quality of your friends, Quinn. It's just, this place is very..."

"Pristine?" he finished for her.

Gemma nodded. "Unsettlingly so."

"Yeah, it took me about three visits before I'd even sit down on the furniture. But, Geraldine is a lot less uptight than she looks."

Gemma continued to look around. "I will have to take you at your word."

As everyone else doffed coats and scarves, Shawn rooted around in Geraldine's kitchen for cookies. Quinn walked down the short hallway to the back of the house and into the living room.

Donald Green sat on the edge of the couch, his knees on either side of Abigail McRae, as she picked her way through the pieces of a large jig-saw puzzle, half completed on a low coffee table. The Inspector, his reading glasses perched on the end of his nose, examined the lid of the puzzle box, which depicted a glowing fairy sitting on a flower.

"No, my love," the Inspector said, looking over the top of Abby's blonde head. "We need to find all the edge pieces first. Then we'll really be in business."

It pained Quinn to interrupt them, but he cleared his throat.

The Inspector studied him a long time over the frames of his glasses. "I'm not sure you should be here, Quinn," he said, finally, and took his glasses off.

Abby looked up when the Inspector spoke, and a smile, the light of which had not been dimmed by all the trials she'd faced, split her face. "Hi, Quinn."

"Hiya, Abby."

The Inspector kissed the top of Abby's head and stood, approaching Quinn. "I will have to speak to the Major Crime team from Nanaimo in the morning, both about your Code of Conduct investigation, as well as a dead man who was last seen alive with you. It will be difficult for me to appear impartial if you are at my house tonight."

"I know, sir, and I don't want to put you in a bad spot," Quinn said. "But Gemma thought it important that she meet Abby."

The Inspector glanced over his shoulder at the girl, who busily separated edge pieces of the puzzle into a small pile. "What does she want with my Abby?"

"She's come to see what it is she can do," Quinn said.

His mouth pressed into a thin line, the Inspector shook his head. "What she can do, what she *needs* to do, is be left alone and allowed to grow up. I don't want anyone coming here and messing with her when she has already given so much." He took a deep breath and rubbed his hand over his nearly bald head. "She is safe here, Quinn, I will see to that."

Quinn blinked, shook his head, then reached out and gripped the Inspector's forearm. "Do you really believe that? That you will be able to keep Abby safe?" The shorter man looked up at him. "You've seen what's out there." He pointed to the nearest window with his free hand. "You know what they can do. If Gemma is right, one of those things is coming for Abby."

"I can't lose her, Quinn," the Inspector said, his voice barely above a whisper. "Not after Patrick."

"We're not going to let anything happen to her, sir," Quinn said, his voice pitched in the same tone. "But this is a world with laws we know nothing about. Gemma is the only one who can help us. If she wants to talk with Abby, I say we let her."

The Inspector glanced over at Abby, then pulled in a long breath and let it out in a rush, his shoulders slumping. After several long moments, he looked up at Quinn and nodded.

Stepping briskly into the kitchen, Quinn found everyone else hunkered around the kitchen island, picking through several colourful cookie tins. Dave had his arm wrapped around Shawn, as they both vied for the tin containing the oatmeal chocolate chip stash.

"Gemma? Bobby?" Quinn said. The big man turned, his eyes wide, crumbs littering the several days of beard growth on his wide chin, a peanut butter cookie half way to his mouth. Beside him, Gemma reached up and brushed the evidence from his face.

"The girl?" she asked.

Quinn nodded. Gemma tucked her hands into the sleeves of her voluminous sweater and stepped towards him without another word. Bobby crammed the last bite of his cookie into his mouth, and then shoved Dave bodily out of the way to grab two more before following.

In the living room, Donald Green stood with his hands in the pockets of his jeans, while he peered down and inspected Abby's work. The child had her mouth quirked as she tried several flat-edged puzzle pieces to complete the outline of the picture. When Gemma and Bobby stepped into the room behind Quinn, Abby glanced up, then stared hard at Gemma and went still.

The Inspector's face darkened and he opened his mouth to say something, but Quinn put a hand on his shoulder. The Inspector pulled in a long breath through his open mouth and then shut it.

"Hello, Abby." Gemma walked around the coffee table to kneel on the floor beside the child. "My name is Gemma."

"You look just like a lady I used to know," Abby said, dropping her puzzle piece on the table and tucking her hands into her lap.

Gemma nodded. "My daughter, Autumn."

Abby's face screwed up and fat tears began leaking from the corners of her eyes. "I'm sorry," the girl said, her voice hitching. "I tried to get her back. I did. But I couldn't find her."

Every time Quinn had tried to get Abby to open a door to find Autumn, the child's response was the same. She could open the door, but there would be nothing on the other side except endless, inky dark, and Quinn's courage to enter would fail. No matter how much he tried to convince her otherwise, Abby clung to the firm belief that it was her fault Autumn was gone, and her responsibility to get her back.

Gemma reached out and wrapped her arms around Abby, pulling her into the folds of her sweater. "No, my dear, no," she said, her face pressed against Abby's pale gold hair. "This is not your fault. But we *are* going to set it right. You and me." She pulled back and looked down into Abby's face. "Do you want to do that?"

The girl nodded eagerly, wiping her face with her hands.

Quinn crossed his arms. This was a side of Gemma's nature that had not been apparent before. He glanced over at Bobby, who only grinned around a bite of cookie.

"All right," Gemma ran a thumb along the edge of Abby's chin to catch a stray teardrop, "will you show me how you open one of your doors?"

Abby's expression turned serious and she nodded. She reached beneath the collar of her t-shirt and pulled out a copper medallion about the size of her palm. It had a crude impression of a feather in the centre of it. The first time Quinn had seen it, the medallion had been strung with an old shoe-lace. Now it was on a fine silver chain, thanks to the Inspector, no doubt.

Abby glanced around, and then selected a puzzle piece off the coffee table. It was the face of the fairy that made up the centre of the picture. She held it between thumb and forefinger. "Would you hold out your hand, please?"

Gemma glanced at Quinn, who nodded. Gemma cleared her throat and held out her hand, palm up. Knowing what was about to happen, Quinn went to the living room's entrance and slid the doors shut.

Abby gripped the medallion so hard she trembled, her eyes narrowed in concentration. For several moments, nothing happened, and then a glow came from her hand. Within the space of a dozen heartbeats, the light became so bright Quinn could not bear to look directly at it, lifting his hand to shield his eyes. Beams of light arched from between Abby's fingers, but directly in front of her clenched fist a black spot appeared so dark it was the antithesis of light.

Into this spot, Abby dropped the puzzle piece.

Above Gemma's outstretched hand, a light flashed. Abby released the medallion and the light in the room instantly died, leaving nothing behind but after-images in Quinn's vision. When he looked over at Gemma, she stared with wide eyes at her open hand. In her palm was the puzzle piece, covered in a thick coating of frost.

"Gigi, are you all right?" Bobby slipped his arm around her shoulder.

"I am..." her voice trailed off with a quiver. She looked at Quinn. "You told me what the girl could do, but I really had not grasped what it meant." She glanced down at the puzzle piece and slowly closed her hand over it. "Oh, my child. She is lost in the black and the cold. Alone." She opened her eyes and locked them on Quinn's. He met her gaze, but had to resist the urge to take a step back.

"We must get her back, Quinn. No matter what we have to do."

He nodded. "No matter what."

Now he just had to figure out how to do that while he fought off the ebony demon and tried to not get everyone in Resolution killed.

He smelled her long before she reached him, and he closed his eyes while he breathed deep. She thought she was being sneaky when she leaned over the back of the chair and cupped her hands on his eyes.

"Guess who?" she said.

He reached up and took her hand gently in one of his own, pulling it to his mouth to kiss her palm. He paused, his breath catching. He could hear his child's heartbeat.

"Are you all right?" she asked, concern in her voice.

He smiled and pressed her hand to his mouth to kiss it. "Yes, my love, I'm fine." He turned in his seat as she settled on the arm of the overstuffed chair he sat in. He placed his hand on her swollen belly and couldn't help but let out a soft laugh as he felt a kick on his palm. "How are you? Our little friend keeping you awake?"

She let out a breath through puffed cheeks. "He hasn't been still once since I laid down in bed. It almost feels like he's trying to kick his way out."

His smile faltered. He had worried, more than once, that the fragile body of his wife would not be able to hold the child growing inside her, and that it would come out in a fashion they'd not intended.

His smile returned when her words settled in his mind. "You said, 'he.' Do you think it's a boy?" They had intentionally not asked to know the sex of the child, although he had secretly hoped it would be a son.

"I think a girl would be more polite. Only a boy would kick me this much." She glanced down at his lap. "What's that you're reading?"

"Oh, this?" He glanced down at the open book in his lap. The page showed a photograph of several dour faced men standing in front of the foundation of what would eventually be Resolution Cove City Hall. "It's a book on Resolution's history that someone gave me."

She reached down and ran her fingertips over the page. "Is it any good?"

"I'm just getting into it, but I have a feeling there might be something important in there."

CHAPTER 14

Quinn sighed and looked around the inside of the detachment's interview room. He glanced up at the camera, mounted high in the corner, pointed at his face, and crossed his arms. He was not used to sitting on this side of the table.

The door opened with a soft *shush*. Dressed in a shirt and tie with the top button of his shirt undone and his sleeves rolled up, Sergeant Bill Davis entered. Dark circles puffed under his eyes, his short salt and pepper hair in unusual disarray, he carried a tall paper coffee cup in one hand and a file folder in the other.

"Hi, Quinn," Davis said as he closed the door with his hip. The sound proofing in the room made his voice a hollow echo that didn't hit the ear quite right.

"Hi, Bill. You look like shit."

The slim sergeant snorted. "Indeed, I do. I'm guessing I got about as much sleep last night as you did." He placed the file folder on the table and slid into the seat opposite Quinn.

Quinn nodded and ran the palm of his hand across his face. Numb with exhaustion, he had to resist the urge to slap himself. After they'd left the Inspector's house, he had gone home with Carrie and their house guests. He had lain down to try and sleep, but spent most of the night staring at the ceiling.

An overwhelming feeling of guilt sat on his chest like a misplaced dump-truck. He felt guilty over the death of the old furniture maker, guilty that a shiny-skinned demon ran loose in his town, and guilty that Autumn was still stuck in the cold black and he had no way to get her out.

Being interviewed by Major Crime was the rotten cherry on a cake made of bullshit.

"So, you want to tell me what happened yesterday?" Bill took a slurping sip from his cup. He grimaced and looked down suspiciously at the contents. "You also mind telling me why the coffee here sucks so bad? I shudder to think of what I might do for a Starbucks right now."

"What part of yesterday do you want me to get into?" Quinn asked.

Bill lifted the cup to his mouth, glanced down at it, and set it on the table beside the file folder. "Look, Quinn," he said, leaning his elbow on the table. "This situation is fucked. We got the Code Of Conduct matter to look into, but we also have to figure out what happened to the old man." He opened the file folder, looking at the first page. "To...Theodore Hill."

"I've noticed, Bill, that you haven't read me my rights or offered me legal counsel or any of the other things you'd do if you actually thought I'd killed Hill." Quinn uncrossed his arms and leaned forward. "So what exactly is my jeopardy, here? Steve Faulk is out there acting like I'm a murder suspect, but I'm not getting that impression from you."

Bill Davis let out a big breath. "No, Quinn, I don't think you and McLeod killed the old man. Although it isn't outside the realm of possibility that McLeod could aggravate someone to death." He turned over the front page inside the file folder to a series of crime scene photos. "In fact, I'm pretty certain you didn't kill him, unless you have the innate ability to grow talons."

Quinn swallowed. "Talons?"

Bill nodded. "We, obviously, have not gotten a full medical examiner's report yet, but the Coroner figures the old man was killed by an animal. His throat was torn, not cut, and the majority of his limbs were broken. Whatever killed him had long talons, and enough strength to break a femur. Even a guy Raife's size couldn't do that."

"All right," Quinn said, as a long huffing breath escaped him. He knew it wasn't right to feel relief in this situation, but he couldn't help it. "If you know I didn't do it, why am I still sitting in this room?"

"Because you know something." Bill pushed the pile of photos towards him, and Quinn tried not to look at them. "Quinn, every time I come here, it's always for something fucked up, and you're always in the middle of it. Crazy guys with guns, heroin addicts twice their normal size breaking into your house, people being eaten, buildings burning merrily to the ground." Bill scooched his chair forward and leaned over the table. Quinn could smell the stale coffee on his breath. "You know something about what happened to this old man, about what kind of fucking animal was able to get into his shop without leaving a mark on the door and tear him into little pieces. You know what it was that took the time to demolish the office with all the computers in it. And I want to know what you know."

No you don't, Quinn thought as he looked at his hands, making a careful study of them. He wasn't sure what he was going to say to this man, a man he liked and trusted. How do you explain to someone that you know exactly what evil looks like, that you've smelled its breath and looked it in the eye? How do you convince someone to believe you when you tell them all the shadows that lurked under their childhood bed are real?

"I wish I knew, Bill," Quinn said, his voice just above a whisper but it sounded oddly amplified in the sound-proof room. "I wish I knew why these fucked up things keep happening around me. If I knew, maybe I could make it stop, but I don't know any better than you do."

"I think part of that is true, Quinn," Bill Davis said. "But I still think you're holding out on me."

They sat in silence for several long moments, while Bill

stared hard into Quinn's face. Quinn met his gaze evenly. Quinn had looked into far more dangerous eyes than Bill's, and nothing the man did would make him flinch.

"Okay, Quinn," Bill said, finally. "I'll have to take you at your word."

"What about the Code?"

"That, you're going to have to talk about a little more." Bill flipped to the back of the folder. "It is alleged that you had a conversation with one Cecil Brown, where you advised him you were working on a special project for the Mayor. That has been proved to be a lie. You were then seen at the residence of a man who was later killed by some sort of animal that can open doors. The reason for that has yet to be explained." He closed the folder. "If you don't give me a statement explaining why you were talking to Cecil and why you made up the story about working for the Mayor, you're going to be found guilty of one count of conduct unbecoming a member, under the Code."

"Okay," Quinn said. "What's the punishment for that?"

"It'll be a twenty day rip in pay, if my memory serves."

Quinn chewed the inside of his cheek while he thought over his options. If he said nothing, he would be out a fuckload of cash, but nothing he wouldn't recover from. If he tried to give some bullshit explanation, which would probably be proven a lie, he would get into even more shit. If he told Bill the truth, that he needed to find a nexus of power in Resolution so he could rescue Autumn from some other plane of existence, he'd probably be apprehended under the Mental Health Act and promptly carted off to the hospital.

"I'll take the twenty days in pay," he said.

Bill Davis blinked. "What?"

"I decline to give a statement," Quinn said. "I'll take the twenty day rip in pay."

"Quinn," Bill said, leaning back in his chair. "You cannot be serious."

"I am."

"For fuck's sakes, man. You realise that if you're found

guilty of this, the loss in pay will be the least of your problems. It'll be career suicide. No promotion board will ever look at you again, and you'll be stuck working the road in some tiny town for the rest of your service."

Letting out a big breath through puffed cheeks, Quinn nodded. "Yeah, that had occurred to me."

"And you're really not going to talk to me about this?"

"No, Bill," Quinn said. "I'm not."

Looking up at the ceiling, Bill ran a hand over his carefully styled hair. "Okay, Quinn. I hope you know what you're doing, 'cause from where I'm sitting, it seems like you're making a colossal mistake. Your Staff was already pissed about all this when I walked in here, and now I think he is going to absolutely shit."

"That had occurred to me as well," Quinn said.

Bill leaned forward and put one elbow on the table. "What's his issue, anyway? Last time I was here, he was all about supporting you and your guys. Now he wants to see you tarred and feathered in front of the post office at high noon. What's changed?"

Telling Bill that he thought a demon had either possessed or replaced the detachment Staff Sergeant was another item on the list of things Quinn didn't want to do today. He shrugged. "If I figure it out, I'll let you know."

With a final shake of his head, the sergeant gathered up the papers in the file folder, dropped the mostly full cup of coffee in the trash can beside the table, and stood up. "Your Code isn't officially resolved until we bring it before the Conduct Authority and complete a Letter of Finding. We're done here, but I would hang around for a few minutes until I talk to your bosses and they decide what your next move is." He switched the folder to his left hand and stuck out his right. Quinn stood and shook with him. "For what it's worth, I know you've been through the ringer with all the shit that has happened here."

"Thanks," Quinn said. "I think."

Bill grinned, a little sadly, and opened the door.

Quinn followed the sergeant out into the hallway that led

into the general duty pit. He found Dave, his hands stuffed into the pockets of his hooded sweatshirt, sitting at his usual desk.

"How did it go?" Quinn asked as he sat down across from Dave.

The other man shrugged. "They told me I either had to explain what happened at Cecil's or cough up twenty days pay."

"And what did you decide?"

"I decided I'm still coming to live with you when my wife finds out I'm losing twenty days pay and she leaves me." Dave ran his hand over the dark stubble covering his scalp. "What about you?"

"Pretty much the same," Quinn said. "Only, minus the divorce."

Across the pit, Quinn watched Bill Davis go into Inspector Green's office with Raife and Steve Faulk.

"How do you think that's going to go?" Quinn asked, tilting his chin towards the closing door of the office.

"I think it's going to go for a quick ride down the nearest toilet," Dave said, standing slightly to see over the wall of the cubicles. "Right along with our careers."

They sat in silence for several minutes, until the door to the Inspector's office flew open with a crash.

"Where are they?" Steve Faulk demanded, his voice bordering on a shout.

With a sigh, Quinn stood up. "We're here, Staff."

The tall, slender man stormed over, his black uniform boots thudding dully on the carpet while the components of his gun-belt jingled. He shook with rage. "What the fuck do you mean you won't provide an explanation?" Raife, Bill Davis and the Inspector filed out of the office and followed.

Quinn glanced at Dave, then back at the staff sergeant. "We were advised that we had the option of providing a statement, or losing twenty days pay. We've both opted to lose the pay."

"Bullshit," Steve Faulk shouted, spit flying from his mouth.

"I want some fucking answers, Sullivan. You're not getting out of this so easy."

"I'd like to suggest, Staff," Dave said. "That losing twenty days of pay isn't exactly easy."

"Shut your fucking mouth, McLeod!" Faulk screamed. The elderly volunteers who manned the front counter all stood from their seats and began drifting towards the shouting, but turned and retreated when the staff sergeant levelled the weight of his glare on them.

"Steve." Inspector Green laid his hand on Faulk's arm. "Lower your voice and calm down."

The staff sergeant jerked his arm free. "No, Donald, not until I get some goddamned answers." He turned his gaze back to Quinn. "Well?"

Standing impassively, Quinn said nothing. He could hear the staff sergeant's teeth grinding together.

"Fine," he said finally, a quaver in his voice. "You go ahead and keep your fucking secrets, but you're going to be keeping them somewhere else."

"What does that mean?" Dave asked.

"It means that you are both suspended for the next twenty days." Steve Faulk eyes darted between the two of them. "By the time you come back, I will have your transfer documents in order and will inform you of your new postings."

"Transfer documents?" Quinn and Dave asked in unison.

"Can he do that?" Dave asked.

"No, he can't," Raife growled.

"Goddamned rights, I can," Steve Faulk said. "I'm the senior NCO and the second in command of this detachment, and staffing is in my purview."

Everyone looked at Bill Davis, who put up his hands. "Don't look at me. This isn't my detachment."

"Steve," Inspector Green said. "We really should discuss this."

"No, Donald, we're not discussing anything," the staff sergeant said. "If you don't sign off on this, I'll take it to Division Headquarters and explain my reasoning, and you know damn well they'll see it my way."

The Inspector's hands flexed helplessly and he gave no reply.

The staff sergeant fixed each man standing there with his gaze, issuing a silent challenge to each of them. None of them said a word, not even Raife.

"I have some phone calls to make," Faulk said. "Sullivan, you and McLeod get out of here, and I don't want to see your shadows darken this place until twenty days from now. Am I understood?"

"Yeah," Dave said, looking at the floor. Quinn thought Dave was probably better off saying as little as possible.

"Sullivan?" Faulk asked.

"Yeah, Staff, understood," Quinn said.

Faulk gave a curt nod, before walking briskly to his office.

When he had gone inside and closed the door, Raife let out a heavy breath that bordered on a growl. "What the fuck is up with that guy?"

"I'm sorry, fellas," Bill Davis said, looking between Quinn and Dave. "This was not my idea."

"We know, Bill," Inspector Green said. "Could you give us a few minutes? I think we have some things to discuss as a team."

"Of course," Bill said. "I'm going to take my team to find a Starbucks, and then get to work on the files we need to finish, so we can get out of your hair." He gave a wan grin and walked down the hallway towards the back door of the office.

Quinn looked at Dave, who gave a nod. "Out of the game," Dave said. "If we thought we were out of the game before, imagine what it'll be like when we're not even posted here anymore."

Afraid to put into words what he thought the landscape of Resolution would look like if they weren't here to defend it, Quinn only nodded.

"This fucking town is going to burn merrily to the ground." Raife rubbed his moustache so hard Quinn feared he'd peel it off his face.

"Sir," Quinn said to the Inspector. "Is there anything you can do about this?"

The Inspector ran a hand over this wispy thin hair. "I don't know, son. He is right. Staffing is within his purview. I could certainly argue that you and Dave aren't eligible for transfer from the detachment, but I believe Steve when he says he'll take this to headquarters. If that happens, we'll have to answer to some investigators who likely won't be as understanding as Bill Davis."

"Then what do we do?" Dave asked.

"If we have to leave here," Quinn said, "there is something we have to do before we go."

The three other men looked at him.

"Get Autumn back, and kill that fucking demon."

He hung up the phone and could feel the smile bending his face. The feeling of nervous apprehension that had niggled at him fell away, and contentment, a surety of purpose, moved in to replace it.

He felt, now, like he knew the way forward. Soon, the Guardian would be gone, in the most convenient possible way. With none of the insight the man received from being in his position at work, he would be easy to circumvent. Not only would he be able to avoid killing the man and creating uncomfortable questions, he wouldn't have to deal with him at all. Once his child was born, the Guardian would be far away and unable to interfere. It was all so delightful he had to suppress the urge to laugh.

Thoughts of his child made him frown. He wondered if the baby would be able to wait that long, and if his beloved would survive. That was a problem he may need to address sooner, rather than later, but, again, he felt like he had a way forward. The book he had taken from the old man would point him towards the place he needed. Thinking of the book made him itchy, like a child waiting to open his gifts on Christmas morning. He bit his lip, considering.

He checked the surface of his desk, to make sure there weren't any tasks he needed to complete, and instantly hated himself for caring. He swore, one day soon, he would be free of the mundane responsibility of this job he had taken. Until then, he needed to finish reading the book.

He slowly opened the bottom drawer of his desk, almost afraid that if he moved too quick someone would discover him. He had taken an enormous risk bringing the book to his office, where it might be seen and link him to the old man's death. He feared leaving it at home where his beloved might read it or show it to one of her friends.

He reached into the drawer, pushed aside several envelopes and random forms he'd placed there to hide his prize, and pulled the book out. Glancing to see that his office door was shut, he opened the book and began to read.

The hours flitted by, until the light outside his window began to fade. His work day was done. He considered giving up and going home to his beloved when he turned a page and found what he needed.

He turned the pages quickly, his lips moving as he read as fast as he could. A warm bloom grew in his chest as certainty filled him. He turned to the last page of the section, and could not help but laugh as he cursed himself for a simpleton. How could he have not known? How could he have not remembered? He had been in this town all those years ago and should not have needed the book.

He laughed until he had tears in his eyes. As he wiped them away, he looked down at the open book.

On the page was a photograph of a group of hard-looking men standing beside the mouth of the old silver mine. Eleven men had died in the fighting, and the mine claimed thirteen more lives a week later during a cave-in. He should have remembered the smell of death around that place; the anger that infused into the rock. After all, he had been there and had killed three men.

He stared at the picture for several long moments and let out a sigh, again cursing himself for his forgetfulness. In the picture before him, in the third row, he saw his face staring back at him.

CHAPTER 15

He waited until he didn't hear any movement outside his office door, sure he was alone. He turned off his desk lamp, left his office and stepped through the back door of his building. Unconcerned about the people he worked with who answered to him, he had spent so long fooling these stupid humans that he hardly had to think about it anymore. But he had something in mind, something that had occurred to him while he looked through the old man's book, searching for a place of power. It reminded him that there were other places of power in this town that could be put to other uses—a very specific use in mind.

He got into his car and drove through the quiet streets. He smiled as he passed houses, warm light spilling from the windows, shadows of lives moving within. He smiled because soon those lives would be irrevocably changed, and they didn't even know what was in store. When his child came, he would change this town, perhaps even the world, to suit him.

He came to a stop in front of a blue, temporary metal fence that surrounded a burned-out husk of a house. He got out of his car and looked around. The houses on either side and across the street, though they hadn't been set on fire, didn't look much better. Resolution's south end was filled with dilapidated houses, occupied by people who looked as ramshackle as their homes. It occurred to him that lighting a few of these shit holes ablaze would probably be an improvement.

Checking around to make sure he wasn't observed, he leapt over the fence. When he landed on the muddy ground, he allowed a shudder of pleasure to course through his body. His old strength had returned, and he revelled in it.

He made his way around several bigger pieces of debris sticking up from the crumbling foundation before leaping off a burnt timber to the basement floor of the old hulk. The dirt floor was nothing more than a sodden patch of mud and ash, but he felt the power of the place pulsing beneath the soles of his shoes. He had to resist the urge to kick them off and bury his feet in the muck. Only the possibility of explaining to his beloved why he was so dirty stopped him.

She would come to know his true nature, but not just yet.

He lifted his arms, spread them out, and tilted his head back, breathing deep. The scent of the Guardian's magic, from his first great confrontation with the infantile demon those years ago, still lingered. Below that, he could taste the violence. The hurt and the misery of all the bad days, of all the death, had permeated the earth here, close at hand when he reached out for it. It made this place strong. Exactly, what he needed.

He gathered the old power to him, summoned it like a well-trained dog, letting it build up in his centre where it mingled with his will. Then he crouched down and smashed his fist into the ground.

The ground shook, a little at first, as though a heavy freight train were passing. Gradually, the quaking grew until the floor of the old basement roiled. He poured out the power he'd gathered until it was almost gone, but stopped a little short, kept a taste. Just in case he needed it.

In the corners, where the shadows were deepest and the light never touched, came a faint glow. As the illumination touched his face, he smiled. He had put out a call that would be heard in both this world and the next. Soon, Resolution would be overrun with his kind. He had effectively removed the Guardian from the town, but this would ensure that he and his stupid friends would be so busy before they departed they'd not even think to look for him. If he was lucky, the Guardian might even die.

He bounded easily out of the basement and started towards his car. As he crossed the fence, his cell phone rang. He dug it out of his pocket and saw a picture of his beloved, holding up a wine glass and tipping a wink. He smiled at the sight and swiped his thumb across the screen.

"I was just thinking about you," he said.

There was no reply on the other end but laboured breathing.

Worry slapped the smile from his face and an icy hand clamped around his heart. "Baby? Are you okay?"

"I think..." Her voice sounded like it came from between gritted teeth. There was more harsh breathing before it sounded like the phone was dropped.

"My love?" Panic made his voice pitch up. "Are you there?"

"I think something's wrong," she said finally, her voice nearly a scream. "It hurts. There's a lot of blood." There was more harsh breathing. "Something's wrong."

Oh no! He rubbed his hand through his hair and staring up at the black sky. The child was coming too soon.

"I need you," she said, her words distorted by pain.

"I know, baby." He stepped past his car, across the narrow street, and made for the tight space between two houses. As he walked, he began letting his true form break through the shell he'd been living in. All his plans had changed in the space of a moment. He did not think he'd need his human form again for a long time.

"I know. I'm coming."

He tossed the phone into the wet grass and began to run.

"Please, Quinn, tell me you're joking." Carrie stood in front of him, one hand on a slender hip, the other palming her forehead.

He shook his head and looked at the worn floor boards of their kitchen. He crossed his arms and leaned against the counter. "No, I'm not joking. Steve Faulk says I'm getting transferred as soon as he can manage it."

"Is that usual?" Gemma asked from her seat beside Bobby at the kitchen table. "For someone to be transferred for this kind of offence?"

"No," Quinn said. "No, it is not."

"Then it can only be as we feared," Gemma said. "Your commander—"

"Staff sergeant," Quinn said.

"Whatever," Gemma said, her brow drawing together as she glared at him. "Your staff sergeant is intentionally working against us. Your departure is a death sentence for this town, and he must know it."

"We can't move, Quinn," Carrie said. "Besides the fact that you need to be here so no one gets eaten, this is our home. This is where Shawn grew up and all my family, *our* family is."

"I wasn't given a choice, Carrie," Quinn said, still looking at the floor. "I don't want to leave here either."

The front door abruptly opened and Raife stomped into the front hall, still in his uniform, wiping his boots on the door mat. A plastic grocery bag dangled in one of his hands, the surface beaded with rain, and he hung it on a hook beside the door. He looked up, his gaze moving between Carrie and Quinn.

"You divorced yet?" the big man asked Quinn.

"We're not married, Raife," Carrie said, her hand finally coming off her forehead to bunch into a fist.

Raife looked back at Quinn. "You single yet?"

Carrie made a furious sound, and then stalked towards the front door. She grabbed a black, bomber style jacket off a row of hooks by the wall and her car keys from a bowl that sat on the end table beside the couch.

"Where are you off to in such a hurry?" Raife asked.

"I have to pick Shawn up from hockey practice," Carrie said.

"Oh, good," Raife said. "It'll give us time to pack Quinn's shit."

She wound up and punched Raife in the arm. The big man squawked, but Carrie stood on her toes to give him a brief peck on the cheek. She reached for the door and paused to look back at Quinn. "I'll be back soon. I love you. Please, please, talk to the Inspector and try to figure this out. Okay?"

Quinn nodded. "I will."

When she was gone, Quinn sat down at the table across from Gemma and Bobby. Raife joined them, the chair he'd selected creaking alarmingly.

"Do you think the Inspector can do anything?" Quinn asked. Once he left the office, he and Dave had retreated to a small diner to discuss exactly how they were going to explain to their respective spouses that they would have to pack their worldly goods and move. Dave had outlined an elaborate plan involving a mime, cutting off one of his fingers and moving to Tibet. Quinn just sat on his side of the booth and wished he were someone else.

"I'm not sure, son," Raife said. "Immediate transfer is one of the things that can be imposed on someone found guilty of a Code of Conduct violation, but I'm not sure if Steve Faulk can make it happen. One thing I am sure of is that if this goes to division headquarters, the Inspector won't be able to protect you."

Setting his elbows on the table, Quinn clasped his head in his hands and pressed hard on his temples. "I feel like the world is caving in on me," he said to no one in particular. "What do I do? How do I fight this ebony demon, get Autumn out of the black and keep my crazy staff sergeant from sending me to Tuktoyaktuk?" He looked at the door that Carrie had recently stepped through and thought of her face. "How do I keep my family together?"

Gemma reached across the table and hooked her hand in the crook of his elbow. "You are not alone in this, Quinn."

"No, you are not," Raife rumbled.

"Whenever I was pissed off at something as a younger

man," Bobby said, his voice almost as deep as Raife's. "My father always told me to figure out what I could control and put a grip on it. Once you have a handle on one part of a problem, the other pieces would fit into place."

Quinn thought about Abby and her fascination with jigsaw puzzles. The image of the girl's smiling face made him smile in turn.

"Okay," Quinn said. "What can we control, right now?"

Bobby looked back and forth between Quinn and Raife. "Can you do anything about your staff sergeant?"

Raife drummed his hairy-knuckled fingers on the table. "Besides beating the shit out of him?No."

"Do we have any way of finding this ebony demon?" Bobby asked.

Quinn shrugged. "Autumn had a way to track things if she had some of its blood." He looked at Gemma. "Can you do that?"

She nodded. "I could, if I had any of the creature's blood."

"Right," Quinn said. "Then, no, we don't have any way to find it."

"Until it kills someone else." Raife ran his thumb and forefinger over his mustache.

Bobby nodded in agreement. "Can we keep searching for this nexus, so we can try and bring Autumn home?"

"Yeah," Quinn said. "That we can do. But where do we look? The only lead I had has been torn into little pieces."

"Oh, Jesus!" Raife slapped his hand against his bald pate with a loud smack. "I got so busy thinking about how much I want to strangle Steve Faulk that I nearly forgot."

"Forgot what?" Gemma's dark eyebrows climbed towards her grey hair.

Raife got up from the table and stomped back to the door, plucking the plastic bag he had brought from the hook he'd hung it on. He came back to the table, reaching into the bag, to produce a broad coffee-table style book, and handed it to Quinn.

The cover was blank and off white, with a simple title in

block letters: *Resolution Cove.*

"It's the old man's book," Quinn said, thumbing open the soft cover. "Where did you get this?"

"The wife of the dead guy gave it to me," Raife said. "I was going to give it to you this morning, but we were somewhat preoccupied with Steve Faulk losing his mind."

"I cannot help but wonder if what that book contains was worth that man's death," Gemma said.

Quinn looked up at her while she stared at the book, her mouth pressed into a thin line. He swallowed and looked down; he really was holding a man's life in his hands—or the remains of it anyway. Taking a deep breath, he flipped over the first page, to the chapter index. The headings were generic, but Raife reached over his hand and tapped the last heading with a thick finger.

"I think we're going to want to look extra hard at this one," he said.

Quinn let his gaze move to Raife's fingertip. "The Dark Days," he read aloud. He looked up at Gemma. "What do you think?"

"If this man was as obsessive as we believe, I don't think that any section of that book should be discounted." She leaned back in her chair and pressing the ball of her thumb into her chin. "The earth holds its own power, but it tends to gather in places that have seen powerful human emotion."

"Like the house in the South End," Quinn said.

She nodded. "Yes, like that place." She held out her hand. "Let me look at the book, Quinn. I know you know more about this town than I do, but I think I will know what we need when I see it."

Quinn thought about arguing for a moment but let out a breath through puffed cheeks and pushed the book towards her. He didn't really want to spend the rest of the night reading. He never remembered feeling so tired. His eyes felt like there was sand in them.

"What do you want us to do while you're reading?" Raife asked in his rumbling baritone.

She opened the book to the first page, the unbent spine cracking softly. "I think you should eat, rest and gather your strength. Before this night is over, I think you will need it."

He cleared the six foot cedar fence surrounding his back yard as easily as a man might step over the curb of a parking lot, ran past the rows of his prize rose bushes carefully covered in burlap sacks, and up the back steps of his house. He burst through the unlocked back door and into the hallway, skidding to a stop on the hardwood floor.

He felt a hot bloom in his chest. The house smelled of blood. And fear. Standing still, he listened carefully and heard a weak moan from the kitchen.

He lunged down the hall and around the corner. He found his wife, lying on her side in a pool of her own blood, her hands cradling the round swell of her belly. He could see movement beneath her skin. She looked like a bubble about to burst.

Her glassy eyes swivelled up to him slowly, and then widened. She let out a weak gasp, then reached out a hand like she was trying to crawl away. He paused, and then looked down at his hands. He was still wearing his clothing, but his skin was almost pitch black, the muscles in his forearms had burst the buttons on the cuffs of his shirt, his clawed hands much longer than a human's. He clenched his fists and summoned his will, turning himself back into the form she knew, and knelt beside her.

Her eyes rolled around in her head like a frightened cow and she made a mewling sound in her throat. "My God," she said, gasping for breath. "What...what was that?" Her eyes fixed on his face. "What...is it you?"

He placed his hand on her forehead, her bloodless skin cold beneath his palm. He gritted his teeth. She was dying. If he didn't do something, right now, their child would kill her before he had time to claim the girl-child and take her to the place of power and have her open a door.

He took a breath and placed his hands on her distended, roiling belly. He knew that he had a deep power in him, but he didn't know what to do with it. But, if he didn't figure it out, he would lose everything.

He summoned his will, pulled the power out of the very air, reached through the floorboards of his house and into the earth below. When he had gathered all he could, he began feeding it into his wife. He felt a pain, a burning in his chest, but he shoved it aside and kept working. He begged the child inside her to still, commanded her heart to slow, ordered the blood around them to seep back into her body and fill her veins. The burning in his chest grew, rapidly, into a rolling storm of agony, and still he pushed.

"I will not lose you," he whispered. "Either of you."

He forged ahead, letting the pain surge through him, until his will was spent and he felt a shell of himself. Until he felt human.

He looked down. The blood from the floor was gone. The pasty pallor of his wife's face was replaced with a flushed glow. Her belly, full and wide, was still. He sagged forward and kissed her stomach.

Her eyes fluttered open and she raised a wavering hand to place it on the back of his head and grip his sweat-drenched hair. "I had a dream," her voice a drunken murmur. "There was blood. And a monster."

He knelt beside her, stroking her hair, allowing his strength to trickle back to him. Once he knew he wouldn't drop her, he scooped her off the floor and carried her to the living room. "There is no monster, my love," he said, as he manoeuvred her carefully down the hallway, avoiding the other furniture in the living room to lay her on the couch. "There is only you and me and our son."

It *was* a son. His wife was correct. He felt it in his bones. An heir, the very first of his line to build his family.

As he laid her down, he pulled a few errant strands of hair away from her face. He summoned a little of his will and wiped across her brow with his thumb. She fell into a deep sleep, her hand resting on the mound of her belly, a small smile playing at the corners of her mouth.

Outside, he heard movement. He breathed deep and smelled his kind, his kindred. Some had arrived, but more were coming—more than enough for the work to come. He kissed his wife's forehead and her belly once more, then stepped towards the back door and allowed himself to shift back into his true shape.

Outside, the shadows were alive with the movement of those he had summoned. He held his arms out in welcome, his ebony skin shining in the moonlight, and he could smell their anticipation.

"The girl first," he said, and felt no objection. "The girl first, then the Guardian, and then we welcome my child."

He bounded off the steps, in the direction of the girl who opened the doors. As he passed through the rows of his roses, he snatched the burlap sack off one and bunched it in a clawed hand.

Donald Green looked down at the top of Abby McRae's head, as she sat at the kitchen table. She zipped through a series of math problems in a colourful workbook as though they were nothing. He could not help but lean down and plant a kiss on her crown.

When his son, Patrick, had been murdered, he felt as though someone had turned off whatever light had existed in the centre of him. But, when he and Geraldine had taken in Abby, whose heart was even more broken than their own, he felt like a little of h is light began to shine again. In the months she had lived with them, they had all healed one another. He loved her fiercely and would do anything to protect her, but with what was happening in his town, he didn't know if he could do it alone.

As he kissed her, Abby let out a small giggle. "Thanks, Poppa," she said, continuing to flit through her math problems. She had taken to calling him that, and he had not for a moment thought to dissuade her.

Geraldine was out at a Rotary meeting, so he was responsible for fixing dinner for him and Abby. He plucked a steaming pot off the stove and dumped a glob of spaghetti into a colander in the sink.

"Are you hungry, Abby?" he asked, squinting through the cloud of steam. "Dinner will be ready in a couple minutes." When she didn't reply, he set the empty pot down on the stove and stepped up behind her again. Not until he stood right behind her did he notice her trembling.

"Abby?" He moved beside her and knelt down so they were eye to eye. The child stared wide-eyed at her page. As he watched, her pencil snapped in her grip. He cupped her face in both his hands. "Abby!"

She blinked and looked down at the pieces of pencil in her fist. She dropped them and shook her hand, then looked at him, her pale blue eyes locking on his own. "Poppa," she said, her voice even. "You need to call Quinn."

He felt his brows draw together. "Quinn? What for, sweetheart?"

"Something is coming, Poppa. Something black."

CHAPTER 16

Before he picked up his phone, Donald Green went into the bedroom he shared with Geraldine. He walked around the wide sleigh bed, towards the closet, but stopped to take a deep breath. The room always smelled of Geraldine's Chanel perfume, and it never failed, even after all these years, to make his heart skip. He smiled, then moved to his purpose and walked briskly to the large walk-in closet. At the back of the room was an innocuous wooden cabinet, half buried behind his suits. Behind the door was the stippled green surface of a very strong gun safe.

He twirled the combination lock back and forth, then torqued down on the handle to pull the safe open. Inside, sat a neat row of long-guns, his duty pistol—for the occasions he had to drag his rickety ass from his bed to go to one of the scenes where Quinn's team had invariably lit something on fire—and his old .38 police special. He picked up the old revolver from the carpeted shelf and hefted it in his palm.

It was the first gun he'd been issued when he'd arrived at Depot, in Regina, more than thirty-five years ago. He'd carried it in the early years of his service, when posted in tiny towns, north of nowhere, and it had never failed him. He glanced at the modern, semi-automatic pistol he was required to carry now. It certainly held more bullets, but he was a better shot

158

with the .38 and liked the way it felt in his hand. He loaded it with one of his old speed-loaders, shoved it into the old clip-on holster he'd kept for it, and clipped it to his belt. He shoved two more speed loaders into his pants pockets, and then reached back into gun cabinet.

About three years prior, he and Geraldine had been in Nanaimo, having a weekend away and doing some Christmas shopping. He had gone into the Cabela's store to kill a few minutes while his wife added to her ever-growing collection of shoes, and had spied something behind the gun-counter. A short-barrelled, twelve-gauge, Browning coach gun. It looked like something from the Wild West, with blued barrels and a hickory stock, but used modern, high-powered shells. He had no practical use for the damned thing, but he liked the way the wooden stock fit his shoulder and he'd wanted it with the passionate enthusiasm of a child. It really wasn't that expensive, and he had tossed his credit card to the pimple-faced kid behind the till without a second thought. When he met Geraldine back in the parking lot, she shook her head, let out a chuckle and kissed his cheek.

He pulled the coach gun from its spot at the back of the gun cabinet, pressed the lever on the back of the stock to open the breech, and dropped in two double-ought buck shells from the drawer at the top of the cabinet. The only thing he'd ever shot with it was old Halloween pumpkins and had done one hell of a number on them. Hopefully, it would have a similar effect on anything that came for Abby.

He hustled back down the hallway and into the kitchen. Abby sat wide-eyed at the kitchen table, her head darting at even the smallest sound. He snatched his phone off the granite counter and scrolled through until he found Quinn's number.

"Sir, are you all right?" Quinn asked when he answered the phone. Donald could hear the concern in Quinn's voice, and it made his heart ache with affection for the young man.

"Yes, Quinn, I'm fine. But you need to come over here."

"Did something happen?" Quinn asked.

"Not yet," Donald said. "But Abby says something's

coming." He paused, to look over at the child. "And I believe her."

"Okay," Quinn said. "I'm coming. You armed?"

"To the teeth," Donald said.

"Don't go anywhere and don't open the door for anyone."

"Or anything," Donald said.

"Yeah, that too," Quinn said. "I'll be there in a few minutes."

After the call, Donald set the phone on the counter. He thought he should keep it with him, but all his pockets were full of .38 rounds and shotgun shells.

Another thought occurred to him and he picked up the phone again. "Abby, love, put this in your pocket. If anything happens to me, I want you to call Quinn."

She looked down at the phone, then back up at him, and took it wordlessly, a fat tear leaking from the corner of one eye.

"No, no, my love," he said, and pulled her to him, kissing the top of her head and breathing in her smell. "Don't you worry about your old Poppa. I've still got some fight in me, and I'm willing to share it with these bloody things."

She looked up at him, wiped away her tear with the palm of her hand and gave a firm nod.

"That's my girl." He took her hand and looked around the house, thinking of the best place to make a stand if they had to. After a moment of chewing the inside of his cheek, he decided on the living room. He grabbed Abby's hand and pulled her in that direction.

The back wall of the living room was red brick and there were three escape routes: the hallway to the garage, the big patio door and the hallway to the kitchen. If he had to face something here, he had a good place to put his back and plenty of ways for Abby to run.

"Abby," he said. She stared up at him. "Do you remember when your teacher sent home that little workbook and we had to plan what we'd do if there was ever a fire?"

She nodded. They'd spent the afternoon carefully drawing a map of the house, planning the routes to take. Then they'd crawled around on their hands and knees, pretending they were avoiding smoke.

"If anything gets here before Quinn, I want you to do what we practiced and get out of the house. Can you do that?"

She shook her head and grabbed one of his hands, the one that wasn't holding the shotgun, in both of hers. Terrified, her body shook and it made his heart crack.

"I don't wanna go anywhere without you, Poppa," her voice hitching as she struggled to hold back tears.

"Don't you worry, my love. I'm not going to lose you."

He bent to kiss her head again, and then threw his arm across her protectively as the big patio door exploded inward in a shower of glass.

He stood upright, dragging Abby behind him, as a tall figure, heavy muscles rippling beneath its ebony skin, stepped into the living room.

"What is it?" Raife asked, already standing from the table as Quinn hit the 'end' button on his phone.

"Abby says something is coming for them." Quinn stood as well, tucking his phone into the front pocket of his jeans.

"Would she know that?" Bobby asked, looking between Quinn and Gemma.

Gemma shrugged and dog-eared a page in the book to mark her place. "The girl is largely untrained. Who knows what abilities she might have? If she says something is coming, then we must go."

"Goddamned rights." Raife stomped towards the door.

Quinn hustled into the bedroom. He walked around the bed to the gun-safe he'd bolted to the wall and floor located in the corner furthest from the window. A massive thing so heavy he'd had to put extra support under the floor, beneath the spot where they kept the safe. It had taken himself, Dave, Raife, Carrie's Uncle Sam, and two of Quinn's neighbours to wrestle the thing into the house and they had to take the door jamb off the bedroom just to get it inside.

He punched the combination into the lock and pulled the heavy door open. He grabbed his own duty pistol and clipped the plainclothes holster and spare magazine holder to his belt, before picking up his Sigsaur .45, complete with a leather shoulder rig and spare magazines, and pulled it on. He picked up the seven shot Remington shotgun and two boxes of shells.

He turned at the clomp of heavy boots behind him and found Raife filling up the doorway.

"You look like you're robbing the place," the big man said.

Quinn jerked his chin towards the gun cabinet. "There's one more thing."

Raife stepped past him and reached into the safe to withdraw an old wooden stock, SKS rifle. "Jesus, Quinn, where did you get this thing?"

"They were selling them at the gun store for a hundred and fifty bucks, so I bought one. There's magazines for it in the bottom of the safe."

Grunting, Raife crouched down and came up with three long, curved magazines gripped in his hairy fist. "What are these, Quinn? Thirty rounds?"

"No," Quinn said. "Forty."

Raife looked at him; one eyebrow climbing so high it looked like it was trying to escape toward the barren plain of his bald head. "You know these are illegal as hell, right?"

"Ask me if I give a fuck right now, Raife."

The big man shrugged. "Fair enough."

Hustling down the hallway, trying to balance his various armaments, Quinn found Gemma and Bobby dressed and ready. Gemma rapidly scanned the history book, while Bobby cradled his axe.

Quinn held the shotgun out towards him. The heavy man glanced down at it, but made no move to take it.

"Do you not want a gun?" Quinn asked.

Bobby shrugged. "Won't do me much good, Quinn. Unless you want me to hit something with it."

"Are you saying," the incredulity in Raife's voice so thick it almost dripped on the floor, "that you don't know how to use a shotgun?"

Again, Bobby shrugged. "I understand the basic concept of pointing it at something and pulling the trigger, but I would not say I'm proficient." He held the axe up. "I'm much better with this."

"Never mind that," Gemma said, her voice cracking like a whip and instantly silencing all three men. "We have to go."

Grunting in agreement, Raife shouldered the rifle. "We'll take your truck, Quinn. They're still making me drive that fucking clown car."

As he got close to the old policeman's house, he could smell the girl's power. He knew its flavour, had tasted it before, but it was always from a distance, just residuals of it, from a building she had walked through or an old use of her magic. Now, in his true form, he could taste it on his tongue, filling his head. It was intoxicating.

He looked into the dark around him, at the others he had gathered. He had left the greatest among them outside of his house, commanding it to guard his wife and unborn son, but the others had followed in his wake like a flock of vultures following a lion. Even more had come out of the dark to join him, as he raced through the dark streets of Resolution towards the old man's house. They, too, could taste the girl's magic, as well as feel his intent, and their excitement heightened his urgency.

He had thought of a subtle approach, take the girl out from under the old man's nose and see the task done before anyone even knew the child was gone. But as he circled the house, he saw that the old man was ready for him.

The time for subtlety, trickery, disguise was all gone. Now was the time for blood and fury.

With a sweep of his arm he shattered the patio door and stepped through, letting shards of glass fall from his shoulders to tinkle on the floor. The old man dragged the child behind him and shouldered a short, double-barrelled shotgun.

He took a step forward, but something made him pause. Something else scented the air of the room, radiating off the old man in waves; Love.

There was no fear in the old man, with his pot belly sticking over his belt, and his thin comb-over coming free of the pomade he'd used to slick it down. Only love and healthy dose of anger filled the air. The old man would die to protect the child and was not afraid to do it.

He held up one hand, the one holding the burlap sack, stopping the advance of the creatures behind him. The other he held out in a placating gesture to the old man.

"Give me the child," His voice strange in his own ears, so long unheard, like a heavy rock bouncing off the walls of a deep well. "I will not harm her."

The old man made no reply, except to thumb back the hammers on the shotgun.

"Please." The word grated out of him. "My wife is with child, and I need the girl to help me birth my son. If I don't move quickly, both my wife and son will surely die." He regretted the words as soon as they left his flat lips. He'd not meant to give away anything of himself, but the power of the old man's love had done something to him. He shook his head, angry.

"Fine, if you will not give me the child—" His words were cut off by the roar of the short-barrelled shotgun. Both barrels flared and lead shot punched into the skin of his face and chest. The force knocked him off his feet and he sprawled on his back. He blinked amid a rush of black blood and gunsmoke.

"Run, Abby!" the old man shouted.

He surged to his feet, seeing the old man snapping the shotgun closed with two new rounds in the barrels. The child skittered on her hands and knees from behind the old man, to a doorway he assumed led to the garage. He took a step towards the doorway, but the old man stepped in front of him and the shotgun roared again.

He was ready this time, and turned away, his arm up to

shield his face. When he turned back, he saw a white light of amazing brilliance, arching from the doorway the child had escaped into.

He realised what it meant and roared. "No!"

The old man dropped the shotgun and yanked an old revolver from a holster on his hip. The revolver barked in the old man's hand, the bullets punched into his face with amazing accuracy. He lunged to the side to escape the angry lead hornets.

The old man thumbed a release on the side of the revolver, dumped the spent shells out, and loaded six more in with a speed-loader. His action was quick and smooth, and his paunchy face had a grim set as he planted himself in front of the doorway. The white light shone brighter now, impossible to look at, and it wrapped the old man in a fearful aura as he began firing again.

Rage filled him, and he charged into the old man, smashing him aside. He lunged into the room beyond the doorway, just as the light died. There was nothing there, save for a square of frost on the linoleum of the hallway.

He stepped back into the living room and roared. The remaining pane of glass in the patio door shattered, and the black shapes that had begun crawling into the house all shrank back. He glanced at the old man who lay unmoving, then looked down at the burlap sack still gripped in his fist. He hissed, tossing the sack to the glass-littered floor, and pointed outside.

"Go," he shouted. "Find the child. Seek out her magic. We cannot lose her."

The black shapes scattered, tearing through the house and out into the night.

Abby McRae was very worried about her Poppa, but didn't think going back home was a good idea. The things that came for her would leave now she was gone and they would leave Poppa alone. Or so she hoped.

She looked around, a little confused. She had only ever gone through one of her doors once—the night her father died. It made her brain spin. When she opened the door, she thought about the park on the way to her school and that was where she ended up, but it took her a few minutes to realise it.

She appeared on the other side of the playground equipment. Wet from falling on the grass, she started to shiver to the cold air. She wished she was still at home, working on a puzzle with Poppa, but her Uncle Raife often said you could wish in one hand and poop in the other and see which one filled up first.

As she looked about, wondering what she should do, she remembered what her Poppa had given her right before the big creature broke the window. She reached into her pocket and pulled out the cell phone and pushed the centre button get it going. The phone gave one bright white flash, flickered a few times, and then went black. She pushed the button again, tried holding it down, but nothing else happened. She guessed cell phones didn't like going through black doors any more than people did.

She had to either find Quinn or go where he would find her. Someplace only Quinn would come look for her. She thought for a minute, as she rubbed her arms with her hands. She wished she wore her warm coat instead of her house sweater, and then thought again of what Uncle Raife said.

After a minute, she knew where she needed to go. She thought very hard about it, and then put her hand on the ground to open another door.

Behind her, in the direction of her house, she heard a sound that sent shivers that had nothing to do with the cold. It sounded like the roar of one of the crocodiles, on the nature shows, if the crocodile were as big as a bus and very angry.

Gritting her teeth, she reached beneath her shirt to grip the medallion her father had given her, and thought about the door.

As Quinn drove, the engine of his black Chevy Tahoe roaring, Gemma kept poring through the furniture maker's history book. Raife sat in the passenger seat, glowering down at his phone, poking the screen with thick fingers.

"Jesus, Quinn," the big man said as Quinn took a turn so hard the tires of the truck gave a little chirp. "If you don't slow down, I'll never be able to dial Dave's number, and I'm going to spew everything I've eaten for the last week into your lap." He tapped the screen several times and held the phone to his ear.

Quinn eased off the gas pedal, just a little, and glanced in the rear-view mirror. "You find anything, Gemma?"

The grey-haired woman shook her head. "There are so many things to find, Quinn. There are so many places that we could look. The laying of the corner stone of City Hall holds power because of the triumph it represented, but the silver mine saw a lot of violence before the final veins went dry. The harbour saw thousands of souls pass through it and would hold a hint of every life that touched it." She looked up and met his eyes in the mirror. "We could search for a week and I still don't know that we'd be sure."

Raife held up his phone before his face, his moustache illuminated in the glow of the screen. "I talked to Dave and he's on his way, with his wife screaming at him in the background. He said he'll call Sandy and Gerritt as well." He turned in his seat, as much as his bulk would allow, to look back at Gemma. "All the experiences we've had here tell me that this neuron—"

"Nexus," she corrected him.

"Whatever, will be in the place where the most people have been shittiest to each other."

She pursed her lips. "Maybe."

They came around one last corner, onto the Inspector's street, and Quinn knew instantly that something was wrong. The Inspector's house was filled with warm yellow light, but Quinn saw that it spilled in a long rectangle where the front door used to be.

He braked hard, yanking the truck over to the curb, and

everyone spilled out. Quinn grabbed his shotgun, while Raife slammed a magazine into the SKS and yanked back on the charging lever.

Taking small, quick steps, his legs bent in half-crouch as he had been trained, Quinn sighted down the barrel of the shotgun, focused on the front door. He didn't have to look back to know that Raife was right behind him.

The front door of the house had been smashed outward and lay splintered and broken on the stone steps leading up to the front door. Quinn stacked to the left of the door, Raife falling in behind him, and listened to the interior of the house. Nothing. Donnel's dagger, always secreted at the small of his back, and the brass knuckles in the back pocket of his jeans, were cold.

He glanced back down the walkway towards the truck. Gemma stood by the front bumper, the book still in her hands, while Bobby stood in front of her, his axe held before him.

"Stay here," Quinn said. Bobby nodded. Quinn leaned towards the door and shouted into the house. "Inspector, are you here?"

Nothing.

"Sir, it's Quinn."

More nothing.

"Fuck," he said to no one in particular. "Raife, you ready?" The big man reached up and squeezed his shoulder. Quinn moved into the doorway.

He peeled left, knowing that Raife would go the other way. He saw nothing in the foyer, and they stacked up again to move down the short hallway. They swept the formal sitting room and were about to clear the kitchen, when Quinn felt a breeze on the back of his neck. It blew from the direction of the living room.

"Raife," he said, and turned away from the kitchen. The big man grunted in assent and followed. Quinn didn't know if Raife felt the same thing he did, but there were no questions asked.

"Ah, fuck," Raife said as they took the three steps down

into the living room area.

There was shattered glass littering the room, and the furniture was in splinters. Large splotches of black blood spotted the floor and walls. Quinn saw a short, double barrelled shotgun lying on the floor. As he reached the centre of the room, he heard a muffled moan from underneath an overturned loveseat.

Raife reached down and grabbed the corner of the loveseat, while Quinn covered it with his shotgun. On Quinn's nod, Raife heaved the furniture aside. Quinn shifted forward, the barrel of his shotgun pointed at a heap on the floor. It took him a moment to recognise Inspector Green.

Using the sling on the shotgun, Quinn shifted it so it hung down his back and knelt beside the prone figure. Raife cursed, then tucked the rifle back onto his shoulder, and stepped down the hallway towards the garage. As Quinn touched the Inspector's shoulder, he moaned weakly, but his eyes fluttered open and he turned his head slightly to look up at Quinn.

"Sir, what happened?" Quinn asked.

"Something..." the Inspector said, and then winced, his breath hitching and a gurgling sound coming from his throat. After a long moment he continued. "Something big, with pitch black skin, came for her."

Quinn did not care at all for the sound of the older man's breath, or the ghostly shade of his skin. Standing up, he turned towards the hallway. "Gemma!" he shouted at the top of his voice, so loud his throat hurt. He knelt back down, his face close to the Inspector's ear. "Did Abby get away?"

Raife stepped back into the living room. "The rest of the house is clear, but there is a big patch of frost on the floor in the laundry room."

Quinn nodded. "Sir, do you know where went?"

"No," the prone man said. "I just told her to run."

"Don't worry. We'll find her." As he said the words, Quinn wasn't sure if they were true.

Quinn heard a crunch of glass and looked up to see Gemma stepping quickly towards them, Bobby hurrying behind her. "Where is he hurt?" she asked as she knelt down beside Quinn.

"Everywhere, I think," Quinn said. "Sir, where do you hurt most?"

The older man's eyes focused on his. "I'm worried about what doesn't hurt." He must have read the question on Quinn's face because he added, "I can't feel my legs."

Gemma put her hand on his forehead, and then yanked it back with a gasp, as though she had touched a hot skillet.

"What is it?" Quinn asked, his voice pitching up in a manner he didn't at all care for.

"He is..." Gemma swallowed heavily. "He is hurt very badly."

"Can you help him?" Raife asked from behind them.

"Yes," Gemma said. "I just don't know how much."

Quinn heard hurried footsteps in the hall, and jumped up, tucking his shotgun into his shoulder to confront whatever was coming for them. Bobby moved beside him, his axe up over his shoulder.

Dave came around the corner so fast, his running shoes came out from underneath him and he sprawled on his ass, scrabbling to his feet as quickly as he had gone down. Sandy and Gerritt were close behind, the former with her pistol in hand, and the latter with a rifle similar to the detachment issue C8 carbines. The recruit also wore an Elmer Fudd style hunting cap.

"Holy fuck!" Dave said as he straightened up and looked around the room. When he saw Inspector Green on the floor his eyebrows shot up even further. "Oh, sweet merciful baby Jesus, is he...?"

Quinn shook his head. "No, he's still alive. But barely."

"What do you need us to do?" Sandy asked, resting her hand on Quinn's arm.

"I need you all to be still," Gemma said from her place beside the Inspector. "I need to focus."

Quinn jerked his chin towards the corner of the room. They all retreated there and were joined by Raife, while Bobby stood guard over Gemma.

"Where the hell did you get that thing?" Raife asked Gerritt, poking the stock of the expensive-looking rifle he held.

The recruit shrugged. "I thought I should buy a gun."

They all looked at him for several moments, but the young man offered nothing further.

"Any particular reason?" Raife asked.

Gerritt shrugged again, and Sandy let out a long sigh.

"And where did you get that fucking hat?" Dave asked.

Gerritt's gaze swung to Dave. "It came with the gun."

"Hard to argue with that," Dave said, then turned to Quinn. "What the fuck happened here, man?"

As quickly as he could, Quinn related everything that had happened since he and Dave had parted ways that afternoon, doing his best to fill in the gaps for Sandy and Gerritt.

"So, they're really going to transfer you?" Sandy asked.

"That's what Steve Faulk says," Dave replied. "I thought about shooting him in his skinny ass, but Quinn keeps telling me 'no'."

"We can worry about that later," Raife said. "What's our next step."

They all looked to Quinn, and he swallowed heavily. The fact they were all turning to him for guidance made his stomach flip. He looked around, hoping someone would tell him what to do.

He was saved from making any explanation when a near blinding glow sprung up behind him. He turned to see Gemma, her head bowed in concentration, her hands pressed onto the Inspector's ribs, and from beneath them issued a pure white light.

Gemma closed her eyes and placed her hands on the body of the man before her. It felt like she touched something scalding and corrosive. His pain was a thing so urgent it almost felt like an entity unto itself, so sharp she felt it bite into the palms of her hands. But floating over that pain, magnifying it, was the taint of the creature who had broken him. The anger, the ancient fury of the creature, rubbed off on her skin in an oily slick.

She summoned her magic, used it to protect her hands—and her mind—and searched through Donald Green with gently probing fingers made of light. Broken bones, organs moved out a place, blood flowing into places it didn't belong. The worst of it, though, was the pain stopped suddenly, as though it were cut off with a knife, just above Green's belly button. Below that, in the picture of her mind, there was nothing but black.

She took a deep breath. She didn't know if she could cast light back into the man's legs, but she had to try.

She sought out the endings of him. They were ragged, as though they'd been bitten off with a mouth full of sharp teeth. Slowly, she smoothed out those endings, made them longer, and stretched them into the blackness of his injury. She felt she traveled down a long, dark tunnel, with only a meagre light to show the way.

She began to slow, to run out of momentum, the well of her magic to running dry. She sucked in another breath and tried to push away the sound of her own pulse pounding in her ears. She pulled energy, from anywhere she could find it, reaching down into her core, into the deepest parts of herself. She brought everything together and heaved against the darkness. Feeble light flickered, but it shone.

She lifted her head to look at her Bobby, to speak to him, but the words fell mumbling from her lips. His broad, constant figure swam in her vision, and she felt herself tumble into a different, deeper kind of black.

The light beneath Gemma's hands died. Quinn lowered his arm from in front of his eyes. Gemma, slump-shouldered, her breath coming in little jerking gasps, turned to look up at Bobby, a smile on her face. It lasted only a moment, before her eyes rolled up and she collapsed on her side, falling beside the

Inspector as though they were spooning lovers.

Donald Green didn't stir, but his breathing was even and clear of the gurgling it had before. Bobby dropped his axe on the glass-littered carpet and knelt beside Gemma. The thick man scooped the grey-haired woman up as though she were a child and held her to his massive chest.

"Bobby," Quinn said. "Is she all right?"

"I think so," Bobby said as he delicately wiped beads of sweat from her brow. "She has just given a little too much of herself."

Quinn reached down and gripped one of Gemma's limp hands, cold as a railway spike that had lain in the snow. He gripped it hard, trying to will some of his warmth into her frigid skin.

He stood and turned back to the gathering of nervous faces.

"What's our next move, Quinn?" Raife's rumbling voice loud in the still room.

Quinn sucked in a breath through his nose. There were so many things that were wrong. He didn't even know how to start to make them right. He looked at the prone form of the Inspector, at Gemma who was only now beginning to stir, and at his friends—his family—who looked to him to give the say so. He wished, for the thousandth time that day, that he had someone to tell him what to do, but there was no one but him.

"Okay," he said. "Sandy, you call 911 and stay here with the Inspector. Tell the responding members that there was a home invasion, and get him to the hospital. Phone Geraldine and tell her he's okay, but a little busted up." He handed her the shotgun he held. "Six rounds in the tube, one in the pipe."

She took the long gun and nodded, then pulled her phone from her pocket and stepped away to dial three numbers.

"The rest of us need to go and look for Abby."

Dave grunted and reached down to scoop up the Inspector's coach gun, pressed the lever to open the breech, and tilted his head away to avoid the two spent shells that popped out. He held it out to Quinn.

"You think that thing with the black skin got her?"

Quinn took the gun. "How big was that patch of frost you saw on the floor, Raife?"

The big man shrugged. "About the size of car door."

Dropping two new shells, taken from his pocket, into the barrels of the coach gun, Quinn snapped it closed. "Then I don't think they got her. She's out there, somewhere, scared out of her mind."

Dave nodded. "You wanna split up to cover more ground?"

"Yeah," Quinn said. "Raife and I will go in my truck. You take Gerritt."

"Who are we riding with?" asked a quavering voice.

Quinn looked over to see Gemma, her face ashen, leaning heavily on Bobby's arm.

"I don't think you should be going anywhere," Quinn said.

"I won't be left behind, Quinn," Gemma said. "You will need Bobby if it comes to fight, and I'm the only one who has read this stupid book." She patted the messenger bag hanging from her shoulder with a hand that was still too pale.

Quinn opened his mouth to object and closed it. If he wanted to find Abby and get Autumn out of the black, he needed Gemma's help. He gritted his teeth, then nodded. "Okay. We go together."

He looked over at Sandy, who punched the end call button on her phone. "Medics are on their way, along with night shift members. You guys are good to go."

On the floor, Donald Green struggled into a sitting position. His face was still pale, but his eyes were focused, and his gaze sought out Quinn's. "Find my Abby, Quinn. I cannot do without her." Sandy crouched down beside him and gripped his hand.

Quinn nodded, looked around at his friends, and blew out a big breath. "Okay. Let's get this show on the road."

As he turned towards the hallway, he heard Gerritt make a harrumphing sound.

"That's odd," the young Mountie said.

Quinn stopped and turned to look at him. In a collection

of circumstances that was already very strange, something that still drew attention could not be overlooked.

"What's odd, Gerritt?" Quinn asked, when the younger man offered no more.

"This," he prodded something on the floor with the toe of his boot.

Dave bent down and picked up a piece of cloth. After he shook it out, flinging glass and debris in all directions, Quinn saw it was a burlap sack.

"What the fuck is this doing here?" Dave asked.

Quinn stepped closer to him and looked down at the sack. He looked at the Inspector. "Sir, is this yours?"

Donald Green shook his head. "No, Quinn. If you didn't bring it, it came in with that thing."

"It's a little story-book isn't it?" Raife asked. "Bring along a sack to stuff children into. Is this the fucking boogey man?"

"Yes," Gemma said. "It is."

"There is something else." The Inspector winced. Once he had caught his breath, he locked eyes with Quinn again. "The thing, the big black-skinned demon, it said something about a child."

"You mean Abby?" Quinn asked.

Green shook his head. "No. It said something about its own child. That it needed Abby to help him birth his child. And if he didn't do it soon, both his wife and child would die."

Gemma's eyes widened. She pulled her arm from Bobby's grip and took a lurching step towards the Inspector. "It talked of its own child? You're certain?"

The Inspector nodded.

What little colour that had returned to Gemma's face fled, and she sagged backwards into Bobby.

"Jesus, Gemma," Quinn said. "What is it?"

The woman tried to speak, but the words hitched in her throat. She licked her lips and tried again. "If this is true, and the demon has managed to breed, we are all in very serious trouble."

Raife blew out a big breath that ruffled his moustache.

"Tell us something we don't know."

Gemma shook her head, emphatically, causing her grey hair to fly around her face. "No!"

The tone of her voice made the skin at the base of Quinn's neck prickle.

"Demons are weak in our plane of existence because they don't belong here. It is unnatural for them. That's why when they are young, when they first cross over here, they are confined to small spaces they know. It takes them years, decades to walk free, and doubly as long to change their shape. But, if a demon child were to be born here, it would be their natural plane."

The realization of what Gemma said trickled through Quinn's veins like ice water. "You mean they would be stronger than their parents."

She nodded. "Unstoppable."

"So what the hell do we do now?" Raife asked.

Gemma looked at him. "We have to find this child and stop its birth."

Great idea, Quinn thought. But he had no idea how they were going to do it.

"Quinn?"

He turned to see Dave reaching into the burlap sack. "I think you should look at this." Dave withdrew his hand, holding it out to Quinn.

In the centre of Dave's palm was a single, red rose petal.

<h1 style="text-align:center">CHAPTER 17</h1>

"Are you sure about this, Quinn?" Raife asked from the passenger seat, as Quinn guided his Tahoe, roaring down the residential roads around the outskirts of the town.

"I am now," Quinn said. He braked hard for a corner and Raife's shoulder thumped the passenger door. "Think about it. Steve Faulk has been trying to take me out of the game since that big black-skinned demon showed up and tried to kill Gemma and Bobby. He's done everything he can to try and ruin my career and keep me off the road all to get me out of the way. Now, we find that fucking rose petal in the sack at the Inspector's house. It has to be him." He took his eyes off the road, for just an instant, to look at the big sergeant. "It has to be."

Raife tilted his head to speak Gemma and Bobby in the back seat, but seemed to be afraid to take his eyes off the road. "Is that even possible?" the big man asked. "I've been in Resolution for almost ten years. Steve Faulk has been here for longer than that. I've never even gotten a hint that there was something off about him."

Gemma shrugged. "If it is as we suspect, no hint would be given. The ebony demon is old, ancient, and powerful beyond our understanding. It would be a simple trick for it to live as a normal human."

"Evil is patient," Bobby said.

Gemma nodded. "Yes. It is."

"What about this kid, thing, then?" Raife asked. "I'm guessing that doesn't happen too often."

"No," Gemma said, shaking her head. "At least I don't think so."

"You don't know?" Raife asked.

"No, Sergeant, I don't know." Gemma sounded exasperated. "It's not as though anyone has ever been able to study the mating habits of the common demon and write a bloody text book about it. I'm guessing here." She combed her fingers through her hair. "The only thing I can say, that I believe to be true, is that a demon having a child in our world, is bad."

"How bad?" Quinn glanced at her in the rear-view mirror.

"End of the world, bad," she said.

Raife shook his head. "I don't much care for the sound of that." He drummed his fingers on the arm rest. "I'm also not sure how I feel about us going to take on this thing by ourselves."

Quinn wasn't exactly a fan of the idea himself, but he didn't see that he had a choice. He'd sent Gerritt and Dave out to look for Abby and regretted he didn't have more people to send for her. She would be terrified and alone, and needed to be brought home as soon as possible.

"Who else would we call, Raife?" he asked the big sergeant. "Who would be able to do something besides us?"

"I don't know," Raife said, shrugging uncomfortably. "Just somebody, is all."

"I think," Gemma said from the back seat. "That if Quinn isn't able to stop whatever we meet, that no amount of armed men is going to make any difference."

Quinn glanced at her in the rear view mirror and knew she was right. If he couldn't stop the ebony demon, then no one could.

As they got close to Steve Faulk's house—a log home on a

rural property with a view of the water–Quinn slowed and pulled onto the shoulder of the road. He put the big vehicle in park and turned off the ignition, killing the lights.

"Are you sure this is the place?" Bobby said, reaching between his feet to pick up his axe.

Quinn pointed at a stone lion beside the driveway. The lion had a brass plate bearing the name 'Faulk'.

The thick man grunted. "I guess that's what people in your line of work call 'a clue'."

Despite the trepidation eating his gut, Quinn grinned. "Yes, I suppose it is."

As he climbed out of the car, Quinn took the Inspector's coach gun and closed the door, very softly, until it clicked. Gemma watched him a moment and then did the same. When he saw her watching him, he nodded. "If I'm right, the thing already knows we're coming, but that doesn't mean we shouldn't be careful."

Gemma nodded, as she stepped towards the front of the truck.

Raife and Bobby both closed their doors carefully and joined them. "How do you want to play this, Quinn?"

Opening the coach gun to ensure it was loaded, Quinn snapped it shut and then looked down the long driveway, to where the warm glow of light was visible between the thick cedar trees. "There aren't enough of us to do much more than go through the front door and get busy."

The big man nodded. "On your word, then, son."

Quinn shouldered the shotgun, pointing the barrel down the driveway, and started up the drive. Raife followed with Gemma and Bobby half a dozen steps behind. In fifty metres, the driveway curved right, around a broad lawn that gave way to Steve Faulk's house.

The structure was, ostensibly, a log cabin in the woods. But as Quinn approached it, he thought that if an English castle had sex with an oak tree, Steve Faulk's house would be the result. It had a wide, wraparound porch, the deck and railing polished to a shimmering gleam in the light from the windows.

A river-stone chimney stuck up from the roof, and Quinn could see through the ten-foot-high windows to the darkness above the water.

"Why does everyone else have such a great house and I live in a twelve-hundred square foot miner's shack?" Quinn asked, his breath misting in the night air.

"Imagine trying to keep the windows clean," Raife said, behind him.

Grunting his agreement, Quinn continued forward. He climbed the steps and pressed himself against the log wall, then leaned over and peered through one of the spotlessly clean windows. Staff Sergeant Faulk sat on a wide couch, watching the news on television. Quinn observed for several more moments, an inkling of doubt crawled into his gut.

"Do you think demons watch the news?" he whispered.

"How the hell would I know?" Raife rumbled back.

Shrugging, Quinn stepped around Raife and planted himself in front of the door. He glanced over his shoulder at Bobby and Gemma, who waited at the bottom of the steps.

"I guess we better go ask him," Quinn said as he lifted his foot to kick the door in.

"What the fuck, Gerritt?" Dave McLeod asked for the tenth time in as many minutes, as he steered his jeep down another side street, looking for any sign of the blonde head of Abby McRae. From the passenger seat, Gerritt did what he always did in response to almost every question ever asked of him, he shrugged.

Dave thought about slapping the kid to get some kind of reaction out of him, but decided it wouldn't actually make him feel better.

Dave hated this, hated all of it. He loved Quinn like a brother, but still wished he had not seen most of the things he'd experienced since Quinn came to Resolution. Quinn was probably the bravest man Dave had ever met, but he wished there wasn't quite so much reason for him to be brave.

"If you were an eleven-year-old girl, who was the victim of a demon home invasion, where would you go?" He glanced over at Gerritt. "And I swear to Christ, Gerritt, if you shrug at me again I'm going to stab you."

The youth swallowed, obviously suppressing the urge to shrug.

"Anything?" Dave asked, almost pleading. "We can't drive around in circles all night. If we don't find that poor kid, then those fucking things will."

"She lost her dad, right?" Gerritt asked, after several long moments, filled only with the sound of the jeep's engine.

"Yeah," Dave said. "When that last, um...thing, was...you know..."

"Eating people," Gerritt finished for him.

"Yeah."

Gerritt shrugged again, glancing at Dave like he was expecting a slap, then cleared his throat. "When my dad died, the only thing that made me feel better was visiting his grave. I was a little older than Abby, but not much."

Dave stared at Gerritt, his mouth open, for a moment, before looking back at the road and jerking the wheel as he realised he'd drifted towards oncoming traffic. He'd never heard the kid say so many words in a row before.

"Jesus, Gerritt, you never told us your dad died when you were a kid."

The youth shrugged again. "You never asked."

Dave opened his mouth again, then shut it, and focused on the road. He made a mental note that when this was all over, he'd take Gerritt down to Sam's pub, get him ripped on Jack Daniels, and get his life story out of him. Provided they weren't all dead, that is.

When Kord McRae had been killed in the summer, by the demon that had followed him and Abby across the country, the detachment members who had fought along-side the slender man had all attended a very small funeral. The Inspector had paid, out of his own pocket, to have the man buried in a plot beside the Inspector's son, Patrick.

Inspector Green had told Abby that Kord and Patrick were together in heaven, while the two of them were together on earth. Family taking care of family. Dave wasn't much for tears, but he'd choked up something fierce at that.

Gerritt was right. If there was any place on earth that kid would go, it would be to her father's grave.

"Okay, man," Dave said, making a U-turn. "To the cemetery we go."

Quinn kicked Steve Faulk's door right beside the handle, and it crashed open. He stepped into a wide foyer, floored with grey tile, and tucked the coach gun into his shoulder. From the living room, he heard the staff sergeant shout.

"What the fuck?" Steve Faulk said.

Quinn moved through the foyer, into the living room. Faulk was off the couch and reaching for a cast-iron poker from a rack beside the fireplace. When he turned and saw Quinn, he paused.

"Sullivan? Raife? What the hell are you doing here? And why did you kick in my door?"

"Get on the ground," Quinn shouted, pointing the coach gun at Faulk's chest.

"What?" Faulk asked, his eyebrows drawing together. "What are you talking about?"

"Quinn," Raife said from behind him, but Quinn ignored him.

"I said get on the ground," Quinn shouted, louder this time. "Or I'm going to blow your fucking head off."

"Sullivan, you're insane." Faulk raised a hand to his mouth and shouted towards the kitchen. "Karen! Call 9-1-1."

"Quinn." Raife put a restraining hand on Quinn's shoulder.

Quinn jerked his shoulder away and stepped around the couch. He was in the grips of what Dave liked to call the 'Celtic Fury'. This creature, this thing, had either taken over Steve Faulk's body, or had been masquerading as a cop, pretending to be one of the good guys for years. He had tried to kill the Inspector, was going to kill Abby, and would unleash a horror into this world that man had never known and couldn't possibly be prepared for. Quinn would not let that, any of it, stand.

Quinn stepped rapidly towards Faulk. Faulk raised the poker and swung it. Quinn ducked underneath the swing and kicked Faulk in the back of the leg. As the taller man lost his balance, Quinn shoved him, like a cross-check, with the coach gun. Faulk fell to the floor, face first.

As Faulk landed, a slim dark-haired woman, dressed in jeans and a t-shirt, but with large pink, furry slippers on her feet, came skidding from the hallway to the kitchen. Her eyes were wide and terrified, a cordless phone in her hand.

"Oh my God, Steven, what's going on?" she asked.

"Karen, run!" Faulk shouted as he craned his neck to look at her.

Karen, turned, but found her way blocked by Bobby. He gave her a wan, apologetic smile, and plucked the phone from her hand. He gave it a sharp squeeze in one thick fist and it popped like a kernel of corn.

"I'm sorry, missus," Bobby said. "Please sit down." He indicated one of the arm chairs near the couch. When Karen didn't move, he took her very gently by the elbow and steered her into the seat.

Putting a foot in the centre of the prone man's back, Quinn pointed the coach gun at the back of his head.

"Jesus Christ, Sullivan," Faulk said, his breath heaving. "Please, don't hurt my wife."

"QUINN!" Raife bellowed.

The big man's shout penetrated the red mist that enclosed Quinn's mind, and he blinked. He looked over at Raife, still keeping the coach gun trained on Faulk.

"What?"

"This isn't right, son," Raife said. His rifle pointed at the floor, and he held up a hand, palm out, towards Quinn. "You know it isn't. Listen to what your gut is telling you, right now."

"But..." Quinn said, looking from Bobby, to Gemma, and finally to Raife. "But weren't we sure?"

Gemma walked slowly across the living room to where Karen Faulk sat, shivering, in the arm chair. "I'm not going to hurt you," she said, as she slowly extended a hand. Karen flinched, but then held still as Gemma placed a hand on her flat stomach. The grey-haired woman closed her eyes in concentration for a moment, before opening them. She looked at Quinn and shook her head.

"There is no life in her belly, Quinn."

"What do you mean?" Quinn asked.

"This woman is not pregnant," Gemma said.

Glancing at Raife, Quinn tossed the coach gun to him. The big sergeant caught it, and Quinn knelt down on Faulk's back. He reached into the small of his back and pulled out Donnel's dagger. At the sight of the knife, Karen let out a short scream.

"Quinn, what are you doing?" Raife asked, his rumbling voice low.

Quinn glanced up at him, then, very carefully, pressed the flat of the dagger's blade against the bare skin of Steve Faulk's neck.

There was nothing. The dagger was cold.

"Ah, fuck." Quinn stood up, releasing the prone staff sergeant. Quinn tucked the knife away at the small of his back and walked over to the couch Steve Faulk at been sitting on. He flopped down onto it and leaned forward to put his head in his hands.

He had been so sure that Faulk was the demon and would know where Abby had gone. Now, he knew nothing and was going nowhere. He glanced up at Faulk, who picked himself up off the floor, a pinched look of fury on his flushed face. Well, Quinn though, he was going nowhere except to jail.

"Raife," Faulk said. "I'm not even going to try talking to this goddamned lunatic." He pointed at Quinn. "So you need to tell me what is going on. And who the fuck are these people?" He jabbed his finger at Gemma and Bobby.

Raife propped the SKS on his shoulder and leaned the

coach gun on the couch next to Quinn's leg. He lifted one hand expressively and opened his mouth. Then he shut it and let his hand drop. "In all truth, even if I knew where to start, I don't think you'd believe me."

Quinn looked up at Raife. "I was sure, Raife. I really was."

"I know you were, son," Raife said.

"When I saw the rose petal, I was sure," Quinn said.

"Rose petal?" Faulk asked. "What goddamned rose petal? Did you fuck with my roses?"

Quinn stood, and Faulk jumped backwards. "No...I...at the Inspector's house we found a sack with a rose petal in it."

"Why were you at the Inspector's house?" Faulk demanded.

"He was attacked," Raife said.

"By Sullivan?"

"No," Quinn said. "By something else."

Gemma lifted the flap on her messenger bag and pulled out the burlap sack, carefully folded into a square. She held it out to Faulk.

"Something attacked Inspector Green," she said. "Whatever it was left this behind, with a single rose petal in it." She glanced at Quinn. "When we saw it, we feared it was you."

Faulk crossed the space between him and Gemma and took the sack from her. "You honestly thought I would attack Donald in his home?" He examined the bag and then dropped it on the coffee table in front of the couch. "I use a framed canvass to cover my roses, I don't use burlap."

Quinn wanted to kick something, to use the coach gun to blow a hole in the floor and crawl into it, anything to avoid facing the reality that, once again, he had been rendered helpless. He was about to collapse back onto the couch and wait for Steve Faulk to call down to the detachment to have them all arrested, when something ticked in the back of his mind.

He looked down at burlap sack and then back up at Faulk. "Do you know someone who uses burlap?"

Faulk edged toward the end table, where Quinn could see a cell phone, but he stopped at Quinn's question.

"What?" Faulk said. "Yeah, lots of guys use them. Say they protect the blooms better than any commercial stuff."

"Can you think of anyone off the top of your head?" Raife asked, apparently catching Quinn's drift.

Faulk shrugged and pointed to a wall of pictures behind Gemma. "There is a group shot from last year's garden show. About half of those guys still use burlap."

Quinn walked around the couch and examined the picture Faulk had pointed to. In his peripheral vision, he saw Faulk snatch up his cell phone and begin punching numbers, but Quinn ignored him. If there was a ghost of a chance he could find Abby, everything else could be damned.

The picture showed a group of men, all smiling, several of them holding ribbons. Faulk held a red ribbon and had his arm draped across the shoulder of a much shorter man standing next to him. The shorter man was holding a blue ribbon and had his chin pointed up as though he were preening.

"Is that the mayor?" Quinn asked. "The guy holding the blue ribbon?" He put his finger on the picture, below the winner's face.

"Yeah," Faulk said, tapping the face of his phone and frowning. "Bastard beats me every year."

Gemma leaned towards the picture. Her eyes narrowed as she examined the spot Quinn pointed at. She looked for several long moments, until her eyes flew open and she gasped.

"Gemma?" Quinn asked. "Are you all right?"

The grey-haired woman turned and fumbled at the flap of the messenger bag. "By all the gods," she muttered, as she finally got the flap open and dug around inside. She pulled the furniture maker's history book out and began riffling through the pages. Near the back of the book she stopped, flipped several pages and then held the book up. She turned back to the picture wall, her eyes flicking from the book to the picture and back again.

"I'll be damned," she said, her eyes wide.

"What is it?" Quinn asked.

She held the book out to him and stabbed the page with her finger. He took it, and looked where she pointed.

Several men stood together, unsmiling, before what looked like the entrance to a mine shaft. Dressed in turn of the century clothing, most of the men held mining implements. At the top of the page was the heading, *The Battle For The Silver Mine.*

Quinn looked at Gemma and shrugged. "So?"

"Look, Quinn," she said. "Look close."

With a sigh, Quinn rubbed his eyes and focused back on the page, examining the picture. Drawn to the man on the end, his chin up as though he were preening for the camera, Quinn thought for a moment that his eyes played a trick on him. He rubbed them again and held up the photo against the picture on the wall, nearly dropping the book.

There, in the black and white photograph, with the same stupid grin and air of self-satisfaction, stood Jay Drummond.

CHAPTER 18

He sorely wanted to kill something. Anything. He looked about him, at the creatures that flanked him, who bent to his will. As if sensing his intent, they shrank away, out of his reach. He snarled and thought about giving chase to the one closest to him, then shook his head to dispel the notion. He had much to do, and no time for self-satisfaction.

He looked down at the ground, at the patch of the earth that was still frosted beneath his feet. He could feel the power still in the earth, just as he had felt it as soon as the child opened this door. But now he sensed nothing. He sniffed the air, reached out with his will, into the ground beneath the soles of feet. He could taste the child's magic, could feel it in the earth about the spot where he stood, but the wind carried nothing, no hint of where she might be.

He wished he knew more about children, what made them do the things they did, but he knew nothing. He was sure he would learn, as his son grew and developed his own power, but for now his well was dry.

What did he know of this child in particular? She would certainly seek out the Guardian and his protection, as she was without a father.

Something clicked in the darkness of his mind and a small light shone on his problem. Humans were always on about their fathers and the bond they shared with their children. He never had a father, or if he had, he'd not known of it, so he could not relate to that particular human frailty. But, the more the thought about it, the more he believed he was correct.

He beckoned to the shadows and three shapes emerged, cowering before him. He had thought that he would have the child and be done before the Guardian even knew she had been taken, but the resourcefulness of the girl-child had ruined that plan. He must eliminate Quinn Sullivan.

"Find the Guardian and kill him," he said to the cowering shapes.

They howled their joy at the order and disappeared into the night. They would scent the Guardian easily enough—the stink of his magic, of the raw power that coursed through him—tainted the air of this town like a mobile garbage dump. He would like this place better when that particular stink was gone.

He had thought his plans ruined after the girl's escape, but he found himself smiling. So long as his child remained in the womb, until he had found the girl-child and employed her magic, all would be well.

Grinning, he surged through the night, on his way to Resolution's cemetery.

Abby shivered and looked up at the cloudless sky, thinking very fondly of the puffy jacket with the fluffy liner that Mama Geraldine had helped her pick out. At least it wasn't raining, she thought, as she hugged herself, hurrying down the narrow, paved path between the rows of headstones.

Most people were afraid of grave yards, but Abby thought that was ridiculous. Her father had always taught her that cemeteries were the safest places in either world; the living and the dead. The first time she had visited the little cemetery near the town she was born in, she'd kept seeing shadows, just at the corner of her vision, and they disappeared if she tried to look at them. She had gripped her father's hand and felt like crying, but he just laughed and brushed the long hair away from his face.

"The ghosts in a graveyard are people who were cared for in their lives," her father had told her. "There might be some bad ones, sure, but most were laid down by people who loved them, and that love is what remains after."

"But they're looking at me," she said. "And they won't let me look back."

Her father had stopped and stared down at her. His mouth quirked and he looked like he was thinking hard. After a few moments, he shrugged and kept walking. "They know that I love you very much, and it calls to them. The same way the smell of your mother's pie calls to you." She giggled at that, and her father winked at her.

She had tried to feel then, to reach out, and to open up the way her mother taught her. When she did, she could sense the spirits around her. Some of them were restless and anxious. A few more were scared, but then, covering all that, was a strong scent like flowers after a good rain. Abby thought it was probably the scent of love.

That smell hung thick in the air as she made it to the far corner of the graveyard. To her father's grave.

They had not buried him in a big casket, like in the movies, but in a jar—an urn she thought it was called—and put him under a big stone with a brass plate on it. She found it with no problem, because her Poppa brought her to visit her father whenever she missed him especially bad. Poppa said it was important to remember the people who loved you, and always let her pick out a bouquet of flowers on visiting days. The last bouquet was still there, although it looked a little ill, now.

As she reached the stone marker, she crouched down in front of it, like she always did. It was too dark to read the brass plate, but she knew it by heart: *Kord McRae; Husband, Father, Friend, Warrior. A Man Who Walked In The Light.*

Poppa had never brought her here at night. Abby always thought that if he did, she might be able to see her father's spirit. She looked around. Nothing.

She sat down beside the stone, drew her knees up to her chest, and hoped that Quinn got here soon.

If there was any place in the world that Dave McLeod hated, it was cemeteries.

His mother would probably blame all the horror movies he'd watched as a kid, but whatever the cause, the place creeped him out something fierce. The fact that he was in this particular cemetery looking for a child who could open doors into a great vast nothing, who was being hunted by a black-skinned demon, only made it worse. Add the fact that Gerritt kept stopping to read the dates on the head stones, pushed Dave's already frayed nerves ever closer to the edge.

"This guy died in 1905," Gerritt said, pointing at a thick granite marker. "I wonder what he died of?"

"Gerritt," Dave said, "I swear to Christ if you don't stop fucking around I am going to stab you."

The pale haired youth shut his mouth with a click, swallowed dramatically, and hurried over to Dave's side.

He had only been to Kord McRae's grave once, the day their Watch, led by the Inspector, had come to put Kord's urn in the ground and allow Abby to start the grieving process. He wouldn't be able to pick out the particular stone in the dark, but he knew it close enough to find a little blonde-haired kid if she were sitting on it.

Dave moved cautiously, his pistol in his hands, his head swivelling back and forth as he checked every shadow. Gerritt, much to Dave's annoyance, walked as though enjoying a leisurely stroll. The youth had his hands tucked into his pockets and his rifle bounced against the fronts of his legs as he walked.

"Are you ready, Gerritt?" Dave asked.

The lanky youth looked at him. "For what?"

Dave could see the headlines now: *Mountie sent to the looney bin for beating an idiot to death with a grave stone dated 1905.* He pinched the bridge of his nose and sucked in a deep breath.

"You know that Abby is out here and we're trying to find her, right?"

Gerritt nodded and tilted his hat back on his head, making him look even more like a cartoon character.

Dave took a deep breath to compose himself so he could keep his voice even. "I need you to remember something, okay?"

Gerritt nodded again.

"We are the only thing that stands between that kid and her being eaten. If something stops us from getting to her, she's going to die." Dave paused, letting the gravity of his words penetrate the bone mass between Gerritt's ears.

The smile faded from Gerritt's face, and his expression grew sombre.

That was promising, Dave thought. "So, I need you to tighten up your game, and get in this with me, all right?"

Gerritt tugged down the Elmer Fudd hat so that it sat level on his head, and tucked the stock of his rifle into his shoulder like he knew what he was doing.

"Ready?" Dave asked.

This time, Gerritt gave nothing but a curt nod.

"Good man. Let's roll."

They carried on down the path. Dave was relieved to see Gerritt focused and clear. "Maybe we won't get eaten after all," he muttered.

"Huh?" Gerritt said.

"Nothing," Dave said, a little louder.

They rounded a bend in the path, past the thick trunk of a maple tree, and saw, up the hill, a small figure sitting on the wet grass.

"We found her," he said to Gerritt

Both men hurried up the hill.

The thing that pretended to be Jay Drummond did not like human graveyards. The spirits of the unquiet dead troubled him. They knew him for what he was, even when he wore his human guise, and his presence drove them to a frenzy.

Some spirits he could put to use; anything that had died well and truly angry, full of hate, could be summoned, harnessed. But most spirits, especially those in a place like this, buffeted him with all the meagre power they could summon. They could not harm him, but they clouded his senses, filled him with trepidation, and made him feel doubt. The moment he set his foot on the consecrated ground of the cemetery, they began to appear.

They howled at him, in their ephemeral way, shoved what little will they had up against him, enough to make him sidestep, like he was in a strong wind, but nothing more. What they did accomplish was to block him from sensing the child. Although, he had scarcely been able to sense her since she left the old man's house. Something secreted her away from him.

As more spirits appeared their shapes little more than pale flashes flitting through his vision, he summoned his will and drove them back. He could not sense the child, but perhaps his other senses, his baser instincts, would find her.

He closed his eyes and breathed deep, but there was nothing. He turned his head and breathed in again, and caught the faintest hint of something. He moved toward where the scent seemed to be originating and breathed in again. A slow smile spread across this face as he recognised the smell—fear.

His smile faltered as he headed towards the smell. He caught the scent of something else, and he swore. He smelled a man's sweat, and anger—overpowering the fear—and...gun oil. He smelled the companions of Quinn Sullivan. He smelled the Mounties.

He paused, his footsteps slowing, and he instantly hated himself for his own anxiety. Whoever these men were, no matter what strength their anger gave them, they would not slow him down. Besides, he might not be able to find the child, but he could find these men, and they would lead him right to Abby McRae.

Snarling, he sprinted between the trees.

"Abby," Dave McLeod called as he got close to the child.

The small figure stood up, clasping her hands in front of her, rubbing them together as she looked at Dave and Gerritt. Dave stuffed his pistol back into his holster and held out his arms toward the child. She took two bounding steps towards him and he caught her up. He wasn't close to Abby, not the way Quinn and Raife were, but it seemed like the right thing to do at the time.

Abby pulled away and turned her face to his. "Is my poppa okay?" There were tears in her eyes.

Dave nodded. "Yes. He's gonna be sore for a while, but he's fine. Gemma, the older lady..." he trailed off, trying to find a suitable explanation for what he'd witnessed.

"She did stuff," Gerritt finished for him.

"That's right," Dave said. "She did, some of her, you know..."

"Magic." Gerritt's timing was absolutely impeccable.

"Yeah," Dave agreed. "What he said."

Gerritt scanned the trees around them, his rifle still tucked into his shoulder. "I think we should go. This place doesn't feel very good anymore."

Dave, his mouth half open to say something else, stopped. The kid was right. Something, suddenly, felt very wrong in the old graveyard. Shifting Abby's weight to his left arm, Dave's hand drifted towards the grip of his pistol.

It was love, the creature who was Jay Drummond realised as he stood in the shadows of the trees, hidden from the pale glow of the lamp that shone down from the paved path and into the cemetery. The humans would not be able to see it, but a muted glow lay upon the small grave marker the girl had been sitting beside—a manifestation of the love Kord McRae had borne for his daughter, even unto his death. The man's love concealed her from Drummond's senses, both animal and otherwise. But it wouldn't do any of them any good now. Flexing his hands and snarling, he stepped into the light.

Dave saw a streak of black, almost faster than his eye could follow, and dove away from it, turning to place his body between Abby and the thing hurtling towards them. The thing still struck him a glancing blow. The force sent him spinning through the air, Abby tumbling from his arms.

Dave rolled into a sitting position, as he heard Gerritt's rifle pop in rapid succession. Dave pawed at his own gun, dragging it from the holster on his hip. At the edge of the light cast by the meagre lamp above them, he saw a black shape streak by, gone before he could so much as point his pistol at it.

"Dave?" Gerritt called out, worry making his voice pitch up.

"I'm fine," Dave said, groaning out the lie as he climbed to his feet and limped over to the younger man. A fine smoke still drifted up from Gerritt's rifle barrel. "How's Abby?"

"Uh," Gerritt said, his head swivelling.

With dawning panic, Dave searched around them. The circle of light was empty, save for the two of them. The bad feeling Dave had gotten right before the demon appeared had vanished. And so had Abby.

CHAPTER 19

Quinn could almost hear the click of the tumblers inside his head falling into place in the silence of the room. He turned to Steve Faulk, who still fiddled with his phone, alternately poking at the screen and holding it to his ear.

"Cecil Brown didn't phone you to complain, did he?" Quinn asked the staff sergeant.

"What?" Faulk asked, looking up from his phone.

"When Cecil called in to complain about Dave and I, he didn't call the detachment, did he? He called someone else."

Faulk shrugged. "No, I didn't talk to him initially, the mayor did."

"And then the mayor phoned you to tell you about the complaint," Quinn stated.

"Well," Faulk said, frowning at him. "Yes."

As Quinn spoke, Raife's thick eyebrows drew together, his moustache bristling. "How mad are you about this, Steve?"

"Mad?" Faulk lowered his phone to lock his eyes on Raife. "I'm not mad. I'm bloody furious."

"Why?" Raife asked, the question rumbling like a small avalanche. "Why are you so mad about a complaint from Cecil Brown, who phones to complain every time he so much as sees a police car?"

Faulk raised a hand with his index finger extended, pointed towards the ceiling. "Because..." the heat in his voice faltered, and he looked confused for a moment. He shook his head. "Because...because of Sullivan! He's a menace. He ruins everything. He's a danger to this town. He..." The heat died again and Faulk lowered his finger. "He..." Faulk licked his lips. "The Guardian has to be stopped."

Gemma's head snapped up, her eyes narrow. She had been reading the furniture maker's history book, but now her entire focus locked on Faulk.

"Quinn, does this man know who you really are?" she asked.

"No," Quinn said, shaking his head. "No one ever told him."

She stepped quickly across the room and laid her small hand on Faulk's forehead. The man flinched, but didn't back away.

"He has been touched by the creature," Gemma said, removing her hand. "And the taint of it has been on him for a long time."

Quinn and Raife exchanged glances. "That would explain why he was so keen to have you transferred," the bigger man said.

"He really was trying to get me out of the way," Quinn said. "Only he wasn't the one making the decisions."

Gemma tucked the book into her bag and reached up to cup Faulk's face in her hands. His wife made another squawk, but Bobby patted her shoulder.

"You know there is a darkness in this town, don't you?" Gemma asked the staff sergeant.

His eyes drifted around, but finally met hers, and he nodded.

"And you know the only one who can stop it is Quinn."

There was a long pause, and another small nod.

"But there has been a voice in your head, making you angry, making you say things you're not sure you mean."

A tear broke from the corner of Steve Faulk's eye, and

rolled down his cheek. Gemma wiped it away with her thumb, and then stood on her toes to kiss the spot where the tear had been.

"We are going to silence that voice, my friend," she said.

"Goddamned rights we are," Quinn said.

Steve Faulk slouched his way to the couch and slumped into it. His wife glanced at Bobby, who took a step back, and then hurried over to Faulk. She sat on the arm of the couch and wrapped him in her arms. Quinn could see Faulk's shoulders shake as he buried his face in her chest.

"What's our play, Quinn?" Raife asked.

What he wanted to do was drive his truck into the front of Drummond's house and chop his head off. But there were too many other things to think about. "We need to find Abby," he said, after thinking for a moment. "Once she is safe, I'm going to hunt down this thing that has been calling itself the mayor." He paused, feeling the anger turn his gut. "And then I am going to do...things."

"You need to move cautiously here, Quinn," Gemma said. She walked over to them, stopping to squeeze Karen's shoulder. "This thing we are going to face is older than we can fathom. If the stories I found are correct, it was ancient when Donnel of Inverness was discovering his power."

"I get that, Gemma, but what do you want me to do about it?" Quinn asked.

"I want you to stop holding back. I need you to start believing." She tucked her hands into the sleeves of her cardigan and fixed him with her stare.

"I do believe, Gemma," he said, frustration lending an edge to his voice that sounded hard even in his own ears. "I believe I'm going to tear that fucking demon limb from limb and send it back into whatever hole it crawled out of, no matter how old it is."

Even as he said the words, he knew them for a lie. He had seen what this thing was capable of. It was twice as powerful as the last demon who had hunted Abby to Resolution Cove, and Quinn hadn't been able to stop it. He was full of anger that felt like it was burning a hole in his belly, but in the centre of that fire lurked an icy ball of fear.

Gemma's mouth pressed into a flat line, and Quinn felt like she was reading his feelings on his face. "You *can* defeat this monster, Quinn," she said. "But until you summon the power that lives in here," she tapped the centre of his chest with a slender finger, "you won't."

He rolled his eyes and opened his mouth to tell her he knew all that, but she surprised him when she reached forward and seized a handful of his shirt with surprising strength.

"You are the last of the Guardians, Quinn. Do you understand me? The last! There are no more like you, and I fear there never will be. I have searched much of this wide world looking for more of your kind, but have found nothing. The power of dozens of generations of men and women who have stood their ground and faced the darkness lives in you. But you doubt yourself. You refuse to believe in the old magic even though you have seen it for yourself. You *know*, but you don't *believe*. It will only be when you find that belief, that you will stand a chance. That all of us will stand a chance."

She released him, and he stood staring at her, stunned into silence.

The quiet, broken only by the sound of Karen Faulk whispering to her husband, stretched on until Raife cleared his throat noisily.

"We need to move," he said and rubbed his moustache.

Quinn nodded, and dug into his pocket for his cell phone. "I'm going to call Dave, and see if they've gotten anywhere with finding Abby."

He looked at his phone and saw the screen was blank. He frowned at it and held down the reset button. It flashed, briefly, and then died again.

"Well?" Raife asked.

Quinn sighed and stuffed the phone back into his pocket. "I must have smashed it somehow. It's an eight-hundred-dollar paperweight. Lend me yours."

Raife pulled his phone out of a holder on his duty belt and tossed it to Quinn. He pressed the home button. The screen lit up, but it was white and blank.

"What the fuck?" Raife said, stepping closer to look down at the screen. "My wife is going to kill me."

The icy ball that had been living in Quinn's gut grew a little bigger as he looked over at Steve Faulk's phone, now lying on the coffee table. It hadn't worked either.

"Quinn, what is it?" Gemma asked.

Quinn saw a flash movement, something catching the light, in front of the big windows.

"I think we have company." Quinn strode towards the front door.

At the small of his back, Donnel's dagger began to grow hot. He opened the front door, and saw a number of shapes moving just at the edge of the light. As he shouldered the coach gun and stood in the doorway, the shapes all stopped, turning their misshapen heads to stare at him.

Red eyes in the dark.

Donald Green gritted his teeth as the medics pulled him from the back of the ambulance and wheeled him into the emergency room doors of Resolution Hospital. It was not pain that set him on edge. The woman, Gemma, and rid him of most of that. What made him ache was being stuck on this damned rattling gurney while his Abby was somewhere out in the dark.

In the parking lot across from the entrance, Sandy Harding came to a screeching stop in her Subaru station wagon. She got out and jogged across the lot towards him.

"Have you heard anything, yet?" he asked, as Sandy fell into step beside the gurney.

"Nothing yet, sir," she said. Sandy pulled her cell phone from the pocket of her coat, checking the screen. "Nope. Not a word."

"Damn," he muttered, as the paramedics wheeled him past

the triage desk and into the main bay of the emergency room. They pushed him into one of the two immediate treatment rooms, and pulled the curtain.

He looked up at Sandy, who had taken up her position at the side of the gurney and had her phone to her ear.

"You trying Quinn?"

She nodded. "Nothing. It doesn't even go to voice mail. When I dial his number, or Dave's, it just goes to a tone."

The curtain was abruptly yanked back, and a bustling figure appeared at the side of his gurney; a short, pretty woman with dark hair and eyes that were almost black. She glared at him with a hand on her hip.

"Hello Doctor Stovern," Donald said.

"What is it this time?" she asked, sticking out one hand which a medic promptly filled with a metal clipboard. She glanced down at it before returning her glare to Donald. The only relief was when she cast a little of it on Sandy, who seemed to be trying to find somewhere to hide in the small room.

"I'm sorry?" he asked, doing his best to look like an innocent old man who didn't know anything.

"What is it this time, Inspector?" Dr. Stovern blew some of her dark hair out of her face. "Every time one of you people—"

"What people?" he asked, trying to look vacant.

She had a pen in her hand, poised to make notes on the clipboard, and he feared she was about to stab him with it. "You Mounties. Every time one of you comes in here, you always have some strange injury that you fail miserably to explain. Especially, Sullivan, that other wise-ass, and your pet gorilla, Mr. Raife."

"I have no idea what you're talking about, Doctor," Donald said, folding his hands carefully across his stomach.

"The last time I saw Sullivan, he looked as though he'd been bitten by something. When I asked him what happened, he said he'd been attacked by a bear."

"There are a lot of bears around Resolution, Doctor," Sandy said.

"It was in December," Stovern said, her voice nearing a shout. "Bears hibernate in December."

"Well...global warming..." Donald offered.

"Sweet Jesus!" Exasperated, she dropped the pen on the clipboard so she could pinch the bridge of her nose as though she fought a headache. "Fine," she said after several moments. "Just tell me what happened today."

"I fell in my home," Donald said, keeping his voice carefully neutral. What he longed to do was shove the woman out of the way, get off the gurney, and go out to look for Abby, but pissing off Resolution's most competent doctor would not do their cause any good.

"You fell?" Stover asked. "Really?" She held up the clip board. "The crew report says your house was demolished in a home invasion. How does that translate into 'you fell'?"

Donald shrugged. "I didn't say I wasn't pushed."

Stovern huffed and made a note on the clipboard. "Are you experiencing any pain from your...fall?"

He reached across his body with his right hand and grimaced as he pressed it to the left side of his rib cage. "Yes," he admitted. "In my ribs and my back."

The doctor deposited the clip board on the gurney between his feet, opened his jacket and yanked up his shirt. Her warm fingers prodded at his ribs. She had him roll clumsily onto his side so she could look at his back. She squeezed his legs and knees, then had him press the balls of his feet into her hands.

"You are covered in so many bruises you look like a high-school football player, but you didn't get them today. They look several days old, at least." She made several notes on the clip board and refocused her glare on his face. "What is it that you are not telling me?"

The idea of telling her that an hour ago a black-skinned demon had hit him so hard he feared he was paralyzed, but was miraculously healed by a woman who liked to wear puffy skirts, fled his mind as quickly as it appeared.

"I don't know what else to tell you, Doctor." That, at least, was the truth.

Stovern pinched the bridge of her nose again, albeit briefly this time. "Fine. There is no winning with you people. You'll have to stay and have those ribs x-rayed, but other than that, I'll give you something for the pain and send you home."

"Thank you, Doctor." He gave her the smile he reserved for the raving lunatics who wanted to yell at someone at the front counter of the detachment, which only made her glare all the more. With a final huff she disappeared back out through the curtain, yanking it closed behind her.

The moment she was gone, Donald pivoted his legs off the bed and stood up, grimacing in pain.

"Sir, what are you doing? You need x-rays." Sandy put a restraining hand on his arm, trying to push him back toward the gurney.

"Did you bring my revolver?" he asked, straightening his back and listening to several unsettling pops that came with the movement.

"Yes. It's in my car with Quinn's shotgun. Why?"

He gently pulled his arm from Sandy's grip, and then grabbed her arm in turn, leaning on her more than he really wanted, but not near as much as he needed. "My Abby, my child, is out there, in the night. I cannot sit idle in here while she might need me." He tried to take a shuffling step towards the exit, but Sandy didn't move. He looked at her and saw her mouth pressed into the thin, hard line reserved for when people were well and truly pissing her off.

"Sandy, please."

Her expression softened a fraction, and she nodded. "All right," she said. "But if it comes down to any kind of a fight, you have to promise to let me handle it."

"If it comes to a fight, we're going to have bigger problems than deciding who gets to stand in front."

The creature, that sometimes called itself Jay Drummond, ran through the shadows lining the streets of Resolution Cove. In his arms, overcome with terror, dangled the unconscious form of Abby McRae.

Drummond stopped beneath a clump of trees as indecision gripped him. He looked north, in the direction of the abandoned silver mine—the place he knew he must go to bring his child into the world. Then he looked west, towards his house, where his wife and child waited. Should he go to her, to his beloved, now, and take both her and Abby McRae to the mine together, or take the girl first and make every preparation necessary to ease his own child's birthing? Every delay irked him, made him want to howl, and the weakness of his indecision pained him doubly.

An idea dawned on him, and he knelt down in the wet grass. He was not alone in this, not any longer. He would call upon those who had come to help him yet again in this task. Knowing that the beings that had come to serve him would do so faithfully, he put out the call, told them the task, and then nodded his shining head.

Soon, all would be done, and this world would be his.

Facing north, he began to run.

CHAPTER 20

Quinn slammed the front door and locked it, and immediately felt foolish. That wooden door would stop a demon about as well as a piece of tin-foil. He turned to Raife.

"We are not alone," Quinn said.

"Of course not," Raife said and shouldered the rifle he carried. "Did you see how many?"

"Is a 'fuck load' a valid unit of measurement?" Quinn thumbed the release on the back of the coach gun to double check the shells were live.

"What are you two talking about?" Steve Faulk asked, as he disentangled himself from his wife, stood and rubbed at his red -rimmed eyes. "A fuck load of what?"

"You know all those times you wanted to know what we were doing and why we were so secretive?" Quinn asked him, snapping the coach gun shut. "You're about to find out."

"If you have weapons, here," Bobby said to Faulk. "You should go get them."

Before the tall man could respond, the window that faced towards the driveway imploded. A stocky shape, a little shorter than Quinn, but hunched, covered in rippling muscle and coarse hair, landed in the middle of the living room. It appeared like someone had crossed a brahma bull with a wolf and doubled its teeth.

Quinn shot it with both barrels of the coach gun, nearly knocking himself on his ass in the process. The thing screeched and black blood flew from its chest and shoulders in thick gobbets. It shook its head, opened its mouth and let out a high-pitched roar that scraped Quinn's ears like a handful of rusted nails.

Raife stepped beside him, his rifle aimed at the creature, when the front door crashed open, and another creature, much like the first, rushed into the foyer. Raife pivoted towards it and started firing.

In the cacophony of gunfire, Quinn dropped the coach gun and reached to the small of his back, drawing Donnel's dagger. The blade flared with brilliant light as Quinn gripped it. The demon he'd shot with the coach gun threw a thick arm across its eyes and backed up several steps. Quinn rushed forward and bowled into the creature, stabbing as hard and fast as he could. The thing let out another piercing roar as the blade punched into its body.

Quinn felt his anger surging in his blood, and he thought about what Gemma had said, and tried to focus that anger into the weapon in his fist. The light from the blade grew brighter, and the demon turned and tried to flee. Bobby appeared in front of it, the wide blade of his axe chopping into the things chest, bringing it up short. Quinn drove the knife into the base of its skull, pushing both with his arms and his will and saw a short gout of flame blast from the thing's mouth.

The demon collapsed, as though all its bones had been sucked from its body, and lay still on the hardwood floor.

Turning, Quinn saw that Raife's rifle had gone dry, and the big man was now using it as a club with his left hand as he drew his pistol with his right. The thing leapt for him, but Gemma stepped beside him her hands thrown up before her. There was a flash of light, and the creature deflected away to land in a heap. It was up in an instant, legs gathering beneath it for another charge, but Quinn threw himself on top of it, gripping it around the neck with his free arm and stabbing it in the eye with the other. The creature screamed, its limbs pin wheeling. Quinn clutched the handle of the dagger as though his life depended on it—which it likely did. He locked his arm tighter about the creature's neck and pulled the dagger free to drive it in a second time, deeper. The creature stiffened, let out a long croak, and fell forward.

Yanking the dagger free, Quinn stood and staggered sideways. His head throbbed and his body ached where it had been bashed about by the two demons. Bobby handed him the coach gun, then put a steadying hand on his shoulder.

"Are you all right?" the thick man asked.

"I'm not dead," Quinn said. "But other than that, I got nothing."

He stood up straight and looked out through the now broken window. Other shapes, at least two, shifted at the edge of the light, but they made no move towards the house.

"Why ain't they coming?" Raife asked as he pulled a new magazine for the rifle from the pocket of his uniform coat and jammed it into the long gun.

"They have witnessed the Guardian's power and they are not anxious to die," Gemma said.

"Now we only need consider if the fear they have for the one that sent them will overpower their fear of Quinn," Bobby said, his axe gripped in both hands as he faced towards the window.

"What do you want to do, Quinn?" Raife asked.

Blowing out a short, hard breath through his nose, Quinn thought a moment. "We need to move. We can't just sit here and wait for the mayor, or whatever the fuck he is, to send more of these things for us. We need to take the fight to him."

"Make a run for your truck?" Raife asked.

"Remember, the dark is their domain," Gemma said. "Once we leave the light of this home, those creatures will get a measure of their courage back."

"What about them?" Bobby asked.

Quinn turned to look at Steve Faulk and his wife. Karen had her head buried in Faulk's chest, and they clung to each other, shaking as though they stood in a brisk, cold wind.

"We can't leave 'em here," Raife said.

"No," Quinn agreed. He turned to Faulk. "Staff, do you keep your car in the garage?"

As it turned out, he did. Steve Faulk owned a huge, white, rumbling Dodge Ram pickup that was roughly as long as an aircraft carrier and probably burned the same amount of fuel. It sat in the wide garage, beside a small import, that likely would have fit in the back of the massive vehicle.

"If we need to kill anything, we can just hit it with this," Bobby said, as he opened one of the back doors and boosted Gemma in.

Quinn saw several sets of keys hanging on hooks by the door from the garage to the rest of the house and snatched the one with the leather tag that said "Dodge" on it. Raife had convinced both Steve Faulk and his wife to put on shoes, but they both balked at the door of the garage like a heifer that was reluctant to take the journey down a cattle chute.

"I'm not going anywhere until you tell me what the hell is going on?" Steve Faulk said, his hand on the door jamb. His eyes were still red-rimmed, but some of the edge had snuck back into his voice. Quinn found it oddly comforting.

"What is going on," Raife said in his rumbling voice, as he hip checked Faulk through the door and dragged Karen behind him, "is that the things that lived under your bed when you were a kid are alive and well, and are coming to eat you."

Faulk's already pale face grew a touch whiter, and Karen broke down into fresh sobs. Quinn and Raife had fought these battles and had seen these strange sights so many times that it was bordering on routine, but for Faulk and his wife this was all a fresh nightmare. Quinn tried to remember what it had been like for him when he first wrestled with the reality that there really were things that went bump in the night. As he did, he found himself softened towards the terrified couple.

"Staff," Quinn said. The tall man's eyes met his. "I know this is insane, but I can't explain until we all get out of here. Just trust me when I say that if I leave you and your wife here, alone, you will both die."

"And be eaten," Raife said, as he scooped Karen under one massive arm and gave Faulk another shove.

"Please." Quinn gestured towards the truck.

Faulk stood still for a moment, his gaze darting between Quinn, Raife and the struggling Karen, and Bobby who stood on the running board of the big vehicle and looked back at them expectantly.

After a long moment, Faulk nodded and moved towards the truck. As he did, a crash sounded from inside the house.

Raife passed Karen to Bobby. Faulk jumped into the back seat after her.

Quinn tossed the keys to Raife. "You drive," Quinn said. "I'm going to try and give Faulk the Coles notes version of our little shit show."

Raife nodded and hustled around the front of the truck to climb in the driver's seat.

The truck was a little older, but immaculate inside. It fired up with a throaty roar as soon as Raife turned the key in the ignition. Quinn hit the garage door opener on the visor in front of Raife, and the door started up with a rattle.

As soon as the garage door was high enough, Raife yanked the gear into drive and slammed his big foot down on the gas pedal. The truck surged forward, the tires squeaking on the smooth floor of the garage. Quinn saw several shapes darting through the headlights, and punched the button to roll down the window, pointing the coach gun in front of them.

One of the shapes leapt forward. Quinn squeezed off a shot, careful to only use one barrel this time. The shape flew backwards into the night. Raife kept his foot pinned on the accelerator and the big truck roared down the narrow driveway. Quinn looked back and saw several shapes, all bathed in the red glow of the tail lights.

When they got to the street, Raife took a hard right turn, pointing the big vehicle back towards city centre.

"Where are we going?" Raife asked, as he guided the truck out of a tail slide and raced down the road.

"Head for the Mayor's house," Quinn said, opening the coach gun to replace the spent shell.

Raife's head snapped towards him. "Forgive me, son, but are you off your fucking gourd? The Mayor is trying to kill us."

"I know, and that's why we're going to take the fight to him." He snapped the coach gun shut. "I'm through running."

He turned in his seat again to peer out the back window. If they were still being pursued, which he was extremely confident they were, then the demons chasing them were far enough back to be out of sight in the dark. He turned his gaze towards Steve Faulk, who was sandwiched between Bobby and the rear passenger door.

"Staff, I am going to try and explain to you what has been going on in this town since I got here, but I need you to shut up and listen."

Faulk opened his mouth to say something, and then apparently thought better of it as he shut his mouth. He took in a deep breath and nodded.

"You remember Scooby?" Quinn asked. Scooby had been the town's eccentric old man who talked to trees, named for the giant purple Scooby-Doo doll he had strapped to the front of his bike. He was also one of the first people to be influenced by the first demon Quinn had killed more than two years prior.

Steve Faulk nodded in response.

"Well, he wasn't just crazy. Something made him that way. Something dark." Quinn glanced over at Raife. "And we killed it."

As Raife drove the big truck as fast as it would go, Quinn told Steve Faulk an abbreviated version of his entire story, starting with the discovery of the creature in the basement of Joe Robowski's house in the South End and finishing with how they determined that the mayor was actually a demon.

Steve Faulk looked like he didn't know whether to shit or yell bingo. His wife, Karen, on the other hand, was quite clear in her emotional response.

"This cannot be real," she exclaimed, making broad gestures with her hands. "Our mayor is a fucking monster?" She looked around at anyone who would meet her eye, and Gemma, sitting beside her, took one of the nervous woman's flailing hands and held it in both of her own. "How could we not have known?"

"Quinn spent a week riding around in a car with one of those things and didn't know," Raife said. "So I wouldn't feel bad."

"It was two days," Quinn said, remembering the plain clothes investigator from Cranbrook detachment, Clara Morgan. She had been killed and replaced by a demon who escorted Quinn while he investigated the death of Inspector Green's son, Patrick. He hadn't known the creature's true nature until it had decided to reveal itself and nearly killed him.

"Whatever," Raife said. "The point is, you, who is supposed to know about this shit, didn't know you were sharing a car with a goddamned demon. So no one else should feel bad for being duped."

"Fair point," Quinn said and looked out the window.

Gemma looped an arm over Karen's shoulders and pulled her close. "Have you ever noticed that when you are standing outside in the dark, you can see into a lighted room but they cannot see you?" Karen nodded. "It is that way with these things. The dark can always see into the light, but the light is often blind."

"What do we do now?" Steve Faulk's voice was soft, barely audible over the growl of the truck's big diesel engine. "Just what the hell are we supposed to do now?"

Quinn twisted in his seat to look back at him. "We do what we have been doing since we killed that thing in Joe Robowski's basement. We fight. We look after our own, and we fight." He turned to face forward again, his hands tightening on the coach gun. "That thing is after Abby, and there is no one to stop it but us."

They left the rural roads that led into subdivisions of Resolution Cove's residential area and Raife slowed the big vehicle.

"You know where the mayor lives?" Quinn asked him.

The big man nodded. "I've been there a couple of times when he wanted to meet with the detachment's senior management. For whatever reason he always wanted to host them at his house instead of have them in the detachment board room."

"It was deepening its cover," Gemma said from the back seat.

"What?" Quinn asked.

"The creature," Gemma said. "By having people into its home it solidifies the illusion of its humanity, both for you and itself. The more it can make you believe that it is human, the more it will, in turn, believe it."

Turning back to Raife, Quinn asked, "What do you think?"

Raife shrugged his shoulders and looked uncomfortable. "You've met the mayor —well, the boogeyman who pretends to be our mayor. He's a likable guy. You can't help but want to talk to him, laugh at his jokes, hear his stories." He rubbed his finger across his moustache. "When I think about how much I told him about myself, and happily, it makes me ill." He glanced into the rear-view mirror. "So, no one should feel bad about not knowing that thing for what it was. Everyone was fooled."

Karen's hands dropped into her lap. Staring at nothing, her face appeared pinched and contemplative.

They pulled on to a narrow street, and Raife drifted to a stop, letting the big diesel engine sit at an idle. "This is it."

The street was narrow and lined with thick maple trees, their bare branches stretching up into the darkness beyond the reach of the short streetlamps. The houses were old, big Victorians with sharply peaked roofs and wrap around porches that gave the impression of wealth. The yards, almost uniformly, were immaculately kept and expensive cars sat on the paved driveways.

Leaning forward in his seat, Quinn peered through the windshield. "I don't know if I've ever been to this neighbourhood."

"Not many calls here," Raife said. "The socio-economic scale goes up, and the crime rate plummets."

"Which house is it?" Quinn asked.

Raife squinted, and then pointed a thick finger to a house on their left. "That one there, with no lights on. With the blue siding."

"Okay," Quinn said and jerked his chin toward the curb at the side of the street. "We leave the vehicle here and go in on foot."

Raife gave the big truck the slightest touch of gas and guided it smoothly to the side of the road where he put it in park and turned it off. They all sat still, every eye focused on the blue house a hundred metres away, the silence broken only by the tick of the engine as it cooled.

Sucking in a big breath and holding it, Quinn wondered for the tenth time that day if he was doing the right thing. Was chasing this thing down and confronting it in its own home a good idea, or was he simply volunteering to meet his own demise? Would everyone involved be better served if he took a breath, regrouped with everyone and came back in strength? He let out his breath in a rush as he watched the rain splatter against the windshield and thought again of Autumn tumbling through Abby's black door and instantly decided. This thing had lived among them long enough and had wrought enough misery on Quinn and the people he called his family.

It was time to shine a light into the darkness that cursed this town.

"Raife, you and Bobby are with me," Quinn said as he reached for the door handle. "Gemma, you stay here with Steve and Karen."

"I think I should be with you," Gemma said, taking her arm from around Karen's shoulders. "You might need me."

"If something in that house bites my arm off, I will definitely need you," Quinn said, looking back to meet her gaze. "But if I can't stop it, you won't be able to either. You will need to find Dave and Sandy, and try to get Abby somewhere safe."

She reached forward and gripped his shoulder. "If you don't prevail in this, Quinn, I fear that nowhere will be safe." She squeezed, her grip surprisingly strong. "Luck to you."

Nodding, Quinn pulled the door handle and slipped to the ground. Bobby did the same, stepping down right behind Quinn. As the thick man turned to close the truck's door, Steve Faulk pushed it back open and hopped out.

"I'm coming, too."

Raife had come around the front of the truck and stopped beside Quinn. "I think that is a poor idea, Steve. You're not prepared for this."

"I'm coming," he said, again, a bit of his old iron creeping into his voice. "That thing fucked with my head and made me into someone I didn't want to be." His tall form stood rigid and his eyes shone in the sparse light of the street lamps. "I cannot let that stand, Quinn, and I won't be left behind."

Quinn opened his mouth to tell him no, to tell Raife to handcuff him to the bumper of the truck, but something in the other man's face stopped him. He closed his mouth and took in the expression on Steve Faulk's face. He saw a mix of anger, fear, determination, but, above all, he saw belief. The staff sergeant believed that they were going to face something evil and wanted to stand with them. Quinn knew how hard it was to come to that belief, and could not refuse the man.

"Okay," Quinn held out the coach gun, digging in his pockets to pass over the last handful of spare rounds. Steve accepted the gun and stuffed the spare shells into the pockets of his jeans. "I need you to remember something, though, Staff. I know that you know how to be a cop, but you don't know how to do this. So I need your promise that you will do as I say, when I say it."

The words, though he knew it was him saying them, surprised Quinn. He had spent so long denying the knowledge of the things that dwelt in the dark, where most people would never see them was still hard for him to accept. He also still wasn't sure that he had any idea what he was actually doing. He glanced around at the faces of the other three men, who looked to him for answers. Quinn hoped that he didn't get them all killed.

"I promise," Steve said, tucking the coach gun into his shoulder. "I'm behind you."

Nodding, Quinn drew the Sig Sauer from his shoulder rig and gripped it in both hands. "Raife, you lead and head for the back door." He looked at Steve. "Guns won't kill these things, but they can hurt it and slow it down. If this thing is in its house, hit it with both barrels and back off. If there is more than one, keep the other ones off me while I try and deal with the big one."

Faulk nodded. "How will I know the difference?"

"Believe me," Bobby said. "If you see the 'big one', you'll know it."

"Are we ready?" Quinn asked, meeting the eyes of each man. They all nodded. "Then let's roll."

Raife tucked the stock of the SKS into his shoulder, pointed it at the front of the blue house, and moved across the street in a crouch, his steps quick. Quinn followed behind him, the Sig Sauer tucked into his chest. He could feel Faulk on his heels. He glanced over his shoulder to see Bobby, his axe gripped in both hands as he tried to mimic the movements of the other three men.

Raife crossed over the sidewalk, onto the lawn of the nearest house, away from the light of the street lamps. When they got close to the blue house, he paused, studying the dark windows.

"You feel anything," he asked Quinn, not taking his eyes off the house.

Neither the dagger at the small of his back nor the brass knuckles in his pocket had any hint of heat. "Nothing." His voice barely above a whisper. "But if the thing is hiding, I wouldn't know anyway."

"Fuck," Raife said. "Okay, ready?"

Quinn glanced over his shoulder at Faulk and Bobby, who both nodded. "Ready." He reached up to squeeze Raife's shoulder.

The big man blew out a big breath, and moved forward, close to the wall of the mayor's house, and headed for the back yard. Reaching over the low fence and flipped up the latch, Raife nudged the gate forward with his knee which made the gate wail like a trumpet in the silence of the night. Quinn gritted his teeth and bit off the curse that burbled up his throat. Raife let out another huffing breath and paused. When nothing jumped out of the shadows to attack them, he started forward.

As they rounded the corner for the back of the house, Quinn saw a well-manicured lawn that gave way to several rows of low bushes, all covered with burlap sacks—the mayor's rose garden. One of the rose bushes stood uncovered, with half the stalks snapped off and the petals wilting on the wet ground. Quinn thought of the sack in Donald Green's living room. He tapped Raife on the shoulder and pointed to the rosebush. The big man turned his head and nodded.

"I see it," Raife said. "What now?"

Quinn side-stepped to see around him and examined the back of the house. He saw a set of stairs leading up to a wide, covered porch complete with a swing beside a single door leading into what was probably the kitchen.

"Hard entry," Quinn said. "Up the stairs and kick the door. I'll be first. You follow."

"Okay, son," Raife said.

He was about to tell Raife to go, when Quinn felt a sudden heat bloom in the small of his back. "Wait," he said, holstering the Sig Sauer. "Something's coming."

A crunch emanated from the inside of the house and the rear door shuddered. Nothing happened for several heartbeats before the door ripped inwards with a crash of broken glass and a peal of ripping wood. A huge shaggy form emerged from the destroyed doorway to stand on the porch. Quinn heard the creature snarl as its huge head turned towards them. Quinn stepped up beside Raife, as he reached under his shirt to draw Donnel's dagger, illuminating the back yard in bright white.

The massive creature stood over seven feet tall, with thick, powerful limbs covered in coarse hair. Its lupine face exhibited a broad snout and pointed tusks sticking up from the lower jaw. When the light hit its eyes, muting the pin-prick of red, the demon flinched before roaring at them.

Slumped in the crook of one of the creature's massive arms, draped an unconscious, obviously pregnant woman.

The creature stooped and set the woman on the porch before charging at Quinn, leaping and crashing through the porch railing as though it didn't exist. As the huge form sailed through the air, Raife started shooting, the SKS spitting a tongue of orange fire. Quinn reached into his back pocket and pulled out Kord McRae's brass knuckles, fitting them to his hand and squeezing.

The demon hit the ground six feet in front of Quinn. Quinn dove towards it, angling slightly to the side. As he passed the creature, he slashed into its leg with the dagger, then tucked forward and rolled to his feet. The creature roared again and turned towards him. Behind the demon, Steve Faulk stepped up beside Raife and fired the coach gun, one barrel followed immediately by the other. The double-ought buck tore into the creature's back and it gave a start, as though surprised, but its eyes didn't leave Quinn. The creature lurched forward, its heavy feet stomping furrows in the damp earth.

Quinn stood his ground and waited for it to come. The demon swung a massive arm towards him. Quinn ducked left, stabbing upward with the dagger, and bit deep into the creature's shaggy arm. The creature screamed, its foghorn voice pitching up an octave. Quinn rushed forward, stabbing into the thick body. The demon turned quickly, flailing, ripping the dagger from Quinn's hand and sending him crashing into the muddy earth. He put his hands out to break his fall and the brass knuckles flew off, tumbling into the rows of rose bushes.

As Quinn fell, Raife and Faulk started shooting again, the SKS an angry bark beside the coach gun's roar. The creature turned its back on them, ignoring the bullets tearing into its body, its red eyes searching for Quinn. The creature charged towards him, and Bobby stepped forward with a yell and threw his axe in a broad overhand motion. The big weapon whooshed through the air and struck the creature in the back with a wet thump. This, too, the creature ignored and leapt, a massive, clawed foot raised high to crash down on Quinn.

Rolling across the muddy earth, Quinn avoided being crushed and pushed himself painfully to his feet. The creature stumbled forward, its clawed hands reaching for him. Quinn ducked underneath the grasping limbs and scrabbled at the dagger, but missed. As the creature lurched past him, he saw the handle of Bobby's axe protruding from its back and grasped it. He gave a hard pull, but the blade was stuck fast. He was yanked off his feet as the creature turned to look for him. He held tight, knowing that if he fell again he might not be able to get up in time.

The creature's massive head swivelled back in forth seeking an enemy until its eyes found the cluster of men still standing by the corner of the house. Steve Faulk scrabbled at his pockets for fresh shotgun shells. Bobby stood unarmed. The creature charged towards them, and Raife fired the SKS, but after two shots it went dry with a sickening click. The creature had momentum now, moving surprisingly fast for its size. Raife, standing out front, turned to run, but Quinn knew he wasn't quick enough to get away.

Quinn gripped Bobby's axe as tight as he could and tried to dig his feet into the soft earth to slow the creature, but he might as well have been pulling on a loaded freight train. He shouted, in fear and anger and frustration. He could not make these men die for him, for his failure. He would not. He closed his eyes and roared again, and something deep inside him cracked.

Sudden, scalding heat burst in his chest, as though he'd been set on fire. A new roar drowned his, and when he opened his eyes, the axe in his grip glowed bright white. Blue-white fire erupted from the wound in the demon's back. The thing lurched to a stop, its clawed hands reaching back for the source of its agony.

Quinn set his feet and ripped the weapon free. The creature turned clumsily towards him and he swung the axe with all his strength. The axe chopped into the side of the demon's head, ripping the top of its skull away in another burst of blue-white fire.

The demon stopped flailing. Its wolfish face took on an almost contemplative expression. Its red eyes found Quinn's and it gave a momentary snarl before the red faded and it crashed forward into the churned earth, the top of its head and the wound in its back still burning.

The light in the axe died, and it suddenly felt to Quinn as though it weighed a thousand pounds. He let it slip from numb fingers and turned towards Raife, who looked at him with a stunned expression.

Quinn opened his mouth to say something, forgot what he wanted to say, and then everything went dark.

CHAPTER 21

The thing that used to think of itself as Jay Drummond looked about with satisfaction. All was almost ready.

Once he had taken the girl, he had made his way, with all its substantial speed and strength, up the narrow roads of Silver Mountain, to the abandoned silver mine. To the place where his child would come into the world that it would soon possess.

The mouth of the mine faced out onto a wide landing, big enough to turn a cargo wagon pulled by a team of four mules. The landing, in turn, gave way to a steep cliff face that looked west, out over the Rivers Inlet, and to the sea beyond.

The mine had been sealed with an old concrete door, complete with a padlock as wide as a big man's hand. He remembered, in the 1950's, when the mining company had opened and instituted exploratory digging to see if there was anything left of the huge silver vein, they had lost four men in a cave-in on the first day and immediately abandoned the place.

He had been in America's Deep South at the time, under a different name, but he had heard about the deaths and had not been surprised. The old ghosts that haunted this place, bound by the earth's Nexus, were angry and always looked to swell their ranks from those that still walked among the living.

Unlike the ghosts in the cemetery, there was no love here. The men who lay in the halls of the mine saw their ends through violence and greed. Angry and fearful, the shades carried their final emotions of life into their deaths, posing no danger to him. When he strode to the concrete door that sealed the mine and ripped it from its old iron hinges, the spirits swirled about him like a pack of obedient dogs.

He made a bed of torn cedar boughs, for his wife to lay on when she arrived, and built a roaring fire in the centre of the landing. He glanced over at the bound child, who lay still at the mouth of the mine. She had not stirred since he dropped her there, but he knew she lived because he could hear her heartbeat. When the time came, he would wake her, gently if he could, otherwise if he could not. She would help him deliver his child, whether she cared to or not.

His reverie was interrupted by a strange feeling, one he had not felt in many centuries, one that made his black blood go cold. Somewhere close, he felt the magic of a Guardian. Not the trickle of power that came from Quinn Sullivan when he gripped one of the puny weapons he had found, but real power. Old magic. As he felt that burst of power, he felt a very human maggot of worry burrow into his heart.

Was it possible that someone else had inserted themselves into this war? Surely, Quinn Sullivan had not come into that kind of power. The man was a buffoon, rollicking through this town as though he were strong enough to make a difference. He mattered so little that he may as well be a bug beneath a boot-heel. Besides, the ones he had sent for him had surely completed their task and the Guardian—or what passed for one in this age—was dead.

He turned his back on the fire and looked out over the water, waiting, but felt nothing else. Growling, he summoned his will and reached out for the one he had sent to collect his family—the most formidable of those who had answered his call—and sought to see through the other's eyes. He found the spirit of the creature, but when he touched it he saw nothing but white fire. The image burned him and set him back on his heels. He almost fell to the earth. Immediately, he broke the connection, his eyes opening to the black night.

He clenched his fists and roared.

Sullivan had killed his kin.

He would make payment in kind.

Slowly, Quinn opened his eyes. His head felt as though it had been beaten with a hammer, and the stink of burned hair filled his nostrils. He blinked several times. Finally, Gemma Donnelly's face came into focus.

"Is he alive?" a rumbling voice asked.

"Yes, Charles, he is alive." Gemma ran a cool hand over Quinn's forehead.

"For Christ's sake, woman, stop calling me 'Charles'."

"Quinn, can you hear me?" Gemma asked.

Quinn tried to answer, but his mouth felt like it was full of chalk. All he managed was a dusty croak. He ran his tongue around the inside of his sour mouth and cleared his throat. "Yeah," he said, finally. "I can hear you. What happened?"

"You chopped a demon's head off," Raife said, his shining bald pate came into view. "Well, most of it anyway."

Squeezing his eyes shut, Quinn remembered the battle with the massive demon, his memory ending in bright white fire. "How did I do that?" he asked no one in particular.

"You discovered your true power." Gemma tugged on his arm to pull him into a sitting position. "And that power helped you defeat your foe."

Shaking his head, he climbed to his feet. The chalky feeling in his mouth remained, but his vision cleared. His hands and feet tingled with pins and needles. On the ground before him lay the demon he'd fought, missing a significant portion of its head. As he stood and looked down at it, he remembered fear and anger and finally fire.

"I don't remember how I did it," he said, nudging the hairy creature with the toe of his boot. "And I don't know if I want to."

Movement from the back porch of the mayor's house caught his attention. His hand dropped to his duty pistol still in the holster on his hip. He saw, after a moment, that Bobby sat on the top step with a pretty, dark-haired woman's head on his lap. The woman lay unconscious. Her petite form heavily pregnant.

Quinn's hands still felt shaky and he didn't trust himself to point. Instead, he tilted his chin towards the woman. "Is that...?"

"The demon mayor's wife?" Raife finished for him. "Sure is. Her name is Emily Drummond, or so it says on the driver's licence we found in the kitchen."

Quinn glanced up at the house to see all the lights inside were on. "You cleared the house?"

The big man nodded. "Once we got Gemma to make sure you weren't dead, Faulk and I checked to make sure there was nothing else inside."

"You find anything?"

"A piss-pot full of books on botany," Raife said.

"And a strange propensity for cross-stitch," Bobby said.

"But nothing that tried to kill us," Raife finished.

Quinn nodded and lowered himself to the step next to Bobby, every muscle in his body vigorously objecting. "So, what do we do with her?"

"I have been thinking about that." Gemma crossed her arms into the wide sleeves of her sweater. "I think it would be a mistake to leave her here."

"You think something like that," Raife gestured to the semi-headless demon, "will come and finish her off."

Gemma shook her head. "Something will come, yes, but I have a feeling that it won't be a danger to this woman. I don't think this creature was sent here to harm her. I think it was sent to protect her, and to bring her to our enemy."

"I agree," Quinn said, remembering through the flashes of fire in his brain that the demon had been cradling the woman like a baby. "I am disinclined to let him have anything that bastard wants."

"So where was it taking her?" Bobby asked, still stroking her hair.

"To wherever the Mayor is," Raife said.

"So what do we do?" Gemma asked.

Quinn stood up off the step. "We get her someplace safe," he said, nodding to the sleeping woman. "Then we go and see the Mayor."

Carrie Dawson ruffled her son's thick hair, the same shade as hers, as they stepped off the sidewalk of the Dairy Queen, heading for her Jeep. Shawn was nearly dancing as he told her, for the third time, how he had scored his team's only goal in a game where they were creamed seven to one.

The coach had offered to buy all the kids ice cream to reward them for the 'hustle' they displayed during their complete shellacking. Carrie had been inclined to refuse, given the latest bout of weird shit that Quinn had been experiencing at work—and everywhere else. But the pleading look in Shawn's eyes had been her undoing, and she had agreed to stop, just for a minute. More than an hour later the team was finally clearing out and heading home.

"Hurry up, baby," she said, as she dug her keys out of her coat pocket. "We need to get home."

"But, Mom!" Shawn said, his legs braced wide and his arms thrown wide. "You should have seen it! It was brilliant." He jumped and did a lap around her, mimicking his stick handling. "Just wait 'til I tell Quinn!"

"He'll make you show him twice."A smile spread across her face. Shawn didn't call Quinn 'dad', but there was no question they loved each other. She had dated other men between the time Shawn's bio-dad hit the bricks and she had met Quinn, but she had never let any of her other boyfriends anywhere near her son. But Quinn Sullivan was something different.

The first time she'd met him, during his drunken 'welcome to Resolution' party, he had asked her out after puking behind the pinball machine in her uncle's pub. Any other guy she'd have told to pound sand, but with Quinn she'd said yes without hesitation, knowing as she said it that she was going to fall in love with him. By their second date, she had brought him to her home to meet Shawn and the two had been thick as thieves ever since. Quinn was the best man she'd ever met, and she wondered if she'd ever be able to tell him just how much she loved him.

"Miss Dawson?"

The voice behind her made her turn, her mass of dangly key rings swinging gently as she held her car key out towards the jeep, her thumb hovering over the 'un-lock' button. The man who spoke was tall, slender, and had a warm, expectant smile. His sand-coloured hair was slightly dishevelled, and he wore a dark, baggy track suit that didn't look like it fit him very well. She looked at him for several long moments, thinking that she recognised him, but not sure where from.

"Oh," she said, as she remembered where she knew him from. "Hello, Mr. Mayor." She blinked again, looking at the man's face, illuminated under the soft yellow spill of light from the lamp situated in the middle of the parking lot. Something was off about his face; like when you see your grade four teacher from an adult's perspective. You know it's them, but they don't look at all the same.

"Mom?" Shawn said, as he approached her and stood beside her, taking her free hand and draping it on his own shoulders. She looked down at him, a frown stealing onto her face. The gesture of him taking her arm was something he hadn't done in years, and only when he had been afraid of something.

When she looked back up at the Mayor, his face was exactly as she remembered it from her last interaction with him, from a summer barbecue at Inspector Green's house. The vague shift disappeared. The Mayor still smiled, wide and warm, but Carrie felt a prickle beneath her breast bone, and she swallowed thickly.

"What brings you out here, sir?" she asked, tucking the hand holding her keys into her pocket and thumbed the unlock button.

"I came to see you, actually," the mayor said, still smiling as he took another step forward. Something white, below the hem of the mayor's dark track pants caught Carrie's attention, and she looked down.

The mayor wore no shoes and streaks of mud covered his bare feet.

She grabbed Shawn's arm and turned, lunging towards the jeep. She only made it three steps before she felt something huge smash into her back. She flew forward, her head snapping back so hard she bit her tongue. All the air was driven from her as she crashed into the rear corner of her jeep. She collapsed to the pavement, her vision blurry. She tried to draw a breath and scream for help, but managed only a moan.

She heard something scrape against the wet, black-top and turned to look for the source of the sound. Above her stood a tall creature, its shining skin as black as the deepest night, its face almost featureless except for a wide mouth filled with sharp teeth and two eyes that glowed like coals. In one of its muscular limbs it gripped Shawn, who stared at her in mute terror.

"The Guardian has someone that is incredibly dear to me," the thing said in a grating voice that didn't sound like it was ever meant to speak human words. "And I need you to ensure he brings her to me."

The thing reached down and scooped her up, like a child with a kitten. If she'd had any breath left in her body, she would have screamed.

CHAPTER 22

Quinn's legs regained a measure of their strength, as he walked from the back of the mayor's house towards Steve Faulk's truck. In front of him, Bobby carried Emily Drummond, cradling her almost as easily as the monstrous demon had.

Up and down the street, people had come out of their homes in response to the gunfire. This was an affluent neighbourhood. People actually paid attention when someone fired off thirty rounds from a high-powered rifle. Raife, who was the only one in uniform, spoke to everyone who approached, laughing deep and slapping arms. It took a while, but eventually everyone went back inside and the lights in the windows started to switch off.

Steve Faulk sat in the back seat with the passenger side door open, speaking quietly to his wife. Her eyes wide, they never focused on anything for more than a heartbeat.

"She looks like she cracked," Quinn said quietly to Gemma, as they got close.

Gemma nodded. "I think that is putting it mildly."

When Karen Faulk saw Bobby gently lift the still unconscious form onto the seat beside Steve, she pushed herself away until her back hit the opposite door.

"Oh God," she gibbered. "Who is that? Why is she here?"

"It's alright, Karen," Steve said, reaching out to gently grip his wife's wrist and pull her toward him. She pushed and scrabbled, but eventually stilled and buried her face into Steve's neck. The staff sergeant glanced at Quinn, a slow tear leaking from the corner of one eye.

Quinn turned when Raife lumbered across the street and joined them.

"What did you tell the neighbours?" Quinn asked.

"That we killed an animal in the Mayor's back yard," he said.

"You think that's going to hold water?"

The big man shrugged. "It will as long as they don't decide to go and have a look."

Gemma snorted. "Yes, I think we might have some trouble explaining the smouldering creature lying on the back lawn."

"What now?" Raife asked.

Quinn opened his mouth to answer when his phone began to vibrate on the dash of the pickup. He hoisted himself into the passenger seat and grabbed his phone. A sense of relief flooded through him as he looked at the screen and saw the picture of Dave wrestling a goat into the back of his patrol car that was the other man's caller ID.

"It's Dave," he said, swiping his thumb across the screen and pressed the speaker button. "Hey, where are you?"

"Where am I?" Dave's voice scratched through the phone. "Where the fuck have you guys been? I've been trying to call you for the last forty minutes."

There was something in Dave's voice that set Quinn's teeth on edge and his heart picked up its pace. "Are you guys okay?"

"Well, we're not dead," Dave said.

"Did you find Abby?" Raife asked, leaning towards the phone.

"We did," Dave said. "But we lost her."

"What do you mean you lost her?" Quinn heart dropped a gear before picking up a little more speed.

"The same time we found her, that black thing we fought at the campground found us." There was a pause of dead air long enough that Quinn feared the call had been dropped.

"Dave?" he said into the phone.

"Yeah, I'm here," Dave said. "It took her, Quinn. That thing has Abby."

Quinn pressed the palm of his hand against the side of his head and gritted his teeth. For every step they took forward, it seemed someone loaded them into a cannon and fired them in the opposite direction.

"Do you know where it took her?" Gemma asked, reaching to grip Quinn's wrist.

"I have no idea," Dave said.

Quinn could hear the frustration in his voice.

"Can you still fight?" Raife asked.

"Of course," Dave said. "Both Gerritt and I are beat to shit, but we're good to go."

"Okay," Raife said. "Meet us at the detachment. We'll regroup there and figure out what we're going to do."

"Copy," Dave said. The line went dead.

Staring at the screen for a long moment, Quinn eventually punched the button on the side that turned the screen off and tossed his phone back on the dash with a disgusted snarl. "This thing has outdone us at every turn. Just when I think we've got it cornered, he gets another step ahead of us."

"We're not done yet," Raife rumbled, smoothing his moustache.

"No, we're not," Gemma said. "Your inspector said the creature wanted Abby to help him birth his child."

Bobby was still tenderly touching Emily Drummond's hair. "But now we have his pregnant wife."

"So as long as we have her," Quinn nodded toward the sleeping woman. "Abby is safe."

"Exactly," Gemma said.

"Now we just need to figure out where the thing is keeping Abby and get her back," Quinn said, finishing the thought he knew everyone shared.

"That's the sixty-four-thousand-dollar question, isn't it," Raife said.

"We can think about it on the way to the detachment," Quinn said. "I want to meet up with Dave and Gerritt and see what we can come up with together."

Raife nodded and turned to walk around the front of the truck, heading for the driver's seat, while Gemma and Bobby gently manoeuvred into the back seat, positioning the sleeping form of Emily Drummond across their laps.

As Raife climbed into the driver's seat, Quinn's phone buzzed on the dash again. He picked it up and saw Carrie's smiling face in the caller ID. He thought about ignoring it, but decided it would do him good to hear her voice and let her know he was still alive.

He swiped his thumb across the screen and held the phone to his ear. "Hi," he said, in the tone he reserved only for her.

A faint crackling responded. Not static, Quinn thought. More like the sound of a big fire.

"Carrie?" Quinn said.

For a long moment all he heard was crackling. Then a harsh voice said a single word. "No."

A terrible cold flowed out from Quinn's heart and into his limbs. His hands began to shake so hard he almost dropped the phone.

Raife's hand was on the key in the ignition, but he stopped as he glanced at Quinn's face. "Are you all right, son?"

"Who is this?" Quinn said into the phone. He already knew who it was.

"You have my family," the voice said. "And I have yours."

An image of Carrie and Shawn, in the hands of the ebony demon, flashed across Quinn's vision, and he squeezed his eyes shut. He took a deep breath and tried to keep his voice steady. "And what do you want to do about that?"

"You will bring mine to me," the voice said slowly, as though it were having trouble speaking the words. "At the silver mine. Or your family dies."

Quinn heard a crunching noise and the line went dead. He pulled the phone away from his face and stared down at the screen, at Carrie's smiling face, until the screen timed out and the phone went black.

"Quinn," Raife said, his hand still gripping the key. "For Christ's sake, who was that?"

"It was him," Quinn said, still looking at the phone.

"Him, who?"

"It was the creature," Gemma said, leaning forward, between the front seats, her elbows leaning on the legs of Emily Drummond. "Wasn't it?"

Quinn nodded, looking up from his phone, glancing at Gemma and then Raife. "Yeah. And he's got Carrie and Shawn."

"The silver mine?" Raife growled, as he drove the big Dodge pickup, the engine screaming through the dark streets of Resolution. "Are you sure?"

"That's what he, or *it*, said," Quinn told him as he stared through the windshield. He perched on the front edge of the passenger seat, as though it might make the big vehicle go faster than its already breakneck speed.

"It makes perfect sense," Gemma said. She had the history book balanced on Emily's legs and used the flashlight on Steve Faulk's cell phone to look through the last chapter. "There have certainly been enough significant events to suggest there is something special about the place. It is near water; there have been fortunes found and lost; dozens of lives snuffed out, through both disaster and violence."

"I should have known that," Raife growled at the steering wheel.

"As should have I." Gemma flipped pages in the book. "I don't know why I didn't see it."

"Why is it important that the mine is near water?" Quinn asked.

Gemma closed the book, keeping her place with a finger, and handed Steve Faulk's phone back to him.

"Water is the source of all life. Without it, nothing could survive, and that deep connection with all living things gives it a certain power.”

“Old Magic,” Bobby said.

“Indeed,” Gemma said. “There are places of the deep magic in the high desert, but if you’re looking for a place of power, water is always a safe bet.”

“So, the silver mine is the place the boogeyman needs to try and deliver whatever it planted into her?” Raife glanced over his shoulder and tilted his head toward the still unconscious Emily.

Quinn looked at Gemma, who stared down at the closed book in her hands, her wavy grey hair falling about her face in a cascade. She sat silent for several long moments. Eventually Quinn reached back and touched the back of one slender hand.

“Gemma?” Quinn asked

She took in a deep breath, audible even over the roaring of the truck’s engine, and turned her face up to meet Quinn’s gaze.

“Yes,” she said. “It is the place the creature needs. It is also the place we need to deliver my child from the abyss she was cast into.”

He gripped Gemma’s hand and met her eyes. “We’re going to get her back.”

She gave him back the same steady look and nodded once.

Quinn turned and faced forward again. “We’re going to get Autumn back just as soon as I kill this fucking demon and throw it into the mine.”

Raife took a hard right, the big tires of the truck chirping on the asphalt, and pulled into the rear parking lot of Resolution detachment. In front of them, in the inspector’s parking spot, was Sandy’s Subaru. Sandy got out of the driver’s seat, while another figure climbed slowly from the passenger side.

“Sweet merciful Christ,” Raife said. “Is that the inspector?”

“I think it is,” Quinn said, putting out a hand to keep from hitting the dash, as Raife brought the truck to a sudden stop. He started to open the door, but stopped as Dave’s truck screeched in beside them, and Dave jumped out.

"The gang's all here," Bobby said from the back seat, struggling out from under Emily Drummond as he opened his own door and slid to the ground.

Opening the passenger door, Quinn hopped out of the truck, wincing as his feet hit the ground. He felt like he hadn't slept in a month and had been beaten with a piece of rebar during all those sleepless nights. When he looked at Dave's face, it was clear his friend felt no better.

"You whole?" Dave asked, placing a hand on Quinn's shoulder.

"Yeah." Quinn gave Dave's arm a hard squeeze. "We're not done yet."

"Good, 'cause—holy fuck who is that?" Dave's eyes went wide as he looked over Quinn's shoulder. Quinn turned and saw the still form of Emily Drummond lying on the back seat of Steve Faulk's truck.

Sandy stopped beside Dave, her arm looped under the elbow of Inspector Green. Raife came around the front of the truck and gave Gerritt a hearty slap on the back, while Bobby reached back into the truck and helped Gemma down. Steve Faulk got out at the opposite side and walked around the back of the truck, while Karen stayed in her seat and stared at them all as though they'd grown second heads.

"Quinn," Inspector Green said, his face a pale mask, as he leaned heavily on Sandy. "Could you please explain to me why you're driving around in Steve's truck with a pregnant woman in the back seat?"

As succinctly as he could, Quinn related everything that had happened since leaving the Inspector's house. Dave filled in the gap with the confrontation in the graveyard, and they all stood in a heavy silence broken only by the crackling of dry leaves as they were blown across the asphalt surface of the parking lot by a low wind.

"So that thing has Carrie and Shawn," Dave said.

"And my Abby," the Inspector added.

Another silence fell, stretching on for long moments, until Sandy spoke up in a clear voice. "What do you want to do,

Quinn?"

He had been staring at the wet patch of parking lot at the centre of the circle they'd formed. He looked up slowly. "It isn't up to me."

That was met with more silence, but it did not last long.

"You know that isn't true, son," Raife said.

Gritting his teeth, Quinn shut his eyes tight and pressed the heels of his hands against them. The resolve he felt settle in him when he'd talked to the thing that took Carrie and Shawn had deserted him. These people who gathered about him now were the closest thing to family he had ever known. They looked to him for answers, but he didn't have any to give. He wanted to shout at them, tell them to look elsewhere, to find someone else to lead them. He wished desperately that some-one would tell him what to do. He wished he were not so afraid.

"I'm not what you think I am," he said, softly. When no one responded he took his hands from his eyes and looked around him, at the expectant faces. "I know you think I do, but I have no idea what I'm doing. And I'm afraid..."

"You mustn't be ashamed of your fear, Quinn," Inspector Green said. "We're all afraid."

Gemma gripped his arm in both her hands and looked up into his face. "You are neither alone in your fear, or what is to come."

"No," Raife rumbled. "You are not."

"We're with you, whatever happens," Dave said.

Gerritt looked like he wanted to say something, but settled on a smile and gave Quinn a jaunty thumb's up.

That made Quinn chuckle, despite himself, and he sucked in a deep breath and let it out in an audible whoosh. He looked at each face again, but this time, instead of seeing expectation, he saw trust, faith and love. They had not changed, he realised. Those things were always there, he just had to recognise them for what they were.

"Okay," he said, after a long moment. "Has anyone ever been to the mine?"

Dave nodded. "Yeah, there is a big clearing up there where we used to have to chase the kids away so they didn't get drunk and fall off the cliff face and into the inlet."

"Used to?" Quinn asked. "I've been here almost three years and I've never been up there."

Sandy shrugged. "When I first started here, we'd be up there a few times over the summer. But now I can't remember the last time we got a call there." She looked at Dave. "In fact, I can't remember the last time I even heard someone mention the mine."

Raife made a growling sound down in his throat. "Yeah, that's weirding me out."

Quinn glanced at Gemma, and then at Inspector Green. "How big a deal is the silver mine to this town?"

The inspector shrugged, wincing as he did so. "As big a deal as the port, I would say."

"The silver mine created this town," said Steve Faulk. He had been serving in Resolution Cove longer than anyone else. "There was nothing here except a camp for people who were on their way further up the coast. When silver was discovered, the town boomed. After that, the port was built, the first sawmills sprouted up, and Resolution became a dot on the map."

"Then why doesn't anyone remember the mine?" Gerritt asked, his mouth quirked up.

"Gemma?" Quinn asked. "Any ideas?"

The grey-haired woman released Quinn's arm and ran both her hands through her wavy hair. "I can't say for sure. Sometimes these old places of power have ways of concealing themselves, for good or ill." She pursed her lips in thought. "Whatever the reason, there is some force at play that did not want the mine to be disturbed."

"Something is going to wind up disappointed," Bobby said.

"You're goddamned right," Raife said. He nodded at Quinn. "All right, son. What do you think?"

Quinn sucked in a deep breath and let it out slowly, forcing his fear to one side. "How many ways are there to get to the mine?"

"Only one," Dave said. "There is a decent bush-road that leads there off the main forest service road, but that's the only way. It's steep, and the mine is basically bored into the cliff face."

"The only other way would be up the rocks from the water," Sandy said."Or down the summit from the top of the mountain."

Folding his arms, Quinn considered this. Stealth it appeared was not an option. There would be no element of surprise, no surreptitious approach to this place. Of all things he felt while he considered a plan of action, relief was foremost among them. There would be no complicated plan, no grand decisions to be made. The only thing they—he—could do was summon their courage and be ready for the fight that was coming.

"All right," he said, looking at each of his friends in turn. "Here is what we're going to do."

The creature looked down at the huddling form of the woman and the child and had a momentary pang of...guilt, maybe? Looking at the boy child made him think of his own son, and he felt a little sorry for involving the boy. His sorrow triggered that old rage in him and pushed all the other feelings aside. The boy's suffering did not matter when compared with the life of his own child.

Besides, once his son was born, Quinn Sullivan's adopted child would die anyway.

The woman, Carrie, sat with her back against the rock of the cliff face, her son beneath one arm and the girl-child, Abby, beneath the other. The woman did not look up at him, would not meet his eye, but cradled the children against her as though she might be able to protect them. He thought about tying them all up, but did not think any of them had the stomach to try and run. And where did they think they would go?

He had put out the call, once again, summoning any of his kind to the mine. Some had come, but his count came up short of what he'd hoped for. The Guardian had proven much more capable than originally believed, but it would be enough to stop the insufferable man and reclaim Emily.

He turned his back on the cringing humans and faced the massive fire that burned in the middle of the clearing. He summoned his will, what little he had left after all the power he'd expelled since stilling his child in his wife's belly so they both did not perish, and cast out his will to find anything nearby that could help him. He made it clear he sought aid, and what was at stake. He felt nothing, besides those who were already on their way. He felt his shoulders sag in disappointment. He did not want to give the Guardian and his friends even the slightest chance. He wanted to use their bones to raze the ground before they even knew they were in a fight. And he didn't think he had quite enough strength to do that—yet.

He was ready to give up, when he felt something, just the barest tickle, at the edge of his mind. Something had reached back towards him, sluggishly, tired, slow to move. He turned from the fire and stared into the gaping maw of the old mine. There, in the dark, down in the very depths of the place, was something he had not noticed before, and it answered his call.

He stalked towards the mine's opening. Exhausted, he dug deep into the reserves of his strength and pulled power from the roaring fire, snatching pieces of will from the unquiet dead who infested this place. He gathered everything he could, focused on that faint call, and reached out to it.

Deep in the bowels of the mountain, in dark places where no light had ever shone, something reached back.

The power of the thing hit him with staggering force, making his knees weak. Whatever spoke to him was ancient, and dark. It had existed in this place long before men ever thought to chisel into the mountain. It had been there when no white man had thought to build a boat capable of crossing the sea, and before the indigenous tribes painted figures on the rock warning others to stay away. The thing in the mine had drunk its fill from the suffering of the men who had come to this place, and had been content to remain hidden. How he had not sensed it before was a mystery, but he imagined a thing of this power would only be known when it chose to be.

Whatever its reasons, it made itself known to him now. From the mouth of the mine, from deep in the rock, it issued a long, slow rumble.

The woman and the children she cradled shrunk away from the mine's opening, pressing themselves back into the rock. As the presence of the thing in the mine grew closer, the demon grew stronger. He glanced at the woman, clenched his fists, looked into the black sky, and laughed.

CHAPTER 23

An autumn storm brewed over the starless night of Resolution Cove. The October wind howled through the streets, snatching at the few people who dared to be out of doors, threatening to throw them to the damp ground, buffeting them with half-rotten leaves. Anyone who snuck a look at the sky through parted curtains snatched their hands back as if they had been burned and looked for lights to turn on; anything to try and push back the dark.

Something moved in the depths of that black night. Every soul in Resolution Cove felt it coming for them.

Inside the Welcome Beaver, Cecil Brown tried to bring himself around to his nightly ritual of staring at himself in the mirror in his mouldy little office, while puffing himself up and telling himself that he was the baddest mother-fucker to walk the earth. After assholes like Dave McLeod and Quinn Sullivan came into his place and threw their weight around, he always needed a good look in the mirror to remind himself how lucky those pigs were that he didn't kick the shit out of them and leave them in the alley out back.

Tonight was different. Every time he looked in the mirror, all he saw was his gut sticking over his pants, telling him he wasn't in as good a shape as he thought. The light kept catching the wrinkles around his eyes, making them look deeper, reminding him he probably had more years behind than ahead. He felt like the spider tattoo on his forehead that he used to think made him look like a badass, now made him look like an idiot who tried too hard to pretend he was something he wasn't. He kept seeing his shitty little office behind his reflection, reminding him that he barely paid the mortgage on a dump that was falling down around his ears.

Instead of the mirror making him feel better, it made him feel like all the hope that had ever been his had been balled up and flushed down the drain.

On the other side of the business district, where you didn't find anyone sleeping in alleys at night, Sam Dawson, Carrie's uncle, was closing his bar. It had been a slow night. It didn't take much to do the final clean-up, so he'd sent the kid he'd hired to help him home. When he retired, after more than thirty years as a Mountie, he'd sunk everything he'd had into this place, and it had been a winning bet.

The bar made money—more than he'd made as a copper—and the people who came through his doors greeted him with smiles, and he treated them like his dearest friends. Everything about the place made his heart glad and never a moment of regret.

Except tonight.

He'd paid a king's ransom for the hand-made brass rail around the edge of the bar. It always made him smile when he polished it to a gleam. But tonight, every reflection in the golden surface was another memory he'd never quite been able to banish.

He remembered all the bad days on the Force: the shattered bodies in the car wrecks, the dead who were bereft of all semblance of dignity, the dirty faces of children who had been broken beyond all repair. He thought of every file he didn't solve, of every shitty thing he'd said to someone that didn't need to be said, every time he lost his temper and moved with a heavy hand. Every image was a bad memory, and it made him feel like a hollowed out, empty old fart that no one remembered.

He looked around for a human face, for something to bring him comfort, but saw nothing except regret. His bar rag slipped from nerveless fingers, and he sat heavily at one of the tables, put his face in his hands, and let the sobs take him.

In Resolution Hospital, Doctor Evelyn Stovern sat on a crate of paper towel rolls in the janitor's store room and wrapped her arms around herself. This hospital had been her life since the time she finished her residency and won a permanent position on the staff. She had let relationships go, never thought to have a family of her own, because she loved this place so much. Every moment of every day, every patient she saw, and every person she helped filled her to bursting. She loved her life.

But tonight was different.

Tonight she felt as empty as a cracked teapot.

The hospital was eerily quiet. The emergency room remained empty for the first time she could remember since she first started working here. As she had paced the halls, checking on patients that probably didn't need to be checked on, she had seen a failure in every shadowed corner. One of the first things she remembered learning from her old Chief of Medicine was that you can't save everyone. She had tried to prove that crusty old bastard wrong every day of her career, but even she couldn't battle death and win every time.

Everywhere she looked, she saw reflections of patients she had lost. As she walked past the ill-equipped trauma room, she remembered the Australian tourist who had fallen off the top of Resolution Falls, hitting every pointy outcropping in the eighty-foot drop. The kid had been barely alive when they wheeled him in. No team of surgeons on the planet could have saved him, but she tried. He lived for twelve hours after she was done working on him, but he was too broken and his heart finally gave out. Nothing more could have been done, but she still saw him glaring at her, her failure shining in his eyes, every time she closed her own.

Every room she passed held another failure, another moment where she should have done better. They pressed in on her until she had found herself fleeing from ghosts that no one else would ever be able to see. She'd stacked everything she could find up against the door and turned her pager off.

She could not face the night.

With the rumbling from the mine came darkness. It crept down the mountain, leaving a taint on everything it touched. All over Resolution Cove, small lights flickered out.

CHAPTER 24

Y ou know your plan is bullshit, don't you?" Raife asked as he guided the unmarked Chevy Tahoe, normally reserved for detachment's traffic section, up a narrow forest service road towards the mine.

Before they left the detachment, Inspector Green had insisted they leave the personal vehicles behind and take 'detachment resources.' If a detachment vehicle gets thrown off a cliff and into the inlet, he could reach into the detachment budget to replace it; not so with Steve Faulk's truck or Sandy's brand-new Subaru that she treated like her first-born child.

"I second that," Dave said from the back seat, as he pushed shells into a detachment shotgun with sharp *snick*. "I'm a little confused about the part where we just drive into the clearing and get it on with the boogey-man."

Quinn turned in the seat to look back at him. The slender man met his gaze evenly as he jacked the action of the shotgun and put a final round into the tube. Beside him, Gerritt looked out the passenger side window, saying nothing for once, his leg bouncing up and down.

"You got something better in mind?" Quinn asked, turning his gaze on the side of Raife's bald head. "Either of you?"

Raife drove in silence for several moments, adjusting the wheel as the Tahoe shuddered over a patch of wash-board road.

"No," he said, finally.

Quinn turned back to Dave who shrugged and tried to look busy by fiddling with the end-cap on the shotgun's magazine tube.

"Well, when you come up with something, I'll be all ears."

The big man harrumphed loudly, his moustache whiffling in his own breeze.

Quinn had thought about the approach from every angle he could think of, even going so far as pulling out the old water-stained provincial forest service maps from the detachment storeroom. There was no point of access other than the main road into the mine site. The only other way was for someone to either rappel down from the summit, or climb up from the water. The only one among them who had any climbing experience was Sandy, and there was no time for her to make the climb or set the rig needed to rappel down. They also had no idea what else would be in the woods waiting for them.

The only way, they'd all agreed, was to drive up to the mine and be ready for a fight.

Quinn pulled the Sig Sauer from the shoulder holster, checked the magazine and the chamber, and then did the same with the Smith & Wesson on his hip. Finally, he reached between his legs and lifted the coach gun, checking to make sure there were shells in the barrels. All the guns remained locked and loaded, exactly as they had been when they'd started the drive up the mountain twenty minutes ago. He shook his head at his fidgeting. When it came time for this fight, those   wouldn't be the weapons he'd reach for anyway.

He twisted in his seat again to look at the car behind them, an innocuous Toyota Venza used by the Serious Crime team. The three members on the team who used the car liked to pretend the vehicle made them 'covert', but every shit-rat in town knew it was a cop car before they'd put the first hundred kilometres on it. The vehicle, driven by Sandy, held the inspector, Gemma and Bobby, and the still unconscious Emily Drummond. There had been a thunderous argument between Raife and the Inspector about the older man's inclusion in this little adventure. Everyone assembled had tried to convince him to stay behind, but Donald Green would not have it, saying that wherever Abby was, he would be, too.

There had been equal agreement that Steve Faulk should stay behind, along with Karen, who fluctuated between hysterical and catatonic. Steve gave no objection to his exclusion. He would put Karen down on the cot in the first aid room and do his best to run interference should anyone ask why the others had taken a bunch of guns and ammo and lit off in two detachment vehicles.

With every turn up the narrow road, it seemed to Quinn that the trees pressed in closer and the headlights grew dimmer. A heaviness descended on his chest, like he was being squeezed by an iron band.

"You feel that?" he asked no one in particular.

"Yeah," Dave said from the back seat. Raife nodded. Gerritt still said nothing, but he rubbed at his chest.

At the small of his back, Quinn felt Donnel's dagger begin to get warm.

"We're almost there," he said. "Pull over."

Without question, Raife slowed and pulled the truck over the side of the road, turning off the headlights and slipping the vehicle into park. In the passenger side mirror, Quinn saw Sandy do the same with the Toyota.

Taking a deep breath, Quinn opened the passenger door and exited the truck. He looked back, over the top of Dave's open door, to see the occupants of the other vehicle doing the same. Sandy had a flashlight in her hand and showed the way for Gemma, who had Bobby's axe clutched to her chest. Bobby cradled Emily Drummond in his thick arms. Behind him, walking slowly and with great care, Donald Green limped up the mild incline of the road.

"Is this the place?" Gemma asked, as they all came together in the space between the two vehicles. There was no other sound except the irregular ticking of the cooling engines and the wind of the coming storm blowing through the tops of the trees.

"Yeah." Raife pulled the magazine from the SKS rifle and held it down in the beam of Sandy's flashlight to check it. "The road opens up in about a hundred metres into a big open space where the old mining camp was."

"And that is where they will be?" Bobby asked, hefting Emily a little higher against his chest.

"That's where they'll be," Quinn said, looking over his shoulder and up the road. At his back, the dagger was almost humming, along with the brass knuckles in his front pocket.

He turned back to face his friends and saw all of them watching him intently. He still balked at the idea that he should be identified as a leader of these people, but they were all looking to him to get started.

The plan was very simple. There was no space for complexity because they had no idea what they would encounter when they reached the clearing. Quinn would walk up the centre of the road while Bobby followed behind, carrying Emily. Raife and Sandy would do whatever they could to get to Carrie, Shawn and Abby. Dave and Gerritt would stick by Gemma and do their best to protect her while they all helped to fight whatever else was in the clearing, beside the demon. Once Raife and Sandy had Carrie and the children, Quinn would kill Jay Drummond.

So long as Drummond didn't kill him first.

Quinn took in a deep breath, trying to think of something to say that wouldn't show his friends how terrified he was, when Gemma held out Bobby's axe.

"You should take this," she said.

He looked down at it for several moments, not responding. "I have weapons," he said finally. "Bobby will need it."

"I'm a little busy," the thick man said, lifting the pregnant woman a little for emphasis.

"Do you remember what happened when you used the axe before?" Gemma asked.

Quinn shrugged. "Not really. I mean, Raife and Bobby told me what happened, but I don't know what I did."

"You summoned your real power, Quinn," Gemma said,

shifting closer to him. "You revealed what lay inside you all along, and you can do it again." She pressed the axe to his chest. "I hate to put it like this, but if you don't do it, then I think we are all going to die."

He sighed, heavily, knowing her words for the truth. What he had been before, the way he had fought the other demons, would not be enough for this fight. He needed more. He needed to reach deeper, or none of them were going to make it out of this.

He glanced around, and then passed the coach gun to the Inspector. The older man took it stiffly, and tucked it under his arm.

Quinn gripped the studded haft of the heavy axe and wrung his hands around it. "I am not what you think I am," Quinn said. "I don't know if I can do this."

"I believe in you, Quinn," Donald Green said, his face illuminated by the downward-pointed beam of Sandy's flashlight.

"We all do." Raife laid a hairy-knuckled hand on Quinn's shoulder. All around were murmurs of assent.

"You pulled me out of the dark once, Quinn," Sandy said. "I know you will do it again."

"I've trusted you on every call we've ever been to, and I trust you now," Dave said.

"You're my friend," Gerritt said, his voice steady. "And I love you."

Quinn nodded, pulling in a big breath through his nose to ward off the tears that threatened, both from gratitude for the belief of his friends and fear that he could be leading all of them to their deaths.

"I love you, too. All of you." He looked at Dave. "Even you."

The slender man barked a short laugh, then wrapped an arm around Quinn's neck and planted a loud kiss on his cheek. "Come on, corporal. There is work to be done."

"Heavy work," Raife rumbled.

"All right," Quinn said, turning and facing up road towards the mine. "Let's roll."

The demon paced around the abandoned mine site, raging, seething, feeling power course through his tired limbs. He had thought himself finished, hollowed out by the effort of will that he had expended preparing for his child's arrival. But, now, he felt reborn.

He raced to the edge of the clearing, ripped several thin trees from the earth, and flung them onto the roaring fire. They caught instantly in the heat of the massive conflagration, the sap exploding to send showers of sparks upward to be snatched away by the wind. He howled along with the storm, feeling as though the tempest thrummed along with his heart.

Whatever it was coming up out of the bowels of the earth in response to his call was something that even he, in all his long years, in a hundred generations of man, had never seen. It was ancient, elemental, and it poured power into him. He could feel it coursing through his limbs, setting him alight. He could hear its rumble coming from the mouth of the mine, and he called out a welcome.

He paused in the act of reaching for another tree, revelling in the strength that pulsed in him, when he heard something familiar, just on the edge of his awareness. So faint, so quick that he wasn't sure it was real, until he heard it again, between the rumbles in the earth. The sound of his child's heartbeat.

His family had arrived.

He ripped the tree from the ground and threw it upon the pyre, then stalked to plant himself in directly before the narrow opening in the trees—the only way the Guardian would be able to approach. There would be no subtlety this time. No trickery. He would face this human like he had faced all the Guardians that he had met before; in open battle, in flesh and steel and blood. He would kill this man, reclaim his family, and unleash his child upon the world to make it anew.

It was time for the Guardian to die.

It was time for his child to live.

CHAPTER 25

An orange glow painted the tops of the trees, and Quinn could feel the temperature had climbed a few degrees.

"This is weirding me out, man," Dave said from just behind him.

Quinn heard him click off the safety of the shotgun.

He couldn't quite see the mine, but Quinn thought they only had one more bend in the road until it came into view.

He turned back to face his friends. From his front left pocket, Quinn took the brass knuckles, which glowed mutely in response to the presence of the demon, and handed them to Dave.

"Are you sure?" Dave asked, bouncing the knuckles in his palm. "What if you need them?"

"If we get to a point where I wish I had those instead of this," he lifted the axe. "Then we're in trouble deep enough we're not going to get out." He reached to the small of his back and unclipped the custom sheath he'd had made for Donnel's dagger. A faint glow emanated from the where the sheath and the cross guard met. He held the dagger out to Raife.

The big man shook his head. "No, boy, that weapon is yours. I've never had it in my hand, and I don't want it now."

"I'll have my hands full," Quinn said. "And this might give you a fighting chance if I go down."

"You ain't going down," Raife growled.

Quinn shook his head and lifted the dagger a little higher. "Please, Raife. Just hang on to it for me until this is done."

The big man huffed, his moustache bristling, and then snatched the dagger from Quinn's hand. "I'm only hanging on to it until we're done. Then I'll be giving it back."

"Deal," Quinn said.

Quinn looked around. "I think we should split up here." He lifted his chin towards the trees on the right side of the road. "Raife, Sandy."

The big man nodded and lumbered into the trees, while Sandy slipped quietly behind him. Quinn glanced over at Dave and Gerritt, who both nodded. Gerritt held out an arm to Gemma, who reached to take it, then stopped and turned. She grabbed Bobby's thick face roughly in her two hands, leaned over Emily Drummond, and kissed him hard.

"I better see you when this is done," she said and kissed him again. "I'm not done with you, yet."

"Nor I you, my love," he said, pressing his forehead against hers.

Gemma turned away again, letting her fingers trace along Bobby's jaw, as she reached for Gerritt's arm with her other hand. She let him lead her into the trees on the other side of the road.

Quinn looked at Bobby, who still cradled the unresponsive form of Emily Drummond as easily as though she were a baby. The only sign the man gave that he was under any exertion was a thin sheen of sweat that covered the top of his bald head and trickled into his fringe.

"Are you good?" Quinn asked.

The thick man tipped him a wink. "Do not worry over me, Quinn. Lead on, and let's be done."

Over Bobby's shoulder, Quinn saw Inspector Green, leaning heavily on a thick branch as tall as himself that Raife had cut for him once it became apparent that he wasn't going to be able to walk more than a couple hundred feet on his own. His breath came in ragged gasps, even though they stood still, and his face had a bloodless hue in the orange glow that filtered in tendrils through the trees. Despite his ragged appearance, his eyes were clear and set with determination.

Quinn did not think to ask the inspector if he could continue. He knew what the answer would be. He gave the older man a nod. Donald Green set his mouth in a hard line and nodded back.

Pulling in another big breath, Quinn turned and walked towards the orange glow. Within a hundred paces, they rounded a corner. Quinn saw a break in the trees where the road spilled into the site of the abandoned mine. Two dozen paces more and they stood at the threshold of the clearing. In that clearing, Quinn got a little glimpse of what hell must look like.

A roaring fire, as tall as a three-storey building, dominated the centre of the clearing, the heat so intense that Quinn had to resist the urge to throw an arm across his face. In front of the fire, the ebony skinned demon stood with its arms crossed. Behind it, showing as brief silhouettes in the fire, the forms of lesser demons flitted in and out of view. Beside the intense heat, Quinn could feel something heavy and oppressive. It reminded him of the first time he approached Joe Robowski's house in the South End where he'd battled the hiding demon. Something about this mine stunk of the dark, and it made him shiver despite the blasting heat of the fire.

The ebony demon looked bigger than it had been the last time he'd faced it, taller, thicker about the chest and shoulders. Whatever it was about this place that curled an icy hand around Quinn's heart, made the demon stronger, feeding it, filling it up.

The demon glared at him, its black eyes showing red around the edges, even in the light of the fire. Quinn spread his feet, gripped the axe in front of him and stilled his breath, pulling it into his belly, and did his best to glare back.

"Give me my family," the demon bellowed, its voice a set of rusty chains being thrown into an aluminum garbage can.

Quinn tried to suppress the urge to look back, but failed,

and glanced over his shoulder at Bobby. What he saw did not inspire confidence. Behind them, flanking them, stood two lesser demons. They both looked like mutilated primates, with hairy, elongated limbs that ended in curving talons instead of hands. Bobby followed Quinn's gaze, and the bald man swallowed.

"Quinn," Bobby's voice was barely audible over the roar of the fire.

"Hold fast," Quinn said to him, even though he battled his own urge to run.

He glanced around the clearing, searching for any sign of Raife or Sandy, but he couldn't see them. The cliff face with the mine opening was to his right and the open air over the inlet to the left and ahead of him. The trees on the right butted against the rock face, extending almost to the opening of the mine. All around were old, collapsed buildings, made up of greyed-out timbers. Plenty of places for an ogre like Raife to hide. Quinn needed to stall until Raife and Sandy had Carrie and Shawn in hand before he brought the fight to the creature. Frantically, he tried to think of something to say to distract the demon.

"You get your family when I get mine," Quinn tried to shout, but it came out halting, nearly a stammer.

"Now!" the demon screeched. "Or your boy dies." He beckoned over his shoulder.

Quinn heard a woman's voice, Carrie's voice, followed by a yelp.

"Shawn?" Quinn looked around searching for the source of the sound, but the crackle from the fire and the open space over the water threw him off.

Coming around the right side of the fire, closest to the mine's mouth, he saw a hunched over shape dragging a writhing form. He lifted Bobby's axe, lunging forward, when the blast of a shotgun and flash of white light stopped him and everyone else in the clearing.

Raife charged into view, the SKS rifle tucked under one arm and Donnel's glowing dagger his left hand. A dark shape scuttled towards him. Raife turned, firing the rifle from his hip—a manoeuvre that might break the wrist of other men, but that Raife pulled off with ease.

Behind Raife, Sandy appeared with Quinn's shotgun tucked into her shoulder. She sighted down the barrel at the same demon that Raife had shot, and let loose a blast. She dropped the shotgun, letting the sling across her chest support the long weapon and drew her pistol. She brought it up in the practiced motion, sighted carefully for the space of a heartbeat at the demon dragging Shawn, and squeezed the trigger. The pistol barked and the creature holding Shawn howled as its head snapped back, black blood flying upward in an arc.

The creature didn't fall, but it released its hold on Shawn's arm. Sandy darted forward to grab the boy and drag him towards the cover of the broken down out-buildings.

Raife stepped in between the two demons and Sandy's retreating form, firing the rifle. The lesser demons shrank back from the light of the dagger. Raife fired at them until his gun went dry. He turned to lumber after Sandy.

"Treachery!" the creature howled. "Guardian, you come without honour, and for that you will pay."

Quinn started to rush towards the ebony demon, when it turned towards the mouth of the mine, and gave a high, screeching call. Inside the mine, a massive shape shifted. Quinn heard a rumbling grind, as though two huge pieces of stone ground together. He saw what a nightmare looked like in the waking world.

The ebony creature stamped its clawed feet into the earth and revelled in the strength he had found in the presence from the depths of the mine. He felt all the exhaustion, the toll of the effort, sloughing away. Full to bursting of his old strength, he felt made anew. All the trepidation he'd felt in confronting the Guardian disappeared, replaced with a hunger for the man's blood.

He saw a shape come into the light at the entrance to the

road; Quinn Sullivan, holding an axe that contained nothing but the barest hint of magic. He snorted dismissively at the man who looked no more formidable than his woman had been. The shape behind the Guardian, though, caught his attention. A short, bald man, with Emily cradled in his thick arms.

Emily still slept, gripped in a shell made by the demon's magic. He could hear her heartbeat, slow and steady. Relief flooded him until he strained his senses, sifting through the noise, to get some hint of his unborn son. Panic sent a hot bloom through his chest as he heard nothing, but then, just at the edges of his ability, he heard another, smaller heartbeat, weak and irregular, barely alive.

There was no more time. He had to get the baby out now.

"Give me my family," he screamed at Sullivan. The pitiful excuse for a Guardian actually quailed and looked back at his companion. They spoke briefly, probably consoling each other in their pending deaths. Then Sullivan turned back to face him.

"You get your family when I get mine," the Guardian said.

The demon snorted, almost laughing at Sullivan's pale idea that he had any control over this situation, any authority to call on. He knew that the Guardian would not harm Emily. The man lacked the conviction to harm someone he viewed as innocent, and that was why he was doomed to lose.

The demon beckoned to one of the lesser creatures he had set to guard the woman and the children, reached out to it mentally, and ordered it to bring Sullivan's brat forward. There was a squawk from the woman, but the creature approached a few moments later, dragging the boy by his skinny arm.

Sullivan took a step forward.

The demon grinned as he stepped to meet the Guardian.

Gunfire popped from the cluster of sunken buildings near the mine entrance.

The demon turned and squinted as he saw a white flash. The huge man, Raife, ran from behind some of the mine's detritus, holding the old dagger in one hand and a rifle in the other. The man started shooting and was joined by the woman that worked with Sullivan. Before the demon could react, the woman dragged the boy away and Raife was shooting again.

The utter contempt that the ebony creature had felt for Sullivan since the man appeared in Resolution burned away in a hot flash of complete hatred. The man had thought to trick him, to bring that pack of fools to try and take what was his.

"Treachery," he screamed, and felt a surge of hatred so strong it brought a sour taste to his mouth.

The demon faced the mine's opening and poured all of his fury and desperation into a call. He summoned the presence from the mine, begged it to aid him, and called it forth into battle. As the creature came into view, he knew that all the darkness that lived in this land had answered his blackest prayers.

CHAPTER 26

There was only one word that Quinn's reeling mind could seize on to describe the horror that stalked from the mouth of the mine. Dragon.

The creature was the size of a small bus and standing as high at the shoulder as Raife could reach while standing on his tip-toes. It appeared as thick as a one of the ancient cedars they'd all passed while coming up the mountain. Covered in dull, stony scales with patches of mottled hair, its reptilian head as wide across as the grille of a Buick, with a huge mouth filled with black pointed teeth. The massive head swivelled back and forth. Two glowing deep red eyes, as big around as dinner plates, settled on Quinn. One of its forelegs, shaped like a dog's, with long, sharp claws, scraped across the gravel and stone of the ground. It spread its feet and roared, black slime flying from its maw.

The sound of the roar struck Quinn like a blow and he staggered, dropping to one knee while his ears rang and his vision swam. Behind him, Bobby fell backwards, crying out as he clutched Emily to his broad chest.

Quinn tried to rise, but the cold evil of the thing, pouring off it in waves, made his legs rubbery and kept him down. The massive fire in the centre of the clearing guttered. An intense cold suffused the very ground, and Quinn could see his breath.

He had seen evil, faced it, nearly died fighting it, but nothing he had ever encountered possessed even a fraction of the power of the creature in front of him. It was ancient and awful in a way that Quinn could not even fathom, and it robbed him of any courage he had ever possessed.

He glanced up at the ebony demon and thought the creature might have been laughing, but he couldn't tell through the ringing in his ears.

Without any apparent urgency, the demon strode towards them, confident with the monstrosity at its back. As Quinn saw it coming, he gritted his teeth and fought against the leaden weariness and heaving nausea that overwhelmed him. He tried to rise, raising the axe up over his shoulder. The demon lunged forward, crashing into him, sending him sprawling in the gravel and mountain pine needles. Through the new humming in his head, Quinn heard Bobby let out another cry. He raised himself up enough to see the demon now cradled the unconscious form of Emily Drummond. If the thing had any of the normal appendages on its face, Quinn would have sworn it gave him a contemptuous glare.

With another laugh—this one Quinn could hear—the creature turned and walked towards the mouth of the mine, past the massive body of the thing that had lumbered out of it.

The dragon shifted, putting itself between the ebony demon and Quinn, and lowered its massive snout towards the ground. It pulled in a deep, huffing breath, and made a rumbling sound low in its throat, a sound of pleasure.

It inhaled Quinn's fear. And it liked it.

Quinn rolled onto his stomach and, with an effort that dragged the last of the strength from him, pushed himself onto his knees. Two booted feet appeared at the edge of his vision, and he looked up to see Dave, the detachment shotgun hanging limp in his hand.

"Quinn," Dave said, clutching Quinn's shoulder, his voice very small in the cold air. "What the fuck is that?"

Behind Dave, Gerritt and Gemma came more slowly, the latter still clinging to the arm of the former. As they reached them, Gemma glanced around in the near darkness, the only light provided by the dying coals in the fire.

"Quinn," her voice coming out in a reedy whisper he'd never heard come from her before. "Where is Emily?"

He glanced up at her, then back at the ground in front of him. He didn't even have the strength to look her in the face.

"The thing took her," he managed to mutter, uncaring if anyone could hear him. "I've failed. We're done."

Raife and Sandy appeared out of the murk, from the direction of the road down the mountain, Shawn clinging to Sandy's hand. The Inspector followed. As he watched the creature in the clearing, he seemed to curl in on himself and his limp became more pronounced. Quinn glanced at them out of the corner of his eye, but could bring himself to do no more.

The massive demon lifted its head, still breathing deep, its red eyes pinched to slits as it glared down at them.

Raife stopped beside Quinn, the rifle tucked into his shoulder and pointed at the behemoth before them, but the muzzle jigged up and down so much he wouldn't be able to hit a barn if he was standing inside it.

"Quinn," the big man said, his normal baritone little more than a papery whisper. "I tried to get to Carrie and Abby." He paused and swallowed thickly. "But there were too many of them. There were just...just, too many."

Quinn could see Donnel's dagger in its sheath, clipped to Raife's belt. In presence of such a power creature, the blade should have been blazing with heat and light, but it was still and cold, as if the massive presence before them had sucked all the power from the weapon, as it had from Quinn.

"It's dark, Quinn," Shawn said, as he clung to Sandy's hip. The sound of his small voice in the silence broke Quinn's heart.

In the distance, beyond the beast, came a short cry, made by a female voice. If it was Carrie, or Abby, or Emily Drummond, Quinn didn't know. He was afraid to ask, even of himself.

As he knelt, with his fist pressed in the dirt, Shawn's words ticked at something in his mind, like a gnat buzzing in his ear on a warm summer night. *It's dark.*

The creature from the mine represented everything that was wrong with Resolution Cove: the cold power that suffused the earth and called other creatures of the darkness to the inlet; the sudden anger that burbled up in your neighbour without cause; hate and fury and malfeasance all made into flesh. What they needed to combat it, was a little light. What it would take, was love.

"Put your hands on me," Quinn said, trying to shout, to put some iron in his voice, but all he could manage was a whisper.

"What?" Dave croaked.

"Put your hands on me," Quinn said again. "All of you."

Beside him, Raife reached down and gripped his shoulder. He could feel the quaking in the big man's grip. Dave gripped his other shoulder and leaned on him, heavily. Bobby shuffled forward, still on his knees, and put his hand on his back. Sandy, Gerritt and Shawn all obeyed, surrounding him and putting their hands on him. Gemma came last, standing behind him, and pushed her fingers into the short hair on the top of his head.

Quinn closed his eyes. He tried to remember all those things Autumn had said to him, about seeing with more than his eyes. About knowing the world for what it really was. He reached out, and felt all of his friends, let the love they had for him, and he for them, flow between them, creating a little light in the dark. Then he reached down into himself, into that place inside him that had cracked in the backyard of Jay Drummond's house. He pushed the small spark of love he pulled from his friends into that place and tried to fan it to life.

Nothing, except doubt, shame and more endless dark.

Then something, a small light in his mind's eye, and it gave him hope.

He seized the light and fed it. He thought of all the love and kindness he'd received from the people who surrounded him, and from all the good people who lived in Resolution. The light inside him grew a little brighter.

He summoned up all of his strength, all of who he was, and everything he might ever be, and fed it into the flame.

The creature in front of him represented everything dark, and it was time for Quinn to cast a light.

He gripped Bobby's axe and surged to his feet, a roar tearing from his throat. He realised the axe in his hands glowed bright white, the heat causing the air around him to shimmer.

The haggard look disappeared from Raife's face, and his huge hands were steady. He snapped back the action on the rifle and added his roar to Quinn's. At his belt, Donnel's dagger glowed in its sheath. Dave pulled the glowing brass knuckles from the pocket of his coat and fitted them on his left hand, then gripped the fore-stock of the shotgun, tucking it into his shoulder.

Sandy stepped up beside Raife, and Gerritt stood beside Dave. All around, Quinn heard the click and snap of weapons and looked around to see the fear gone from the faces of his friends, replaced by the same hard-eyed determination he felt. If they were to die tonight, they would do it on their feet, and they would do it together.

He turned and tossed the axe to Bobby, who caught it deftly, and reached to Raife's belt to yank the dagger free. He took whatever was inside him and pushed some into the dagger. The blade, all made up of heat and light, seemed to grow as long as his arm.

The Inspector hobbled forward and shouldered in beside him.

"It's time to finish this, son," Donald Green said.

"You're damned right it is," Quinn said, lifting the dagger above his head.

In front of them, the massive demon lowered its head and hooded its eyes as the brilliance from Quinn's magic played across its face. On either side of it, smaller, red-eyed shapes appeared. With a sudden, agonizing howl, the demon charged.

Surging forward, Quinn howled back.

There was something so reassuring in the presence of the massive creature that dwelt in the bowels of the mine, that the demon could not keep the smile from his face. He walked around it and to the spot in the rocks where he had left the Guardian's woman and the special child. The fire he built had gone cold, but he did not need light to see.

The woman, Carrie, cradled the girl-child in her lap. Her bound hands looped over Abby McRae, as she pressed her face into the top of the child's head and rocked her back and forth. He knelt beside them and the Carrie woman shrank from him, pressing her back into the rock and turning, trying to pull Abby out of his reach.

"I said I would not hurt the child," he growled. It might be a lie, but he was happy to tell it. The child's life depended wholly on what happened with his wife. Any harm that befell Emily would be visited on the woman and the child ten-fold.

He knelt and set Emily on the rough bed of tree-boughs he had made for her. He could feel the will of his child pressing up against the barriers he had set to keep Emily and the baby alive. If he did not get the child out soon, they would both die.

He held out a clawed hand to the Abby child. "Come here," he said, in as soft a tone as he could manage. The child made no response and buried her face beneath the woman's chin. He growled in exasperation and lunged towards them, faster than their eyes would be able to follow, yanked the woman's arms up and snatched the child away. The woman screamed in pain and the child gasped.

He dropped the Abby child to the ground beside Emily and knelt beside them both. "I need you to create a door and help me birth my child." He kept his voice low, soft, imagining how he would talk to Emily. "Can you do that?"

The Abby child made no response, only stared at her bound hands. He kept his anger in check and reached forward with thumb and fore-finger, using his clawed fingertips to slice the old rope that bound the girl.

"Is that better?" his voice still soft.

The child rubbed her wrists but did not as much as look at him.

Any patience that he had ever felt, in his entire existence, fled from him. He lunged towards the Carrie woman, lifting her off the ground by her hair, digging his claws into the soft flesh beneath her chin. The woman screamed, louder this time, and whimpered as he gave a sharp shake.

"Help me or this bitch dies," he snarled.

The Abby child said nothing, but stared at him with eyes that shone white in the dark. With shaking hands, she reached beneath the tattered sweater she wore and drew forth an old bronze medallion attached to a leather cord.

He dropped the woman to the ground and knelt down beside the blonde girl. "If my wife and child survive, so do you and her." He jerked his head towards the Carrie woman, who lay in the fetal position, her hands pressed to her scalp where he had just grabbed her.

He reached down and placed his hand on Emily's forehead and drew back the glamour he had used to still her and the child. Her eyes opened slowly, and she winced in pain.

"Emily?" His voice soft once again.

"Jay?" she croaked. Her eyes opened wide and rolled in the sockets. "Oh, dear God, what's happening? Where are we?" Her hands flew to her distended stomach and she howled in pain.

He pressed his hand down on her chest to hold Emily still as her legs thrashed. He lifted the hem of the shirt she wore and the skin of her stomach bulged alarmingly. He felt his heart slap up against the inside of his chest with a nearly unbearable stab of fear. By all the Dark, he hoped he was not too late.

He gave the Abby girl a shove towards his wife. "Do it now," he snarled.

The child glanced up at him, and he saw fat tears roll down her cheeks.

He worked his mouth a little. "Please," he whispered in a

raspy tone that even he hated. "Please, or they'll die."

The child leaned forward, and one of those fat tears dripped off her chin to patter against the rolling skin of Emily's stomach. The girl placed one hand on Emily's belly, while she gripped the bronze medallion in the other. Within a few seconds, a bright white light appeared from her clenched fingers and from under her palm. The light seared his eyes, made him wince, but he forced himself to keep looking, ignoring the pain. He would gladly suffer much more if it meant that Emily could live.

The light from beneath the girl's hand slowly spread, trickling out from her palm, and following that trickle of light was a growing black space. Inside that space, he saw a small hand. His child's hand.

He smiled and reached toward the black space, when he heard a howl and the ground beneath him rocked violently. The child lost her balance and toppled sideways, the light from her hand disappearing, and the portal above his wife's belly abruptly snapped shut.

"No!" he shrieked.

He stood and turned. Beyond the dully glowing coals of the nearly-dead fire, he saw a bright white light that filled the clearing, setting every stone and tree into stark relief. Gunfire exploded and voices, both human and otherwise, lifted in fury and pain. Shapes darted in and out of the light and white fire burst into the night.

He looked down at Emily who gripped her stomach and kicked her heels into the hard ground. He clenched his clawed fists as indecision gripped him.

"Hold on, my love, I'll be back," he said, dashing into the searing glow of the white light.

The earth rumbled beneath Quinn's boots, as he ran towards the monstrous demon. The thing's reptilian head hung low to the ground, its mouth open to reveal black teeth and a mottled tongue. A black shape appeared at the edge of Quinn's vision, but it staggered and fell as Dave shot it with his shotgun. To his right, he heard the chattering report of Raife's rifle. All about, howls of the creatures and the roar of his friends, but Quinn ignored it as he charged towards the beast.

When he was within a step of the monster, he dove to his left, swinging the elongated dagger with his right hand. The demon's head snapped out, trying to catch him, and the tip of the fiery blade raked across its snout. Quinn rolled and sprang to his feet as the thing scrabbled and turned to pursue him.

Before the demon had its balance, Quinn lunged in and chopped into one of its forelegs, then scored a long gash in its side. He began to think he was doing very well, when the creature twitched its serpentine tail and slapped Quinn's legs from underneath him. He landed badly, his head and shoulders striking the ground first, his breath fleeing him in a rush. The dagger tumbled from his grip, the light of the blade fading to a muted glow.

His ears rang and his vision swam. Quinn tried to get to his feet, his hand groping blindly for the dagger. He felt the thundering crash of the demon's lunge and flipped onto his back in time to see the black maw streaking towards him. He rolled instinctively and felt the fetid wind as the massive jaws snapped shut on the space where his head used to be.

He felt something hard beneath him and scrabbled for it. He found the grip of the dagger and felt the searing heat as it burst to life in his grip. The creature lunged for him again. This time Quinn surged up towards it, throwing himself to the side at the last moment and stabbing down with the fiery knife.

The blade chunked into the bone of the creature's face. It howled in agony and tried to pull away. Desperately, Quinn held onto the blade and was yanked from his feet as the demon shook its head back and forth. Quinn latched both hands onto the dagger as the demon screeched and snapped at him.

Quinn brought all his fear, all his anger, every bit of his love for his friends, gathered it into his centre and pushed it down into the dagger. He felt the heat of it burning through his veins, lighting up every fibre of his body. White fire exploded from the blade, the brilliance of it blinding Quinn. He shut his eyes and continued to shove his will into the weapon. The demon howled, its huge legs spasming, scrabbling at the hard earth. Quinn gave no quarter. He took everything that made him who he was and put it into the power of the weapon, until it felt like something tore inside of him. The creature reared up on its hind legs and then fell backwards. Quinn fell with it and tumbled to the ground, the dagger finally coming free of the massive head.

Quinn lay on his side, looking at the still form of the dragon as it burned with white fire. Around him, the sound of gunfire slowed, and then stopped.

"Quinn?" he heard Raife bellow.

He lifted the hand that didn't grip the dagger and tried to answer, but his voice was little more than a croak. He worked his sandy tongue around the inside of his sour mouth, and opened it to try and call out again, but stopped.

In front of him, silhouetted against the white fire that consumed the massive demon, was a tall, ebony shape.

<h1 style="text-align:center">CHAPTER 27</h1>

A h fuck," Quinn muttered, rolling onto his knees. He lifted the dagger in his right hand and realised it hung cold. He looked down at it to see not a blade, but a melted stub protruding from the hilt.

"That's not good." He dropped the ruined weapon onto the dirt.

"Why won't you bloody die?" howled the demon, its clawed hands outstretched in an imploring gesture.

Quinn remembered his pistol still hung on his hip and he tried to draw it, but the ebony demon streaked forward, smashing into him and knocking the pistol from his hand. Borne backwards in the demon's grip, they both crashed into the mountain face beside the opening of the mine. The demon's hands locked around his throat.

"No more tricks, Guardian," the demon snarled. "No more plans, and no more of your old weapons. I'm going to kill you and erase your memory from the world I will create with my child."

Quinn groped for a weapon. The pistol on his hip was gone, and he could not reach past the demon's thick arm to get to the Sig-Sauer in the shoulder rig. He kicked and gouged, but the demon's grip didn't slacken.

He had a moment to think that it was ridiculous for him to

come so far, only to die like this. As he thought of the distance, he realised that he was no longer the man he was the day before, or even the hour before. He shouldn't be fighting like he was either.

There was not much strength left in him, but he summoned what little there was and brought it to his centre. He reached out with both hands and locked them onto either side of the demon's head. The creature snarled and tried to shake Quinn's hands off, but Quinn held fast.

Quinn focused on his grip, feeding his power to his hands. White fire exploded beneath his palms and the ebony demon howled in pain and surprise. It staggered backwards, releasing his hold on Quinn.

Lunging forward, Quinn attacked the creature with all the savagery he could muster. The demon put its hands up, but Quinn's fists, wreathed in white fire, streaked forward, smashing through the creature's feeble defence. The demon fell, scrabbled backwards, came unsteadily to its feet, and Quinn struck it again.

This time the demon didn't try and rise, but rolled onto its hands and knees and crawled away into the darkness, towards where Quinn heard Carrie's scream.

He started after it, when he heard someone call his name. He turned to see his friends come limping past the body of the dragon-thing.

Raife had one arm looped around the Inspector, but was limping himself. Sandy's brown hair was matted to the side of her head with what looked like blood. One of Dave's eyes was swollen shut and he had lost the shotgun, gripping his pistol in one hand. Bobby's bald head was covered in bloody scratches, but he still held his mutely glowing axe, and Gemma walked beside him, gripping his arm to keep him upright.

Only Gerritt seemed unhurt. He held Shawn's small hand in his own, and when he saw Quinn, he gave him a thumb's up.

"I think we did it," the young man said with his honest smile.

"Did we do it?" Raife asked in his rumbling growl.

"Is it over?" Donald Green asked, then winced and pressed a hand to his side.

Quinn looked at each of them, suppressing the urge to weep in relief, and held his hand out towards Bobby. The thick man slapped the haft of his axe into Quinn's palm without a word, and the weapon flared to brilliance.

"Almost," Quinn said, wringing his hands on the axe. "We're almost done."

The ebony demon's head echoed with his own howls as he fell back from the Guardian's burning hands. He didn't know where the man had summoned such power, but it raked through him and set him alight. All his strength was gone. All his reason was gone. Through the haze of pain that covered him he could only think of one thing; getting back to Emily.

He flipped over and tried to stand, but his legs gave out. With nothing else to do, he scrabbled, like a rodent, on his hands and knees, towards his beloved.

His vision was half-ruined from the Guardian's fire, but he found his way back to Emily through her moans of pain. The Carrie woman knelt beside Emily. She had freed her hands and one rested on Emily's sweaty brow and the other on her distended belly. The woman's head turned at his approach and she shrank away, scooping up the blonde child and cradling her, as Carrie put her back to the rock wall and stared at him. He ignored them both, his focus only on his wife.

He crawled forward until he was beside her, looking down into her wide and terrified eyes. "Emily," he croaked. "I am so sorry."

"Jay?" she wailed, her head rolling from side to side. "Jay, where are you?"

"I'm here," he said, reaching for her face.

She slapped feebly at his hand, turning her face away. "Jay! I need you."

"I'm..." he said, starting to reassure her, to tell her he was with her. But was he? The creature he truly was bore almost no resemblance to the face he had worn on the day they met, the day of their wedding, the night they conceived the life inside her.

As he was now, could he be there with her at all?

He dropped his hand and sagged, his head hanging between arms that quaked as he tried to hold himself upright. "If everything else about my life is a lie, the one truth is that I always loved you."

He heard the crunch of boots on the coarse ground behind him, and felt a wash of heat as the Guardian's bright magic touched him.

Then, all he knew was the dark.

Quinn saw the ebony demon on its knees beside Emily Drummond, and he halted. The creature reached out a clawed hand, a tender gesture, and tried to touch Emily's sweating face. The woman cried out and turned away, and the creature's shoulders sagged in defeat.

The demon said something, then, in a soft, almost human voice. Quinn didn't catch all of it, but he was certain he heard, *"always loved you."*

Quinn hefted the axe, but paused before he committed himself to stepping forward. If it had been him, trying to save Carrie and Shawn, were there any lengths he would not go to? Is there anything he would not do?

No, he decided. He would let the world burn if it meant Carrie would be safe. But no matter how he might sympathize with the creature before him, it could not be enough to stay his hand.

Quinn lifted the axe high above his head and took two quick steps forward. He brought the blade down, with all the strength he had left, and chopped into the demon's neck at the base of its skull. The white fire of the weapon shot across the demon's skin in a crackling blur, and the creature slumped to the ground. It gave one convulsive shudder, and then lay still.

"Quinn?"

His head snapped up at the sound of Carrie's voice. She appeared out of the gloom, Abby in her arms. He let go of the axe, still fixed in the neck of the demon, and held his own arms open while she rushed into them. He squeezed both of them as hard as he could, kissing both Carrie and Abby several times. He heard Carrie sob, and realised they were all crying.

"Now, it's over," Raife said as he came up behind them all, wrapping his big arms about both Quinn and Carrie, until Quinn felt as though he'd been crushed.

After several long moments, Quinn finally lifted his head and looked at his friends. Their faces, lit only with the muted glow from the fire that still consumed the monstrous demon, were bloody and haggard. But he did not think he had ever seen anything so beautiful in his entire life.

"What do we do with her?" Dave said, looking down at Emily Drummond, who still cried out weakly and clutched at her stomach.

Quinn had a momentary thought that the world would be better off if both she and the creature growing inside her were to die, but even he did not have the bloody constitution to do the work himself.

"We have to help her," Bobby said, stepping forward and wrenching his axe from the smouldering body of the ebony demon.

"Help her what?" Raife asked, releasing his hold on Quinn and Carrie.

"Help her birth her child," Bobby said.

Dave glanced over at Quinn and Raife. "I thought that was what we were trying to prevent here. I mean, doesn't that child coming into the world mean the apocalypse?"

Donald Green stepped forward and held his hands out to Carrie, who handed him Abby. The girl looped her arms about the inspector's neck and pressed her face against his. The old man tottered, but Gerritt put out a steadying hand, and they all stayed upright.

"As much as it pains me to say so," the Inspector said, "I

agree with McLeod. Whatever is inside that woman was important enough to that thing," he nudged the ebony demon with his toe," that it was willing to kill all of us. I'm disinclined to help it live."

Bobby stepped between all of them and Emily and set his feet apart. His usually friendly face had the same look that Quinn had seen when he thought Raife had insulted Gemma, only a couple of shades darker.

"Whatever is inside her, she did not ask for it," he said. "If the child is a danger, we can deal with it, but she is as much a victim of this creature's deception as any of us. We cannot stand here idly while she dies."

No one responded for several heartbeats, until Quinn cleared his throat. "Bobby is right. Emily didn't ask for any of this. We can't let her die."

"Okay," trepidation thick in Sandy's voice. "Do you want me to go get the car so we can get her to the hospital?"

"This is not work for a hospital," Gemma said, stepping forward to place a hand on Bobby's thick arm. "For good or ill we must do it ourselves." She looked to Abby. "Will you help me, child?"

The blonde girl glanced from Gemma to Inspector Green.

"It's up to you, baby-girl," the Inspector said. "Do you want to help?"

Abby pursed her lips and looked at the ground for a moment, then back into the Inspector's face. "Yeah, Poppa. I do."

Wincing, Donald Green set her feet on the ground, and she stepped forward, reaching for Gemma's hand. Together they knelt beside Emily Drummond. The woman's breathing had become shallow and she was almost unconscious, her eyes only half-open as she moaned weakly.

"All right, love," Gemma said, addressing Abby. "Whenever you are ready."

Abby picked up the bronze medallion where it rested against her chest and gripped it in one hand, while she put the other Emily's belly. Abby's small face took on a look of intense concentration and the medallion in her hand glowed with a warm white light. Beneath her hand on Emily's belly, a white glow emerged. The edges of the bright spot grew, and in the centre was the deepest black.

As Quinn looked into the black space Abby was opening, he saw that it was not the dark emptiness of other doors she had opened. He also saw a small, curled shape, lying very still.

Gemma summoned her own power and sheathed her hands in a dull white glow. Reaching past Abby's hand, into the small doorway, she gathered up the curled shape and carefully pulled it free. Once the baby was in the open air, Abby let the door close and stood up to reach for Inspector Green.

Gemma only glanced at the thing in her hands and then held it out towards Quinn. "Take the child," she said. "Before we lose the mother."

After a moment's hesitation, Quinn stripped off his tattered jacket and folded it around the wet bundle that Gemma offered him. He clasped the bundle to his chest, while Gemma went to work on Emily Drummond with her skilled and powerful hands.

Folding back the jacket, Quinn looked down at the creature he held, fear and revulsion making an acidic ball in the pit of his stomach. But what he saw was not a monster, it was not strange, it was not dangerous or terrifying. It was a baby. A small, pink, human baby. And it was a boy.

After a handful of heartbeats, Quinn realised the child, while it appeared to be human, wasn't moving. Or breathing.

He held the child close to his face, thinking frantically of what he should do. He cradled the child in his left arm and reached his free hand into the bundle to place it on the baby's still chest.

"Work with me here, little guy," Quinn said, rubbing softly. Nothing happened. Trying to remember what little first aid training he had ever received, he dipped his head and put his nose and mouth over the child's. He tasted blood, and something else, but gave a small puff of breath and felt the tiny chest rise. The baby still did not move.

"Come on," Raife said from over his shoulder. "Come on, baby."

Quinn looked up to see everyone gathered around him, their faces tight with concern. He saw a hint of something else, too. Something he felt himself, a strong dose of guilt. It was not a handful of moments before they had seriously considered letting the child and his mother die. That, Quinn decided, could not happen.

He rubbed the child a little harder, trying to force his warmth into his hands and into the child. He dipped his head again and gave the boy another small, puffing breath. He felt as though something passed between the child and himself, something small and nearly undetectable, but he felt it just the same.

With a jerk of his small leg, the child gave a bleating cough, and then began to cry softly. This time when Quinn glanced up, he saw tears of relief brimming in more than one eye.

Gemma appeared in front of him, dressed only in her voluminous dress, her arms wrapped around herself. Quinn looked past her to see Emily covered in Gemma's thick sweater, still sweaty and pale, but breathing evenly.

"How is she?" he asked.

"She is alive," Gemma said. "What we will find when she wakes up, is unknown. I did what I could, but there was a great deal of damage done. I fear the pain of the betrayal she suffered may be almost as dire as the pain of the birth." She looked over her shoulder at the sleeping woman. "Whatever comes, we will do what we can."

Quinn saw the faintest lightening in the sky above the peak of the mountain. The temperature seemed to have dropped in the space since the battle, and he let out a shuddering breath that misted the air in front of him.

"We need to get off this mountain," he said as he noted the shivers consuming several of his friends.

Bobby stood at his shoulder, looking down at the now mewling baby in Quinn's arms, waggling a thick finger in the air above his face to no effect. Quinn could not help but smile and held the child out to the thick man, who took the bundle without hesitation with a smile that suggested he'd just received a fine prize. Raife hulked past them both and bent to scoop up the still form of Emily Drummond, while Quinn bent down and held his arms out for Abby. Arms were linked and hands held as the small band turned for the walk to the vehicles.

With Abby in his arms, Quinn stood and saw Gemma staring at the mouth to the mine—a darker hole against the shades of grey and cobalt.

"Gemma?" he said to her. "Are you all right?"

The grey-haired woman pulled in a long breath, her shoulders rising, and let it out in a hitching exhale while she pressed her closed fists to her chest. "I thought this would be where we'd claim my child from the black." She turned and looked at Abby, who had her head pressed into Quinn's shoulder. "But I think everyone has given too much already, and there is nothing left in any of us."

The sharp stab of guilt that Quinn felt every time he thought of Autumn, of her endless tumble into Abby's black door on the night she saved his life, raked through him as he watched Gemma drop her chin to her chest. Abby lifted her head and gripped her medallion in one small, pale hand.

"Put me down, Quinn," she said, very softly. When Quinn didn't do so, she turned her face to his, her eyes intense. "I need you to put me down." Her small voice held a vein of command he had never heard in a child, and he moved to obey.

Once her small feet were on the ground, Abby walked past Gemma towards the mouth of the mine.

"What's she doing, Quinn?" Raife asked.

"Abby, don't," Inspector Green said, taking a hitching step to follow the child. He opened his mouth to say something else, but Quinn put a hand on his arm.

"No, sir," Quinn said. "I think we have to trust her for a minute."

Abby stopped in front of the entrance to the mine, spread

her small feet and lowered her head. A strange, static hum filled the air, making Quinn's scalp tingle. A light began to bloom from Abby's chest, where she gripped the medallion. Instinctively, Quinn followed. He didn't need to turn and look to see that everyone else did, as well.

As the light grew, Abby lifted one of her hands out in front of her. From her palm, first a light, and then a black spot, darker than any shadow in the depths of the mine, grew. In moments, the space appeared taller than Quinn and twice as wide. Inside it, he saw nothing but endless black.

"You need to call her, Quinn," Gemma said, as she gripped his arm. "You have to call out to her and bring her to this place, before Abby's strength fails. "

He glanced down at the child. The light at the edges of the door she'd opened was steady, but her small hand quaked in the air.

Call Autumn? he thought. *How the hell do I do that?*

He opened his mouth, and then shut it. He knew that would not be the way. He took in a deep breath, then another, like he would do if he was making a long shot with a rifle, and held up his hand close to Abby's. He closed his eyes and reached down into his core, to that place he was still not familiar with, and thought of Autumn. There was not much left in him. His centre felt hollow, but as he searched he found a little spark, enough to cast a light.

He took that small light and sent it out into the endless black of Abby's door. He silently called out to Autumn and imagined her, not as it had been when he'd watched her fall, but in all the kind moments where she'd shared a smile. He stepped forward, extending his hand past the steady light of the door's border, and felt a hard cold envelop his skin.

He stood like that a long time, sending out that silent call. Nothing. The intense cold made his skin feel like it would crack. It leached up his arm to encase his heart, making it hard to breathe. He stood there, gritting his teeth against the pain, and listened with all his will. But, there was no voice that called back.

Quinn opened his eyes and glanced down at Abby, whose small hand violently shook. He was about to tell her to close the door, that he had failed, when something brushed across his numb fingers.

He snatched his hand back, startled, and saw a glimmer of muted colour beyond the door. He reached for it. His hand closed on something stiff that crackled beneath his touch, and he pulled hard. Something heavy and frigid fell into his arms. As he grabbed, he staggered backwards, knocking into Abby. The child's eyes fluttered open and the light from her medallion died as the black door closed with a soft *snik*.

Quinn looked down to his arms and he saw Autumn Donnelly. Small crystals of ice covered her hair and eyelashes, glimmering in the pale light of the coming dawn. Her cheeks were pale as new snow, and her lips had a bluish tinge. Her clothing, frozen stiff, cracked audibly as he lowered her carefully to the ground. He put his hand on her cheek, but found it stony and frigid.

"Jesus," Dave said, over Quinn's shoulder. "Is she dead?"

"No," Gemma said, kneeling down by Autumn's head, facing her feet. "But she will be if we don't do something." She placed her hands on either side of Autumn's face. "Quinn, you have to help me."

"What do I do?" he said, the elation he'd felt at finding Autumn rapidly replaced by a ball of helplessness in his gut.

"Do what you did with the baby," Gerritt said.

Quinn turned his head and saw that everyone was looking at the young man. Gerritt glanced around and shrugged.

"It seemed to work," he said. "Whatever it was."

Turning back to Autumn, Quinn leaned forward. He placed his hand in the centre of her frozen chest and brought his face down to hers.

"I'm sorry, Autumn," he whispered to her, as he dug into himself to see if there was anything left at all. "I'm sorry I left you in the dark."

Closing his eyes, he leaned down, further, and placed his forehead against hers. He pushed aside the icy ball of worry at his centre, and again remembered the way he'd felt when he'd watched Autumn tumble into the black door while she saved his life. She had given everything to save him. He could do no less for her.

Lowering his lips to hers, he gave a long, hard breath. In the centre of his chest, he felt an icy stab of pain. He grunted, unable to find the breath to cry out, and fell sideways, trying to support his weight on his hands. He succeeded for a moment, until his quaking arms gave way, and he fell onto his face. In that moment, he saw Autumn's pale blue eyes flutter open.

Before the darkness took him, he knew that the cost had been worth paying.

CHAPTER 28

The sun rose pink against the breaking clouds over Resolution Cove, but the dawn did a little to warm the earth.

In a run-down hotel in the centre of town, a skinny man with a spider tattoo on his forehead stepped away from the haunted image he'd been staring at in the mirror all night and walked out the front door. He stood on the sidewalk and turned his face up to the bright rays of sunshine that peeked over the top of his place. Perhaps it wasn't so bad, this place of his. He could do a little more to fix it up. Although, he decided he might actually have to pay someone to help him, before that stage he'd built inside collapsed and killed someone.

He resolved, also, to go down to the laser tattoo removal place later that day and see if they could do anything about his forehead.

Near the water, a heavyset man stood in the middle of his bar, his favourite place in the world, and rubbed a hand across his tired face. The morning sunlight hit the stained-glass windows on the east side of the building—that he'd got for a steal when the glazier had agreed to build and install them in exchange for the elimination of his ancient and monstrous bar tab—and filled the bar room with a soft glow that made everything in the place look polished and perfect.

It had been a long night, but he had plenty to do before he opened at ten o'clock for the Saturday brunch crowd. It was bound to be a long day of telling stories and hearing woes, but there was nothing in the world he would rather be doing.

In front of the hospital, a dark-haired doctor stepped out the doors of the emergency room and filled her lungs with cool air. The ghosts that had followed her all night couldn't survive the light of morning. She shook herself to be rid of the lingering sensation of their grasp.

This was still a good place, she decided, as she looked at the pink sky. There were people here that needed care, and she was glad to say she would be the one to provide it.

A smile broke over her face as a large, black SUV pulled to a screeching halt in front of her, and a familiar, hulking figure climbed out from behind the driver's seat.

"Sergeant Raife, you moustached baboon," Doctor Stovern said, completely unable to push the smile from her face and gave the huge man the glower she saved only for him. "What brings you to my door?"

"We got problems, doc," the big man said. "All kinds of 'em."

She reached up and gripped his chin to examine a long gash on the side of his bald head. "Don't you always." She lifted the emergency call button that hung from her neck and pressed it firmly. "Come inside and we'll see what we can do."

CHAPTER 29

Hypothermia, apparently, is hard to get over. Despite numerous arguments with Raife, where the words "baboon" and "moustache" and "empty bald head" were used often, but with a barely concealed smile, Doctor Stovern refused to release Quinn until he'd been the hospital for three days.

The doctor had asked several inconvenient questions about how Quinn had come to have severe hypothermia. The explanation that he had fallen into the inlet had not flown, as he was completely dry when they brought him in. They also had a hard time explaining the numerous scrapes and abrasions that covered almost every inch of his body.

"Are you ever going to tell me what actually happened to you?" Doctor Stovern asked him on his second night in the hospital. She had abandoned her brusque tone and stood at his bedside after visiting hours, her hand on his arm and a sombre look on her face. "Are any of you people every going to tell me what has actually happened all those times you've come through the doors of this hospital and I've patched you up."

Quinn looked at her and sighed, then took her hand off his shoulder, held it in his own for a moment and kissed her knuckles with cracked lips. He had not known he was going to do it until after the job was done. The gesture surprised them both, but she did not pull her hand from his.

"What happened, doc," Quinn said, slowly, looking past her and out the window at the dark water of the inlet. "Is we did something important. We discovered, all of us together, that love, above all things, is what is really important. And then you saved me. Again." He moved his gaze to her face. "Is that enough telling for today?"

"No, Corporal Sullivan, it is not. But I will take it." She stood on her tip toes and turned off the light above his bed. "Get some rest. I'll see you in the morning."

His team visited him every day, and for some reason Gerritt always insisted on bringing him flowers. They came so often that Doctor Stovern threatened Dave and Raife with catheters if they didn't let Quinn rest. It did him good to see their faces. Despite all they'd seen, all the things they'd done, their spirits were high, completely unburdened by the darkness they had fought.

Inspector Green brought Abby by. The child had crawled onto his bed and gazed at him with a very serious expression that was far too old to be on her smooth face. Then she hugged him carefully, her arms around his neck. Carrie had dinner with him every night, and Shawn sat on the bed between Quinn's feet, until Quinn had read him at least ten pages from the *Fellowship of the Ring*.

Everyone he knew came to see him, always asking too many questions about how he got hypothermia. There was a face that he had been hoping to see, but did not appear. Every time someone walked through his door, he hoped it would be Autumn. But she did not come.

On the third time he asked about her, Raife ran a thumb and fore-finger over his moustache and blew out a long riffling breath.

"I stopped in at her shop this morning," the big man rumbled. "She's been staying there with her mum and Bobby. She looked fine. When I told her I was coming to visit you she smiled in that weird way she has and told me to give you her love."

"But she didn't want to talk to me," Quinn asked.

Raife shrugged. "Not that she let on, no."

On the morning of the fourth day, Doctor Stovern pronounced him fit to be discharged.

"I'm quite convinced you are going to die of some manner of misadventure," she told him as she removed a blood pressure cuff and glowered at him. "But it won't be from this particular one."

Raife, who was already there to visit him, pulled out his phone. After glaring at the screen for several seconds, he reached into an interior pocket and settled a pair of reading glasses on the end of his nose. He tapped laboriously with one finger for several seconds, growling, and then put his glasses away. "I told Carrie you're allowed to come home, and I'll drive you."

Getting dressed felt like a narrowly won battle. Between the fights he had fought, the beatings he had taken, and what he had given to both Drummond's child and Autumn, Quinn felt as though he'd paid a heavy toll. He felt like had aged a decade in the last week, with glass in his joints and his muscles stiff and protesting at the slightest movement.

And when he thought about it, maybe he had.

He had found that strange magic deep inside himself. Tapping into it, he felt as though a piece of him had been freed while another had been shattered. He had not reckoned there would be such a cost, but he felt it every time he moved and saw it in the lines of his face every time he looked in the mirror.

Quinn finished dressing as Doctor Stovern appeared with a wheelchair. He made weak protestations that he didn't need it, but had to repress a relieved sigh when he gave up to her insistence and carefully lowered into it.

As she pushed him through the front doors of the hospital and onto the broad sidewalk where the black Tahoe sat by the curb, she stopped the chair and crouched in front of him. She put her hand on his knee and looked at him wordlessly for several long moments.

Raife got out of the driver's seat and came around the front of the big vehicle to stand beside her. She glanced up at him, then back at Quinn, and drew in a long, slow breath.

"I don't know what you did," she said, and her eyes flicked to Raife again. "What any of you did, but you've changed this place."

"The hospital?" Quinn asked, glancing over his shoulder at the grey building.

She shook her head. "No. The town. Resolution. I've always known that you, the skinny guy who curses too much, and your pet baboon here are up to strange things that you refused to discuss. I let it go because I always thought you would do something horrifically stupid and I'd read about it in the paper one day. Now I'm glad it didn't turn out that way."

She stood, folded her arms and turned her gaze the water. "I've lived in this place my whole life. Couldn't wait to come back here once I'd finished medical school, and thought it was the best place on earth. But since you came in here, nearly dead, four days ago, Resolution is different. Even the air feels new. I didn't even know there was anything wrong before. It's like we were living under a cloud we'd all gotten so used to we didn't even notice it anymore."

"You never realise how dark it is until you step into the light," Quinn said.

Doctor Stovern looked down at him. "Yeah. Whatever you people did, you pushed away the shadow that darkened this town."

She slipped a small hand under his arm and helped him stand. When he was steady on his feet, she cupped his stubbled jaw line with her warm palm and smiled, then took the wheel chair and hurried back into the hospital.

"How do you feel about that?" Raife asked, as they watched the doctor's retreating form.

"I don't know," Quinn said. "But I hope she's right."

As Quinn opened the front door of his house, he was greeted

by a chorus of cheers.

"Aw, fuck," he said as he glanced at Raife, and let his head droop. The last thing he wanted was a surprise party.

His entire watch was there, along with the Inspector, Abby, Gemma and Bobby. A stack of pizza boxes and several cans of Guinness sat on the kitchen table. He looked down at himself, at the pyjama pants and old t-shirt he wore, and thought he should go and put on some clean clothing. But when the smell of the pizza hit his nose and his stomach gave a rumble, he decided he could look like a vagabond in his own house. If anyone didn't like it, they could leave.

Carrie put her arms around him and squeezed him gently. "I tried to tell them you needed to rest, but Dave yelled nonsense until I said they could come and see you arrive."

Quinn looked over top of Carrie's head, to where Dave poured can of Guinness into a pint glass, watching it cascade. The slender man caught him looking and gave an exaggerated shrug.

"I watched my best friend nearly die," he said. "If your coming home isn't cause for celebration, I don't know what is."

Despite his exhaustion, Quinn felt a smile amble across his face, and started to make his slow way toward the table. As he passed the end of their long couch, he turned and saw a single figure sitting on the far end. Autumn Donnelly sat with her legs crossed and a baby held in the crook of one arm, while the other tilted a bottle up to the tiny mouth.

When he stopped, she looked up at him and met his eyes. She gave him the knowing, patient smile she had shown him so many times since they'd met, and he knew she was all right.

"I'll be just a minute," he said to Carrie, who squeezed him again and stood on her toes to kiss him before sashaying over to the table and plucking up the beer Dave had poured. She grinned at him wickedly, as she began to drink it.

Quinn turned and approached Autumn, settling himself on the couch beside her. He looked at her, opened his mouth to speak, and then shut it again, at a loss for where to begin. Did he apologize for letting her float in a frozen oblivion for months before finally coming to get her? Did he offer up excuses and explanations? What did you say to someone who sacrificed themselves, without hesitation, to save your life?

"Hi," he said, finally.

"Hello, Quinn Sullivan," she said, and gave him that patient smile again.

"Um." He rubbed his hands across the tops of his legs. "How are you feeling?"

She looked past him, to where her mother stood, both of her slender hands wrapped around one of Bobby's arms, as the thick man told Gerritt something that made the young man blush.

"I am well," she said. "I have been...working with my mother and collecting myself. Clearing my mind and reclaiming anything I might have lost." Her eyes met his again. "I am sorry I did not come and visit you in the hospital. I understand you were there because of what you did for me. But I was not ready to see anyone, let alone you."

"No, Autumn," Quinn said, lowering his head and looking at the hardwood between his feet, unable to meet her eye. "I'm the one who should apologize to you." He worked his mouth around, fighting a sudden dryness, and a catch in his throat. "I left you in that place. You jumped on that demon's back to save my life, and then I left you in the black."

She pulled the bottle from the baby's mouth and settled it between her knees, then reached up a hand and grasped his chin, turning his face towards hers.

"Is that what you think?" she asked him, her blue eyes narrow.

He nodded, his chin still in her grip.

"Oh, Quinn." She pulled his face forward and kissed the corner of his mouth. "No, that is not what you did." The baby began to make small, unhappy noises, so Autumn picked up the bottle again and continued to feed him. "To tell you the truth, I do not remember much of my time on the other side of Abby's door. I remember fear, and falling, and being very, very cold. But it is just small flashes, a sense of it rather than a complete picture. The thing I remember most is a glimpse of your face as I fell, thinking I'd failed you."

He began to object, to say he was the one who had failed, but she cut him off.

"I know what you would say, but I would not near it. The important thing is that you nearly gave your life to bring me back, and now I am here. What we have to do now is find our way forward."

He nodded, letting her words sink in, along with a healthy measure of relief. As the guilt he had been carrying for the months since he'd thought he'd lost Autumn sloughed off his shoulders, he felt a little less tired. He thought he might be a little less broken.

"Speaking of the way forward," he said. "What are we going to do with the baby? And where is his mother?"

Autumn smiled down at the child in her arms. "His mother is at my store, with a couple close companions my mother called from home. Her body is fine, but her heart and spirit are broken. She has a long way to go until she is steady again. Until that happens," Autumn ran her finger down the child's smooth, pink cheek, "we will care for her child."

"Okay, but what about the child?" Quinn asked. "Isn't it, you know, a demon?"

She met Quinn's eyes, and then looked back down at the baby. "That has been a topic of heated debate amongst my mother and her friends." She took in a big breath and blew it out in a rush. "His parents are of different worlds, both the light and the dark. And while his father sought to use him for dark ends, he was, ultimately born of love. His father truly did love his mother, despite whatever else he might have planned, and that is important." She looked at Quinn again. "And from what everyone who witnessed it say, something passed from you to the child when you got his heart beating. Your power comes from the light. If he were purely a creature of the dark, your power would have destroyed him, not brought him to life. So, he will always carry the potential for evil, but he will also have the capacity for good."

"Just like all of us," he said.

"Like all of us," she agreed. "We just have to hope that it is the light that wins."

"Does he have a name yet?" He slipped one of his scarred fingers into the child's tiny hand.

"His name is Jason Quinn Drummond," Autumn said, turning to smile at him. "Named for both his father and the man who saved him. When my mother told Emily what her husband was, and what happened up on that mountain, that is the name she chose."

"Will you guys keep him here?"

She didn't say anything for a long time and busied herself fussing with the now-empty bottle and the blanket.

"Autumn?" he asked.

She met his eyes again, her mouth quirked down. "No, Quinn. We will all be leaving."

He pulled his chin back as though he was avoiding a punch. "Leaving? All of you? Why?"

"The magic you spilled across that mountainside will be like a beacon to any creature of the dark who is powerful enough to know such things. While you destroyed that ancient presence that had affected this town, we think you might have awoken something else."

"Awoken something?" he asked. "What are you talking about?"

"My mother told me the power you displayed has not been seen in many lifetimes. It was the power of the Old Guardians. The ones who held back the Dark when magic wasn't a myth and the veils between the worlds weren't as thick as they are now. As with all things, there must be balance, so as the power of the light grows, so will the power of the dark." She looked down at the baby again. "And when it is discovered that one of the demon-kind gave life to a child, something might try and claim him. So we will ensure he is well hidden, in a place that is far from here." She looked at him again. "I think you and your family should move on too, Quinn. This place, Resolution doesn't need you anymore. But there will be some place that does."

A sigh escaped him as he sunk back into the cushions of the couch, feeling the air go out of him. "I don't know how to do this without you," he said, his voice thin and bewildered in his own ears. "When you were gone I couldn't find my way until your mother arrived."

She showed him that patient smile. "You are stronger than you know, Quinn. And besides, we won't be any place that we can't get to you if you need us."

He opened his mouth to say more, but was interrupted when a heavy hand gripped his neck and a heavier moustache made contact with his ear.

"I have to run an errand," Raife said, quietly. "But I'll be back."

Quinn stood, slowly, and turned, but the big man was already closing the door behind him and stepping out into the cold, sunny afternoon.

Autumn got up, the baby still cradled to her chest, and moved towards the kitchen, where Quinn's friends, his family, were eating and drinking and telling their stories. As he approached, he felt their laughter wash over him, smoothing out the wrinkles of his trepidation, easing his fear of the changing future.

While he lay in his hospital bed, he had hoped that all of this—the tumult that had been his life since he was first posted to Resolution Cove—was over. But, maybe, it was only another beginning.

Ah well, he thought as Dave handed him a still-cascading pint of Guinness. Let the changes come. They would not find him unprepared, nor would he be alone.

ABOUT THE AUTHOR

Award Winning Author, Tyner Gillies,
works and lives in British Columbia,
Canada, with his beautiful wife and
three moderately chubby cats.

http://www.tynergillies.com

"...[a] thrilling story...a page-turner right to the end. Tyner Gillies presents his debut novel with a fresh voice—an exciting new Canadian talent!"
– kc dyer, Author and Director of the SIWC

Constable Quinn Sullivan thought, when he transferred to Resolution Cove, that it was the perfect place: low crime, nice people, easy shifts, and finding the girl of his dreams. But something is happening in Resolution Cove. Violent crime, committed by sane, reasonable people is on the rise with no discernible connection between the crimes except for ramblings of 'eyes in the dark.'

Something is feeding upon its victims' and it must eliminate the emerging Guardian or else be banished into the netherworld to await a new time and place to strike. Autumn Donnelly knows what is plaguing the city. Can she convince Quinn of the truth before evil blankets Resolution Cove, destroying the sleepy town in a confluence of Hell on Earth.

Get Book One of the Resolution Cove Trilogy!
Available in paperback and ebook
Everywhere fine books are sold.

"Taut writing, gripping action, and sly wit in a perfect blend of police procedural and demonic horror. Gillies has hit another one out of the park!"
– CC Humphreys, Winner of the Arthur Ellis Award.

Quinn Sullivan has vanquished the Demon of Resolution Cove, armed with only Autumn Donnelly's dagger. Now, new forces conspire to test the Guardian once more as he is sent to discover who, or what, was behind the suicide of Inspector Green's son. Little does he expect what awaits for him in the mountain town of Cranbrook.

Devoid of the Guardian's protection, Quinn's fellow RCMP constables are set in a trap they cannot escape as piles of human bones begin turning up. A serial killer is on the loose, searching for a little girl with abilities that will release others of its ilk to rain Hell down on earth. To win, Quinn must make a sacrifice. For him to succeed, someone must fall.

Get Book Two of the Resolution Cove Trilogy!
Available in paperback and ebook
Everywhere fine books are sold.

Jake Ross has dreams of breaking back into a boxing career.

One night, after a promising match, he is drawn into an unseen world where the Fates transform him, unwillingly, into a tool for Their works, guided by a mysterious man named Mac.

Vanessa Rain, a stripper at a nearby club, has been running most of her life, hiding and making do so as to protect the only person she loves–her son–from forces that threaten to steal him away from her. Gareth is a pawn but is much more than his mother ever dreamed. It is he that dark forces conspire to capture and turn towards their destructive aspirations.

The Fates lead Jake and Vanessa into a chance encounter with one purpose–to save Gareth. But are they too late?

Available in paperback and ebook
Everywhere fine books are sold.

"Canadian Dreadful showcases some of Canada's best voices in horror fiction. This anthology is a harrowing tour of the northern landscape that will leave you both dazzled and terrified."
~ David Morrell, New York Times Bestselling author of Murder as a Fine Art.

In the pages of this anthology, you will not find the Canada you are accustomed to, nor a Canada that the world has grown to know and love. Between the covers, you will discover a dark landscape that will challenge your perspective. From sea to shining sea, stories of a darker Canada will arise, and within them all a kernel of truth. Stories of sacrifice, cannibalism, ghosts, and mystical forests, the authors will plunge you into the country that is Canadian Dreadful.

Available in paperback and ebook
Everywhere fine books are sold.

BOOKS

To see a full list of our amazing books,
please check our website:

www. darkdragonpublishing.com/books.html

All Books Available At The Following Retailers:
Amazon.ca
Amazon.com
Amazon.co.uk
Amazon.com.au
Barnes and Noble
Books A Million
Book Depository
Powell's Books
Chapters/Indigo

And other fine book retailers.